Lost American Fiction

There are no firm guidelines for selection of the Lost American Fiction volumes. The only rule is that to be considered for republication a book must have been originally published at least twenty-five years ago. One quality we look for might be called "life": does the work live?—does it have a voice of its own?—does it present convincing characters? Another test for including a work in this series is its historical value: does it illuminate the literary or social history of its time?

The editor and the Press feel that the Lost American Fiction series has largely achieved what it set out to do. Twenty-eight books have been given another chance. Some have found new audiences. Some will vanish again. We do not claim that all of the volumes are lost masterpieces; and there has been considerable disagreement from readers about individual titles. We never anticipated uniformity of response. That readers would find the Lost American Fiction volumes worth reading and would be prompted to make their own appraisals is all we expected.

M.J.B.

Lost American Fiction
EDITED BY MATTHEW J. BRUCCOLI

Salt

or

The Education of Griffith Adams

By Charles G. Norris

Afterword by Louis Auchincloss

Southern Illinois University Press
Carbondale and Edwardsville

Copyright 1918 by E. P. Dutton & Company
Afterword by Louis Auchincloss Copyright © 1981 by
　Southern Illinois University Press
All rights reserved
Printed by offset lithography in the United States of America

Library of Congress Cataloging in Publication Data

Norris, Charles Gilman, 1881-1945.
　Salt: or, The education of Griffith Adams.

　(Lost American fiction)
　Reprint of the ed. published by Dutton, New York.
　　I. Title.　II. Title: The education of Griffith Adams.
PS3527.0485S34　1981　　　813'.52　　　80-25152
ISBN 0-8093-1011-2

TO MY WIFE
Kathleen
WHOSE UNTIRING FAITH IN THIS EFFORT
AND
WHOSE ENCOURAGEMENT AND LOVE
DESERVE A FAR MORE ENDURING TRIBUTE
THAN THIS DEDICATION

CONTENTS

	PAGE
BOOK I.	1
BOOK II.	123
BOOK III.	249
BOOK IV.	317

AUTHOR'S NOTE

It may seem to some of the readers of this story that certain of its episodes are overdrawn or exaggerated to prove the purpose of the novel—if it may be said to have one. While many will contend—and with these I have no quarrel—that the story of Griffith Adams' life is not typical, I wish to state that the incidents upon which it is based are founded upon fact—or less than fact. The book represents a painstaking effort to transcribe the results of personal observations over a number of years, and to make the principal character of the tale a type of American youth which is, I believe, to all unfortunately familiar.

C. G. N.

New York City,
February, 1918.

SALT
BOOK I

SALT

OR

THE EDUCATION OF GRIFFITH ADAMS

BOOK I

CHAPTER I

I

THE education of Griffith Adams was begun, as far as he, himself, could remember, by his sharp-featured nurse, Carrie, seating him firmly upon a high straight-backed chair, after he had been tubbed, combed and arrayed in one of his stiff, starched piqué dresses, and given a long nail file and told from between firm lips, to clean his nails, and that if he rumpled his dress, he would be locked in the closet. The nurse always finished the operation of manicuring him, herself, and frequently hurt him, because at the very last, she was apt to be late and his mother to be waiting. Carrie was not unkind; she was capable. She was spoken of as that "capable Carrie"; she had become so capable that she seemed to lack other attributes. Griffith had heard his mother assert time and again:

"I never worry about the baby as long as Carrie's there; Carrie can rise to any emergency, she's so capable!"

But Carrie was not as amusing nor as sweet nor as kind as the little round French nurse, Pauline, who succeeded her and taught her charge nursery rhymes in her own language. Pauline was Griffith's nurse for a long time; then, when he was seven, something distressing happened. Pauline was sent away, after much weeping, and hugging, and kissing of Griffith, and Leslie, his half-brother, left home at the same time. The incident might have contributed materially to the boy's education had he been able to understand it, but he did not and only cried bitterly because Pauline had gone away.

Leslie's departure on the other hand brought Griffith a great deal of satisfaction, for he thus acquired a set of fencing foils, a long unused English saddle and bridle, a pair of Indian clubs, and a folding-bed which shut up and became a bureau with imitation drawers by day, and he could feed Diana, the cat, whenever he wished. Leslie had always regarded Griffith as an unavoidable nuisance and treated him accordingly, while the earliest emotion the child could remember was a feeling akin to hate for his older half-brother. Once when Griffith had hid behind a door that opened off the dark hall-way upstairs and had suddenly sprung out from his hiding-place with a shrill little piping scream to frighten Pauline, he had encountered Leslie instead, and his brother had twice struck him, with the full sweep of his open palm, on the side of his head.

The going of Leslie and Pauline marked the end of one and the beginning of another chapter in Griffith's life. Pauline came to see him occasionally and cried over him, but it was years before he met Leslie again.

After Pauline there were no more nurses. When she went, his mother sent the boy to a neighboring kindergarten where he spent his mornings, and at eight years of age, he entered the primary class of the public school. But it was the education he obtained at home rather than that of his text-books and associates at school, during the following five years, which contributed more essentially to the formation of his mind and character.

II

The Adamses lived in Cambridge in an old, square, cream-painted brick house on Main Street, before dignity was added to that thoroughfare by changing its name to Massachusetts Avenue. The dwelling was on the corner on the sunny side of the street, not more than ten minutes' walk from the Square. Griffith's grandfather had built it nearly sixty years before the child was born,

THE EDUCATION OF GRIFFITH ADAMS

and it had been patched, mended and made to serve ever since. It still presented a comfortable, substantial appearance, and when the lovely Mrs. Paul Wagstaff changed her name to Adams and became its mistress, she brought to it an air of life and gaiety as well. She tore away the white picket fence which sagged its way in front of it and up the side street, and built in its place a four-foot brick wall, beside which she planted Virginia creeper that soon covered it luxuriously with foliage in summer and clung to it in winter with many black and tenuous adhesions like a malignant fungous growth. To the house she added flower boxes full of bright geraniums, and red-and-white awnings; the windows appeared to be open all summer, the soft white curtains billowing out into the cheerful sunshine that perpetually flooded the square old house.

Cabot Adams, the grandfather, had been one of the trustees of Harvard College and had bequeathed half his wealth to that institution to establish a Biological Laboratory. Richard, his son, was still considered a rich man on the remaining half, and, after idling about the world for six years subsequent to his receiving a Harvard degree of Ph.D., returned to Cambridge and commenced the compilation of *The History of Boston Town in Revolutionary Times*. His secret ambition was that posterity should consider him an historian, if not of equal rank with Mummsen and Gibbon, at least one whose life-work deserved a place in the same library. Busts and engravings of these idols, with others of Tasso, Thucydides, Cæsar, Carlyle and Guizot had places on his study's walls.

As Griffith remembered him, he was a tall man with a thin face and deep-set eyes. His hair was of a lovely, soft quality, a gray mop, and swept away from his forehead in waving abundance. He was a sensitive man, shy and silent, who would have been much happier if he had spent all his days alone in the musty, book-lined library of the dark, old Adams homestead, and had never thought of marriage. There was a detached air about him as if he were constantly surprised to find himself alive upon the earth, functioning like other human beings, associating with them, and,—strangest of all,—that he had formed and possessed such actual human ties as a wife and son. He was at ease only when alone in the library, endlessly smoking cigar-shaped weeds which he purchased at a dollar a hundred, scratching his way slowly from one sheet to another of his interminable manuscript. At other times he regarded people warily as if, not understanding them, he mistrusted them. He looked on at life, which swept past him; never did he seem a part of it.

When Griffith was eight or nine years old, his father arrived home one day in strange agitation, calling for his wife, waving a book above his head and displaying an excitement which alarmed his son. Mrs. Adams was serving tea in the long, oppressive drawing-room to three of the younger Harvard instructors and a fat, jolly woman in a gay, flowered hat. They looked up in mild surprise at the intruder as he stopped in the doorway, and Mrs. Adams said solicitously:

"Why,—what *is* it, my dear?"

Her husband glanced swiftly from one to another, his eyes betraying his dismay, while he attempted to conceal the emotion unguardedly revealed. He murmured something, repeated the word "pardon" several times, and drew back into the hall where Griffith stood gazing up curiously at him. The father's troubled look encountered the boy's stare and for some moments they regarded one another without speaking. Then a sweet interested smile broke over the man's face, and he put his hand out to take his son's, stooping a little as he said:

"Would you like to see something that father found to-day,—something extraordinary?"

Griffith nodded his head, still fascinated by his father's lapse from habitual reserve. Some vague realization came to him at the moment that this silent, shy man who lived in the house with his mother and himself and who was his father, was capable of being glad or sorry, like himself. He accompanied him curiously into the leather-smelling library and there Mr. Adams awkwardly drew him upon his thin leg, and pulling out one of the slides of his desk, laid the book upon it. The boy, conscious of the unfamiliarity of his father's lap, was acutely uncomfortable but the man did not notice; he was aware only of his treasure.

"Look, Griffith," he said, his voice once again showing feeling, "do you know what this is? I found it in a queer, dirty, book-shop down in Boston. It—it must be the only copy in existence. Do you see that date, 1774? You remember when the Revolutionary War began? *Well!*"

It was a broken-backed, leather-covered book containing the affidavits of the citizens of Boston made at a time just before hostilities began when the feeling against England was daily becoming more intense. Those sworn statements attested to the affronts and indignities to which the towns-people had been subjected by British troops quartered in their midst. His father read many of them aloud to Griffith, chuckling delightfully over the peculiar old-fashioned wording.

His son listened for a long time, shifting his uncomfortable position as frequently as he dared. At the first movement in these attempted adjustments, his father's arm would grip him, hugging him closer, while the man, unconscious of the boy's distress, read on and on.

Griffith heard his mother's guests taking their departure, the sweet murmur of her voice and their succeeding laughter. He was sure she listened at the study-door after she was alone but she did not enter. Griffith endured the situation after that as long as he was able, then with a desperate wiggle, he squirmed out of his father's hold. Instantly he saw the swift change which came over the man's face. Mr. Adams never again permitted his son to observe him without his cold, shy reserve.

III

If his father contributed but little to the boy's development, his mother was by far the most important influence in it.

Maybelle Griffith had been born in the little town of Taunton, thirty-four years before the son she bore Richard Adams came to bring her alarmingly close to death's door. At seventeen she had married the school-teacher of her native village and become Mrs. Paul Wagstaff. Leslie—her first son—arrived two years later and the young mother began to wonder whether a girl with excellent health who was generally considered pretty, had been fair either to herself or her husband in marrying at so early an age. For a decided change had come over Mrs. Wagstaff with the arrival of her child. At seventeen, while she had been thought pretty, she was thin and angular and her complexion waxy. Maternity played a delightful trick upon her; she rose from her bed of confinement a beautiful woman. It was a miracle, just as her baby was, and she settled herself to enjoy both. Shortly afterwards, her husband obtained a position in the public schools of Providence and a year later the family moved to that city.

The beauty of Mrs. Paul Wagstaff was of a remarkable quality and particularly appealing to men. There was just a little boldness about it which prejudiced the minds of her own sex against her. Mrs. Wagstaff was fated never to have an intimate woman friend; not that she wanted one, although there were times in her life when she bitterly regretted the fact. The attention and devotion of the male sex became for her the sum and substance of her being. She craved admiration and wherever she went she had it. There were invariably two or three men admittedly in love with her. She permitted them to make their declarations; she even went so far as to encourage them to commit themselves, but there it stopped. After that it was:

"Don't be silly, Jack. You're a dear, good, nice boy and I shall always like to have you as one of my dearest friends, but there's my husband and my little boy, you know, and they were all the interest I had in life—until *you* came along. Let's be good friends,—*real* friends, and stop this silly way of talking."

Frequently it did stop there. Jack followed her about until he found other Jacks imitating his example; then either he grew sullen and hurt, or else saw that he had made a fool of himself and disappeared. Either way was equally satisfactory to Mrs. Paul Wagstaff.

In the few instances in which the situation got beyond her control, there were of course, unfortunate consequences. They always brought distressing and uncomfortable thoughts to her, so she refused to allow herself to think of them. There was a young Pole whose foreign temperament was further complicated by his passion for music. It was his encouragement, his own rich voice, his knowledge of methods, which awakened her interest in singing. She made the pleasing discovery that she had a light, lyrical soprano, and after a year's study, began to sing French *chansons* and simple English love songs with pretty charm. She worked hard over her French and her music, until her singing master, ignorant of the devotion of her other admirer, brought everything to a distressing climax by falling in love with her, himself, and insisting that she elope with him.

For the first time during the course of her many flirtations, Mrs. Wagstaff was frightened. Both men were infatuated and inclined to be violent; she foresaw a scandal and the thought of the publicity was too much for her. In a desperate mood, she borrowed money from her Polish admirer, and promised to meet him in London provided he would agree to go there by another steamer. She lied to her slow-witted husband, persuading him she needed a rest and a trip abroad, and with her boy, Leslie, took a steamer for Italy. A month or so later, she learned that the Pole had committed suicide in Paris, and that the singing teacher had been arrested and jailed for accepting partial payments on pianos he had persuaded people to buy but which had not been delivered. Sobered, Mrs. Wagstaff returned with her son to Providence and for some time devoted herself to her husband, who began to show a rheumatic tendency. With alarming and staggering rapidity the disease fastened itself upon him and he was obliged to give up his teaching. There was little money saved and Mrs. Wagstaff began to have terrifying misgivings as to the future.

A famous specialist who lived in Boston brought the Wagstaffs to that city for consultation. In the waiting-room they encountered a shy, retiring man with a sensitive face and a waving mop of blue-gray hair. Mrs. Wagstaff was too distressed over the situation she faced with her husband, to find any satisfaction in the grey-headed man's attentive study. Events followed rapidly. Dr. Lloyd-James prescribed a long and arduous treatment which involved a daily visit to his office; Mr. Wagstaff, it seemed, was in a serious condition and only powerful anti-toxins whose effect must be carefully observed, could save him.

Poor, lovely Mrs. Wagstaff gave way to her grief in the doctor's waiting-room and the nurse in charge did her best to console her. The next day there was a note left in the nurse's care and a check inclosed for three hundred dollars, an offer of more when it was needed, and a request, delicately and beautifully expressed, to allow

the writer to be her friend in "the dark hour of her adversity."
It was signed "Richard Adams."

A year later, Paul Wagstaff died and his golden-haired widow consented to become Mrs. Adams after a becoming lapse of a few, intervening months. On the day of her second marriage, she was just thirty-three years old.

IV

With the atmosphere of the old Cambridge home about her, the impressive dignity of the Adams' name which was now her own, the recent Mrs. Wagstaff decided on more circumspect deportment. Whether it was the effort she made, or the refining influence of her shy, quiet husband, or the effect of her new environment, her nature underwent a belated development and Griffith's birth which brought with it months of pain, and long hours of reflection, added a much needed depth to what she came herself to realize had been a shallow, pleasure-loving nature.

Griffith's mother was an intelligent though a selfish woman, and she recognized that while the actions of a public school teacher's pretty wife might provoke small interest in a city like Providence, in Cambridge, the wife of a man of the standing of Richard Adams, the son of old Cabot Adams, would be under the watchful eyes of every woman in the community. She wanted to take her place among them and provide for some kind of social recognition upon which she could fall back when her beauty faded. Already there were distressing lines beneath her chin and occasionally she discovered a terrifying white hair among her golden ones. She sensed that with these wives of professors, doctors and writers she needed an advocate; they were all too afraid of one another to assume the responsibility of her introduction.

It was these considerations which led her to become a member of Christ Church congregation and make a friend of its English rector, Doctor Cook. It took her longer to win his regard than she anticipated for Mrs. Adams was an extremely pretty woman and Doctor Cook was cautious; he was anxious not to give any cause for idle gossip. He admired her exceedingly and was not loath to show her in private how deep his admiration was. He was wary however about openly advocating her. She met with more immediate success with Professor Castro Verbeck and his frail nervous little wife, who accepted the new Mrs. Richard Adams entirely on the Professor's account. Mrs. Verbeck was afraid of her handsome, black-haired, black-mustached husband, and would have championed an Indian if he had wished it.

But Griffith's mother never felt her position secure. She still possessed a coquettish manner with men, still valued and sought their admiration. She tried to disarm the women by affectionate demonstrations toward her husband in public,—tender love-pats, endearments, adoring glances,—which brought him infinite embarrassment,—and by speaking of him with true wifely devotion behind his back. She frequently attended the eleven o'clock service at Christ Church and, when he was four, Griffith, accompanied to the church by Pauline, entered the infant class in the Sunday School. Except when they were away for the summer or he was actually sick, Griffith was rarely allowed to forego this Sunday duty.

A source of constant anxiety to Mrs. Adams was the behavior of her older son, Leslie. He had been disposed of at the time of her remarriage by being sent to a boarding-school. Griffith could remember the day when he had unexpectedly arrived home and announced that he had been expelled from the institution. There had been a dreadful scene in which Mrs. Adams had violently upbraided her wayward son behind the locked door of her bedroom. There had followed an effort to get him into college which had failed, and an experiment with a clerkship in a commission merchant's office in Back Bay which likewise met with no success. Griffith had witnessed a terrible struggle one night when, standing in his night-drawers in the doorway of his nursery, he had seen his mild erratic father, trembling with anger, force his drunken stepson into his room, which had been unoccupied for three days, and there fling him upon the floor, lock the door upon the outside, and with more sternness than Griffith had ever seen him show, order his wailing wife, who was lying half prone upon the stairs, to control herself unless she wished the neighbors to hear her. The boy was deeply impressed by the scene. The sordidness of it, the angry, obscene language of the offender, the strange violent passion of his mild father, the noisy outcries of his mother terrified and shocked him.

It was shortly afterward that Leslie and Pauline were both sent away. A position in the passenger department of a great railroad in New York was obtained for Leslie and Griffith vaguely understood he would not come back. Pauline's mother, to whom a letter had been sent, came and after an unintelligible harangue in French to her weeping daughter, took her home, leaving behind her a train of indignant sniffs which were obviously intended for the Adams household in general.

With Leslie's and Pauline's departure, Mrs. Adams began to show a genuine affection for her younger son. Up to that time he had been capably superintended, kept immaculately clean, amused, fed and dressed by competent nurses. After Pauline's regime, she decided to try the experiment of attending to him herself. There was a certain charm the boy possessed at this age which may have accounted for her awakened interest in him. He had a black, curling mane like his father's grey one that clung in a thick cluster to his head, a lovely mass no matter in what disorder. He had soft large eyes with a sooty shadow beneath them, an incongruous bunch of red freckles across a short snubbed nose, and a trick of distorting his mouth into what was more a grin than smile. It was his wistful expression which drew people's attention; he had something of the wonder and bewilderment that belonged to his father's, and a certain eager hopeful expectancy, unusually appealing. Griffith never forgot the day when coming in to dress him in the early morning, clad in a blowy, blue silk dressing-gown trimmed with eider-down, his mother had suddenly caught him in her arms, and rapturously kissing him, had exclaimed:

"He's a darling little fellow! Griffey dear, 'cute' is no name for you! You're going to be mother's pet!"

The child's early passionate love for his mother dated from that moment. To him she was the embodiment of everything good and beautiful. Her arms, her cheek and the curve of her neck seemed to him the smoothest and the softest things in the world. He was particularly susceptible to affection of any kind and a tender caress from his mother's hand or a swift pressure of her lips would transport him with delight. There was always a faint exquisite perfume about her that enchanted his childish senses. But it was not often she permitted him to crawl into her lap or to twine his thin little arms about her neck. Half-smiling, half-pettish, she would recoil from his embraces, pushing him from her with an annoyed:

"Don't Griffey! You'll muss my hair!" or "I'm all powdery, now, Griffey dear, and you'll spoil my gown."

The boy was not offended by these rebuffs. He readily understood that his mother was an exquisite creature and took a great deal of trouble with her appearance. Her unapproachableness made her all the more wonderful to him and often he was deeply happy, silently watching her as she swept about the room, her soft floating draperies trailing behind her. He enjoyed too hearing her sing the children songs in French and listening to the stories she told him about them. Of these his favorite was "Malbrouck" which he was never tired hearing. The romantic figure of the knight who failed to return from the war became the hero of his childish dreams.

Whatever discipline Griffith knew in these early years was administered by his mother. His father distrusted himself too much to correct his son.

V

The boy's happiest days were spent with his mother and Professor Castro Verbeck. The Professor had a small sail-boat which he kept at one of the boat clubs on the Charles River and he frequently asked Mrs. Adams and Griffith to go sailing with him. The boy was included for propriety's sake as Griffith's father detested the water and Professor Verbeck never saw fit to ask his own nervous little wife. These excursions always embodied a picnic for which Griffith's mother took great pains to prepare.

If there was no wind, the Professor used his canoe, but by either craft the little party was able to get a few miles up the river where either seated in the boat in the shade of overhanging trees or comfortably stretched on a grassy slope of some bordering estate they hungrily ate their lunch. Afterwards Professor Verbeck read aloud and Griffith went to sleep or if a convenient bush was available slipped out of his clothes, pulled on his swimming trunks and splashed about in the water.

On one of these excursions when he was just ten years old, he woke suddenly from his sleep and saw the dark head of the Professor bent over his mother's beautiful face. Only the lovely lines of her throat and the tip of her white chin were visible. It did not impress him as wrong for his mother to permit this. To him she was faultless, but he experienced an angry resentment against the man. He was unusually silent on the way home and he answered petulantly his mother's solicitous queries as to what was the matter with him.

He was still disturbed and unhappy when they reached the house. He said a sullen good-night to Professor Verbeck and crawled into the hammock on the screened side porch. His mother went upstairs to brush her hair and put on something cool for dinner. Griffith lay in the hammock, his hands locked behind his head, idly kicking a porch pillar every time the slow oscillation of the hammock brought him within range.

His distressing thoughts were interrupted by the silvery tinkle of the dinner-bell. He heard his mother calling him to come and wash his hands and slowly he obeyed. Presently he found her in the dining-room alone at her place at the table, pouring vinegar into the bowl of a large wooden spoon, mixing the salad dressing as he had seen her mix it a hundred times. At that moment as he gazed at her, the first doubt of her absolute perfection occurred to him. It made him shut his fingers tightly into fists and breathe hard. He did not hear her when she spoke to him and it was necessary for her to direct him a third time to call his father to dinner before he understood.

He squirmed out of his chair and crossed the hall, knocking on the study door before he opened it. His father lay on the floor beside his desk, his open, staring eyes fixed glassily on Griffith. The boy knew at once he was dead. The swivel chair in which he had been sitting was overturned, its three bent ungainly legs sticking up like the crooked branches of a misshapen tree. When the doctors arrived, they agreed that death had been caused by heart failure.

CHAPTER II

I

GRIFFITH was half a year past his tenth birthday, when he entered the Fairview Military Academy situated a mile or so from the city of Lowell, Massachusetts. After his father's death, his mother and himself had spent the summer quietly in a rambling little white cottage down on the Cape. Griffith always carried with him in after years, the picture of his mother during these days. She was four years past forty but even her own sex did not suspect it. Her skin which seemed never to have known a cosmetic was of a creamy translucence. Color fluctuated in her cheeks, flickering suffusions like the quick play of rosiness at eighteen. Her eyes were clear, the whites behind the dark pupils still transparent and shining. Her golden crown held all its fresh silkiness and early luxuriance. Griffith knew what efforts these effects required. He had seen her rubbing cold cream upon her face half-a-dozen times in a single day. She had her reward. In her black lace with touches of white at throat and wrists and her shining yellow hair, framing the perfect oval of her face, she was a lovely thing to look upon. There was besides a certain sadness in her expression that Griffith knew was not altogether assumed. Mrs. Adams really missed her shy, eccentric husband. At the same time she was keenly aware that in her rich black she was a most appealing figure and that never in her life had she been more beautiful. The rôle of bereaved widow she foresaw would be a fascinating and interesting one.

In August Mrs. Adams and her son returned to Cambridge and the process of dismantling the old homestead was begun. Within two weeks thereafter it was sold, and Mrs. Adams engaged a suite of rooms at the Brunswick Hotel on Boylston Street and began to inquire for a good boarding school for Griffith.

To the suggestion of Mr. Rufus Clark who lived at the Brunswick and whose wife's cousin had married one of the instructors there, Griffith owed the selection of the military academy to which he was sent. Mr. Clark, who was fat and tried to conceal it, and who brushed his hair in black wisps across his bald forehead, thought the lovely creature who had come to live at the hotel, a charming acquisition and was only too pleased to interest himself in the selection of a school for her polite little son who impressed him as being unusually "heady."

Griffith may have had some claim to this qualification, but one could not have called him either good looking or attractive. He had already begun the lengthening process by which he attained six full feet at seventeen. He was thin and looked frail, his ribs stood out across his narrow chest like the corrugations of a washboard. His wavy black hair was much too long and gave his face a look of emaciation, with its dark smudge beneath the eyes and the band of freckles across his brief nose. But he was an extraordinarily healthy boy despite his distaste for exercise.

Left to himself, he developed a tendency to read. It was slow process with him and it took weeks to progress from sentence to sentence and from page to page until a book was finished. His first long novel was curiously *The Cloister and the Hearth*, little of which he understood and it bored him at times almost to the point of abandonment. Mr. Clark put into his hands those books known by heart to every English school-boy: *Eric, or Little by Little*, and *Julian Home*, and Griffith was absorbed in them when his mother took him to Lowell and thence by hack to the Fairview Military Academy.

The boy was overwhelmed with grief when his mother left him in the keeping of the Reverend Dana Ostrander. If Mrs. Adams had any misgivings, as she turned to look back at him from the hack window as he stood behind the beaming head-master, rubbing his thin little wrists into his streaming eyes, she dismissed them by reminding herself that a hotel was no place for a growing boy and that Mr. Rufus Clark, who appeared a kindly gentleman, had given the school an excellent character.

II

The Fairview Military School consisted of three buildings: the head-master's house where the mess hall was located, a long dor-

THE EDUCATION OF GRIFFITH ADAMS

mitory with some fifty rooms on its second, third and fourth floors and class rooms on its first, an armory and gymnasium where were the Assembly Room and additional class-rooms. These buildings faced three sides of a rectangle of beaten earth in the centre of which was a tall flag-pole and piece of field artillery. Behind the armory and the gymnasium were the athletic field and the tennis courts. The Academy faced a well-travelled strip of road which led straight into the heart of Lowell. There was a bordering high brick-wall along this road and a tall grilled gateway with the name: The Fairview Military Academy worked in flowing iron letters over its top.

Some eighty boys were enrolled in the school, averaging in age between fifteen and sixteen. Griffith's room-mate was a boy six years older than himself who because of his blundering helplessness, sluggish wits, and odd appearance was the butt of the school. Otto Pfaff was a slow moving, hulking fellow, stoop-shouldered soft and fat. He had pale yellow close-cropped hair, white eyebrows and eyelashes and peered from small eyes through spectacles whose lenses were a quarter-of-an-inch thick. He was a simple-minded boy, protected to a certain extent from the bullying of his school-mates by his inability to be teased. Boys found they could not anger nor annoy him, and that never aspiring to be one of them, he uncomplainingly accepted whatever they dictated. He was kind to Griffith but he was incapable of helping him.

III

Within the first twenty-four hours of his coming to the Fairview Military Academy, Griffith had the process of human generation explained to him in one brutal question flung at him from a group of his new school-mates who sought his acquaintance by circling about him, butting him with their shoulders in the back as he turned and tried to avoid them. The question met with a gleeful shout from his tormentors but it meant nothing to him at the moment. It came back to him later when, after the bugle had ordered lights out, he lay in bed staring up into the darkness. Among the confused recollections of his first turbulent day, the incident of the foul interrogation protruded itself like a reptile rearing from the muck of tangled, swamp grass. It arrested him sharply, his curiosity at once aroused, his mind instantly alert, aware in an instinctive way that under its vulgarity, lay the key to what he knew had been carefully hidden from him, day in and day out, for the ten years of his life.

He continued his speculation all the next day as he took his place among his fellows and moved from mess hall to class-room, to parade-ground and back to his own room again, a cycle of petty duties that was to become his uneventful daily experience. He found himself looking from face to face among the boys at their desks in the Assembly Room, even to the impassive, hard features of Captain Marcus Strong who occasionally lifted his eyes from the pages of the book he read and slowly swept the room. Did each one of them know? Did that one and that one and that one know? Was he the only one of them all who did *not* know?

There were many more dangerous sources from which the knowledge that Griffith sought could have been obtained than his literal and slow-speaking room-mate. Pfaff sat on the edge of his own bed, squinting through puckered eyes at Griffith when he asked for enlightenment. Readily and unemotionally he told him, expressing himself in few words and without a suggestion of morbid interest in the younger boy's ignorance. Nor did he palliate the information. In his thick way of speaking he stated the facts baldly, almost coarsely, and Griffith heard them with a sickening sense of their truth.

Hours later as he lay in the darkness, wide-eyed and filled with loathing and disgust, he could hear Pfaff's clumsy phrases and see his fat lips form the words that had so shocked him. His outraged mind could only think of his lovely mother and again and again with teeth tight-clenched, he shook his head upon the pillow, refusing to accept the fact that she who was so warm, loving and beautiful could possibly be a willing party to a process so degrading. He would not believe, either, that his shy, sensitive father was ever capable of an act so revolting, a deed about which a vulgar crowd of school-boys could jest and jeer his son, shrieking their amusement at his embarrassment.

The knowledge he acquired made him acutely ashamed. He was ashamed of his mother, of his father, of himself, of the boys,

THE EDUCATION OF GRIFFITH ADAMS

and the head-master, and under-masters, of Mrs. Ostrander with her wide hips, of the fat Irish cook and her pimply-faced helper. He shut his hands over his face in the darkness as, with burning cheeks, he thought of the ordeal he must endure in the morning when he should have to stand before them, knowing their secret, and they looking at him, should know his. It seemed to Griffith that if this monstrous fact were so, the world was too dirty a place, was one in which he did not desire to live. He never wanted to see his mother again. Not that she appeared less modest and pure to him, but he felt that he, in possession of his knowledge, was now besmirched, no longer fit to breathe the same air with her, no longer worthy to touch her hand or accept her kiss or the soft pressure of her cheek against his.

IV

The discipline at The Fairview Military Academy was of a most rigid character. Captain Marcus Strong was a man of iron who ruled through fear, and Griffith soon came to realize that it was he who owned, managed and governed the Academy and not the Reverend Dana Ostrander.

A system devised by the Commandant provided for the whereabouts of every member of the school being instantly ascertained. Each day certain boys were detailed on what was known as guard duty and it was their business to keep track of their fellows. At any moment it was possible for Captain Strong to know where a boy was and what he was doing. If it so happened he could not be located, Strong proceeded to credit him with a demerit under the charge "Unaccounted for."

For each demerit imposed, the transgressing youth was required to sit at his desk in the Assembly Room with hands clasped and eyes front for fifteen minutes. Working off demerits took place Saturday afternoons and if the five hours were not sufficient to dispose of the number accumulated in a single week,—and this was frequently the case,—the afternoons of week days were so employed. If a boy succeeded in obtaining less than ten demerits during the week he was permitted to leave "bounds" for five hours on Sunday afternoon. He could wander over the hills back of the Academy, or visit friends in Lowell. In all the time that Griffith spent as an enrolled cadet of the Fairview Military Academy, the fewest number of demerits he ever received in one week was eleven. Demerits were sometimes given in quantities of four or eight or twelve. A third offense or infraction of a rule generally brought a "twelver,"—a three-hour punishment. A boy caught smoking received twenty-five. If the number of demerits rose over fifty within a single week he was put in the "jug."

Griffith inspected the jug when he had been only a few days at the school. Captain Strong put no obstacles in the way of its examination and there was a general eagerness on the part of the boys to impress newcomers with its terrors. They were all somewhat proud of the jug. A school-fellow who had spent three days in it was a hero among them thereafter.

The jug was located in the center of the attic of the long dormitory building: a room twelve feet square with two apertures on either side, window-sized and heavily iron-barred; there was also a grilled door. Light filtered in from the far ends of the attic where in the peaks of the roof were two small windows. Piles of trunks, the boys' luggage, mitigated even this pale diffusion, so that within the jug there prevailed a semi-darkness in which the bars across the apertures could be but dimly discerned. On the floor of the cell lay a heap of tumbled quilts and a lumpy mattress. Griffith was told that in hot weather the jug, directly beneath the low, hanging roof, became a suffocating oven, and in winter there was no protection against the cold except the torn and ragged comforters. There was no ventilation; the air in the attic was close and permeated with the pungent scent of moth-balls and camphor. Thrice a day when the cell was occupied, Strong, himself, brought the imprisoned boy three slices of unbuttered bread and a glass of water. The incarceration lasted from one to three days.

Griffith turned away shuddering. He wanted to escape from the building as quickly as possible and fill his lungs with the air outside. The boys who had invited him to view the jug, were delighted at its effect upon him. As he backed away toward the stairs, they ran after him and, dragging him by his thin arms, flung him into the blackness of the barred room, pushed to the bolt in the iron door, and clattered gleefully down the stairs, leaving him screaming his entreaties. It may have been five minutes, it may have been ten,—it seemed a long black hour of terror,—before it occurred to him that the door must have been merely bolted by the boys,—not locked,—and that he could reach the bolt through the grilling. The experience left an indelible impression. During the night that followed, he tossed and moaned, and once woke suddenly to find himself sitting up in his bed, his teeth clenched, his heart pounding, holding his breath.

It was after this that he came more and more to understand the shifting, side-long, evasive glances of his school-mates. He soon became aware that he, himself, had come to have the same look. Once when Captain Strong had abruptly entered the Assembly Room, Griffith felt it upon his face, felt it as if some unfamiliar twist of his features, while within him rose that fear and hatred of the man he grew to cherish with vindictive satisfaction.

It was some three months after he had entered the Fairview Military Academy that a boy was "jugged." The unfortunate youth had broken bounds and as this was his second offense, he was ordered to the jug for forty-eight hours. For a long time after his imprisonment was over, Griffith was haunted by the wild, roving look in his eyes. He imagined he acted a little queerly after the experience and felt sure his suspicions had been correct when the boy came down with a high fever a few weeks later and his uncle came and took him away in an ambulance.

Before the close of the spring term, the jug was again occupied. One of the older boys, a youth by the name of McGinnis, a hulking young Irish lad, one of the Academy's football stars, struck Captain Strong with his clenched fist. The Commandant was sitting in his swivel chair at his desk in the Assembly Room and McGinnis was standing on the platform beside him. It was the study hour and the boys were bent over their books under the cones of light that streamed from the shaded oil lamps. Griffith recalled afterwards hearing McGinnis' voice haltingly raised as he urged some point in a long argument with Strong. At the end of a short final question, there came the Commandant's sharp, imperative "No," and it was then the boy struck.

All his life Griffith remembered the gigantic figure of the man as he rose towering from his seat, and the dull bronze suffusion of his copper face. For a moment he stood with his arm upraised as McGinnis crouched before him, hands above his head, and the rows of boys' faces at their desks shone in the white light of the glaring lamps like the bright bowls of polished spoons. Then came the swift descent of the huge fist and McGinnis crumpled up on the floor like a suddenly deflated bag. Strong stepped over his body, thrust his fingers into the boy's collar and dragged him out of the room. Griffith put his head down on his desk and tried to control a violent sensation of nausea while a wild hubbub broke out around him.

McGinnis spent three days in the jug. After his confinement was over he was as buoyant and as cheerful as ever, and seemed to cherish no ill-will. He became the idol of the school and was elected captain of the football team for the following year.

V

Griffith was not unhappy at the Academy. There were the football and baseball games with other schools, dances two or three times a year when the girls from Lowell and from Miss Chadwick's Seminary came to the Armory and two-stepped and waltzed upon its freshly-waxed floor in the arms of the cadets uncomfortable in their be-buttoned full dress. There was the tennis in which he commenced to take an interest, and there was Professor Horatio Guthrie. This was his music teacher who came to the Academy on Tuesdays and Thursdays to give lessons to those boys whose parents were willing to pay the extra ten dollars a month.

Professor Guthrie was an extremely young man with a high-pitched voice and long sensitive fingers. He was distressingly thin and his lips trembled whenever he began to speak. The boys of the Academy made a great deal of fun of him but Griffith conceived a genuine affection for him, partly because of his own awakened interest in music, partly because of Professor Guthrie's kindness and gentleness to him. Griffith often spent the free hours, after school was over, in the music room, practising his scales and working over passages bracketed for his attention, beside which, in his teacher's gentle handwriting, appeared the underlined and repeated command: *"Count."*

THE EDUCATION OF GRIFFITH ADAMS 23

Griffith remained three years at the Fairview Military Academy. He learned many things there. He was like a reedy young plant that sucks up the bad with the good in the soil packed about its roots. He had long roots and they went down deep, stretching out their tendrils, reaching, investigating, absorbing.

He learned how to study and how to obey; he learned how to deceive and how to lie; he learned to fear and to hate; he learned to love music and to be happy when he was alone. If during the first few days at the school his innocence had been brutally affronted by the coarseness of his fellows, if he came to know indecent language and to listen unshocked and unmoved to obscene stories, the rigid discipline of the school protected him from anything worse. His purity was untarnished. If there was corruption in the Academy he neither knew it nor saw it; Captain Strong drove his boys too hard to give them time for mischief; the arduous routine of the school day tired them out; he studied to keep them active.

Griffith was quick-witted and because he could think faster than the other boys, could invent excuses and fabricate misstatements with glib and ready assurance, his gift came to be recognized, and he was nicknamed "Anny," a contraction for Ananias. All the boys lied,—bold-facedly and shamelessly. If a demerit could be avoided by lying, they lied without compunction. Griffith was proud of his title and was himself sometimes astonished at the quick and plausible explanations he was able to invent at a moment's notice. At the end of his second year, however, there occurred an instance when this habit of untruthfulness that had grown upon him made his blundering room-mate accept a punishment which should have been his. The "twelver" Captain Strong gave Pfaff for the offense brought that unfortunate youth's weekly total of demerits over the fifty mark and he was sent to the jug for twenty-four hours. Griffith, frightened by what he had done, waited too long: he waited until he knew his confession would have sent him to the jug in Pfaff's place. He had not the courage to spend a night in that black den of terrors, neither was he able to bring himself to say anything about the matter to Pfaff when he came out, but he knew that Pfaff knew he had lied and he despised himself as a betrayer and a coward. He was just thirteen years old.

VI

There was only one boy in the school of whom Griffith made a friend. His name was David Sothern and he did not enter the Academy until Griffith's third year. He was two years older than Griffith: fair-headed, lantern-jawed, tall and loose-jointed, with a clear, sharp pair of blue eyes, heavy eyebrows and a way of bringing them together in a quick frown when he was thinking hard. David radiated strength,—not so much physical strength as mental. He electrified Griffith by his readiness to pass judgment upon the boys, upon the Reverend Dana Ostrander, Captain Strong and the instructors. Because they said a thing was so, or this was right and that wrong, did not settle the matter for David; he wanted to know the why and wherefore. What Captain Strong said was law to Griffith but not to David. Once in the Assembly Room, David rose in his seat and found the courage to question one of Strong's verdicts. Respectful in his manner, he asked the reasons for the rule which seemed to him unfair and unnecessary.

Griffith saw the steely look he had come to know so well glisten in Strong's eyes. David was chalk white as he faced it but he remained standing until Strong answered him slowly and with an even deadly tone.

"It is because *I* say so. . . . Take your seat."

And although David sat down as he was told, he still believed it was his right to see the justice of an order before he obeyed it. Griffith knew that Strong had the boy marked from that hour. At the first opportunity, the Commandant would attempt to break his spirit.

David's father had been the editor of a daily newspaper in Topeka, Kansas. Both he and his wife had been killed in a cyclone that had caught them unawares in a frail buggy as they urged the horse to a mad gallop in an effort to reach their home and their children. David was eight when this catastrophe occurred and his sister, Margaret, five. There was not even a life insurance, so the boy went to work in the newspaper office at three dollars a week and rich neighbors, named Barondess, adopted his sister. Adolph Barondess was a Hollander who had come to America with his wife many years before and had prospered at farming. Coal had

THE EDUCATION OF GRIFFITH ADAMS

been discovered upon his land and he had turned from agriculture to mining and grown rich. Shortly after the adoption of David's sister, he had decided to close out his coal interests in Topeka and establish himself and his family in New York. David was not to be abandoned and Barondess undertook to arrange for his education. But the relationship between the boy and his benefactor was not happy. Barondess was dictatorial and domineering, and he believed David should show and constantly express gratitude for his generosity. He had none of the affection for him that he had for his little sister. The boy felt this and resented accepting favors from a man who gave them as charity. He had been too long adrift in the world not to resent any curtailment of his freedom. At eight he had had to shift for himself, feed and clothe his body out of his three dollars a week. In the five years he had knocked about Topeka after his parents' death, he had learned a great deal about life and had set his small mind to a firm determination to become rich. After his experience as printer's devil in the newspaper office, he had sold papers, hawked fruit, run an elevator, worked as a "puddler" in a foundry, driven a farm truck, become a bell-hop in a hotel, and, saving money, launched himself as a laundry agent. He was struggling to make a success of his little business when Barondess offered him an education. School and tutors followed, but David and his benefactor speedily reached the conclusion that they could not get along with one another. Boarding School was suggested and the Fairview Military Academy selected.

VII

David chafed under the restrictions and regulations of the institution. His spirit rebelled against the rule that he must not step beyond certain established lines that bounded a definitely prescribed area. He begrudgingly accepted Strong's mandates and obeyed the school's laws with a bad grace. Griffith's undisguised admiration won his friendship, and he poured into the younger boy's sympathetic ears his indignant protests and rebellious anger. Griffith listened to him, drank in his confidences and mused over the stories of his short fifteen years, till it seemed to him that

David was the most wonderful person in the world. He conceived for him that blind idolatry which only a young heart can know. Even the Fairview Military Academy became a paradise under the influence of this new and splendid friendship.

It was a startling suggestion to Griffith when David proposed they run away together; but he did not hesitate. David was determined he would no longer endure Captain Strong's obvious persecution. The Commandant was goading the rebellious boy into an outbreak that would furnish him with an excuse to jug him. Griffith believed that Strong enjoyed the process of subjugating a recalcitrant spirit and David promised him an unusually pleasant experience. Together they assembled four dollars and sixty cents and this, the self-reliant David assured his friend, was ample to take them as far as Boston. There something would turn up and they would begin to make their fortunes.

Griffith never doubted. He packed his satchel and slid out of his window on an improvised rope of knotted sheets to meet David by the laundry, behind the Armory. They knew well enough that Captain Strong would make a vigorous effort to overtake them. Time and again he had dealt with runaway boys, and the police of Lowell had aided him in their capture. David decided therefore to strike off in an absolutely opposite direction and, making a *detour* of the city, hit the highway to Boston below it.

The boys trudged until early the following morning and slept the next six hours under a tree in a field of stubble. They had left the coats of their blue-gray uniforms behind them; when they woke they ripped off the heavy, black braid which ran down the outside of their trousers; neither wore a hat. Their efforts to disguise themselves were pitifully futile; every boy who had run away from the Fairview Military Academy had done exactly the same things. The first farmer they met on the road driving to market his early spring load of radishes and peas, waved to them, grinning broadly.

"Hope you don't get caught!" he shouted.

If misgivings began to enter Griffith's heart, he left them unexpressed. His feet began to be sore and he grew hungry. At a saloon at a cross-roads' juncture they bought a loaf of bread, a bag of green apples, and two five-cent bottles of sarsaparilla, whose foaming pink contents could be drunk after banging the iron staple-like stopper against a hard surface. David's spirit was indomitable; he kept buoyantly on, enjoying his freedom, planning what they would do when they reached Boston.

Toward the late afternoon, Griffith commenced to have severe cramps in his stomach. His sufferings rapidly increased and presently he was in agony. He lay down in the grass by the side of the road and with knuckles dug into his eyes, prayed that he might die. Even David's resourcefulness failed in this unexpected difficulty. Griffith writhed and moaned, panting with exhaustion between the sharp pains.

A man driving by in a buggy, pulled up his horse and asked what the matter was. David alarmed and at a loss to know what to do, explained. The man ordered him to put Griffith into the seat beside him. They were both sure that the boy had in some way been poisoned and that he would die in one of the convulsions that seized him every few minutes. The horse was urged to a brisk trot and David ran along behind, holding on to the tail-board of the rattling vehicle. They presently reached a drug-store which was also a corner grocery and a village dry-goods store, situated at a cross-roads in a group of white cottages and farm buildings. The proprietor,—a bespectacled, unshaved New Englander,—shook his head and rubbed his chin dubiously as he listened to Griffith's moans and watched his writhings. David began to cry and the man in the buggy to swear. There was no doctor to be had within three and a half miles.

In the tumult of these lamentations there suddenly appeared a red-faced, enormous female with round bulging cheeks and an abdomen which protruded like an inverted bottom of a wash-tub. She listened silently to David's broken story, then decisively and with a convincing finality, uttered the words:

"*Sour apples!*"

The diagnosis boomed from her like the report of a cannon.

She gathered Griffith in her arms, carried him upstairs into the room over the grocery and presently, supporting his head in the great cup of her hand, she poured a scalding drink of Jamaica ginger into him.

With the cessation of pain, he almost instantly fell asleep and when he awoke, Captain Strong stood grimly looking down at him. Pinned to his shirt was a pencilled note from David.

"They have sent word to the school. Write me care of your mother. I will go to see her as soon as I reach Boston. Good luck.
"DAVID."

VIII

Griffith drove back to the Fairview Military Academy with Captain Strong. Neither spoke as they jogged along in the school's two-seated rig with its fringed and ragged top. Griffith was too deep in utter despair to care what became of him. Now that it was certain that he was to be jugged, he no longer feared the man beside him. He felt that he had been deserted by his mother and his friend and nothing now mattered.

When he reached the Academy he followed Strong up the four long flights to the attic in the dormitory building and heard the snap of the bolt and the turn of the key in the iron door, without a disquieting sensation.

He slept and woke and slept again. He listened to the bugle calls and heard the shouting of his school-fellows as they raced to be first upon the tennis courts when school was out. The commands of the cadet officer at drill hour reached him, and the tinkle of the piano in the music room filtered up through the intervening floors. Toward the middle of the day it became excessively warm in the attic and the odor of moth balls and camphor grew noticeably more suffocating. The water-pipes clacked and gurgled throughout the day and pigeons cooed on the roof incessantly. At night Griffith could hear the scuttling of many rats and their sharp, angry squeaks. Sometimes before the light entirely faded he was able to coax them out from behind the protecting piles of luggage where they hid by throwing bits of bread to them through the iron bars of his window. Once he awoke sharply in the night to feel the scurrying feet of one of them upon him and to hear the sound of the intruders mad flight.

It was the end of the second day before he gave way. He was convinced that Strong would let him out when forty-eight hours had passed but when taps sounded and the Commandant did not appear to order him to his room, it seemed that another black night in the rat-ridden garret was more than his mind could endure. He cried until his eyes hurt, and his face was swollen and puffed. The blood pounded in his head and hunger gnawed at his stomach. He called for Captain Strong at the top of his voice, promising he would "be good." His clamor frightened the rats and the profound silence of the night enveloped him like the great folds of a thick blanket. He sank a quivering heap beside the iron grilling of the door and lay moaning and sobbing until the rats, growing indifferent to his noise recommenced their squeaking and drove him into another paroxysm of terror. Toward midnight he fell asleep from exhaustion, a worn-out little organism, crushed and broken.

Captain Strong hauled him to his feet in the morning and pulled him into the light that streamed through the open attic door. He seemed satisfied that the limp and drooping little boy he held up by the arm had been sufficiently punished. Griffith, stumbling and dazed, staggered down the stairs, found his room, and dropped upon his bed. One of the cadet officers came to see him presently and told him to take a hot bath and get into bed. Griffith was physically unable to make the effort. Mrs. Ostrander came later and regarded him speculatively with folded arms and lips puckered like the mouth of a draw-string bag; and then there was the doctor.

"Just rest," the physician recommended, "he'd better stay in bed for a few days. You could fix him up in a quieter room. He's rather young . . . a little careful nourishment . . . he'll be round again by the end of the week."

They carried Griffith over to the head-master's house and put him to bed there in a vacant room adjoining Dr. Ostrander's, and gave him soup, creamed chicken and preserved peaches, and it was here, three days later, his mother found him.

She came into the little gray room in which he lay, a glorified vision of soft loveliness. As she knelt beside his bed and gathered him into her arms and held him close against her fragrant breast, Griffith's love for her was overwhelming. They both were crying, the boy sobbing passionately, the tears upon his mother's lovely face leaving wet lines behind them as they washed away the fine powder upon her cheeks.

"Oh, Griffey . . . Griffey!" Mrs. Adams cried, hugging him to her, "why didn't you tell me? All these years! Your little friend came to see me. . . . I didn't understand at first. . . I thought he was trying to sell me something. Then he told me! I wouldn't believe him at first but he seemed such an honest little fellow I couldn't help but be convinced. . . . But you had never said a word! Griffey, dear . . . I came as fast as I could! My darling boy! You're a perfect *sight!*"

"You'll take me home, mother dear?" Griffith sobbed. "You'll not make me stay here any more?"

"Just as fast as you can pack your trunk, my own boy. You're to come home with mother and mother'll take care of you. We'll go down to the Cape as soon as ever we can get away."

CHAPTER III

I

FOR the next two years Griffith attended the public schools in Cambridge. Mrs. Castro Verbeck had become a widow, her black-headed husband having unexpectedly made her one following an operation for appendicitis. Mrs. Adams was anxious to go to Europe and Mrs. Verbeck's straitened circumstances made leaving Griffith in her keeping appear a charitable as well as a convenient arrangement. A hotel was no place for a growing boy, and certainly travelling about from place to place was not the right kind of an atmosphere for him.

Life in Cambridge in Mrs. Verbeck's shabby little house on Trowbridge Street became a curious interlude in Griffith's development. There were other boarders, mostly Harvard students, who, if they noticed him at all, resented his presence among them. He was interested in his rabbits which he kept in a converted dog-house in the back yard and in Susie White, a spoiled, petulant little girl who lived next door. He liked to stroke the rabbits and feel their soft fur under his palm, and he would have liked to touch the little girl's cheek and drew his finger-tips ever so gently down the side of her face. He persuaded himself he was in love with Susie White, who was an undeveloped child and accepted his adoration as she did that of her grandmother and her aunts, with casual indifference. Griffith kept a diary in these days and vented his passion for his little straight-haired neighbor by covering its pages with extravagant expressions of it.

Mrs. Verbeck did not concern herself too closely with his welfare. With her husband's death she began to assert herself for the first time in her life. The petty demands that the conduct of a boarding-house made upon her, awoke a self-expression and an independence she herself and everyone else believed had long ago died within her. She devoted herself with a fierce joy to the management of the details of her business. Twice a year she took

Griffith to Jordan & Marsh in Boston and bought clothes for him extravagantly, charging her purchases to his mother's account. Otherwise she left him to himself. She could find no fault with his behavior; he came and went to school regularly and amused himself after school was out; he gave her little cause for worry. She devoted considerably more thought to the timely arrival of the sixty dollars a month from his mother's attorney than she did to the boy himself.

Fortunately Griffith did not need supervision during these days between his thirteenth and fourteenth years. His development was slow, but he grew amazingly tall. Little Miss Bates, who was Mrs. Verbeck's cousin and who occupied the parlor suite, declared every morning at breakfast that she could "just *see* that boy grow."

Griffith found the time hung heavy on his hands and he began to read again. He read Dumas and Thackeray and Dickens; interspersed with literature of this kind were books by G. P. R. James, Fenimore Cooper and Archibald Gunther; surreptitiously he read the stories of Horatio Alger and G. A. Henty. He got his books at the Public Library and was obliged to apply in the juvenile department for those by the two last named writers, which was always an ordeal for him.

He found he was older than most of the boys at the Grammar School he attended. It was one of the best public schools in Cambridge and unusually well-bred children attended it. He made few friends among his school-fellows however. The habit of ready and unnecessary lying which he had acquired at the Fairview Military Academy clung to him. It was this perhaps as much as any other definite cause which made him unpopular with both teachers and pupils. At this public school, the classes, or grades as they were called, were divided into sections. Thus there were two halves to the eighth grade to which Griffith belonged: Section A and Section B. Griffith was the "bad boy" of Section B. Miss Street, the teacher, a hard-featured, sharp-nosed New Englander, conceived a strong dislike for him. He had a contempt for her shrill reprimands and mild punishments after Captain Strong's brand of discipline, and showed it. He knew she was powerless and he openly enjoyed her discomfiture. He used to stare at her fixedly for long intervals while she bit her lip and tried not to notice his steady scrutiny.

THE EDUCATION OF GRIFFITH ADAMS

At the mid-year, Miss Street and the teacher in charge of the other section of the Eighth Grade, Miss Fisher, decided on the experiment of exchanging "bad boys." Miss Fisher's incorrigible was a hulking young negro named Shaw. Griffith pretended to be diverted at the trade but in his heart he was offended, and entered Miss Fisher's class with the same belligerent, sulky attitude toward his new teacher that he had employed against his former one.

A new experience was in store for him. Miss Fisher was considerably younger than Miss Street—a woman about twenty-four or five. She was a Radcliffe graduate, and had a better understanding of boys than Miss Street, despite the advantages of the other woman's additional twelve years' experience as a teacher. Miss Fisher still aspired to reach ideals; she took her work seriously and tried hard for results. She was moreover a pretty woman with heavy masses of dark hair, coarse and wavy; her eyebrows and eyelashes were thick and black, her lips were crimson and nicely shaped, and she had white and unusually beautiful teeth. The bloom of her cheeks in her dark olive skin suggested the coat of a russet apple.

Griffith never forgot the moment when Miss Fisher, walking up and down along the aisles between the desks, paused behind his seat, which was at the rear of the room, the last in the row, and rested her hand upon it as she held the text-book in the other, calling upon the various pupils in recitation. The curve of the woman's arm fitted the back of Griffith's head and instinctively he leaned against it.

The contact had an amazing effect upon him. The woman by accident had found a vulnerable spot in the hard casing of his youth. The pressure of her arm against his head was for him a caress and he responded instantly. As day after day the same thing occurred, he began to conceive a strong affection for Miss Fisher; he thought her beautiful and watched her covertly. He used eagerly to wait for the moment when she would rise from her desk and begin her slow threading of the aisles which would bring her eventually beside his seat and to the casual, careless placing of her arm behind his head.

Responding to her interest and affection, Griffith became metamorphosed. From being Miss Street's "bad boy," he became Miss

Fisher's "favorite." He was chosen to be monitor when she left the room; it was he who was called upon to shut and open the high windows with the window-pole and it was his privilege to water the geraniums in the window boxes. He resolutely refused to whisper and became daily filled with an increasing desire to try to please his teacher.

Suddenly he was aware that something had happened to him. Without warning or premonition he was sexually awake. It was a startling and perplexing experience which thrilled and at the same time distressed him. He did not understand it. But Miss Fisher recognized only too clearly the change that was taking place in him. He had responded so instantly to the little affection she had shown him, at first she had felt intensely sorry for him; presently however she began to be conscious of a more definite emotion. The attraction for her which she had easily recognized in his gaze of devotion, she was forced gradually to admit to herself she experienced in return. Something drew her to this tall gawky, ambling boy with his unshaved chin, wistful eyes and tumbling hair. She wanted to push back that hair from his unhappy eyes and draw his head down against her breast and fold him in her arms.

One afternoon he stayed after school and when the last of the boys had gone home, she questioned him about himself, asked about his mother and father, where he lived and how. She seemed to think his story unusually appealing; repeatedly she told him how sorry she was for him. As Griffith described his life at Mrs. Verbeck's, she shook her head slowly, her heavy eyebrows twisted into a troubled frown, her lips moving sympathetically. Later he walked home with her to the little house in which she lived with her mother north of the Square.

Often after this, Griffith stayed when school was over and walked home with Miss Fisher. Their attraction for each other troubled them both. The boy was vaguely unhappy without knowing why; his dreams at night bothered him; he passionately hungered for Miss Fisher's caresses. When she stroked his hair or held his hand, he was transported into a paroxysm of delight. It was a different matter with the woman. She fully understood the attraction that drew them toward one another, but she could not forget the great disparity in their ages. She considered their affection

THE EDUCATION OF GRIFFITH ADAMS 35

unnatural, and yet she found Griffith's charming adolescence strangely appealing. Continually waves of troubled conscience overtook her, and she would brusquely withdraw her hand from Griffith's ardent clasp, and summarily send him home. Humbly he obeyed her, upbraiding himself for having, in some inexplicable way, offended her again.

One rainy afternoon in March he accompanied her home, carrying her books and a heavy bundle of examination papers. He stayed while she made tea, and gave him huge wedges of chocolate cake. It was after he had put on his overcoat, and was standing, hat and umbrella in hand, just inside the front doorway, that she suddenly drew his head down, put her arms about his neck, and kissed him ardently upon the mouth.

The effect upon the boy was electrical. His head was in a mad whirl of intoxication as he stumbled homeward. He lived in a sensuous state of delight through the evening that followed and far into the night. He believed himself to be madly and desperately in love. Marriage awaited him: marriage with the most desirable and beautiful woman in the whole world.

II

The next day his mother arrived in Cambridge unexpectedly. She brought with her a third husband, a man thirteen years younger than herself, of Italian and American origin. Paolo Santini's mother came from Cincinnati, his father from Naples. He had the Continental manner and a clever American mind. Griffith liked him in spite of his narrow waist and small delicate mustache with its waxed points. Santini took pains to win his stepson's affection. Griffith was full of his mad infatuation; he talked eagerly of his marriage to the lady of his dreams; he spoke confidently of it as if it were to occur within the month. His mother, interested and surprised at this evidence of her son's maturity, listened to him until his rhapsodies on Miss Fisher's charms bored her. Then she commenced to laugh at him and ridicule what she spoke of as his "puppy-love." The boy deceived by her first show of interest, had poured out his young love in a passionate avowal. The lightness with which his mother dismissed his hopes and plans hurt him deeply.

Santini however was full of sympathy. He urged Griffith's cause with his wife, speaking rapidly in Italian until the recent Mrs. Adams suddenly became annoyed and angry. Her emphatic reply to his animated plea elicited a hurried and conciliatory shrug. She proceeded to deal with the situation summarily. Griffith never saw Miss Fisher again. The day his mother arrived, he quitted Mrs. Verbeck's sheltering roof and moved to the hotel in Boston with his mother and stepfather. That night he wrote a long, passionate letter to the woman he believed was the eternal mistress of his heart. It was a weird epistle of blots and scrawled writing, vehement assertions of his love and reiterated declarations of his enduring constancy. His tears dropped upon the paper as he wrote and he fell asleep convinced that his heart was forever broken and his life ruined.

The next week the Santinis left for California and took Griffith with them. At fifteen the boy had reached an awkward, clumsy, unattractive age that was a source of great annoyance and chagrin to his exquisite mother, who, nearing fifty, appeared no more than her husband's age. Griffith had grown so rapidly he had become distressingly round-shouldered. It was impossible for him to stand erect; he slouched and shambled when he walked and he drooped over his plate at table so that his mouth was but a few inches from his food. His manners were atrocious and his habits were not cleanly. Mrs. Verbeck had not concerned herself with these. His teeth had become discolored from neglect, and his breath usually was bad. Lastly his complexion of which his mother had been always proud, deserted him; it became waxy and unhealthy-looking, small white pimples appeared upon his forehead and about his nostrils and chin. His mother eventually might have overcome the distress his appearance caused her, but she found it impossible to tolerate his clumsiness. Everything Griffith handled he dropped. He was forever stumbling over people's legs, stepping on the train of her gown, knocking over his drinking tumbler at meal-time.

He grew ashamed and daily more unhappy; he lost faith in himself. He loved his mother; he admired her immensely and was anxious to please her, but he saw he failed completely. He strove to do what she wanted, but succeeded only in irritating her. Her dissatisfaction with him was becoming almost aversion. The four months spent in the West left an impression upon Griffith's mind only of rebuffs and corrections. His mother would continually break out with:

"Oh . . . Griffith . . . *don't!* Mercy me, boy! don't you realize what you are doing? . . . You *mustn't, mustn't, mustn't* do such things! . . . Why don't you *think* a moment? If you will only use your brain! . . . I don't know *what* I'm going to do with you!"

III

It was at the Hotel del Coronado that Griffith met Archie McCleish. He was a boy a few months older than himself, thick-set, sandy-haired, sandy-faced, quiet and undemonstrative with dull, opaque, gray eyes. His father, Archibald Walter McCleish, was a national figure in financial and railroad circles,—a powerful money-making genius, and a millionaire, whose name at times figured prominently in the newspapers of the country. The private car in which the McCleish family travelled had been backed on a railroad siding on the beach below the hotel. Beside the stern, clean-shaved, square-shouldered, compact financier, and his pale-faced, gentle wife, there were two older sisters like their mother in manner and appearance, and Archie, the only son, the centre of the family's pride and solicitude.

Archie was like his father. He was Scotch in appearance and temperament. Already there radiated from his fifteen years a certain reserved force and dependableness. He had a strong personality but was hampered by a stubbornness inherent in his character. He spoke infrequently and had a slow delivery that was sometimes irritating.

"He's an uncanny child," Mrs. Santini declared. "I can't make him out. He gives one the feeling he's forever taking one's measure, —judging you; I'm actually uncomfortable when I'm rattling along about something and see those dull gray eyes of his fixed upon me. But he has exquisite manners! He acts like a grown man, doesn't he, Paolo? Rather British, I should say. I'm so glad you're friendly with him, Griffey; I wish you were more like him. Do take a leaf from his book, and imitate his ways!"

Winter is the season at Coronado and in July there are few guests at the Hotel. Griffith made Archie's acquaintance as the natural result of both boys' desire for companionship. They had few interests in common; besides lacking imagination, Archie had little sense of humor. He took things literally, seldom smiled and when he did, Griffith usually failed to find anything particularly amusing in what he considered diverting.

In the natural course of events the boys' mothers met and mild Mrs. McCleish found nothing but what was pleasant and agreeable in the talkative, pretty woman who joined her frequently on the hotel veranda. Inevitably they discussed the subject of schools and one day Griffith's mother said to him:

"Mrs. McCleish told me about a wonderful school which Archie attends; it's in Concord, where all the poets and great writers used to live, you know. There are only twenty-five boys, and Mrs. McCleish says they watch over them just like a father and mother; it's not a *military* school, it's a *home* school; just like one big family. It's called the Concord *Family* School. I think it would be an excellent place for you, Griffith, . . . if it isn't too expensive."

During the next few weeks it was decided to give the new school a trial. Mrs. McCleish continued to praise it to Griffith's mother; Archie said the boys had a lot of fun with their canoes. It did not open however until mid-September which was unfortunate as Mr. and Mrs. Santini were anxious to return to Italy. An uncle of Paolo was failing in health and there was much talk between Griffith's mother and his stepfather of the possibility of a reconciliation before the old man died. Signor Gualtiero Santini was wealthy; there were not many heirs; if the old disagreement could be patched up, . . . Paolo had been his favorite nephew. . . .

Eventually it was arranged that Griffith should go and stay at the school for the month before its fall term began and so allow the Santinis to sail for Italy without delay. The boy was eager for the new experience. He had grown almost sullen and surly under his mother's constant fault-finding.

IV

Early in August Mrs. Santini took her son to Concord and left him in Mr. and Mrs. Garfield's hands. She went away perfectly satisfied. It seemed to her that nothing could be more desirable for Griffith at this gawky, unformed, undeveloped period; she was convinced that the influence of the refined "homey" school would do more for her boy than she could do herself.

The Concord Family School was situated on the outskirts of the historic town, beyond the river that winds and winds its way about it. Griffith shared his mother's confidence that he was going to be happy in his new environment. Mr. Garfield, a short, bearded little man with a somewhat uncertain eye, impressed them both as being kindly and intelligent. He showed them over the grounds and buildings and Griffith was enchanted with the house-boat down beside the bridge on the river-bank where the boys kept their canoes, particularly when his mother promised she would order one and have it shipped to him at once. Behind the Garfield home, —a rambling old delightful, white New England homestead,—was a large, yellow, glaringly-new, barnlike building where the boys ate, studied and lived. Mr. Garfield explained at length his reason for limiting the number in his school to twenty-five; not only did it carry out his ideas of individual supervision and personal interest, but, he added laughing, it was all he had room for!

Downstairs in the school building, the floor was divided into class-rooms, a kind of parlor, a large dining-room, and kitchen. On the second floor, arranged on three sides and opening on a large general lounging room in the centre, were the quarters where the boys slept. These were small affairs, like cells, but open at the top. They had no doors, a portière hung over the entrance; there was a window, a bed, a bureau, and a chair; the thin walls of tongued and grooved painted boarding rose ten feet above the floor, leaving an open space of four or five feet between the top of the partition and the ceiling. These quarters were called "cubicles." Mr. Garfield explained they allowed each boy a certain necessary privacy without eliminating the supervision that was equally desirable. An under-master slept at either end of the lounging-room, and there was also a matron.

Griffith kissed his mother goodbye dutifully and unemotionally; he was eager she should not forget about his canoe; he shouted a reminder of it as her carriage rolled down the strip of gravel road before the house. He experienced no pang at parting from her; rather he felt a lifting of a heavy weight from his shoulders. He was intoxicated with his freedom; exuberant with the thought of his own independence.

V

On the fifteenth of September, the pupils and the two under-masters,—young Wesleyan graduates,—arrived. Most of the boys came from Boston, some from Providence, Springfield and Hartford, a few from New York. They were a different lot from those that had attended the Fairview Military Academy; all were rich men's sons; frail youths for the most part, domineering and arrogant. They proceeded at once to make Griffith's life miserable.

The school was divided into two natural groups: the older and the younger boys. Griffith fell between. Largely due to his wide reading, he was mentally as old if not older than boys two or three years his senior. His age put him with the younger members of the school, but he could not bring himself to associate with them. McCleish, who arrived a week after school opened, and whom Griffith was overjoyed to see again, held himself aloof from either group. The effect of his quiet, reserved, forceful nature was markedly evident among his school-fellows. They respected him and he was popular with them.

In less than a fortnight's time, Griffith became the butt of the school. His new associates took offense at many of the same things his mother had railed at him to correct. The smaller boys followed their elders' lead. There were seven of these young devils and they formed a band which became Griffith's daily and nightly torment. He was easily teased, quietly enduring, and their obvious success in annoying him and his failure to retaliate, made him an ideal object for their persecution. At any hour of the day when no other amusement presented itself, the younger boys would commence their programme of "getting after Adams." He could hear their whispers and giggles at his back, and knew at any moment a missile might strike him on the head. He tried to hide from them, but they soon discovered his attempt to avoid them and enjoyed all too well the game of finding where he was concealed. He resorted to going to bed early in the evening, immediately after the study hour, to escape their persecution, but shortly after he retired pieces of fire-wood, coal, and presently logs would come clattering, crashing down into his cubicle over the partitions. The under-masters saw the abuse to which he was subjected but they only interfered when the regulations of the school were infringed or the noise became too violent. Griffith was unpopular with them as he was with the boys. During the first week of school he was caught in a flagrant and unnecessary falsehood; within the next few days he was apprehended in another. The curling lip of Mr. Sanborn eloquently expressed his contemptuous opinion of the new boy. From that day he was dubbed the "sneaking liar" by the boys and Mr. Sanborn approved. Griffith's stoop-shouldered, ungainly length, his shuffling walk, his bad complexion and unpleasant breath were all subjects of derision among his schoolmates. Whatever self-confidence he possessed deserted him entirely; he grew timid and was easily frightened; he became what the whole school considered him: a sneak.

VI

Several weeks passed at the Concord Family School before Griffith became aware of certain vile practises of a few of the older and most of the younger boys. He was fascinated and curious at first; the ring-leaders among his tormentors were the worst offenders. His nature revolted in disgust when he discovered that the little boys were being debased by their seniors. He was horrified and repelled; his position in the school might have been considerably ameliorated had he not shown his repugnance so openly. The iron rule of Captain Marcus Strong had prevented the possibility of any such bullying or viciousness at the Fairview Military Academy. Griffith would have been glad to go back there.

VII

The first year at Concord was a long and dreadful ordeal. He dragged out his life, counting the days until June should come and bring to an end an existence so miserable. Once a fortnight he received a letter from his mother: she was still in Naples; Uncle Gualtiero was failing; he might die any day; a complete reconciliation had been effected between the old man and his favorite nephew. She was sorry to hear that Griffith did not like his school; it was a great disappointment to her. Wouldn't he try and make the best of things? He might grow to like it in time.

It was a staggering blow to the boy on a day in May when the apple blossoms were dropping from the trees behind the school dormitory, and the air was heavy with the smell of new grass, that Mr. Garfield sent for him to come to his study, and there told him that his mother had written she would be obliged to remain in Italy and desired to make an arrangement by which Griffith could stay with the Garfields during the approaching summer. In a subsequent letter to himself, she explained how impossible it was for her to return to America while Uncle Gualtiero continued so ill, urging him to be a good boy and she would try to come over in September, and find a new school for him.

But September brought a similar communication and Griffith faced the opening of school with bitter hatred and dread. He had not been unhappy during the summer months for he had spent the long, hot days in his canoe paddling up and down the beautiful Concord River, and in roaming the hills behind the school with a small twenty-two calibre rifle, purchased with some extra money his mother had sent him. As the return of the boys grew more and more imminent his fear of their cruelty and abuse was a daily and nightly terror; he became like a wild thing that feels the approach of its natural enemy; he hugged his rifle in his arms, dreaming his retaliation, imagining his persecutors' ignominious rout, his fearful revenge.

Upon the night of the first day of the opening of school the hectoring and abuse were resumed, the old boys being anxious to show the new ones the established methods of handling the school "sneak." Lyman, the chief of Griffith's former enemies, swaggered

THE EDUCATION OF GRIFFITH ADAMS 43

up to him and struck him with his open palm upon the side of his head.

Griffith turned with a snarl and with fingers hooked and teeth bared flung himself upon the bigger boy. Both went down upon the floor. Griffith did not use his fists; he did not know how. The animal in him, spurred by terror, suddenly rose insensate and uncontrolled, sweeping away his accustomed fear, rendering him blind to consequences. His nails sunk into the boy's face and his teeth buried themselves in his neck.

An uproar followed. Lyman had been severely bitten; his face terribly mutilated. Griffith was regarded with horror; he would be expelled from the school, arrested and sent to prison. Lyman's father came down to Concord and withdrew his son from the school, promising he would bring an action against the institution and against Griffith. The nicknames of "the sneak" and "the liar" to which Griffith had become accustomed gave place to "the dog" and "the biter." The school held a meeting and the boys decided to ostracize him: no one was to speak to him; he was to be left entirely to himself.

His crime however brought no further results. Mr. Garfield considered the matter of his expulsion, but decided this step was "hardly practical." The boy's parents were in Italy; the school's revenue had already been depleted by several hundred dollars through the loss of one pupil; nothing would be accomplished in doubling this loss by sending another away. Mr. Garfield finally decided that the boys themselves had handled the situation in a highly creditable manner, and their ostracism of the offender would be more efficacious as a punishment than any which he himself might inflict. At the same time he felt sure that their concerted action undoubtedly would raise the *morale* of the entire school.

But his ostracism by his school-mates was a great satisfaction to Griffith. He heartily enjoyed his enforced isolation, and was happier than he had been at any time since he had come to the Concord Family School.

Fortunately Archie McCleish had not been present at the school when his outburst occurred. Griffith heard that Archie had had typhoid and was slowly recuperating somewhere in the South; he would not return to Concord until after the holidays. When he once more appeared at the school, his presence did much toward lifting the ban of Coventry that had been imposed upon Griffith. He declined to respect it, asserting he had always disliked Lyman whose habits he and all the rest of the school well knew. He considered he thoroughly deserved the treatment he had received from Griffith. His slowly uttered declaration that *"he* wouldn't have bitten Lyman for a farm" was considered extremely humorous and the attitude of the school commenced gradually to change toward his friend.

Griffith feared what might follow the end of his ostracism. He was determined to resort again to the methods by which he had escaped persecution if the necessity arose. He found at the first evidence of an intention to annoy him, he had only to crook his fingers into claws and emit a savage snarl, baring his teeth, to instill a wholesome dread into the hearts of his would-be tormentors.

As a result of McCleish's championship, Griffith's admiration and affection for him became intense devotion. He worshipped and idealized him; Archie became his hero, his defender, his God; he found real happiness in a supreme and abject adoration. Archie, though somewhat mystified, accepted his devotion. He did not understand Griffith's ardent attachment, but gradually grew accustomed to it, and unconsciously it had its effect. Through the rough, Scotch, matter-of-fact exterior of his nature, Griffith's affection penetrated and slowly he came to depend upon it, eventually to return it in an unimaginative, stolid way.

VIII

The result of their cemented friendship was an invitation from Archie to Griffith to spend the summer with him at his brother-in-law's ranch at Beowoee in Nevada. One of his sisters had married a cattle-man who bred steers for the market. Griffith's mind was full of the visions of the rodeo and the free life of the cow-puncher, but in June, a week before the closing of school, his mother returned to America.

The year before Griffith would have regarded her advent as a manifestation of heaven's answer to his passionate prayer for deliverance from misery. Now he saw in it only an awkward complication of his plans.

Beyond being a trifle heavier and rounder, his mother had changed but little in two years. She had acquired certain foreign mannerisms and her voice contained a suggestion of an accent—which Griffith suspected she cultivated. Uncle Gualtiero had finally died, but Griffith gathered that Paolo's devotion had been unappreciated, that he had been treacherously deceived. He was ill, poor fellow, and had gone to Ostend for the summer, quite run down from his long and exacting attendance upon an ungrateful uncle. She was much impressed with the improvement in Griffith. He had begun to fill out; his complexion had cleared and the ragged white down upon his chin and upper lip had disappeared with his first shave six months before. There still remained an uneven edge of fine colorless hair along his cheek which marked the line of the razor. He was neater and trimmer in appearance; the shamble was gone from his walk and he had lost much of his ungainliness. He was still stoop-shouldered, used his hands clumsily, and there was a quick shifting look of apprehension in his eyes which his mother did not like. He was far more presentable however than he had been as she remembered him, and she was pleased at his willingness to remain at Concord until he graduated. But his preference for Archie's society and his desire to accept his invitation for the approaching summer instead of falling in with her own plans, offended her. She wanted him to spend the three months with her in Europe, but Griffith could not disguise his eagerness to accompany his friend to the land of the round-ups and bucking broncos, nor his distaste for the programme she proposed. Mrs. Santini shrugged her plump shoulders. She had been accusing herself of neglecting her son, had crossed the ocean especially to make amends to him. If he preferred other society, she had at least done all that a mother could do under the circumstances. Archie McCleish was a fine fellow, of course, and she was glad her son had formed so desirable a friendship, but her pride was hurt; there were few boys who had the opportunity of going to Europe offered to them. Grudgingly she gave way and proceeded to rejoin her husband at Ostend.

The summer that followed was a wonderful experience for

Griffith. On the limitless stretches of prairie, mounted on his own sinewy mustang, he galloped after the cowboys with Archie. All day long he was in the saddle, and at night, in a hammock swung out on the porch of the rambling ranch-house, he slept under the clear light of a galaxy of stars. It was the only life of exercise he had ever known and it whipped his sluggish young blood into life, swept away the waxy look from his face and brought him a strength and energy in which he exulted.

IX

A different boy returned to Concord in September. He hated the school, and he would always cherish a bitter resentment against it. He had a contemptuous opinion of the evasive Garfield, his calculating, practical wife, the placid, ineffectual matron, and the two apathetic instructors. He thought of them all as lying hypocrites, who had stood by and seen him bullied and hounded by his school-mates but had not interfered. He knew they were aware of what practises went on among the boys placed in their charge but they dared not take the vigorous steps necessary to stamp out the evil. Youth might be corrupted, injustice and cruelty might prevail, but nothing must be done which would affect the number of boys enrolled; the attendance must be maintained, the school's reputation protected.

Griffith continued his sullen defiance toward the boys. Some of them still found pleasure in telling the new-comers of his criminal tendencies; he was to be avoided; no one dared provoke him; it was better to placate and humor him. His own resentment smouldered but he had learned the futility of showing it. He was especially annoyed by a boy named Snyder, who had always had a hand in his persecution; but the moment of squaring scores with this particular tormentor did not present itself until the following February.

The river had frozen solid and the skating was at its best. Griffith enjoyed long solitary spins on the ice, following the winding course of the river about the town, past old homes storm-sashed for the winter, beneath round spans of small compact stone bridges, to pause a moment perhaps before the staunch figure of

THE EDUCATION OF GRIFFITH ADAMS 47

the Minute Man with gun and powder-horn edged with a fine crustation of frozen snow. Hockey on the ice was popular with the boys; Griffith liked to play, but he was only asked when someone was needed to fill out a side. Returning late one afternoon from a long trip on the river, he was in time to see the finish of an exciting game. As he stood watching, the ball came spinning toward him; he struck out hastily to get out of its way and violently collided with Snyder. Both were flung sprawling on the hard ice, Snyder coming down flat upon his back, the impact driving the breath out of him. He was several minutes recovering, struggling in helpless agony. When he caught it again, he came directly up to Griffith and struck him with all his strength. The blow sent Griffith down upon the ice again. It was a vicious swipe and for an instant a black congestion played before his eyes. It was the meanness of the assault, the suddenness of the attack without giving him a chance to defend himself, rather than the blinding concussion of the blow itself that roused Griffith's fury.

The fight that followed was a long-cherished memory for those who considered themselves privileged to see it. It lasted the better part of an hour and was unique in that it was fought on the ice and both boys wore their skates. There were no rounds nor rests. They lost their balance continually and tumbled to the ice, but prone or standing they continued their struggle until dragged apart and helped to their feet by those who formed the ring about them, when they went at one another again with undiminished purpose.

Griffith fought with a ferocity which only the previous years of humiliation and tyranny, the accumulation of indignities and insults, the hate and rage stored up within him made possible. He was conscious of nothing except his enemy. Blows and bruises, pain and fatigue for some time possessed no sensation for him. He was eager only to strike and if possible maim his adversary. He had dreamed many times of this moment of retaliation and he relished the brutality of the conflict with fierce joy. As his mind cleared after the first savage frenzy, he became aware of both delight and wonder; it was an amazing discovery to realize he was not afraid! This heartened knowledge came to him when for the twentieth time eager hands about him helped him to his feet; it brought a confident smile to his lips. At the same time he became conscious of the encouragement, the enthusiastic shouts of the group around them. He felt the moment had come at last for him to vindicate himself before the school.

It could not be said that either boy won the fight. Both were brutally punished; nose and lips, eyes and ears were puffed, bleeding and battered out of shape. Griffith's shin was laid open by the point of Snyder's skate,—a long, ugly rent below the knee. It was this accident that brought the fight to an end, the older boys interfering. But Griffith's unaffected eagerness to resume the contest after the rent had been bandaged with handkerchiefs, and Snyder's equally apparent willingness to have it over, gave Griffith the victory in the eyes of many witnesses. All he hoped he might regain in the estimation of his school-fellows was realized. He had put up a plucky, aggressive fight and they were eager to acknowledge his ability; their praise was music to him. For a day or so he was ordered to bed while the jagged wound in his leg healed after the Concord doctor had drawn its edges together, with half-a-dozen stitches. The boys flocked into his small cubicle to see him, crowding about his bed, discussing the fight tirelessly. His bruised lips hurt him when he smiled, but he enjoyed the pain. Scraps of conversation he overheard thrilled him with delight.

"Would you have thought he could put up a scrap like that? . . . The way he tore into him! . . . Snyder's got the science, all right, but there was nothing could stop him. . . . That's fighting that counts! . . . Science ain't much good against a wild cat!"

CHAPTER IV

I

GRIFFITH and Archie had planned to spend the following summer in Beowoee again. They had talked of the prospect all year and Griffith had written his mother and obtained her consent. A few weeks before the close of the school in June, however, an entirely different project suggested itself.

It had been decided from Archie's earliest boyhood that when his time came for college, he should go to the University of St. Cloud from which his father had graduated and to which he had made liberal donations. St. Cloud was one of the big railroad man's hobbies, and Archie confided to Griffith he suspected his father secretly hoped he might one day receive an honorary degree from its faculty. It was a state college in the Middle West, having an enrollment of over five thousand students, half of whom were women. It competed in athletics with the Universities of Chicago, Wisconsin, Kansas, Missouri and the Colorado School of Mines.

Another year at Concord had to be endured before the two boys could graduate. Archie shared Griffith's opinion of the school and his contempt for Garfield; nine months more under his petty jurisdiction was a dismal prospect for both. It was McCleish who proposed they forego their trip to the ranch and spend the next three months "boning up" for the entrance examinations to St. Cloud, and it was Griffith's warm endorsement of the plan that decided them to attempt it.

June, July and August were hot, dusty months in the little village of St. Cloud. The University was closed, its wide, bare campus deserted. Even the established residents had gone away for the summer. Griffith who was familiar with the green enclosure of the Yard at Harvard hemmed about by classic buildings, and who had visited Yale and Princeton and admired the established dignity of the old ivy-covered structures of brick and stone, was taken aback by the rawness, crudeness and newness of St. Cloud.

The buildings, arranging themselves informally about a great flag-pole, stood on a bare hill looking down on the village from which the University took its name. The surroundings were not inviting. Concrete walks wandered aimlessly from one empty barracks to another; there was no foliage nor grass, but behind the buildings, following the crest of the hill, was the edge of a thick pine forest. The line of trees made the only pleasing aspect the view of the rambling college buildings possessed from the streets of the village of St. Cloud below; a dark, irregular, jagged-edged strip against which the gray edifices were silhouetted, poking their roofs and gabled peaks into the blue background beyond the tree-tops. Some fifty structures composed the University proper, varying in size from the mammoth octagon-shaped gymnasium which squatted like a giant toad at the bottom of the hill, to the cozy, square brick building tucked behind the gaunt tower of the Library where Philosophy was disseminated. Toward the north, half a mile from the group about the flag-pole, was located the Agricultural Department and the experiment stations where cows, poultry and swine were kept; between and just over the brow of the hill, which dipped momentarily to allow the little St. Cloud creek to bubble out of the fastness beyond and worry its way down the slope of the campus under rickety, picturesque bridges, were the Botanical Gardens.

The two boys had found a student boarding-house near the campus and had been fortunate enough to secure one of the assistant professors in English as coach. He was a pleasant, red-faced Englishman with close-cropped blond hair, small flaring mustache and pale blue eyes, not more than thirty-three or four. His name was Hugh Kynnersley and he took a keen interest in his pupils, particularly in Griffith. The boy amused him, he was diverted by his vehemence, his extravagant assertions and enthusiasms. Griffith answered the twinkle in his eyes; he was aware his instructor liked him and he purposely indulged himself in mannerisms he knew entertained him. But there were times when he thought he caught a look of sadness in the older man's face, a puzzled concern that was almost distress.

"You have too many illusions, Adams," Kynnersley said to him one day, shaking his head. "I'm afraid you have many disappointments in store for you. You'll find that what seems so wonderful

THE EDUCATION OF GRIFFITH ADAMS

and beautiful to you now is nothing but Aladdin's fruit. I wish you were not quite so ardent,—so eager."

Griffith's intimacy with Kynnersley grew. One morning after a three-hour tussle with algebra, the professor invited him to lunch with him at the little Faculty Club that stood high on the bank of the St. Cloud creek surrounded by a dry cluster of ragged pines. The young Englishman and his guest talked well into the afternoon. The boy told him unreservedly about his experience in Cambridge, at the Fairview Military Academy, and the Concord Family School. He spoke of his music and discovered his host played the 'cello and was a passionate music-lover. They derived more enjoyment still, in a discussion of the books they had read, for both had the same favorites: *Quentin Durward, Les Miserables* and *Our Mutual Friend*. The last of these each knew intimately and presently were shouting with delight as they reminded one another of certain of its characters and passages. It was an enjoyable afternoon and Griffith was glowing with high spirits as he walked back to his boarding-house. Kynnersley acompanied him part way. As they stood a moment, shaking hands and saying good-night, the older man suddenly became grave.

"Adams . . . you know, I am sorry for you!" he said kindly, one hand on Griffith's shoulder. "You are making a mistake to enter this university; college was not intended for such as you. I wish you could go to Oxford or Cambridge; there they would know what to do with you. The American university is a coffee-mill: young men and women are dumped into it and some one spins the handle, and out they all come mixed together, individuality gone; all just the same: little grains the same size, the same color, the same smell. I have taught in many Western colleges,—six to be exact. They are all alike; this great university is typical of the lot. I say again I am sorry. I have seen it before,—ah, so many times! You seek culture here; you will not get it; you will not follow your natural inclinations; you will do only the conventional things; so and so is proper; it is not good form to do otherwise. That is the undergraduate attitude. Your friend, now, McCleish—it will not matter with him. He is not seeking culture; he has not imagination; he comes to be made a smart business man like his father. He cares nothing for poetry, music nor literature. It is different with you; you are a blotter; you will absorb the evil with the good; you will accept the wrong standards of the undergraduate here and you will worship his false gods. . . . It is a pity!"

Griffith was vaguely puzzled. He was flattered by Kynnersley's differentiation between himself and Archie, but he did not like the simile about the blotter; it implied that he was easily influenced, that he was weak. Griffith believed he had an unusually strong character.

II

When the throng of eager applicants for admission to St. Cloud had arrived for the entrance examinations, Griffith had been considerably impressed, and when a few days later the great horde which composed the other three classes descended upon the college town that was so proud of its big institution, he became suddenly aware of his own insignificance and the gigantic proportions of the great school which he had been holding in light esteem.

On the opening day, the entire student body gathered about the flag-pole and listened to President Hammond's vigorous and plainly-worded address. As the square, bald-headed, robust man drew the picture in his swift incisive words, Griffith saw it as a vision for a brief moment. It was an inspiring sight to see five thousand young men and women together at one time,—an eager army gathered there with a singleness of purpose,—a surprising and a stimulating thought to realize that in four years another five thousand would be standing there, and in four years again another five thousand, and another and another, and so on and so on. In a hundred years, two hundred thousand men and women would have passed through the gates of St. Cloud, and become clear-thinking, disciplined, able citizens of the nation! And this was going on all over the country. The youth was gathered up from city and farm, poured into the great hopper the Universities provided, vomited out at the end of four years, belched broadcast over the country, future fathers and mothers to breed new harvests for the educators.

Griffith was still under the spell of the man's impassioned phrases, when, suddenly, as he ceased, a roar burst from the thousands of throats about him and he listened for the first time to his college

THE EDUCATION OF GRIFFITH ADAMS 53

yell and heard the prolonged note and rhythm of "U. of St. C." Something within him made his breast heave and his breath quiver as the swing and tumultuous rush of the yell caught him. They gave it twice and cheered their smiling President. Then—abruptly, in an instant,—there was a hush. Every hat and mortar-board came off and the crowd stood bare-headed in the sun. Griffith raised wondering eyes and saw a student standing on the steps of the little platform beside Doctor Hammond, arms extended, fingers outstretched. Swiftly he looked right and left as the silence grew; then when he had their attention, he brought his hands down together above his head as if they pulled a bell-rope, and simultaneously there rose from the sea of upturned faces the swelling, stately measure:

> "When sad and lonely I shall be,
> With eyelids closed and shoulders bowed,
> I'll see again in memory
> The battlements of old St. Cloud. . . ."

Griffith felt his heart grow big with something he did not understand. He blinked up at the sunny heavens.

> ". . . we flaunt our banners in the sky,
> Unfaltering, onward, fearless, high,
> Vic-tor-ious, . . . triumphant!"

The song was rich with a deep, full resonant melody. It rose powerful and sweet, ringing out over the bare hill. There was something primitive about it, something that sprang from virgin hearts, unspoiled, unsnared, as yet untarnished; it was pregnant of purity and young love, rampant, trustful, magnanimous, loyal.

With his arm linked in his friend's, Griffith walked soberly back to their boarding-house. He could not explain why he had been so deeply stirred; he was aware only of a sense of regret for his recent patronizing attitude toward the University. In that hour he knew he had pledged his undying love and loyalty to the institution which was to be his alma mater. Harvard, Yale and Princeton were a collection of hoary and antiquated halls of learning. Out at St. Cloud life was down to the buff; it was vital and free; here one *made* tradition, not followed it. McCleish, stolid, unimaginative, experienced none of his emotion. The song and college yell meant no more to him than college songs and bleacher "rah-rahs" usually did. To Griffith they had represented a hymn and a battle-cry.

III

The boarding-house where they had lived quietly all summer became crowded to its capacity long before the university opened. It was occupied mostly by freshmen, clear-eyed, well-mannered youths for the most part, eager to plunge into the college activities awaiting them. Farm and city were equally represented; they came mostly from the state which supported the university. They were a heterogeneous lot, typically Western. Already they talked excitedly about football practice and discussed the big freshman rally that was to be held that night in the Gym.

As Griffith and McCleish came up, a group was on the porch steps, filling their pipes and smoking. A senior,—Griffith knew his class by the battered silk hat he wore,—had stopped in front of the house. He was obviously making an inquiry, for his head was tilted forward at an interrogative angle. As the two boys appeared, Griffith heard one of the freshmen say:

"There he comes. He's the short one."

The senior turned and came toward them holding out his hand.

"Mr. McCleish? My name's Crittenden. My father knows your father pretty well. I had a letter from him the other day—he's in New York—and he said he'd seen your dad, who mentioned that you were entering here this fall. So I thought I'd look you up, and see how you were getting along."

There was something magnificent about the senior's manner. It was the embodiment of benignity, friendly interest, graciousness and good-fellowship. Griffith looked at him with awe and admiration. Instinctively he knew that he stood before a man tremendously important in the college world he was about to enter,—a leader, a dictator. Crittenden's attire was perfection. He affected all the undergraduates' carelessness of dress, which is so thoughtfully conceived and so casually assumed. On his silk shirt there dangled a

THE EDUCATION OF GRIFFITH ADAMS 55

heavily jewelled, diamond-shaped fraternity pin. He had a thin face, and regular features; his mouth was small, and when he smiled it stretched taut over glistening, even teeth. Good breeding radiated from him; he appeared to Griffith the perfect, finished gentleman.

McCleish shook hands, and introduced Griffith. They turned toward the boarding-house, and Griffith was aware that the freshmen on the steps were watching them.

"I'd like to have you come up to the house for luncheon, Mr. McCleish, if you haven't anything better to do," Crittenden remarked. "And you, too, Mr. Adams, if you'd care to."

Griffith could not control the flush he felt creeping into his cheeks. He understood the situation perfectly. Crittenden was a fraternity man. He had seen the dangling pin; the senior had come purposely to find McCleish,—McCleish, whose father was widely known, as financier and millionaire. He was not interested in Griffith Adams, a nobody.

The two boys had discussed the question of fraternities at considerable length. It was a subject that ordinarily must never be touched upon in public, never be mentioned even to a school-mate, one of those sacred topics, which according to the code they knew, may only be whispered in the most intimate fashion to one's closest friend.

There were some thirty-five fraternities at St. Cloud. The university was honeycombed by the system, and located about its campus were some of the strongest and richest chapters of certain national, college Greek-letter societies. Gleaned in schoolboy fashion, just how neither of them could have explained, both Archie and Griffith knew that there were six fraternities at St. Cloud that mattered. Failing election to one of them, it made little difference which one joined. Of these half-dozen societies, the two most powerful were the Delta Omega Chi and the Gamma Kappa Delta. They knew also that only the members of these favored six were ever elected to the exclusive Sophomore society of Theta Nu Epsilon: T. N. E. No other undergraduate, no matter how desirable or popular could become a member of this inter-fraternity organization; one had to belong to the "big six" before he was even considered.

Griffith and Archie secretly hoped they would be asked to join one or the other of the two most powerful clubs, or failing these, to "make" one of the other fraternities through which membership in T. N. E. might be gained. During the hot summer they had frequently walked up along Fraternity Row and speculated as to the interiors of the mysterious and attractive houses that lined the college street. Some of them were massively built and beautifully designed; handsomer by far than any of the college buildings. A few of the fraternity houses were of brick or stone, with colonial door-ways and white pillars supporting overhanging porticos.

Crittenden's invitation—extended to include himself—placed Griffith in the embarrassing position of wanting to accept and yet feeling it had been tendered merely for politeness' sake. Instinctively he felt he should decline. Instead, he paused in awkward silence, his cheeks growing bright, his face working. He wanted so much to go! He might never have another chance!

Crittenden's hearty: "Good; that's fine" to his hesitating acceptance reassured him to some extent, but he was ill at ease as he fell into step with Archie and the senior as they turned up the street toward Fraternity Row.

During the last weeks of summer, just before the university opened, Griffith and Archie had avoided the neighborhood of the fraternity houses as if the district were an infected area. To be seen anywhere in that vicinity would be inexcusable and suicidal to their chances of election to even the lowliest of the societies. Earlier, when they had reconnoitered the forbidden precincts they had found the houses closed, shuttered and the street empty. Now things were amazingly different. The steps and porches of every fraternity house were crowded, men called to one another, exchanging greetings; the jangle of pianos in adjacent houses vied inharmoniously with one another and the odor of food cooking for lunch drifted appetizingly to the street while bicycles leaned against fences and stone walls. In almost every club the windows were wide open; on the sills on upper floors young collegians lolled and through others shirt-sleeved forms moved to and fro or were to be seen in the process of shaving or struggling before a mirror with collar and tie. Express wagons and in some cases furniture vans were backed up against the curb, disgorging trunks and pieces of furniture wrapped in excelsior and sacking. One lawn was littered with the ladders and pails of a paper-hanger; a pile of matched boarding lay in the road before another.

Continually Crittenden and the two freshmen encountered men who had not met the former since the opening of college. They greeted him delightedly, inquiring how the summer had gone, how his "leg" was, and whether or not he had as yet been over to the "Wid's." Griffith drank in their phrases and studied their attire. Most of them were in red sweaters, a few bearing a great white "C" on their chests, a smaller "St" in its center. The seniors all wore black silk plug hats, battered and mashed down upon their heads. The juniors affected grey plug hats gaudily painted with college symbols and similarly crushed out of shape. A small purple cap with a white "C" on its visor distinguished the sophomores.

Griffith as he stared about him, fascinated by these details, could not but be aware that his and Archie's companionship with Crittenden was being observed and causing comment among the groups around the doorways. He even suspected that occasionally Crittenden was surreptitiously joked about the fact by those who stopped to greet him.

"Hello Crit! How's the fruit and flower mission? I hear most of the fruit is rather green . . . sort of sour, hey? Looks good for a late season . . . but no windfalls this year? . . . Shopping early to avoid the Christmas rush? I trust you don't mistake lemons for peaches; get Doc Parsons' advice over at Cow College, if you're in doubt; I understand they did awfully poorly over your way the year you entered."

Griffith watched Crittenden and the speakers closely. If their words referred to Archie and himself there was not a flicker of an eyelash or a glance to confirm his suspicions. He marvelled at the senior's genial and easy manner; it was clearly apparent he was extremely popular.

Half-way down the block Crittenden turned in before a wide brick house. A row of fluted Corinthian columns arranged in a semi-circle about a fan-topped doorway, skirted a wide curving front porch. Two substantial wings of the building balanced each other on either side of this columnar entrance, the white window trimmings making a pleasing contrast to the red brick façade. Let into the pavement immediately in front of the curving steps appeared the black Greek letters: Δ O X

Griffith's heart rose on a happy sigh. Crittenden seemed to him the most wonderful being he had ever met. He had hardly dared to wonder to what fraternity he belonged. It made everything perfect to know he was a Delta Omega Chi.

He and Archie were introduced to the group lounging upon the porch and seated upon the low steps. At once it was plain to Griffith that there was a difference between the way McCleish was greeted and the manner in which his own hand was accepted and introduction received. They were eager to meet Archie and obviously anxious to ingratiate themselves with him; they were merely politely gracious to his friend.

Griffith was plunged into an agony of spirit. In his life he had never met such wonderful fellows, so attractive, so charming, so infinitely amusing. It seemed almost unbelievable that all of them could belong to the same fraternity. They appeared to him rarefied beings whose society it was a privilege to enjoy even for a moment, just to listen to them, just to watch them, just to laugh with them, to sit and worship! Such a circle was not for him; it was presumption even to think of their wanting him!

He realized all this at the luncheon table,—a great board twelve feet across about which thirty of these fresh-faced, noisy, captivating youths gathered. He realized it when he saw where Archie sat toward the head of the table, between Crittenden and another senior, while he himself was placed more than half-way down on the other side next to a silent junior and a sophomore who turned his back upon him in eager conversation with a classmate. At the head of the table burst followed burst of uproarious mirth, and once Griffith caught Crittenden's voice as he leaned across the table to say:

"Did you hear what Mr. McCleish just said?"

The repetition of Archie's witticism escaped Griffith. He tried to think of some funny story with which he could regale his hosts when he had their attention but his mind was a blank. There were other freshmen being entertained besides himself and McCleish. All sat nearer to the head of the table. One pug-nosed, bright-eyed, sharp-featured youth sat opposite to him; he was of the same cut as his hosts and Griffith listened to his easy flow of words and ready "come-backs" in bitter fury.

After luncheon there were loud shouts for "Pikey" Robbins. "Oh you, Pikey! . . . Come bang the box!" A wiry little fellow, with sandy hair and a peppery freckled face, responded, leaping down the wide flight of stairs in the square entrance hallway. With a series of springs he bounded into the great, comfortable lounging-room, hopped upon the piano stool and flung himself upon the white row of keys. A wild, mad explosion of ragtime music burst from the instrument. It was terrific, irresistibly infectious, marvellously executed. The performer's fingers flashed over the key-board like scurrying water-bugs. Griffith had never heard such rag-time playing. His whole body responded to the rhythm; his blood throbbed in his veins to the beat. One syncopated melody followed another, now a march, now a song. The group around the piano hummed and whistled the one, and shouted the words of the other. The room rocked with noise.

Griffith listened in misery, his heart sick with longing to be one of this band of favored creatures. He glanced over to where McCleish sat surrounded by an attentive group. Crittenden had one arm flung over his chair-back; two or three others were leaning toward him listening with interest to what he was saying. For a brief moment hatred of his friend rose up within him. God! What had Archie McCleish ever done to deserve such consideration! He happened to be the son of a rich man; that was all.

Since luncheon the junior who had sat next to him at the table, had continued his dutiful and rather awkward attentions. He had followed Griffith into the lounging room, seated himself beside him on a high-backed wooden settee, and continued the labored effort of asking him polite questions during the silences which grew longer and longer between them.

Griffith felt his golden moment was passing and that unless something happened which would impress him in some way upon his hosts, they would never think of him again. A few were already getting their note-books together for the first recitation of the afternoon. Little Pikey Robbins was playing "Nearer my God to Thee" in rag-time. He brought the piece suddenly to a flashing and staccato finish and in the abrupt silence that followed, Griffith said to the junior beside him:

"I play the piano—a little."

He could have bitten out his tongue the minute the words were spoken, but several who were standing near heard him. They turned toward him politely interested, pleasantly surprised. Pikey Robbins bounced off the piano stool and came over to him cordially while the junior beside him said brightly:

"Oh! Please play something for us."

The room swam before Griffith's eyes. His terrified and hurried protest was drowned by what seemed to him a hundred voices. Hands grabbed him by the arms, pulling him to his feet, dragging him toward the piano. For a brief moment he caught sight of McCleish's face; it seemed to him to be deathly white, stricken with horror. He felt himself being forced down upon the stool; he opened his eyes and was confronted by the hideous green cover of a popular song upon the rack before him bearing the title: "Coon—Coon—Coon" diagonally printed across it. A hush fell upon the room; Pikey Robbins leaned against the piano, one arm resting on its top.

There was no time for him to think. In some inexplicable way he had been suddenly plunged into this terrible situation. There was no way of escape; he raised his eyes hopelessly. Over the piano in a great plush frame hung a crayon portrait of a be-whiskered man; across one corner in a flowing hand was written: "Fraternally to the boys at St. Cloud,—T. Alfred Vernay." Griffith stared at it; the room grew more silent; someone smothered a cough. He raised his trembling fingers to the key-board. The gentle, kind face of Professor Horatio Guthrie rose before him and the bare little music room at the Fairview Military Academy. Then feebly, shakily, he began a little waltz of Grieg's.

His attempt was a dismal failure. His fingers slipped upon the notes and interfered with one another. The music sounded thin and tinkling like the playing of a child. He stumbled and hesitated, reached vaguely for the notes in the bass, striking them inaccurately. With tightly pressed lips and trembling chin, his head bent over the key-board, he forced himself to go on to the end. It was a dreadful, an awful,—a ridiculous performance! He rose dizzily, the

THE EDUCATION OF GRIFFITH ADAMS 61

room whirling about him. Blindly he groped for the doorway; he could not bring himself even to turn his head for a moment to acknowledge the ripple of perfunctory hand-clipping; he wanted to get away, to sink out of their sight, to efface himself forever from their lives and vision!

Presently he found himself out on the street, hurrying along Fraternity Row, brimming tears in his eyes, setting everything dancing, multiplying outlines. And then somehow he reached the boarding-house where he lived and was on the last flight of stairs, feeling for the china knob of the door of his room in the dark hallway. He had opened it, closed it and locked it behind him, and then leant against it, while his utter humiliation and misery gave way in a torrent of bursting, choking sobs and tears.

IV

The succeeding days were full of forlorn unhappiness. Archie immediately became "dated up" for weeks in advance. All his spare moments were spent at the "Delta Om" house. Every night there was some engagement. The bustling little village of St. Cloud boasted two theatres and there was the big metropolis fifty miles away which could be reached in less than two hours by the transcontinental flyer which stopped at St. Cloud at five-ten. Archie made the trip, two and sometimes three times a week, the guest of his enthusiastic hosts. Invariably, when he and Griffith came out of their class-rooms together, there was a member of the fraternity waiting for Archie and together they would wander away. Griffith was frequently asked to accompany them but he declined. He knew that never again could he enter that house where he had disgraced himself. He hated Pikey Robbins with all his soul.

He was constantly making new acquaintances however, and he tried to be friendly; but with those he thought worth while, he felt he did not succeed, and those with whom he succeeded, he felt were his inferiors, mentally and socially. A big-framed, red-headed freshman named Hendricks who lived at the same boarding-house, was rather an interesting fellow to talk to, Griffith thought, but his table manners were abominable, and he made noises with his mouth when masticating. There was a Jew, named Silverberg, whom he would have liked to know better because he found him one afternoon reading *Barnaby Rudge;* but Silverberg had a hooked nose, thick lips, small ferret-like eyes, and Griffith felt instinctively that it would be wiser not to start a friendship. It might prejudice the fraternity fellows against him if seen in such company. He responded more readily to the advances of a sophomore, named Atkinson, who was re-taking freshman "math" and on several occasions pointedly sat next to him in the class-room. Griffith was aware that Atkinson was a "Pi-eye," a member of Pi Iota Phi fraternity. This society did not rank with the best; it was generally regarded as second-rate if not third. One day Atkinson asked him to "come on up to the house for lunch"; Griffith made excuses the first time, but he accepted the second invitation.

The Pi Iota Phi house was at the very end of Fraternity Row. It was new and suggested only too clearly, even to an uninitiated observer, that it had just managed to elbow its way on to the street. Griffith found its members a hospitable group of boys who banged him on the back and told him again and again how glad they were to meet him, urging him vociferously to make himself at home. The cold appraising glances that had made him so uncomfortable at the Delta Omega Chi house were conspicuously absent from their eyes. They treated him as if he were already one of them, solicited his opinions, listened attentively to what answers he ventured, and laughed uproarously at a story he attempted. Griffith's heart was warmed. These new acquaintances might be uncouth, perhaps even a little vulgar,—but they liked him, they wanted him to be one of them.

The next evening he was invited by his new acquaintances to go to the theatre with them in St. Cloud. The offering was a burlesque,—a troupe of girls and a comedian,—the performance tawdry and suggestive. The students from the University who were in the theatre applauded loudly; Griffith joined in the hand-clapping, eager to share the apparent enthusiasm. In his excitement he attempted a shrill whistle through his teeth. This proved eminently successful and he was pounded on the back and his example generally imitated.

After the performance was over, his entertainers led him to a house of prostitution. He had never seen women of this type

THE EDUCATION OF GRIFFITH ADAMS 63

before, although he was familiar enough with the fact of their existence. Their heavy coils of carefully arranged hair, their waxy, rouged faces, their fat, uncorsetted bodies beneath the blue and pink satin wrappers they wore, filled him with disgust. His companions stayed to "josh" the girls, a round of beer was bought, and presently they all tumbled hilariously out into the street. As Griffith hastened to go with them, one of the younger woman caught him by the hand, detaining him, leering at him significantly. He laughed shakily, drawing back, intensely embarrassed. Precipitately he joined the others, filling his lungs with the sharp night air outside. He was shuddering, shocked and full of loathing of himself, the women and his companions; but he dared not express himself. This was college life, the recognized order of things. He soon would get used to it and accept the standards about him.

His new friends found such visits highly diverting and another was proposed; they would all go up to Tillie Belmont's. But this did not transpire. On the way there they passed a dark alley which reminded one of the party of a restaurant where beer was sold "on the quiet." They were admitted into a dingy back-room after a talk with the proprietor through a crack in the door, and it was here that Griffith drank beer for the first time in his life. He was disappointed with it, finding it bitter and unpalatable, but he managed to swallow a steinful. He carefully concealed his dislike and pretended to enjoy it with the others. Several rounds were ordered and drunk, but presently the party became noisy and the proprietor turned them out. It was a little after two o'clock when they went home.

Toward the end of the week Griffith was invited to become a member of the Pi-eye fraternity. He asked to be allowed to think the matter over, and the same night Archie coming home late, his dull grey eyes alight with the only sparkle Griffith had ever seen in them, awoke him and announced he was a pledged Delta Om. The next day Griffith accepted the Pi-eye's invitation and a pledge pin was fastened upon his vest.

No sooner had he committed himself than he became obsessed with misgivings. He was not proud of his pledge pin. He kept his coat buttoned over it and delayed on one excuse or another moving over to the fraternity house. The hurt, the humiliation at failing to make the same fraternity as Archie rankled in his heart. Added to this disappointment, was the sad realization that he and his friend would drift apart. Belonging to different "frats" would bring their intimacy to an end, and though he knew Archie, too, regretted it, there was nothing to be done about it. Archie's place was among the Delta Oms and even had he suggested it Griffith would not have permitted him to jeopardize his opportunity of becoming one of them by delaying his answer in the hope that Griffith, also, might be included in their invitation. He told himself fiercely that he did not wish to belong to any fraternity where he must win his election through pressure; but it was hard to think of the next four years ahead of him without Archie's companionship.

Having pledged him, his prospective fraternity brothers left him to himself while they bent their energies on others of his class whom they hoped to persuade to join them. Griffith was lonely. He was full of uncertainty as to the wisdom of the step to which he was committed; the more he saw of the members of the fraternity, the more he became filled with disquieting doubts. He longed for advice. Was it better not to join any fraternity at all than to belong to one he knew to be of inferior quality and rank?

V

He was a prey to these fears and one day was making his way heavy-heartedly toward his class-rooms when a large hand was laid roughly upon his shoulder and he was swung sharply around. His first impression was of a pair of beetling brows over flashing blue eyes, a sophomore cap and a lean lantern jaw. His own eyes searched the face that confronted him for an instant, and then the other's name sprang impulsively to his lips.

"David Sothern!"

It was six years since they had seen one another. David had matured even more rapidly during the interval than Griffith. He was taller and leaner, big-boned and loosely built, and lines had come into his face, lines of thought and character.

If Griffith was delighted to meet his old school chum again, David seemed pleased in no less degree. In the swift moment of their meeting Griffith had the sudden conviction that this friend of his boyhood really cared for him,—perhaps was the only one who did. It was a rare experience to discover that David was ready to pick up their old friendship where it had been interrupted at the little four-roads' grocery store a few miles outside of Lowell. They had much to tell one another. Both cut the classes for which they were bound, climbed up the hill behind the University, and down the other side, making their way to the Botanical Gardens in the hollow beyond, where rows of specimen shrubs and cereals were grown by the Agricultural Department. There was a turbulent little creek here that came foaming down from the higher hills, and a stone and wooden bridge; ferns and lush undergrowth covered the banks and the trees met overhead. David and Griffith sat on the bridge and dangled their feet over the bubbling water, while they rolled cigarettes out of fine cut tobacco, and told each other what had happened to them since they had separated.

After David had left Griffith in the corner country grocery, he had tramped on to Boston and at once secured a job as a wrapper in the shipping department of a large department store. He had gone to see Griffith's mother at the Hotel Brunswick as soon as he had earned enough money to make himself presentable, and had told her of the cruelty to which her son was being subjected. He had remained at the department store for three months until he was discharged for refusing to obey an order which seemed unjust. For some time he was without work, but finally got a position as janitor's helper in a large office building. One day there was an accident: a heavy crate containing an electrical contrivance designed for physicians' use, fell while he was assisting in unloading it from a delivery van. It crushed his foot, splintering some of the small bones. The doctor to whom the crate had been consigned, set and dressed the foot, and sent him to a private hospital he owned. From that time onwards he took an interest in David and when the boy was completely well, he was set to drive the buggy in which he went about on his daily calls. He persuaded David to write to Barondess and the following summer the choleric, rich Hollander came to Boston. A conference followed. The doctor had a brother in Cincinnati, a teacher of physics in the High School. It was arranged that David should go West and live in his brother's family, take the High School course and fit himself for Rush

Medical College in Chicago where the doctor himself had graduated. Barondess agreed to this programme willingly, though the boy's indifference to his wealth and patronage had angered him. David's sister had become the apple of his eye, and it was for her sake as well as the wish to assist deserving youth that he continued to take an interest in David's welfare.

For three years David remained in the family of the physician's brother in Cincinnati. Part of his time he spent in a local doctor's office and in the evenings he studied *Grey's Anatomy*. As he grew older he became more and more convinced that he did not want to become a doctor; medicine did not interest him. He was strongly attracted by politics and asked permission to study law. Barondess wrote, expressing through the medium of a stenographer, his irritation and vexation at David's change of plan. He enclosed a cheque for five hundred dollars and informed the boy that thereafter he might determine his destiny as he saw fit, without further aid or advice from him. David returned the cheque and decided to enter the University of St. Cloud and work his way through. He borrowed two hundred dollars and had matriculated the year before. Since then he had managed with comparative comfort. He had joined a fraternity and became its caterer, buying its provisions, planning the meals, engaging and directing the help. By this service he earned his board. He wrote college items for a daily newspaper in St. Cloud and also for a morning daily in the neighboring big city. He obtained discounts on clothing and haberdashery from the local merchants who advertised in *The Trumpeter*, the college weekly of which he was the Assistant Business Manager. During the summer just past, he had peddled aluminum ware through Ohio and Indiana and had returned to St. Cloud only a few days ago, a month late for the commencement of his class work, but with three hundred and seventy dollars in commissions.

The story of his friend's adventures again stirred Griffith's imagination. David's was a romantic life; it would always be so, and Griffith envied him. There was something admirable about his courage and independence. Griffith thought of Archie,—the product of a totally different social environment. His two best friends were as widely as possible separated in their sympathies and traditions; McCleish was stolid, honest, loyal, obstinate, radiating integrity;

David was eager, active, fearless, indifferent to conventions, a child of pioneers, an adventurer.

VI

While David had been recounting his experiences, it had occurred to Griffith that his friend was just the one to advise him in regard to the matter uppermost in his mind during the last few days. He was waiting for a chance to mention it, when David turned to him and asked abruptly:

"Done anything about a frat yet?"

Involuntarily Griffith shook his head. He could not have explained why he did so; the action he meant to be non-committal.

"Well . . . let's go up to the house," David said; "it's about lunch-time; I'd like to have you meet some of the boys."

Confusion possessed Griffith. Instinctively he knew he should immediately appraise David he was a pledged Pi-eye, but as he hesitated, the passing moments made the confession difficult; as they turned together to climb the hill it appeared to him an impossibility.

His heart was beating rapidly as they reached Fraternity Row and sauntered side by side down the street. He had no idea to what fraternity David belonged. He tried to listen to him as he expatiated on the college spirit at St. Cloud, but all the time he glanced nervously about fearing that at any moment he would meet a member of the fraternity to which he stood pledged. As they approached the Delta Om house, he looked up and saw Archie on the steps with Crittenden and little Pikey Robbins. He nodded pleasantly and even managed a careless wave of the hand.

Then his heart stopped beating altogether and he experienced a sudden vertigo. David turned in.

CHAPTER V

I

GRIFFITH was initiated with Archie McCleish and another freshman named Hyde into the Delta Omega Chi fraternity early in October. He broke his pledge to the Pi-eyes. At first he regarded it a grave, a dishonorable thing to do.

When the unbelievable came to pass, and Crittenden had drawn him into the little library in the rear of the lounging room and, closing the door behind him impressively, had asked with his mouth stretched taut across his even rows of teeth in as wide a smile as he could manage: "How would you like to be a Delta Om, Adams?" Griffith thought the world had gone crashing to pieces. He saw the door to the paradise of all things desirable, which he had believed hermetically shut to him, suddenly flung wide and himself cordially bidden to enter. This group of college men who were to him the finest, the most attractive, the most wonderful lot of glorified beings in the whole world had asked him to be one of them—and he was bound to another fraternity! He had given his word! Their invitation had come too late!

He saw Crittenden's genial smile slowly fade from his face as his own grew white and stricken.

"I'm pledged already," he said dully, forcing his words from his lips. "I've promised the Pi Iota Phis."

"You're not *initiated* yet?" Crittenden asked sharply.

"No . . . I . . . I'm only pledged . . . I've . . . I've promised."

Mechanically he unbuttoned his coat and exposed the pledge pin. Crittenden's genial smile returned, amusement twinkled in his eyes. His fingers went to Griffith's vest and he unpinned the emblem; then he drew from his own vest pocket a Delta Omega Chi pledge pin and fastened it in its place.

"There," he said, and offering Griffith the little gold insignia

THE EDUCATION OF GRIFFITH ADAMS 69

he had removed, he added: "send this back to them. Tell 'em you've changed your mind and that you are going to be a Delta Om."

Griffith's eyes alight with the pleasure he made no effort to conceal, looked up into the smiling senior's.

"But . . . but I promised them. . . . I accepted the pledge."

"Break it," the other said lightly. "Pledges don't mean anything here; they're broken constantly; there's never a rushing season goes by without half-a-dozen of 'em being broken."

He turned to the closed door of the little library and opened it. A dozen men in the lounging room looked up expectantly.

"Welcome a new member to Delta Omega Chi," he announced theatrically.

II

Griffith trod on air during the days that followed. The attentive consideration he received, the atmosphere of open-handed hospitality of which he was made subtly aware, was intoxicating and perplexingly delightful.

But the dream that he had been an ugly duckling and that the days of his swanhood were at hand, was short-lived. His awakening came upon the night of his initiation.

The moment the ceremony came to an end, his new fraternity brothers proceeded to put immediately into effect the humiliating discipline that it was the custom to mete out to all freshmen. Griffith had been specially marked for their subjugation; he was considered too assertive, too "lippy," too fresh.

The sudden change in the manner of his new associates was bewildering. He did not understand it; he was hurt and frightened. The terrifying thought persisted in recurring that his fraternity mates regretted having asked him to become a Delta Om. He could hazard no opinion now that was not met by either a blank stare or a curt, humiliating snub.

But new influences, new thoughts, new experiences rapidly entered his life—which left him less and less time to wonder how his fraternity brothers regarded him. These new factors crowded so fast upon him that it was impossible to receive or accept them with the consideration he should have liked to have given them. He was confused, staggered, overwhelmed. His old standards of living were ripped away and discarded; new ones took their place. Every day his widening mental horizon showed him how pitiful and absurd had been what formerly he had revered and esteemed. Scales dropped from his eyes; things he had considered white, he now saw to be black, and the black things he discovered had always been white. He labored to accept the better, more manly, broader principles of the boys who had made him a member of their club. He strove to imitate their example, and manner, to acquire their point-of-view, to accept their codes, to act like them.

St. Cloud was supposed to be a temperance community. There was a state law that no liquor could be sold within one mile of the University, but this did not prevent two "blind pigs" from flourishing almost within the shadow of the college buildings. One of these was operated by a fat little German named Gus Braüser, who cheated his patrons unconscionably. He had the custom of the college trade outside of the fraternity men who had banded together to boycott him. The club men obtained their beer from the Widow Concannon—or as she was intimately known, the "Wid." Both of these establishments were ostensibly small tobacco shops, where a few magazines and some dark-brown candy resembling chocolate creams in wide pasteboard boxes languished for purchasers. Each had a back-room identical in its appointments: four white oil-cloth topped tables against the walls were flanked on either side by kitchen chairs beside which upon the floor stood shiny, dented brass cuspidors; a heavy linoleum covered the floor and the cheap wall paper was of a large florid pattern. There were no pictures or other furniture. The rooms were designed strictly for the purpose of drinking beer. No other liquor was sold.

On the night the members of the Pi Iota Phi fraternity entertained him, Griffith had had his first taste of beer. He had often drunk claret at his mother's table and on two or three occasions had been permitted to sip champagne, but his experience with intoxicants ended there. Archie McCloish had an agreement with his father by which he was to receive a gold watch and chain on his twenty-first birthday provided up to that time he had not smoked, touched liquor or had any sexual intercourse with women. Griffith's close intimacy with Archie had served him also as a protection from these temptations; but he had no principles in regard to vice. Drunkenness had always seemed coarse and shocking to him; smoking made him dizzy, and he was afraid of contamination from immoral women. He found nothing particularly repellent, however, about Pikey Robbins or "Fat" MacFarlane when they came rolling home after midnight, maudlin and boisterous. They were ludicrous and amusing even when they dragged him out of bed and compelled him to do freshman "tricks." With rare exceptions all the fraternity men drank; some crowds "boozed" more than others; the Alpha Sigma Zetas were generally characterized as "a gay bunch." One fraternity, Delta Upsilon, was avowedly opposed to all forms of intoxicants; liquor was never permitted inside its club house and the members were for the greater part teetotalers. But its name was a by-word among the other fraternity men, and if an undergraduate refused an invitation to drink he was accused of being a "damned Delta U."

Griffith carefully concealed his dislike for beer and controlled the shudder that ran through him after he had swallowed as much of it as he was able at one time. He disliked the smell of it, and the sticky feeling of it upon his fingers was particularly obnoxious. But he became drunk for the first time in his life some six weeks after he had become a Delta Om.

It was a warm October day and the windows of the class-room were wide open. The fragrance of ripe apples and a rich blending of autumnal smells reached him as he sat tilted back in his chair in the last row of the room. Lolling next to him was a ferret-faced, wiry little freshman named Yerrington, who had recently become a Gamma Kappa Delta and ostentatiously displayed his diamond-studded pin upon his vest. Presently this youth leaned over and whispered:

"I say, Adams, let's cut the rest of the morning and go down to the 'Wid's' for a bottle of beer. I've got a thirst you could lasso."

They found the Widow's back-room deserted, but settled down by themselves. Griffith was much impressed by his companion's knack of drinking direct from the bottle. He tried to follow his example but succeeded either in choking or in spilling the beer over his cheeks and down his neck. At his sixth pint he fell asleep.

Vaguely he recalled being supported by Yerrington out into the alley behind the Widow's, and being helped, stumbling and staggering along, until he reached the Delta Om house. He was carried upstairs to his room and thrown upon his bed by his amused fraternity brothers, where he remained inert and asleep for the rest of the day.

The fact that he still retained his purity, as far as intercourse with women was concerned, was a matter of much good-natured joking by his club-mates. Archie's virtuousness was understood and respected: he had promised his father. There were other boys in college who were likewise bound and such reasons for being "on the wagon" and for chastity were accepted as good and sufficient. No attempt was ever made to induce a boy to break his word to his parents if he chose to keep it; but if he broke it of his own free will, he was not condemned. Griffith had retained his purity through lack of opportunity for losing it. He frankly acknowledged that he had no principles in the matter; no one had ever given him any beyond the memorizing of the seventh commandment in the Christ Church Sunday School in Cambridge. He hated ugliness, and adultery to him was ugly; naturally he shrank from defilement; vice possessed small lure for him because of its nastiness. His innocence was an almost constant subject of jest among his companions. He was twitted with being a "virgin," and was told that it was high time he became a man; he was assured his health demanded it. Griffith was imaginative, temperamentally inquisitive, and after years of adolescent speculation he was eager to satisfy his curiosity. It was inevitable he should follow his friends' advice. The only impression the experience left upon him was one of utter disgust. He was half drunk at the time.

Griffith set himself determinately and passionately to win the favor of his own fraternity brothers, and to make himself popular with the members of other fraternities. Every afternoon he formed one of the devoted "rooting" band, seated on the windy bleachers to cheer the football team at their hard practise, and he learned to sing the songs to be used in the big contests to encourage the team. He unsuccessfully attempted to learn to play ragtime on the piano, that he might share some of Pikey Robbins' glory. One day, hoping that after becoming familiar with the kind of music he could play, his fraternity brothers might grow to enjoy it, he got out from the bottom of his trunk his old "pieces." Patiently, self-consciously he played through the simple things he knew by Grieg and Schubert till gaining confidence he tried something more difficult by Chopin. He had played only a few bars, when a pillow struck him from behind and an upper classman shouted:

"For God's sake, freshman, cut out that long-haired stuff! If you're going to bang that instrument, give us the Lew Dockstader thing!"

But Griffith could never catch the rhythm of rag-time; whenever he found the house deserted he practised it, but the delayed beat puzzled him; he could not understand the principle of syncopation. He finally gave up, and never touched the piano in the fraternity house afterwards. He found no time for reading either. He was no longer interested in books; none of the fellows in the house did any reading outside their text books.

III

There were compensations. David, Archie and himself formed a close three-cornered friendship from which he derived unfailing pleasure; they referred to themselves as the "triumvirate." It was a strange combination of personalities, each so singularly different from the others.

Archie conscientiously attended his classes and filled page after page of note-books with his round handwriting. Griffith often watched him affectionately as he sat among the fellows in the fraternity house. Occasionally he wondered how much Archie caught of what was being said. Sometimes he was convinced that he had understood little of it; at others he was surprised by his astuteness. He loved him best when he and David were successful in persuading him to do something reckless, when his innate reserve and caution were thrown aside.

David, on the contrary, impressed Griffith as always using his vigor and forcibleness to their limit. He was ever ready to attempt the daring thing, take chances, try a new way. He had studied human nature and he understood it, and it made him a natural leader among his fellows. He cared nothing for what was taught him in the class-rooms, for he was not interested in education. College for him was a ladder by which he hoped he could climb faster socially. He could not bring his active brain to the study of books; he was interested in men and in what happened about him; more and more he became absorbed in college affairs and in college politics. He chose and elected the president of his class during his sophomore year; he was a member of the board which managed the Co-operative Store; he arranged the tours of the Glee Club; he was on the Advisory Committee of the Associated Students; he took the advertising contract for space in the souvenir programme of the football games. Shrewd and calculating, he made it a point to call once a month on "Prexy" Hammond on his day at home.

McCleish was ploddingly fitting himself to fill his father's shoes. He took courses in Political Economy, in Jurisprudence and in Banking. It was inevitable that Archibald Junior would be as important a figure in the financial world as Archibald Senior; his destiny lay directly ahead of him.

David was the adventurer. His purpose was equally definite, equally determined. He was getting out of college whatever was going to be of use to him when he began to carve out his fortunes in the business world; he was fitting himself to deal with men, to handle situations, to make money.

In entering St. Cloud, Griffith had been actuated by no such motives as had impelled his two friends. He had drifted into college, would drift through the four years and drift out again. He did not know what he wanted to do after he graduated; he was not artistic, yet he hated the prospect of business. He did not think much one way or another about his future.

Eighty per cent of the men Griffith knew at St. Cloud possessed similarly vague ideas as to what they were to do after graduation. "Some job in some kind of an office" was the prospect to which most of them looked forward. A few had their futures cut out for them: they would go into "the business" or the "old man" had something "fixed up" for them; some were taking courses that would turn them out mining or electrical engineers; others were studying farming, training themselves to become agricultural experts. The fraternity men who came into the last two classifications were generally in earnest about their work, but they were the exceptions. The great majority was drifting through college like Griffith; they knew no more than did he, what they were going to do after graduation. The business at hand was to graduate; after that something would "turn up."

Cheating in examinations had always prevailed at St. Cloud; it was an established practise among the fraternity men. Archie was one of the few who rarely did it, but even he was not above glancing at a neighbor's examination book when in need of an important fact. The greater part of the undergraduate body preferred to cheat their way through their work, or at least to be allowed the chance to do so if—as Terry MacFarlane expressed it—"a fellow was up against it." David made no bones about cheating; he did not hesitate to peek into a book, or glance over a class-mate's shoulder.

"I haven't got time to learn the rot the faculty of this University compels me to take; I'm not interested in learning that Pi is 3.1416+; I don't care to understand Sartor Resartus; that kind of knowledge will never do me a particle of good. I'm forced to take these courses, so I get through them as easily as I know how. But you take Doc Eisemann's Political Economy 1, . . . that's the kind of stuff that interests me; you won't find me cribbing in *his* exams."

Most of the unprescribed courses for which Griffith had registered and which he pursued in a desultory manner, were known as "snap" courses. Not being permitted to take the lectures he preferred, he followed the example of other undergraduates and filled up the rest of his "card" with "snaps."

Such a course was Entomological Ecology, the study of the environment of insects; another was Oriental Languages and Literatures, a series of rambling, disconnected talks on modern conditions in China given by a mumbling white-bearded earnest little man who occupied the chair endowed by a misguided patron of the University, interested in the Orient; another was Biblical Archæology, conducted by a venerable Jewish Rabbi whose voice could not be heard beyond the first row of seats in the class-room; lastly, and what was considered the best "snap" of all, was a series of lectures known as Ethnology 4, for which one need only register at the beginning of the semester: it was not necessary either to attend the lectures or take any final examinations.

IV

It was toward the end of his freshman year that Griffith met Hugh Kynnersley again. He had often waved to him passing on the campus, but the opportunity for a chat had not presented itself. Now they walked together down toward the squat, octagonal gymnasium below the University buildings, Kynnersley full of interested inquiries as to how Griffith was getting on.

"You promised me that we should have some duets this winter," he said reproachfully. "You have not been near me since college opened: eight months! Come 'round tomorrow night to my little cottage and we'll have a pipe and some beer and a little music,—what do you say? There will be one or two others there—good fellows with brains who are not afraid to think for themselves and say what they think. I do not know whether you know any of them but you should. Will you come?"

Griffith promised, but the next morning he remembered it was the night of his fraternity's fortnightly meeting so he telephoned Kynnersley postponing his call. When the date of the next engagement came around, he again telephoned his regrets, explaining there was an examination impending for which he was obliged to study. The truth of the matter was that he had been playing ten-cent poker with Sam Hyde, Barry Andrews and Terry MacFarlane all afternoon and had lost over fourteen dollars which he was hot to rewin during the continuation of the game that evening. The third appointment fell upon the night that the Kappa Gamma Delta freshmen gave their annual "beer bust." Griffith sent a note to Kynnersley—he had not the courage to telephone—giving as an excuse a bad toothache but promising faithfully he would be 'round the following evening. All the next day he was ill from the effects of the beer he had drunk the night before, but wearily he dragged himself across the campus after dinner, afraid to offend the young Englishman with another evasion of his well-meant hospitality.

Kynnersley lived alone with his blind grandmother in a quaint

THE EDUCATION OF GRIFFITH ADAMS

ivy-grown, brick cottage he had built for himself behind the University buildings, and beside the turbulent little creek that bubbled its way through the Botanical Gardens.

Griffith found him picking at his 'cello, replacing a broken string. There was only candle-light in the room, which was so small, that the old square piano, tinkly and discolored, occupied more than a quarter of it. There were rows and rows of books, and on the walls were dark-framed pictures of buildings, quaint in architecture, and a great number of photographs of distinguished-looking people many of which were autographed. In the corner in a low rocking-chair sat the old grandmother, motionless, silent, her eye-lids closed, her hands folded peacefully in her lap. The wrinkled lids fluttered a moment when Griffith was introduced, there was a slight inclination of the head and her lips moved. Besides her sightlessness she heard with difficulty, and Kynnersley was obliged to shout to make her understand him.

His raised voice made Griffith's head throb. He turned to his host's music with relief, but his eyes troubled him and he could not find the notes with his uncertain fingers. They attempted to play several duets together. Kynnersley patient and encouraging, Griffith becoming more and more irritated and disgusted.

Unable to control his jangled nerves, Griffith suddenly broke off in the middle of a song whose accompaniment he was executing abominably. He was relieved to find the white-haired, wrinkled face in the low rocker had disappeared. Kynnersley good-naturedly drew a large green cloth bag over his instrument, gave the drawstrings a jerk, and proposed they smoke their pipes and have their beer in the tiny dining-room adjoining.

But Griffith's system revolted at the odor of beer, and the first inhalation from the long-stemmed clay pipe made his head spin. He substituted a cigarette but his mouth and tongue were still too tender from the previous evening's immoderate smoking, for him to derive any enjoyment from it. His host asked him about his college work and wanted to hear what he had been reading; but Griffith felt in anything but a confiding mood. Kynnersley would not understand the care-free good-fellowship, the gay geniality of American fraternity life. A description of how he spent his days would give an unfair impression of what his life really was like;

it would make it appear almost degraded. It was not possible for anyone not a part of it, to form any idea of its wonderful irrationality, its irresponsibility, its delightful jovial sociability.

Griffith made it apparent he was not in a communicative mood. Kynnersley tried to interest him in tales of the undergraduate life at Cambridge and Oxford, and finally resorted to reading Kipling aloud. At the end of twenty minutes Griffith's head slipped forward abruptly. He recovered himself with a sharp jerk, broad awake upon the instant, gazing apprehensively at his apparently absorbed host, hoping his drowsiness had been unobserved. If Kynnersley was aware that his guest had nodded, he gave no sign, but continued to read on in the same mellow voice. Presently Griffith interrupted with a question to show he had been listening closely, but when the story was finished, of which he had completely lost the thread, Kynnersley did not offer to begin another. At half-past ten Griffith was able to get away. He said good-night with a troubled heart, and walked homeward across the deserted campus, miserably conscious that the evening had been a failure and that Kynnersley was disappointed in him.

V

But the approaching election to Theta Nu Epsilon and the bare possibility of election to that exclusive inter-fraternity society, soon drove what concern he experienced for the young instructor's possible loss of respect for him, out of his head.

Only freshmen belonging to one of the "Big Six" were eligible for Theta Nu Epsilon. Election to it occurred at the end of the first year, the initiation taking place on the night before Class Day. Sophomores were the only active members and their identity was a guarded secret until they became juniors. On Class Day they appeared flaunting their new shining pins, attempting to appear unconscious of its conspicuousness, receiving the congratulations of their "co-ed" friends with deprecating airs.

It was almost the end of May when Griffith received an innocuous looking envelope, and opened it to find it unexpectedly contained the engraved notice of his election, with instructions as to what to do, and how to conduct himself before the initiation ceremony took place. The sudden gift of a great fortune would not have contained for him half the pleasure conveyed by the information chastely inscribed on the sheet of stiff paper.

A subtle air of secrecy, an atmosphere of conspiracy, averted glances, significant remarks pervaded the fraternity house for the following two weeks. Griffith admired the unconcerned way in which Archie comported himself, and he tried to disguise his own elation and appear equally unconscious. He could not forbear from slapping him on the back one night when he was alone with him in his room and smiling happily into his eyes. The other looked up puzzled, inquiringly.

"You stupid old idiot," Griffith said affectionately, "aren't you glad, . . . aren't you pleased about it?"

"About what?" Archie looked blank.

"About T. N. E.," Griffith said with good-humored impatience. "Didn't you know *I* made it, too?"

McCleish stared at him a moment unsmiling and said laconically: "I'm glad of that, Grif, . . . but I didn't."

Griffith returned his steady look, his gaze shifting back and forth from one eye to another in his friend's impassive face, the happy grin whipped from his lips.

"*You* didn't!"

Archie shook his head.

The strained silence was the only embarrassment each had ever experienced in the other's company. Griffith was amazed. He could not believe that McCleish, who was many times more popular than he, had failed of election, and that he instead had made the coveted society. For the next few days he went about perplexed and heavy-hearted, but at the same time he was aware of a certain sense of satisfaction, a subtle feeling of gratification that he had been considered more desirable than his friend.

It was Barry Andrews who first spoke to him directly about the approaching initiation.

"Your oldest clothes tomorrow night, Grif; wear only what you're ready to throw away; we start right after dinner."

Griffith nodded and smiled with understanding. After a moment's silence he mustered up courage to say hesitatingly:

"I'm sorry about Mac; I though he'd surely get in."

"He doesn't drink," Andrews said shortly.

"Why . . . I don't understand; how do you mean?"

"Only fellows that can drink get into T. N. E. There are no teetotalers in that bunch."

Griffith eyed him a moment, a light breaking in upon him. So that was it! Archie's abstemiousness kept him out of T. N. E. It wasn't then because he, Griffith, was better liked! He was surprised to realize to what an extent he had been flattered by his supposed preferment.

VI

The incidents of the night of the third of June of that year, were never forgotten during the rest of his life.

At about seven-thirty in the evening he appeared behind the fraternity house as directed, dressed in his oldest clothes, a ragged blue sweater under his coat. A dozen members of his fraternity were waiting for him, and Griffith happily recognized David's big loose-jointed figure before his eyes were blindfolded. Stumbling and sometimes falling, he was led a long distance, a hand firmly grasping his. He was aware he crossed the top of the hill where the University buildings were, followed the line of pine trees behind them, dipped down on the far side through tangled underbrush and over uneven ground. After that he lost his sense of direction. About half a mile farther on, he heard distant shouts and a confused jumble of sounds. A few minutes later the smell of fire reached him and presently he could distinguish the rushing, crackling sound of flames and the snapping of wood among the other noises, while he caught the glare of fire through the folds of his bandage. An uproarious din prevailed as he approached: excited voices, cries and calls, trampling feet, the wild clamor of forty eager youths. It rose and fell, now dropping unexpectedly, now breaking out with fresh vigor.

As he and his fraternity brothers appeared in the circle of light there was a general outburst. The rush of approaching feet was accompanied by wild yells of greeting. Griffith was pushed suddenly and roughly from behind. He staggered forward uncertainly toward the snapping fire, conscious of the heat but a few yards away. A dozen hands laid hold of him; a dozen voices commanded:

"Bend over there, freshman."

He doubled himself as he had been instructed, putting his head down, groping blindly for the ground with outstretched fingers. A shower of blows sent him sprawling upon his knees. In an instant he was jerked to his feet again.

"Bend over there, freshman!"

The whistling sticks bit deep into his flesh. He clenched his teeth, shutting his lips tight to check the cries of protest that filled his mouth. Again and again the punishment was administered.

"Bend over there, freshman!"

The blows were given mercilessly, ruthlessly; behind them was all the strength of young arms.

"Bend over there, freshman!"

He dug his nails into the palms of his hands and ground his teeth. Then when he felt that the limit of his endurance had been reached, and his quivering flesh could stand no more, he was shoved violently forward and pushed into a tangle of legs, arms and bodies, down among which he sank, exhausted and faint with the stinging smart of the blows.

From the hoarse breathing around him, he realized that about him lay other freshman who had endured the same punishment. There was comfort in their proximity; they lay huddled together in a confused heap, while new arrivals occupied the attention of those about the fire. Presently a body fell sprawling upon Griffith and lay inert across him. Hot breath fanned his cheek; faint gasps sounded in his ear. Involuntarily he crooked his arm about the slender figure above him. The rapid breathing was checked for an instant and a choked young voice whispered:

"Who're you?"

"Adams, . . . Delta Om."

"I'm Sawyer . . . Kappa Gamma."

"It's fierce . . . isn't it?"

"Oh, *God!*"

An interval ensued; the jumble of bodies occasionally moved concertedly, disentangling arms and legs, easing constrained positions. An authoritative voice, supplemented by others, brusquely issued a command:

"Get up there, freshmen! Stand up . . . stand up! . . . Get in line . . . get a move on. . . . Form in lock-step; hands on shoulders. . . . Hurry!"

Clumsily they disengaged themselves and rose staggering to their feet, groping for one another's shoulders. Hands shoved them, pulled them, pushed them; twenty voices shouted directions. Griffith grasped a pair of shoulders before him and felt the grip of other fingers upon his own. The line moved and turned from the fire, following a path through the trees. Branches brushed his face and presently he recognized the rough, rocky surface of a road beneath his feet. Then came the jingling sounds of harness chains and the smell of the hairy coats of horses. The lock-step halted. A bedlam of noise arose: the creak of wheels, the stamp of horses' hoofs, running feet, the quick interchange of raised voices and the loose laughter of merry-makers. Suddenly there was a general shout, a sharp whip-crack, a driver's "Gee!" and the crunching sound of heavy wagons moving over a stony road. The shoulders of the boy in front were nearly torn from Griffith's grasp, as the line of freshmen abruptly surged forward.

As the march began, the belaboring of the neophytes was resumed. The blows were directed against the fore and rear part of the leg between hip and knee as the only fleshy part of the body easily struck. The last boy in the line received the hardest beating as more of his body was exposed: in consequence there was a constant shifting of the order, the tail-ender being made the head of the line after he had received sufficient punishment in the somewhat uncertain judgment of his initiators. In turn Griffith became the ultimate unfortunate. As he stumbled on, clutching desperately the body of the boy in front of him about the waist, the stinging, lacerating blows struck him anywhere between neck and knees. At the very moment he felt his fortitude slipping from him, he was roughly jerked free of his hold, rushed quickly forward, staggering blindly at a half-run up the sharply-rising rocky ground. Brusquely he was ordered to "hold tight" to the tail-board of the wagon ahead of him.

From the feel of the heavy construction of the part of the

wagon to which he clung, the sound of slow grinding wheels, the frequent shouts of a driver, the hard impact of many hoofs, Griffith gathered that the big truck was being drawn up the steep, rutty hill road by four struggling horses. The clatter of another four-horse team with the accompanying clamor of a second band of freshmen and their initiators rose from further down the hill. In the wagon, to which he was obliged to struggle to retain his grip, there were many cases of beer. With every heavy jolt he could hear the clink of the bottles. Sophomores, juniors and seniors constantly clambered upon the tail-board before him, swung themselves into the swaying truck and helped themselves. A little later, after he had lost his place at the head of the line and dropped further down its length, Griffith realized that some of those with sticks in their hands had become befuddled with what they had drunk. One blow aimed at his legs, crashed across his wrist and knuckles; another hit him at the point of the knee-cap. Frequently as the halting march progressed, beer was squirted in his face and poured over his head; his hair was dripping and the collar of his sweater was soaked about his neck; it was sticky and cold and the smell nauseating. He became dizzy and sick presently with pain and fatigue. He lost his sense of time and place and held only to the thought that sooner or later the ordeal must cease, the fearful agony of blows upon his bruised and mangled thighs come to an end. On and on he stumbled, swaying blindly from side to side, staggering and reeling, clutching tightly to the beer-soaked coat of the boy before him.

"Whoa! . . . Wait a minute there. Hi, driver, pull up a minute . . . here's a guy that's out."

More and more frequently the cry arose. Invariably it was the signal of a general outburst.

"The damn quitter! Who is he? Make him get back in line. Stand him up there. What the hell's the matter with him? Make him get back in line."

"I tell you he's all in, Butch. He's not any of my freshmen; he's a Chi Phi, I think; he's really hurt; I saw Hudson crack him with a fence-rail."

Griffith heard, but he was only dimly conscious. Somehow he kept his feet and held to the dripping coat before him, plunging onward. But in a moment when his mind cleared, he grasped the meaning of the frequent stops and altercations. With a little moan of relief he crumpled down upon the ground and, unheeding, let the others behind tumble over his prostrate body.

"Whoa there, driver! Wait a minute; here's another."

He felt the weight of the bodies being lifted from him and himself caught up by the feet and shoulders and carried forward toward the wagon; they lifted him in and threw him down upon the straw-covered bottom. There were others there before him, inert forms, sprawling at various angles across the wagon's floor. Griffith's head found a level spot beside a grimy boot and a beer case.

He knew nothing more; an exhausted sleep fell upon him. The heavy truck bumped and jolted on, the wild confusion of sound prevailed about him; he was indifferent to everything. After a long time he became dimly conscious of his name being persistently repeated; his shoulder was being shaken with increasing violence. Struggling, in the grip of an agony of fatigue, he managed to open his eyes. The soaking bandage across them had been removed.

"Griffith! . . . Griffith! Come on, kid. This is David talking. How are you, boy? Sorry I couldn't look out for you; they made me stick down with the other wagon. Did they beat you up bad? Pretty sore? Barry said you stood it great. All the rotten part's over. Now comes the ceremony and it's all hunky-dory."

Griffith smiled cheerfully and attempted to rise. A hundred pains seized him; his back, his thighs, the fore and hind part of his legs throbbed with pain; his thumb and knuckles were swollen and aching. Blood had dried across the back of his hand. He was cruelly stiff but he managed to get upon his feet, David's arm about his waist, his own about David's neck.

Three hundred feet away a great bonfire with tossing, leaping flames shot upward among tall, encircling pines. The yellow light flung long shafts of flashing brilliancy through the surrounding trunks, the red glare played shiftily upon the underside of the fringed branches of trees spread fanlike overhead. About the fire black figures moved, their exaggerated shadows thrown in dark masses against the thick underbrush that screened the enclosure. A sound of singing, young and boyish, rose musically above a din of minor noises. The blending voices prolonged a happy harmony and ceased abruptly in a gay burst of laughter. From the truck in which Griffith stood, the remaining beer cases were being lifted and carried down toward the fire; a dozen silhouetted forms bent to the work. The driver was flinging blankets over his steaming horses, their noses already thrust into their feed bags; twenty feet away the other truck was being unloaded, the horses whinnying hungrily for their oats.

Griffith, with David's help, slid to the ground and limped painfully down the hill to the crackling fire of great logs. He sank in the grass in the warmth of the blaze and little Pikey Robbins brought him something to eat, delighting him by telling him he was "all right" and that Delta Om was proud of the way he had borne himself. He felt amazingly refreshed and cheered after he had eaten two smoking hot frankfurters, munched some soda crackers and drained, on David's advice, two tin mugs of beer. The heat of the fire dried his soaked clothes and warmed his cold body. With each succeeding minute the pain in his legs lessened and his spirits rose.

High above his head suddenly, through a rift in the trees, a red glow appeared. At first Griffith thought a spark had caught the dry under-brush far up on the hillside, for the deep crimson light grew, widening rapidly, touching everything with the ruddy reflection of its opulent color. Even the yellow brilliancy of the fire was outshone. The roseate glow became a glory. In its center shapes commenced to detach themselves, red figures in hurried action. Abruptly two fountains of sparks spit themselves out of the crimson heart lightening the whole night,—and the unearthly illusion vanished.

At once Griffith saw the face of a great cliff that rose sheer above them, a hundred feet or more above the tops of the tallest pines. A quarter of the way up on its unbroken façade was the egg-shaped opening of a cave; red fire was burning in two pots at either side of its mouth and beside these stood devils holding roman-candles from which showers of sparks fell pierced through at intervals with flaming balls of color.

Up the face of the cliff, through the spray of sparks, a rope tied under their arms, the neophytes, one by one, were hauled. Inside the red-illuminated cave, the initiation ceremony took place.

Afterwards by a steep, rocky passage-way that wound down inside the cliff, the new members of Theta Nu Epsilon rejoined the circle about the fire. When the formal rites were over, the entire company proceeded to drink up the beer. Griffith was too stiff and sore to make any effort to be convivial, and when no one was looking he surreptitiously poured the contents of his tin mug upon the ground.

At four o'clock the home journey began. The upper classmen, heavy with beer, slept torpidly, swaying to and fro on the improvised seats on either side of each truck. The newly-made members of the society, exhausted by pain and fatigue, lay piled one on top another on the soiled straw-bottoms of the wagons. Griffith, his head in David's lap, did not wake until at six o'clock in the morning the blowing horses stopped in front of the Delta Omega Chi house.

Wearily he sought his room, eager for his bed. When he came to undress he found that his underclothes were stuck in places to his bruised legs. With a quick jerk he freed them too tired to save himself the extra twinge of pain. But he was aghast at the sight of his purple, misshapen thighs, the fore and hind parts of his legs above the knee. Great welts swollen to the size of heavy ropes criss-crossed one another like the woven strands in a doormat. In many places there were abrasions like the broken surface of decaying fruit, the raw meat protruding through the rents. A flow of blood started by the quick rending of his underclothes from these ugly bruises, trickled in thin wiggling streams between the fine hairs upon his legs.

Griffith stared at himself, his eyes wide for an instant. He was greatly astonished, somewhat concerned and shocked, a little proud. He reached for a bottle of witch-hazel and began to dab the lacerations with a saturated bit of cloth.

"Well, it was worth it," he said aloud. "I'm a T. N. E."

CHAPTER VI

I

AFTER the beginning of his second year at St. Cloud an incident occurred which frightened Griffith and left a strong impression upon him.

He had spent part of the summer with Archie at his brother-in-law's ranch at Beowoee, riding horse-back and chasing beeves, and part at the boarding-house at St. Cloud where he had stayed as a raw freshman, studying for one of his re-examinations. He had been disappointed in finding that Kynnersley was away; he had been looking forward to spending much of his time during the quiet weeks before the University opened in the young Englishman's company and re-establishing their intimacy. Kynnersley, he was told, was in Europe.

The Delta Oms had decided upon an energetic campaign to obtain new members with the beginning of the new semester. They were determined to secure the cream of the incoming class. The previous year they had taken in only three freshmen: Archie, Griffith and Sam Hyde. Hyde had failed to pass his examinations and had been dropped from the University's roll. To run their expensive house, and keep out of debt, it was necessary to have at least thirty men living in it, an average of eight from each class.

Their efforts were unusually successful. Money was spent recklessly; entertainment lavishly provided; graduates of other years returned for days to help with the "rushing"; Crittenden came back for a fortnight. The combined factors resulted in eleven new Delta Oms.

Of these Griffith took a particular liking to Lincoln Potter. He had been much sought after by all the fraternities as his father was a United States Senator. He was an eager, ardent youth, excitable and enthusiastic. He made Griffith think of a bird, liberated suddenly from its cage, intoxicated with freedom, entranced with the power and beauty of its wings. Young Potter was rather under-sized, with curling close-cropped brown hair, sharp, alert eyes, nicely, almost prettily made features, and a complexion as fair and as delicate as a girl's. He was not effeminate though not physically strong, impetuously foolhardy, frankly craving the experiences of life with the undiscriminating rapacity of stark hunger. Griffith was drawn to him, seeing something of what had been his own fervent ardor a year ago. He foresaw that Potter would inevitably get himself in trouble, and the prospect seemed unusually regrettable to him. The boy was so clean, so fresh and innocent, so blinded as yet by youthful illusions.

The richest and most important fraternities rushed little Potter; he was extravagantly entertained; one club out-did another in providing him with amusement. The members of a certain fraternity took him in their zeal to a notorious house in the neighboring city where nothing but champagne was ever ordered or served, and where the inmates of the establishment appeared in elaborate *decolleté* costumes. Like Griffith, up to that period of his life Potter had never been in such a place before. He was overwhelmed, swept off his feet, drunk with excitement.

Not until after he had become a member of Griffith's own fraternity, did the disease he contracted on that occasion develop. It had been the only experience of the kind he had ever had. During one of Archie's periodic flying trips to meet his father and mother, little Potter occupied his bed. Griffith never forgot the night when he awoke suddenly to see in the middle of the floor, the slender figure of his room-mate clad in his scant pajamas, his legs drawn up tight against his chest, his hands locked above his head, teetering back and forth upon his knees, muttering incoherently in the grip of excruciating pain.

The stricken boy was afraid to tell his father. The local physician treated the case to the best of his ability but complications appeared, and presently symptoms of a far more dreadful nature began to develop. The physician told Griffith, who had accompanied Potter on several occasions to the doctor's office, that the boy's parents should be informed. Griffith, aghast and terrified, went to David, who after consultation with some of the seniors, wrote to Senator Potter. Five days later the ponderous, be-frocked, square-toed Senator arrived from Washington. There was something poignantly tragic in his grave, immobile face and sharp, accusing eyes. Griffith quailed under his piercing glances. He saw the outraged father turning upon those he believed were the cause of his son's contamination, and annihilating them in one mighty expression of insensate wrath and condemnation. A long session followed between the Senator and his son behind the closed door of Griffith's room. Tiptoeing in the hall outside, while the other boys in the house gathered silently about the fire in the lounging room downstairs, Griffith could hear the plaintive whimpering of the boy, alternating with the deep rumble of the man.

An hour later they came downstairs, little Potter with his overcoat on, hat in hand, his father's leviathan arm laid protectingly about his young shoulders. For a moment the two stood in the doorway, the man glancing under his gray bushy eyebrows from face to face of the room's silent occupants.

"Lincoln wishes to say good-bye," he said heavily. "He feels badly about leaving you, and wishes to thank you for your kindness to him and your friendship. For myself I want to thank you,"—here he found David's face in the group,—"to thank *you* particularly, sir, for communicating with me so promptly."

Then they went out of the house and down Fraternity Row, and Griffith climbed the stairs soberly to his room, and, dropping into the arm-chair before the littered table, gazed wide-eyed at the blank wall before him.

His own fraternity might so easily have been directly responsible. It might so easily have been himself.

II

The affair persuaded him to bring to a speedy termination a relationship which he had previously hoped would mature into a liaison such as he was aware other members of his fraternity maintained, and of which he had often heard them boast. The girl was a "co-ed," a member of one of his classes. He had first seen her in his freshman year when he had indulged in a mild schoolboy flirtation with her, one of smiles and glances across a safe interval of intervening chairs. In his sophomore year he met her again in one of his English courses which occupied the hour between three and four on Tuesdays and Thursdays. The interchange of covert smiles and flirtatious looks became too much of a bore to be everlastingly maintained. Griffith grew tired and more to bring this phase to an end, than any particular desire to develop a relationship more interesting, he sauntered home with her one afternoon after the class was dismissed. He had an uncomfortable feeling as he walked alone by her side and would have regretted meeting anyone he knew. The girl was not prepossessing, although she was undeniably pretty, in rather a cheap, tawdry comeliness, a beauty slightly tarnished.

Griffith kissed her before he parted with her that afternoon, and thereafter when he went to see her there were more fervent embraces. He derived a certain momentary satisfaction and pleasure from these osculations but they left him dissatisfied and ashamed.

The relationship might have terminated as he had begun to hope during his excited moments, had it not been for the incident of Lincoln Potter. After that he pointedly avoided her.

III

College life carried him through his sophomore and junior years uneventfully. His fraternity occupied all his interests and he cared little for the events that occurred outside of it: college politics, class meetings, college socials. Few of the fraternity men concerned themselves with these things. The only functions that stirred their interest were the annual dances in the giant gymnasium given by each of the classes.

In Griffith's third year an uncouth footballer was elected President of the class. He was openly a bitter foe of the fraternities and declared that the "Prom" should be a dance in the management of which no fraternity man should have anything to say. He appointed a committee of his personal friends and excluded all members of the Greek letter societies. In retaliation the fraternity men decided to have a dance of their own and boycott the "Prom."

The plans for the affair rapidly reached proportions which indicated that the dance would be the most elaborate thing of the kind ever given in St. Cloud. More than half the fraternities decided to keep "open house" which meant that the club-house would be turned over entirely to the visiting girls and their chaperons. The Odd Fellows Hall in St. Cloud being the only available place in which to hold the dance, much time and money were spent in making its dingy interior attractive. A twelve-foot green lattice fence was built within a few inches of the walls of the barren hall; artificial vines were trained over this and concealed green electric lights disseminated a pale, verdant radiance from behind the lattice work. Everywhere hung yellow Chinese lanterns and cleverly arranged calciums gave the effect of silvery moonlight in a conservatory. A caterer was engaged to furnish fifty waiters and an elaborate supper.

It was at this affair that Griffith met David's sister. It was David's last year at St. Cloud; he was still uncertain what he was going to do after graduation and the probabilities were that he would have little opportunity of seeing much of his sister. He had met her for the first time in six years the previous summer in New York, and now a passionate devotion for each other filled both their hearts. Margaret had been educated in London and Paris; three years had been spent in a French convent, and when she was eighteen, Barondess and his wife had taken her for a year's trip around the world.

She was not in the least like David, except in the coloring of her eyes which were of the same limpid blueness. Her hair was glossy brown, of a rich, burnished quality, and in sun-light, warm glowing tones of deep red appeared in it. Her lips were thin but beautifully shaped, the line of the mouth long with a little turn-up at the corners. She was rather pale but her skin was of unblemished smoothness. It was her expression that made her beautiful. There never was a more honest face, softer, sweeter, or kinder eyes, a more gentle, ready, sympathetic smile.

So Griffith thought when he and Archie met her and David at the station. He caught the first glimpse of her standing in the vestibule of the Pullman. A blue-coated porter, foot-step in hand, was on the step below her waiting for the slacking speed of the train to cease, while David's lantern-jawed face peered over her shoulder, his keen blue eyes roving from side to side under his contracted brows as he searched the station for his two friends. Griffith never forgot the picture she made as she came tripping toward them after the final screech of brakes, a hand stretched out to each, laughingly turning from one to the other.

"So *this* is Archie and *this* is Griffith!"

Her manner was different from that of any girl Griffith had ever known. At the very first moment of his meeting with Margaret Sothern he wanted to take her in his arms. It was the paramount emotion she inspired; she was so radiant, so beautiful, so sweet! It was hard to believe that this airy, charming, finished person, so exquisitely dressed, so superbly poised, could be any possible relation to the tall, loose-jointed David they knew so well. She was the product of a French convent, precise in speech, gay and spontaneous in manner, cultivated and assured. Her brother was of the West, forceful and vehement, an adventurer, rough, raw, big-boned. Yet there was something about the twist of the neck, the shape of the head that marked their close blood relationship.

IV

Margaret Sothern was the acknowledged and accepted queen of the fraternity dance. She was as popular with her own sex as she was with the eager youths who swarmed about her. Coupled to her sweetness she had an unaffected gaiety which drew people to her. Her spirit spread itself over the room until everyone felt it, and responded to its infectious influence. The dance became a confusion of music, laughter, lovely eyes and throats, a whirling succession of white shirt-bosoms and floating scarves of colored tulle about young pink shoulders. At supper Griffith decided he had never been so happy.

After it was all over, fur-coated and be-wrapped, the Delta Oms and their guests walked slowly back to the campus and to the fraternity house in the fresh, early morning air, and lingered over the last words of good-night. David, whose face was transfigured with pride in his sister's conspicuous popularity, took the occasion to ask her to sing. She smilingly swept the room with a half-hesitating, half-willing-to-oblige look, and sat down unaffectedly upon the piano stool, letting her soft, gold-embroidered wrap slip loosely from her shoulders, raising her white limp fingers to the smooth cold ivory keys, and began "Mon cœur, s'ouvre a ta voix." It was then that Griffith realized he was hopelessly and desperately in love.

He sat on the edge of the broad wooden settee in the big lounging-room, while the others—some thirty in number—grouped silently about the piano, on the steps outside and in the square entrance hallway. One of Griffith's elbows rested upon his knee, his forehead, dropped forward, was supported by his hand, the long fingers and thumb gripping his temples. He was always able to recall the scene afterward as if, detached from the bowed figure upon the settee, his sub-conscious self gazed about the room, noting the hastily taken attitudes of rest the tired dancers had assumed, availing themselves of table-edges or chair-arms, as the first suggestion of a song interrupted their gay chatter, the detached form of David, nervously glancing from face to face, his own black back and bent head, the long tapering white arms and the shining hair of the exquisite figure at the piano. The perfume of crushed flowers, sachet and the fine scent of cigarettes pervaded the air, and from without came the faint laughter and final good-nights of other groups breaking up on the steps of neighboring fraternity houses.

He did not go to bed that night. After he had held her slender fingers in his own for a moment and dumbly, in agony of spirit, gazed into her smiling eyes, unable to answer her warm-hearted good-night, he had followed the others down the street, and hanging back, had been able to turn abruptly into a side street unnoticed. He climbed the slope of the University hill, threading his way between gaunt, black deserted buildings until he reached the edge of the trees beyond. There was a well-worn path there skirting the line of the thick pine growth. It followed the brow of the hill that curved gracefully down to a round symmetrical hollow, like the bottom of a bowl, where was located the dairy farm belonging to the University, then rose precipitately beyond to the crest of another hill, similar to that on which the college stood, but bare as the palm of a hand except for an even stubble of white grain stalks that swept up over the mounting surface of the ground like a foaming tide-tip brought suddenly to a stop by the sharp line of pine trees.

It was on the brow of this hill that Griffith gave himself up to the reverie of his first love, and the intoxicating haunting memory of her golden voice.

"Oh God . . . God . . . God!" he murmured brokenly again and again. He could not bring himself to speak her name or voice one syllable to express the overwhelming yearning that filled his bursting heart. His breath rose in long quivering inhalations of the crisp clean morning air until his lungs were filled to their capacity; it left him in an explosion, his chest heaving, his fists in knots, his body swaying from side to side, his head shaking hopelessly.

So this was love—this was love! This was what they had written about; this was what they said made the world go 'round! He was in love! He, Griffith Adams, was in love! There could be no mistaking the paroxysms that possessed him; it was so,—and he was in love! The thought thrilled him; but more than any other consideration, borne in upon him was the crushing conviction of the hopelessness of his passion. Griffith rolled upon the clean, stiff stubble and buried his face in the crook of his arm. He wanted to die.

Slowly the morning broke. The murky gray of earliest dawn first changed by imperceptible degrees to a thin pale light in which objects loomed black and bulky. In the west the round faces of a few puff-clouds turned pink, touched here and there by brighter tones, deepening gradually to faint vermilion and presently the interstices between them were shot through with long penetrating pencils of yellow radiance. Simultaneously, vague shadows began to take shape upon the ground, indefinite, elongated narrow streaks that lay in serrated rows across the flat landscape. A chorus of cocks maintained an increasingly clamorous interchange of morning salutations, and birds trilled and piped, calling incessantly to one another in the under-brush along the edge of the pine wood. Other noises commenced to make themselves evident: small, tinkling sounds, faint murmurs, a fine, delicate hum,—the distant clamor of men astir. Gradually these became welded into a pulsing, minor vibration which mounted the octave-scale by eighth- and quarter-tones, ascending higher and higher with increased volume.

Suddenly, straight as the course of a bullet, a beam of sunlight caught the top of the hill on which Griffith lay. He rolled over and sat up to blink at the scintillating, iridescent spot of fire which glowed in a notch on the opposite horizon, rearing itself seemingly by swift spasmodic jerks like a thing pulling itself out of a hole. Down the face of the hill flooded the yellow radiance, the elongated nebulous shadows, swiftly taking shape, growing blacker and sharper, more and more definite as the descending tide of sunlight swept down upon them. Slowly, gradually, the great ball of flame climbed upward, clearing at last the distant barrier of the earth that blocked its rays, mounting into the blue expanse of the heavens above it.

Griffith buttoned his overcoat over his evening clothes and walked slowly back toward Fraternity Row. Early risers were already threading their way across the campus, janitors were busy with brooms on the steps of the bleak, echoing buildings. Israel, the Co-op boy, was taking down the iron screen frames from the windows of the store. Griffith paused a moment as he passed his fraternity house, to gaze up at David's room, where he knew she was asleep. His aching heart contracted fiercely. She was not for him; she would never care for him; he would never win her love.

V

At the late luncheon, served the following day at the Delta Omega Chi house, he saw her again. He sat next to her, McCleish upon the other side. Neither of them was able to talk to her; Archie was always reticent in the presence of women, and Griffith had never seemed to himself so tongue-tied. Conversation was generously supplied by the rest at the table. Pikey Robbins was amusingly obstreperous, and MacFarlane, Griffith thought, never said so many clever things in his life. They all roared at his remarks except Griffith who was too miserably conscious of his own dumbness to do more than smile half-heartedly.

After luncheon she sang once more, an aria from a new opera

and some of the same delightful French songs Griffith's mother used to sing to him. The girl sang these with infinite charm, and they brought back the atmosphere of the old gray house of his boyhood, the long, heavily-curtained drawing-room with its tea things and china ornaments, where his mother had sat at the ebony square piano, a lovely vision in the light of two wax candles that burned in tall black candlesticks on either side of her.

Griffith was deeply moved, and when the girl turned toward him as she finished, he made no effort to conceal his emotion. For a moment they were alone together by the piano.

"My mother used to sing those children songs," he said awkwardly. "They bring back a lot I thought I'd forgotten. Do you know 'Malbrouck?' "

"Malbrouck s'en va-t'en guerre . . . ne sais quand reviendra." She lightly sang the words and Griffith's eyes glistened. "I don't know the accompaniment. It's a dear little thing; there's nothing in English like the French nursery songs."

"My mother sang it; I liked it best; she used to invent the adventures of Malbrouck when he went to the wars. I suppose that's why I was so fond of it."

He told her about his father and his own meagre experiments in music with Professor Horatio Guthrie at the Fairview Academy.

"Will you please play something for me?" she asked him with interest.

Griffith gasped.

"No . . . no, I couldn't, really I couldn't. . . . I never play any more . . . they wouldn't understand. . . ."

He broke down in confusion. She looked at him inquiringly. He felt she was swiftly studying his face, but she did not urge him again and he was grateful.

"You have given me . . . an awful lot of pleasure," he said abruptly, painfully embarrassed. "I have never heard anyone sing . . . that way. It was wonderful."

She smiled at his eagerness.

"If you'll come to see me when you're in New York, I will sing for you as much as you like."

"Will you?"

She had no opportunity to reply for David interrupted them.

If she was going to be ready for the 'bus when it left for the station she had only fifteen minutes to pack her suitcase. She rose at once, but before she turned away she laid her slim hand a moment on Griffith's sleeve.

"Thank you for your praise. You'll come to see me in New York? Soon?"

She followed her brother and hurried upstairs, but Griffith felt his heart was breaking. The room swam before his eyes; blindly he found a window and stared mistily out into the sun-flooded, vacant street. There was no satisfaction, no fun in love like this! There was only suffering! She would be gone presently; when would he ever see her again?

He would have liked to go to the station to say goodbye to her, but there was only room in the 'bus for the girls and the chaperons, all of whom were taking the same train. David hung on to the back step. Griffith held her gloved fingers a moment and there was a separate wave of her hand for him from the 'bus, but he found it small satisfaction. One might have supposed all of his fraternity brothers to be in love with her by their manner; they crowded about her saying goodbye over and over. She was equally gracious to all, distributing the favor of her glance and smile to each, quite impartially.

There was a final surge of the youths crowding about the 'bus for a last hand-clasp with its occupants, a shout from David to clear the wheels, a swiftly swelling clamor of laughter, shrill exclamations and goodbyes, and the crowded wagon rolled away from the curb, to disappear, a fast diminishing shape at the other end of the street.

She was gone. Griffith went back to the house, desolation settling about his heart. His club-mates, freed from the restraint of women's presence, flung themselves in abandoned attitudes in the chairs, loosening the tight formal clothes they wore, unfastening the high-starched collars to which they were unaccustomed, drooping legs over chair-arms, yawning generally. An interested, leisurely discussion of the entertainment began. One voice volunteered:

"Gosh! David's sister's a hummer, isn't she?"

To refer to her so glibly, so familiarly, in such a group was a desecration. Griffith turned away in resentment. The house, his life, the world generally was a useless, vacant, eviscerated shell. The heart had gone out of things; nothing was worth while.

VI

The prospect of empty days to come seemed insupportable to Griffith; he did not see how he was going to endure them. Yet one followed another, and at the end of a week he was absorbed in helping Archie arrange the details of a wonderful beer-bust his friend planned to give in the fraternity house on his twenty-first birthday, when his promise to his father would be fulfilled.

The affair when it finally transpired, made for itself an important place in the traditions of fraternity life at St. Cloud for several years to come. It was a magnificent carouse to which most of the fraternity men were invited. Archie provided with prodigality, though he imbibed only moderately himself. It was expected that the taste of alcoholics for the first time in his life would produce immediate results, but his Scotch temperament proved equal to the test.

Griffith woke late next morning, his head aching, a bitter, foul taste in his mouth. He could not drive thoughts of Margaret Sothern from his mind. There rose before him a picture of himself in the boisterous part he had played during the previous evening's entertainment, and an infinite regret swept over him. For the first time in his life there entered into it an incentive to adhere to his natural instinct for finer things.

Dreaming sentimentally of Margaret, revelling in the secret of his love, the months fled by, and presently June with its final examinations found him as usual unprepared, the ordeal and the prospect of hard study impressing him with more repugnance than ever before. But David changed all that. One day he came to Griffith and Archie, many sheets of a long letter fluttering in his hand. Barondess had rented a place for the approaching summer on Lake Geneva in Wisconsin, and Margaret had written to ask if he and his two friends could not manage to spend July with them; there would be boating, bathing and excellent black bass fishing. Archie interrupted joyfully; there was nothing that interested him more than sport.

"You can count on me!" he exclaimed.

For twenty-four hours Griffith lived in a tumultuous transport over the prospect. The following day a letter arrived from his mother: she was coming home; she was ill; she had been outrageously deceived and cruelly treated. Paolo Santini had deserted her. She was coming home to her boy for his help and comfort and protection. She enclosed a money order; he must meet her in New York; the steamer arrived the end of June.

CHAPTER VII

I

GRIFFITH had not seen his mother for four years. His gaze shifted uncertainly from figure to figure, returning with vague disquietude to the round little person in a long white coat and voluminous white veil that swathed head and shoulders, as step by step, the file of disembarking travellers haltingly descended the gang-plank. He remembered his mother as an active, brisk woman; she had always impressed him as being large, bigger than himself. Perhaps it had been his boyish idea of her dominating personality. As he waited, he grew more nervous and embarrassed, suddenly afraid of the swiftly approaching meeting. When the round, little figure in the white coat and veil marked his face among the waiting crowd and sent him a fluttering greeting with a small gloved hand, he experienced an actual sensation of sickness. Mechanically he raised his straw hat and smiled back. Presently he squirmed past an intervening couple and caught her in his arms as she made the last step off the gang-plank.

His first impression was of a delicate perfume. It was the same powder she had used ever since he could remember, and a flood of boyhood sensations swept over him. There was something about this woman that was familiar, something that reminded him of his mother,—but it was only the vaguest suggestion. Her voice with its foreign accent first thrilled him.

"Griffey . . . Griffey . . . how like your father you are! Oh my dear, my dear! . . . You're nicer looking than he was. You're tall and strong! Oh Griffey, you're going to be such a comfort to me. You're going to take good care of your poor old mother, aren't you?"

She was loosening the veil that hid her face. He noticed her trembling fingers. She seemed so little, so shrunken!

"I'm not pretty any more, Griffey! Your mother's old and

wrinkled; I'm not the way you remember me; I'm old, . . . old . . . *old!*"

The poignant distress in the last word was pathetically appealing. It roused his first feeling of affection for this woman, still so like a stranger to him. They had wandered a little away from the confusion about the gang-plank and stood alone by a pile of crated freight.

His mother freed the veil at last and swept it from her with a dramatic gesture, turning her face up pitilessly for Griffith's scrutiny, her eyes shut, her expression abject but determined. He only half guessed what a terrible ordeal it was for her, or suspected that during every waking moment of her days upon the sea, she had been dreading it almost with terror.

Her son kissed her gently, tenderly. Her face was not greatly altered. She was older, he saw that, but she was still pretty. The affection, the appeal her voice awakened increased; he felt sorry for her—*exceedingly* sorry for her.

Mercilessly she kept her face turned up to meet the strong light that her son might behold once and for all what she considered to be the devastation of her beauty. It distressed Griffith that she should value his opinion in this respect. Whatever natural attraction drew him to her,—and he became more and more conscious of his affection as the minutes of their meeting lengthened,— it did not depend in any way upon her physical appearance. There was nothing wrong with his mother. She had still the face of a pretty, pretty woman.

Her skin was still lovely and blooming, her mouth still red-lipped and perfectly moulded in its doll-like cupid's bow, her nose, eyes and chin still possessed their youthful freshness and firmness. Only on either cheek in a space that might be covered by a twenty-five cent piece appeared a few tiny red veins the carefully applied rouge and powder would not hide. A few fine wrinkles criss-crossed the barely defined pockets beneath the eyes, and just below the chin hung a lean little pouch of flesh. There was no denying she was old. She was past fifty; Griffith could only guess how much.

"Is it so dreadful, Griffey? Am I such a fright?"

"Oh mother! Don't talk so! You . . . you're all right!"

Both had changed in the four years. Far more than his mother's, Griffith's aspect had altered. To his early height, breadth had now been added. The shambling walk and stooping carriage had disappeared. It could not be said he carried himself with rigid erectness, but he had an easy, pleasing deportment. He dressed well, had acquired a certain elegance and smartness from his fraternity associates, and he affected the careless, inconsequential manners of the collegian. His face was still youthful, and lacked character; it contained a suggestion of weakness, but the lower jaw was well-formed and ended in a firm, strong chin. His boyish grin had grown into a wide, expressive, likable smile, a few freckles still lay scattered across his short nose, and his hair, parted in the middle in the college manner, swept his temples in wavy, blue-black graceful abundance. The shifting, uncertain look in his eyes which had succeeded the wistful expression of his boyhood, had in turn given place to a boldness, an affected indifference which first drew his mother's liking, but later puzzled and distressed her.

II

Madame Santini, as she now styled herself, had returned to her son and to America to prepare for a becoming and as-happy-as-possible old age. She had maintained her struggle against departing youth for many years longer than she was entitled. The past decade had been a daily conflict, at which she had been worsted with increasing frequency. She acknowledged to herself at last that she was defeated; there was no use in fighting longer. Her efforts during the past few years had only made her ridiculous, and she was resigned now to grow old with what dignity she could command. She counted on Griffith. He was to be the foundation stone on which she proposed to reconstruct her life. She felt she was entitled to reap the interest of what she had invested in his support and education.

She was thinking of this as they crossed the ferry together after the requirements of the custom-house had been met. She was pleasantly surprised with her son on the whole. She had decided to take him out of college;—one year more or less would not matter,—and had planned to establish him with herself in a "snug little apartment somewhere,"—in New York or Boston,— where he could look about and begin to "carve out his career." But she felt now, he would oppose such a plan. She sighed heavily. Life was a difficult problem. She had spared no expense in her son's upbringing, had sent him to the most expensive schools and had allowed him to choose his own college, denying him nothing, in order that he might be a comfort to her when she needed him! Now it was plain that none of his plans for the future included her, that he was ready for anything rather than a happy, intimate companionship with his mother!

The Hotel Kenningston, a modest, inexpensive hostelry on Fifth Avenue and Sixteenth Street, was selected by Madame Santini. Griffith soon became aware that money was not so plentiful as it had been. Reluctantly he accompanied her to this dingy, old-fashioned abode and mother and son began the process of adjusting themselves to one another. They had three small rooms looking out upon a dreary well. The experiment was fore-doomed to failure. Madame Santini's pride had been violently shocked by her husband's dereliction. She could not bring herself to confide in her son; she kept her grievances and her affairs to herself; though she eagerly longed for reassuring compliments and affectionate attentions from him which were not forthcoming.

Griffith never heard the details of his stepfather's defection. Santini had always found someone who would support him, and his extravagant tastes and love of luxury had been responsible for the constantly dwindling size of his wife's income. When it proved insufficient to meet his demands, and when her age commenced to be apparent even to the casual observer, he proceeded to replenish his fortunes with the undepleted resources of a woman to whom the latter objection did not apply, and who was only too ready to fall in with his suggestions. Madame Santini's meagre allusions to him were always replete with bitter invectives, and invariably ended with equally bitter self-reproaches. He was an unfeeling, selfish, ungrateful, deceitful wretch,—and she,—ah yes,—she had been a fool, a trusting, silly *gobemouche* whom he had wickedly betrayed!

Nothing in the arrangements his mother made was to Griffith's liking. He resented his upset plans for the summer; he **chafed** at being "cooped-up" in three rooms in a small New York hotel during the hot season that he might have been spending on Lake Geneva with Archie and David,—and Margaret! He still dreamed of her by day and night, and his mother who was not long in suspecting his secret, persuaded him to confide in her. In possession of it, she gently but effectively ridiculed his emotion as a boy's immature passion, and joked him about his inability to support a wife, and the consequent absurdity of his dreams. She had no intention of permitting Griffith to marry anyone for many years. He was absolutely necessary to herself and she proposed to crowd out of his life every interest she could not share. She wanted him to grow to care for her, to yield the affection that was hers by natural right, the love other sons bore their mothers,—and she strove for patience and self-restraint when he flatly denied the truths she herself had learned from the hard experiences of life. He thought her cynical and unwarrantably distrustful, her vision and her opinions colored by her long residence abroad. She viewed everything from the standpoint of a foreigner. He resented this and came to a point where he would not or could not discriminate. He discounted her advice, and rejected everything she said. Most particularly her lack of money nettled him. He had never in his life known money stringency. His father had been rich; his mother had inherited his money; he himself was known as a rich woman's son. And now to have her continually exclaiming:

"We can't afford this, Griffey! That's too much! . . . Money does not grow on trees! It's not to be had for the picking! . . . No . . . that would be too expensive . . . no theatre this week . . . we have our meals paid for at the hotel, it would be foolish not to go back for luncheon. . . . Perhaps the cotton one would do as well!" It sounded insincere; he did not believe her; it fretted and angered him.

In August they went down to a small farmhouse on the banks of the Susquehanna River, where they could live cheaply, and it was here that the question of whether or not Griffith should return to college was thrashed out. Griffith had suspected his mother's intention from the first days of their reunion and she had been equally conscious of his determination to oppose it. Anger, reproaches, and tears marked the discussion. Madame Santini averred she could not afford to send him another year; Griffith suspected rightly that while the expense might be a consideration, it was not her real reason, which he did not attempt to fathom, though convinced in his own mind that it sprang only from a consideration for her own pleasure. He was in despair for fear she would tie the strings of her purse and so compel him to do what she wished, when by a lucky chance he stumbled upon a threat which completely routed her. Dramatically, he declared he would follow David's example, work his way through college for his last year and cut himself off from her entirely. Griffith had neither the ability nor the courage to do this, although he did not admit it even to himself, but his mother was not so sure. She was impressed by his passionate desire to return and began to fear he might carry out his declared determination. More than anything she had ever feared in her entire life Madame Santini dreaded a solitary old age. It was not so much her son's companionship she wanted as that Griffith should bring to her the atmosphere of youth, keep her in contact still with what was young.

A compromise was reached: Madame Santini agreed to finance Griffith's last year at St. Cloud on a slightly smaller allowance; after graduation he was to live with her in New York or Boston, wherever he could find the work for which he was best suited, adjusting himself to the best conditions she was able to provide, applying himself diligently to his business and to being the comfort to her she had always hoped.

Griffith promised without reservation. He had never speculated on what was to happen to him after his four years were over. St. Cloud constituted for him the entire world; the things affecting him in college were the most important of his life; with graduation consequential matters ceased; he was indifferent to what happened to him then.

III

If he returned to St. Cloud with a shortened purse, the fact had no effect upon his manner of living. On the contrary he spent more money during his last year than in any previous one at the University. He shut his eyes to what was to follow after he graduated. The prospect was dismal in any case, and a row about his debts could not make it much worse. He might as well have a good time while he had the chance.

An influence which contributed to Griffith's recklessness in spending money was the friendship he formed during his last year with a boy named Jack Taylor,—a freshman. Taylor was the son of a rich man who had tried again and again to divert the boy from the primrose path he found so attractive. He disciplined him repeatedly but weakened too soon; he cut down his allowance for months and then in a burst of generosity and affection paid all his debts. The son was a waster and rapidly becoming a thoroughly debauched young person. He entered the freshman class at St. Cloud when older by several years than most of the seniors. Some of the fraternities rushed him but he was not seriously considered by any of the best clubs. But Taylor was clever. He wanted an invitation from the Delta Omega Chi fraternity and set about to get it. His methods for ingratiating himself with the members were as obvious as they were objectionable to the undergraduate code. He would call at the club-house to inquire for someone he knew was not in and after loitering about a little while would depart, intentionally leaving a note-book behind him to serve as a pretext for another visit. Frequently he was at the house when luncheon or dinner was announced, and accepted hesitatingly, with a deprecating air, the unavoidable invitation to remain for the meal. He was not ill-mannered; in fact he was quiet, a readily-amused listener and good company. When opportunity permitted he entertained regally, throwing his money about with lavish indifference. Everyone liked him well enough, but no one to the extent of wanting him in the fraternity. He was not a gentleman.

He conceived a particular attachment for Griffith, and seemed to possess an uncanny faculty for intercepting him on the campus, as classes were dispersing, or in the village streets. Side by side they would stroll back to the fraternity house, where he would linger for an hour or more, borrowing one of Griffith's books to serve as an excuse for another visit when he returned it. Griffith's good-natured indifference to Taylor's company led the way to an unforeseen intimacy which gradually became a nuisance. Taylor was constantly proposing expeditions to the neighboring metropolis on which he urged Griffith to accompany him. Once there he proceeded to throw his money to the four winds, insisted on buying everything which might contribute to his guest's enjoyment. He engaged the best rooms at the big hotel, ordered champagne, and bought a box for the theatre.

Griffith was gratified by Taylor's preference for him, and found it difficult to offend him after having accepted so much of his open-handed generosity. Archie in his slow, clumsy way argued against the growing intimacy, and David asked him impatiently:

"What the hell is that guy, Taylor, always hanging 'round you for?"

To both remonstrances, Griffith hardly knew what to answer. Taylor had no permanent hold upon his friendship and their close association continued solely because of the other's clever insistence. The direct and most important effect of it so far as Griffith could see was the drain upon his small allowance.

IV

When Griffith returned to St. Cloud in September he had been eager to hear of Archie's and David's summer. The former had been able to spend only the last two weeks of July at Geneva Lake, but McCleish Senior had invited Barondess, his wife and daughter, to accompany him in his private car on a trip to the Imperial Valley where some irrigating experiments were taking place in which he was deeply interested. David could not accompany them, for since his graduation the previous June he had been offered the secretaryship of the Board of Regents of the University of St. Cloud, which carried a salary of a thousand a year. He had decided to accept this, for he had unavoidably run into debt, and the position would permit him still to live at the fraternity house, manage its affairs, and save money enough in a few months to pay up what he owed. His new duties took him back to St. Cloud on the first of August but his sister and her foster-parents went with Archie and his family to the Imperial Valley.

They had a wonderful time. Griffith listened sick-at-heart to Archie's descriptions of their experiences. A fierce jealousy possessed him. His friend's easy references to the girl who had filled his thoughts and dreams for the past six months were like knife-thrusts in his heart. Archie's clumsily-expressed, enthusiastic account of their joint adventures was torment, yet he drank up the details as a man parched for thirst drinks of a poisoned well. There were snapshots, a great number of them, but Archie, like all beginners in photography, had wasted his films upon the scenery. They had spent three days at the Grand Canyon: here was the view from Inspiration Point, that was their hotel, this was an old fallen tree that looked just like a dragon and if one bent close there was a horned toad upon it, this picture showed a straight-away bit of track across the desert, here was the Colorado and that white spot was Margaret's horse; this was Margaret on the steps of the car, Barondess was the man with his back turned.

Griffith bent over the picture, the blood pounding in his temples. Yes,—it was Margaret! It was she! Suddenly it blurred before his eyes. . . . Were there any more?

Of the many dozens, there were only a few in which the girl appeared; one of these plunged Griffith into a veritable agony of spirit. It showed Margaret and Archie on horseback ready for a ride over the Mexican border at El Paso. It was an indifferent picture of the girl suggesting her only slightly, but what struck at Griffith's heart was the graceful, romantic figure Archie presented. In puttees and riding breeches, a wide sombrero upon his head, his white shirt open at his throat, the very horse arching its neck in the manner of horses in all equestrian statues, Archie appeared superb. It was a happy pose, beautiful and heroic, however unconsciously assumed. Griffith expressed his admiration, and persuaded Archie to give it to him. He put it away in a bureau drawer and for several weeks took it out daily to torture his soul with its inspection. Fortunately, jealousy had no effect upon his affection for his friend. Archie would always be first with him whether or not he won the girl he loved. She was far too wonderful, too good and beautiful for himself; Archie of all men he knew came nearest being worthy of her.

V

Aside from his unhappy love and the pain of his jealousy, Griffith's last year at St. Cloud was by far the happiest he had known. As the only seniors in the fraternity, he and Archie dictated its affairs and enjoyed its best advantages. They shared the largest, most comfortable room in the house, and Griffith used to think that the most perfect moments of these idyllic days were those when the bright, warm sunlight, creeping across his bed, reached his face and woke him in the mornings. It would be nine o'clock by that time, yet the house was generally still. Archie would have gone to an early recitation leaving the room in delightful confusion. The sunshine would pour in through the wide open windows, and the musical rattle of a mechanical piano would come faintly and pleasantly from further down the street. Drifting vagrantly up from the dining-room below would rise the fragrant smoke of cigarettes. There never was a perfume like that, Griffith used to think: the first whiff of aroma-laden smoke! It was a delicate invitation, a suggestion, a gentle elusive incense, subtly provocative of sensuous delight. He would lie stretched out upon his bed, his eyes closed, his arms flung wide, waiting to catch the exquisite fragrance which came to fill his nostrils with its tantalizing, entrancing scent one moment and be gone the next. Frequently, as he lay half-dozing, surrendering himself to the perfect enjoyment of this moment of waking, Jack Taylor would hail from the street. Griffith might lazily stumble to the window, yawning and stretching himself, kneel there with the morning breeze blowing open the neck of his pajamas, and an idle colloquy would follow:

"What've you got on for today?"

"Oh, . . . nothing much."

"There's a ripping good fight in town tonight. We could catch that slow accommodation at ten-ten. Today's Wednesday and there's sure to be some sort of a matinee if you feel like it? Gans is the cleverest coon in the ring!"

"I haven't had any breakfast yet."

"Well, we'll eat on the train; there's a buffet service with the parlor-cars."

"I . . . I don't feel much like it to-day, Jack; we went over there only last Saturday; I don't dare cut any more."

"Aw . . . c'm on! I'm crazy to see that coon work; his speed's phenomenal. . . . We'll have a bang-up dinner at Luchetti's. . . ."

"No-o, Jack, I don't dare; I'd like to, . . . you know that. Come in while I eat; I'll put on a bath robe and be right down."

Perhaps some of these discussions would end by Griffith falling in with the plan; perhaps his well-meant effort to attend to his neglected class work would prevail for a moment, only to be sidetracked into a visit to the "Wid's" where a bottle or two of beer was consumed, many cigarettes smoked and the morning as effectively wasted.

It was a life of complete irresponsibility; there were no exactions, no standards to maintain, no compulsory rules to observe. It was an existence of uninterrupted idleness, self-indulgence, indolent drifting. Once or twice a fortnight there was a gathering at one or other of the fraternity houses for an hilarious, boisterous evening, in which much tobacco was burnt and considerable beer imbibed. Griffith rarely drank to excess. His discomfort the next morning was too acute to be easily forgotten, and besides he did not care for the taste of beer. He was content on these occasions to fill and light and smoke his pipe, refill and smoke it again. He enjoyed watching the others, but even this amusement began to pall. The affairs did not vary in their character: the freshmen lapsed early unto unconsciousness, the sophomores yelled, stamped and sang off key, the juniors reprimanded and directed, mollifying offended feelings, settling disputes. Most of the seniors, like Griffith, were bored.

VI

The days slipped by. January and February came with ice and snow, March dragged itself miserably to an end, April unexpectedly brought early warmth and clear, heartening sunshine, and before anyone realized it, Spring was upon them and but a few weeks remained before Class Day and Commencement.

Griffith woke on the morning of his twenty-second birthday,

towards the end of April, with a sudden, awkward, disturbing realization that there remained less than seven weeks of college, that he was heavily in debt, that final examinations would soon be upon him, and that failure of graduation was inevitable. In any case his time of dreaming and idling about his fraternity and college halls was rapidly approaching a close, and there awaited him at the end of a brief interval only the prospect of rejoining his mother, adjusting his life to existence in a stuffy hotel-apartment of three rooms, and looking about for a job that would keep him bent over a desk day in and day out at work he knew he should detest.

He shut his eyes tightly, impatiently shaking his head at the thought. He had enough to bother about already without worrying over the future. His first concern was the problem of graduation. None knew better than himself how serious that was. He had idled all the year; he had cut flagrantly; he had treated with indifference the warnings from the Recorder's office. Only by getting brilliant marks in his final examinations could he hope to win his diploma. Unfortunately, he did not have Archie's notes to fall back upon, for his chum had specialized on banking and finance in his senior year. Griffith had chosen subjects which he had anticipated would not require any work. Having attended considerably less than half his lectures, he realized he would have small chance in the final examinations. The idea of failure was exceedingly repugnant to him; it was humiliating. He did not value a diploma especially; it meant no more to him than a piece of engrossed parchment; but he disliked the thought of not being able to fall in line in gown and mortar-board on Commencement Day to march into the Gymnasium with the rest of his class for the closing exercises of their undergraduate career. He shut his teeth together and frowned irritably. He *must* pass his examinations somehow!

Searching his mind for some means by which this might be accomplished, he remembered Hugh Kynnersley, and as the vision of the red face and pale-blue, friendly eyes of the young Englishman rose before him, he flung back the covers of his bed and jumped to the floor with a little exclamation of happy exultation. Kynnersley would see him through; he would coach him in the subjects he required just as four years ago he had coached him for the entrance examinations! Griffith congratulated himself upon his lucky thought.

VII

He found Kynnersley early in the evening in the kitchen of his little cottage behind the Botanical Gardens, washing up the dishes after a solitary dinner he had cooked for himself and only just eaten. A year ago, Griffith had heard of the old grandmother's death. He had meant to go at once and see Kynnersley, or at least he intended to write him a letter of condolence, but one thing after another intervened and then suddenly he realized it was too late. He was sorry now for the lost opportunity to re-establish himself in the other's good opinion.

Kynnersley gave the wet dish-rag a final twist as he wrung the water from it, dried his hands quickly on a roller-towel, and taking both of Griffith's shook them heartily. He was full of his usual interested inquiries, and listened with rapid little nods of sympathy and concern to Griffith's answers. All the time the boy felt he was studying his face, glancing searchingly from feature to feature, but the scrutiny, though obvious, was not embarrassing. It was prompted too obviously by affectionate interest.

Kynnersley, however, could not help him with his examinations. He was familiar with the entrance requirements, having studied them so that he could coach intelligently, but he knew nothing of the subjects Griffith had been taking. Even if he did, he had no time to go over them with him now because his own examinations in English Literature would require all his attention.

Griffith had banked on Kynnersley's assistance. It had not occurred to him that the young Englishman would not be able to help him. His concern and distress showed in his face. The only chance now for passing the final tests was the uncertain possibility of his being able to read the answers to the questions from a neighbor's book. He must risk the correctness of these, and the danger of being caught.

Kynnersley laid his hand sympathetically, affectionately upon his arm.

"Don't let it worry you tonight; think about it in the morning;

THE EDUCATION OF GRIFFITH ADAMS 113

perhaps you can get a fellow class-mate to coach you. Tonight I want you to spend the evening with me; some of the boys are coming 'round; friends and members of your class: Red Hendricks and Silverberg and Gordon Cherry and others. We shall have some music and some good talk, and afterwards beer and cheese."

Griffith reluctantly consented. He followed Kynnersley through the swing door into the little dining-room where three years before he had nodded and fallen asleep over his host's reading. As he watched him now putting away the few dishes and pieces of silverware he had used at his dinner, he wondered what it was about the young professor that baffled him. He entertained a sincere admiration and liking for Kynnersley, and was sure that the other was sincerely interested in himself. They naturally attracted one another; their sympathies were alike, and yet Griffith always felt ill at ease in Kynnersley's company, constrained, awkward, unable to express himself frankly and unaffectedly. Kynnersley embarrassed him; he felt himself continually at a disadvantage.

As he passed into the disordered, book-lined study and sank uncomfortably into a deep-seated couch, he regretted having consented to stay. Kynnersley puttered about, lighting candles and busying himself with small preparations for the entertainment of his coming guests; Griffith foresaw he was going to be dreadfully bored. The men his host had mentioned were all known to him slightly. He had met Hendricks and Silverberg in the little boarding-house where he and Archie had lived when they first came to St. Cloud. Since then he had not spoken more than two or three times to either of them. None of those who were to be Kynnersley's guests were fraternity men and Griffith had no interests in common with any of them. He was a "Greek"; they were "Barbs." He did not consider himself better socially than they, but just of another world with different laws, different customs, different interests.

Hendricks was editor of the "Lit" and of the college weekly; he was red-headed and strongly socialistic. Griffith knew he had attacked the fraternities in the columns of both journals he edited and that he was invariably arrayed against the societies in college politics. Silverberg was a Jew and the college debater; at University gatherings he was always ready to spring up and make a speech. Gordon Cherry was in the Glee Club; Griffith barely knew him by sight. He had an instinctive aversion to them all.

He was a little surprised by their easy cordiality when they arrived. He was prepared to be dignified, reserved in his manner, to let them see at once that his presence there was accidental. But they gave him no opportunity to be supercilious; they greeted him warmly, unaffectedly.

With them came three or four others, sophomores and freshmen whom Griffith met for the first time. None of them were fraternity men; all seemed somewhat uncouth and grotesquely dressed; two of them were Jews.

A general chatter began at once; everyone seemed to be talking at the same time. Without urging, they made themselves comfortable, settling into the few deep-seated chairs, perching on their broad arms, or finding places upon the floor where they could lean against the wall. Kynnersley produced steins and beer and all drew their pipes and proceeded to fill and light them. A few availed themselves of the long-stemmed clay pipes the host had provided. In a few minutes, the air was thick with clouds of slowly drifting smoke.

The talk, at first divided among two or three groups, shortly became general in a sharp criticism of the government's policy in the Philippines. It switched to the bugaboo of the Japanese menace and presently was diverted to a discussion of free trade, the tariff and the probable platforms of the political parties two years hence. Hendricks interrupted by reading a brief sketch he had found in a square envelope-sized booklet published by a socialistic visionary somewhere in the East. It was entitled *"Why I Murdered My Mother"* and was diabolically clever and funny. His audience was convulsed with mirth; they rocked to and fro, exploding with noisy shouts of appreciation. Griffith was swept away by their hilarity; he laughed until the tears stood in his eyes and his sides ached. Someone next recited a trenchant, daring poem on the Christlessness of Christianity which provoked a heated argument on the value of the Church as a social institution. There was a general repudiation of the subject as soon as it became evident that it was merging into a debate between Silverberg and a sophomore who had been a divinity student at Princeton before he entered St. Cloud. A red-faced little Canadian whose nose turned up at its end like the snout of a young pig, produced a copy of Stephen Phillips' *Herod* and read a portion of it that amazed Griffith with its exceeding rare beauty. It prompted Kynnersley to pull down from his book-shelves Oscar Wilde's *Salome* and to read another poet's treatment of the same subject.

After this there was a general demand for Kipling. Kynnersley good-naturedly consenting, began *The Mary Gloster*. He read *Tomlinson*, *The Ballad of East and West*, *The Native-Born*, *Boots*, *Chant-Pagan* and *Mary, Pity Women!*

Griffith listened, stirred to the depths of his soul. He knew Kipling: he was the author of *The Vampire* and he had read *Soldiers Three* and some of the stories in *Plain Tales from the Hills*. But the Kipling he knew was a different person from the man who had written the poems Kynnersley read aloud. Griffith had but a slight acquaintance with poetry. He had never heard of Stephen Phillips and he had an idea the name of Oscar Wilde had only one significance. That there was such a thing in poetry as Kipling's verse he had never dreamed; he was electrified, profoundly stirred. The compelling cadences, the pictures and fancies, the bold fearless, unembellished words, the absorbing stories the poems told, kindled in him a fire of enthusiasm.

He was still in the grip of the poet's masterful lines when Gordon Cherry got up to sing. He sang Kipling's *The Gypsy Trail*, and then another ballad with a swinging, reeling, rollicking lilt that was irresistible. A freshman played Cherry's accompaniments and the next song was a duet in which he added a fresh, boyish tenor to the other's unusually fine baritone. Kynnersley got out his 'cello after this. There was first a solo and then an obligato to the singers' combined voices. After that they all grouped themselves about the piano and sang in harmony some of the college songs with which they were familiar. It was one o'clock when they finished with *The Battlements of Old St. Cloud*, and in happy mood trooped off together calling grateful good-nights to their host over their shoulders, breaking into song again as they threaded their way along the pebbled path skirting the Botanical Gardens.

Griffith followed alone. He hardly heard the blended harmony of receding voices or caught the aromatic incense of exotic blooms about him. A great weight lay upon his soul. The little world of tinkling gods and images he had so long venerated and worshipped, tottered upon their pedestals. He looked back over the four years of his college life, a vista of empty, idle, profitless days. Happy? Yes, they had been happy; they were the happiest he had ever known, and infinitely dear to him because of that. But something was wrong with them, something was false. Suddenly he felt as a man who has travelled many miles,—a thousand or so,—in a wrong direction, confident, trustful, hoping in good faith to reach his goal, to whom comes startlingly the first suspicion that he has perhaps made a mistake, that all the miles and miles and miles he has traversed and put behind him are wasted ground!

The doubt that entered Griffith's soul persisted during the immediately succeeding days, insisted upon acceptance, clamored to be received, again and again attacking his peace of mind, giving him no rest. In the end he crushed it, blindly and unreasonably. He found it impossible to turn aside from the things he had so long admired and reverenced; habit was stronger than the desire for truth. If he had been all along deceived, if college was not what he had come to believe it to be, if in reality he had wasted in sloth four golden years of his youth, worshipping false ideals, if there were more wit, brains and beauty outside of the fraternity life than in it, if the Delta Omega Chi club-house, instead of being the home of the best spirits at the University, harbored the most indolent, and frivolous, and if not the most dissolute, certainly the most deluded element at St. Cloud, then he preferred to remain in his delusion, duped and deceived, the wool to remain where it lay, across his eyes. He loved his gods, he loved his fraternity, its traditions and atmosphere; he loved the friendships it had given him. To uproot these was to tear out his very heart-strings.

VIII

But how to graduate was the immediate problem. Taylor called for him at the fraternity house, a few days before the examinations were to take place, and they discussed their mutual misgivings:

Taylor's concerning his freshman year examinations, and Griffith's of his graduation.

"I haven't a chance in the world to pass 'em, Griffith," he complained drearily. "The Governor will raise the devil; he swore this was the last opportunity he'd give me! But say," he added, in a cautious tone, "come out and take a little walk with me. I've got a scheme that may help us out. There's just one chance in a hundred of our pulling it off, but if we do, neither of us need worry about passing any examinations!"

Griffith gloomily followed him out of the house.

They set off toward the campus, climbing the University hill and descending the other side into the Botanical Gardens. Taylor refused to divulge any details of his plan, assuring Griffith he would explain them later on. They strode silently and rapidly along, until they had crossed to the other side of the Gardens, and were passing in the rear of a small brick building, which Griffith had always been aware stood there though he had never paid it any attention. Taylor abruptly halted and glancing to right and left to make sure they were unobserved, told Griffith to look through the window of the little building.

It was somewhat smaller than the ordinary window, and was covered with a heavy wire screen screwed to its sash. Half of it was below the level of the ground, a small concrete well in front, permitting light to penetrate into the cellar. The window had not been opened for years, and the dirt and dust were thick upon its glass while much debris had collected at the bottom of the well.

"Look down there and tell me what you see," Taylor directed.

Through the almost opaque window glass, Griffith peered. In the half-light within he presently made out several rectangularly shaped bundles, wrapped in heavy paper and stoutly corded. On the top of each, thrust beneath the encirling hairy rope, were single sheets of white paper somewhat soiled and crumpled. Printed matter was upon these and, bending close, with difficulty Griffith read:

"Mathematics 2 A." On the next he deciphered: "Philosophy 14"; on the next: "English 9."

Griffith straightened up and caught Taylor's eye.

"They're the examination papers; they just arrived yesterday.

I saw 'em being carried in here. The State printer at the Capitol does all the printing for the University; they keep 'em in here until they hand 'em over to the professors."

Griffith nodded.

"This is a pipe," Taylor went on. "All we've got to do is get a couple of those electric hand flash-lamps, come up here to-night, unscrew that wire screen, loosen the putty 'round one of those panes, reach in and slip back the lock, climb in and help ourselves! But there's one thing you've got to swear to, Grif: no one else is to be let in on this little graft. It's got to be done carefully and just one sheet of questions removed from a bundle. They're sure to have 'em all counted, and if any suspicions are aroused, they'll spring a new set of questions, . . . and it's all up with us. This has got to be between you and me. I've three more years, and if we do the job right, it'll save me from burning midnight oil during the rest of the time I'm here."

IX

At a quarter past two that night, Griffith, exerting all his strength forced upward the lower half of the window, and dropping upon his hands and knees, slipped his legs through the aperture, and reached for the floor with his feet. Once inside he used his pocket flash. Taylor joined him in another minute and together they carefully made their way between the long tables on either side of which the bundles of papers were piled in considerable disorder, just as they had been received from the printer, still redolent of fresh ink. One sheet to mark the contents of each bundle was slipped beneath the thick hairy rope with which each was tied. Taylor had little difficulty in finding the sets of examination papers in which he was interested. They were the largest bundles, as the freshman class had little choice in the matter of selecting courses. Griffith was obliged to look for a long time for his own. There were nearly two hundred bundles, and in some cases two, often three or four different examination papers were tied up in the same package. Eventually he located all but one. It was a nervous, tedious business, and daylight was upon them as they crawled out of the window, replaced the glass pane,—holding

THE EDUCATION OF GRIFFITH ADAMS 119

it back in place with pins—and screwed the heavy iron screen back into position.

Just after the last screw had been securely driven home, and Griffith had risen with a growing elation and thankfulness in his heart that the job had been successfully accomplished, he saw Kynnersley. The young professor was standing not twenty feet away, leaning upon his cane, the long cape he affected hanging loosely from his shoulders. A quick, low exclamation came at the same instant from Taylor as his eyes encountered their observer. For a few interminable moments, the three stood motionless and silent. Griffith could not raise his eyes; he knew the other's gaze rested upon him, not upon his companion. Presently he heard Kynnersley move and looked up to see him turn his back upon them, and without speaking, walk slowly away in the direction of his little brick cottage on the opposite side of the Gardens.

Taylor's wild alarm the instant Kynnersley was out of sight and hearing, disgusted Griffith. He knew well what was passing in the young professor's mind, and detection, exposure, even failure to graduate, were insignificant in comparison with the pain and disappointment he had caused the man who had always been so well disposed toward him. Kynnersley had understood him, had read aright his mind and heart as no else had ever done. Now he was stricken with the realization he had irretrievably lost his regard, had hurt him grievously. Taylor's bleatings and craven apprehension as to what Kynnersley would probably do about the matter, enraged Griffith. Exasperated, he turned angrily upon him and told him to "shut up!" He was sick of Taylor; he never wanted to speak to him or see him again.

The next morning the letter he expected arrived from Kynnersley:

"My dear Adams: I want to ask you and your friend not to take the examinations which confront you this year. I am sorry it means another six months' work for you, but you will understand my position I am sure. I hardly blame you for what you attempted; I blame conditions, your environment, the influences of this place which have robbed you of your ideals. I am very sorry for you. But do not be discouraged. Hold whatever you have gained here you believe of value; try to forget the rest; begin anew. I believe in you; I believe in your destiny; eventually you will succeed, for the material is there; you have been given the vision to see where others cannot. Follow your own instincts; do not trust to others; you are right, they will be wrong.

"I shall say nothing to anyone about what I observed this morning. I ask you to see that whatever papers were taken from the basement of the warehouse are destroyed.

"Affectionately your friend,
"Hugh Kynnersley."

X

His failure to graduate was a keen disappointment to Griffith. He knew he could not return in the fall for another semester's work; his mother had reminded him too often in recent letters of his promise. He faced an unavoidable long angry scene with her when he should confess his debts; after that there would be no persuading her to give him six months more at St. Cloud.

The Class Day ordeal proved even harder than he expected. It was particularly humiliating because of Margaret Sothern's presence. Archie's mother and father and one of his married sisters came to St. Cloud to see him graduate, and they invited Margaret to accompany them. The friendship between Barondess and the elder McCleish was rapidly becoming cemented by investments in similar enterprises and by close business relations.

Griffith found that his love had not abated. He had not seen Margaret for over a year, but many times each day his thoughts reverted to her, and at night before he fell asleep his last moments of consciousness were hers. But in the fifteen months her personality had escaped him. Thinking so much of her, dreaming dreams of her, cherishing his memories so constantly, she had become for him a creature of the spirit, a being without either flesh or blood. He realized this the instant he saw her. The Margaret he had been worshipping was only a figment of his brain, a ghost of the real Margaret. What he had supposed to be the anguish of love had been a form of mental intoxication, and the personality he believed he loved was as formless, as incorporeal as a verse of poetry or a phrase of music.

The real Margaret Sothern plunged him back into the agony

THE EDUCATION OF GRIFFITH ADAMS

of spirit he had known at first. His heart had been beating wildly enough before he saw her, but when he held her hand a moment he thought she must surely feel the throbbing in his veins.

He sat with her alone in the gallery of the octagonal gymnasium during the graduation exercises on Commencement Day. As became a generous benefactor to the University, Archibald McCleish, his wife and daughter had been asked to occupy seats with President Hammond and the faculty on the platform. David was busy looking after the Regents who arrived bearing themselves with pompous dignity. Archie in mortar-board and gown sat with the seniors just beneath the platform, listening to the addresses. The other classes ranged themselves behind.

Margaret reached out and laid her hand on Griffith, as the seniors began to file up in line to receive their diplomas. His fingers closed over hers and she let her hand remain in his. Together they sat there silently, looking down on the great gathering, the flags and bunting, the rows of black mortar-boards, the girls with white dresses showing underneath the black gowns, and the flash of programmes in the hands of too warmly dressed women who gently fanned themselves, flopping the limp-covered books indolently to and fro.

An infinite sadness possessed Griffith. It seemed that everything was passing away, deserting him, that he was losing all he cherished and loved, even the girl beside him whose hand he held. A wild impulse to blurt out his love for her then and there, to tell her that she represented all there was in life for him, to beseech her to wait a little while until he had the chance to prove himself, rose up insistently in his heart. He turned to her, white, with trembling lips. At that moment Archie stepped forward to receive his diploma, and the girl withdrew her hand to join in the applause which followed Dr. Hammond's sonorous pronouncement of his name.

"Why don't you clap?" she asked reproachfully.

He did so, jealousy flooding his heart as he watched her, eagerly bending forward, vigorously applauding, her face bright with animation.

The exercises dragged on to a close. The entire assemblage rose and sang *The Battlements of Old St. Cloud;* the seniors gave

U. of St. C. for the last time; a reverend gentleman in a sudden hush made the closing prayer.

Griffith reached for his hat beneath the seat and rose stiffly to his feet. He turned to the girl offering his hand to assist her to rise. As she stood beside him an instant looking down at the now fast disintegrating throng, he felt the pressure of her fingers again.

"I am leaving Saturday," he said simply.

She looked at him, her eyes full of concern.

"That will be the last?"

"That will complete my undergraduate career."

"And there is no chance of your coming back next year to finish?"

He shook his head.

"My play-time is over; I'm supposed to be educated even if I didn't graduate. It isn't the learning, it's the experience you get here that counts. I shall have to begin to work now; my mother expects me to live with her and find something to do."

He shrugged his shoulders indifferently. There was a moment's silence between them. He felt the girl's eyes upon his averted face.

"You'll come and see me, Griffith, when you're in New York?"

There was a quality in her voice he had never heard before. He looked up eagerly.

"Oh, Margaret . . . oh, Margaret, may I? You *will* let me come sometimes?"

"You'll always be welcome, Griffith."

He helped her on with her loose Spring wrap and, with his hand beneath her elbow, guided her toward the choked exit through the crowd that had filled the balcony and was inclined to linger in the aisles. Together, slowly moving through the throng, they descended the well-worn stairs.

End of Book I.

SALT

"Ye are the salt of the earth: but if the salt have lost his savour, wherewith shall it be salted?" Matthew v: 13.

BOOK II

SALT
OR
THE EDUCATION OF GRIFFITH ADAMS

BOOK II

CHAPTER I

I

THE following Monday morning Griffith arrived at a Broadway hotel near Central Park to which his mother had moved some months before. He had travelled as far as Chicago with a half-dozen of his fraternity brothers, and their companionship had mitigated somewhat the wrench of parting from Archie and David, and leaving forever the spot where he had known the only happy years of his life. He dreaded meeting his mother, the upbraiding which was sure to follow the admission of his debts, the awful monotony of an existence with her shut up in the confined limits of the hotel.

The clerk glanced at him, impertinently, Griffith thought, when he asked for his mother. He knew she expected him as he had written when he was leaving St. Cloud. He was annoyed by the man's manner. It aroused a suspicion that his mother had involved herself in some way, had made herself conspicuous; perhaps she had married again!

"You had business with Madame Santini?"

Griffith hid his smile. The question and the clerk's frank attempt to determine his status, fanned his irritated mood into ugly anger. He leaned toward him, looking him directly in the eyes from beneath sharply contracted brows, emphasizing his words with firm taps of his gloved forefinger upon the counter between them.

"Yes, I have business with Madame Santini; kindly inform her Mr. Griffith Adams is here."

He thought with satisfaction of the clerk's dismay when he should learn their relationship.

The clerk returned his angry look, then gave him the benefit of a twisted smile and an indifferent shrug.

"Madame Santini's dead; she died Saturday."

Griffith did not change his pose. He continued to lean across the counter, one arm extended, his gloved hand supported upon a rigid forefinger, his eyes riveted upon the other's face. The two stood so, glaring at one another for some seconds, the clerk's mouth twisting slowly in a contorted smile. With a small commotion, the telephone operator who sat at the exchange board in the rear of the office rose abruptly to her feet. Griffith, though he did not shift his gaze, saw her quick movement and her nervous struggle to free her hair from the nickel head-piece. She gave it an impatient tug, snapping the few entangled hairs, and stepped close to the man opposite him, whispering to him sharply. At her words the clerk's expression underwent a sudden contortion. It was as if a high voltage of electricity had seized him. His head jerked, his features contracted, his hands flew out toward Griffith, the palms extended, the fingers twisting. The action was intensely ludicrous.

Griffith thought:

"He won't get over it for days; he'll tell everyone he knows what a damned fool mistake he made."

Swiftly followed the thought:

"So . . . she's dead . . . Did she leave me her money? . . . How much is it?"

Then:

"There'll be a lot of trouble arranging the funeral; what will I have to do? There ought to be somebody to tell me."

Lastly came the thought of Margaret Sothern:

"She'll be kind; she'll be full of sympathy."

The clerk began to mumble. Griffith turned away. He was conscious of shock, but had no feeling of loss; rather his immediate sensation was of relief.

The hotel parlor opened off at one side of the foyer. Automatically he entered this room and crossed over to a curtained window, where he stood looking out upon the traffic of the street. He was aware there were other people in the room,—a couple seated upon the sofa behind him. A woman's voice rose and fell stridently.

Griffith remained at the window trying to adjust his mind to what had befallen him. He tried to feel sorry but he could not. He kept repeating to himself that he ought to feel sorry; to lose one's mother was a terrible thing. He was left alone, now, in the world and he assured himself that soon it would sweep over him how dear she had been and he would get the full significance of his loss. She had taken care of him; she had loved him; she had been generous and good. But among these reflections, persistently there bobbed up in his mind speculations as to how much money she had left, what he should do with it, how he should live, what Archie and David would say when they heard the news.

An immense coal wagon, with three huge lumbering clumsy horses had backed up to the curb in the street outside; the driver had lifted off the covering over the man-hole in the sidewalk and adjusted the iron chute between the aperture and the tail of the wagon; now he opened the small gate in the rear of the great van, and the coal poured out in a thundering, rushing black river.

Griffith absently watched him, his thoughts busily turning round and round. On the sofa behind him he could hear the sibilant whispers of the two women's voices, rising sharply now and then as they interrupted one another. Dimly audible above the roar of the coal outside he could distinguish the merry jangle of a hurdy-gurdy.

He could pay his college debts. That was the main thing. There would be no wrangle over them now. He hoped there would be some loose bills and change among his mother's effects as he had only sixty cents in his pocket. Perhaps the hotel would trust him until matters were straightened out. At the back of his mind, the desire for some older person's guidance persistently troubled him. During all his life, there had always been someone to go to, someone to obey, someone to tell him what he could and what he could not do; now there was nobody. His mother was gone; he was alone. Suddenly he felt frightened; there was no satisfaction in the thought; he had always counted upon his mother. Unconscious of what he did, he dropped his head upon the arm that rested against the sash of the window, and shut his eyes. He wanted his mother.

II

A hand,—a soft, small hand,—was laid upon his shoulder. He turned about. A little man with a pale expressionless face stood before him. He wore an unkempt Van Dyke beard, and the mustache covering his upper lip hung long and ragged over his mouth. The hair upon his face and upon the top of his head where it had begun to thin was darkly red. His eyes were sunken and sombre, with no light in them. Griffith was struck with his unhealthy paleness. The face above the thick, untidy beard was colorless as white paper.

"Hello, Griffith," he said holding out his hand. "I'm Leslie."

Griffith accepted the proffered palm, and for several swift seconds his mind grappled with the statement, and with the personality of the man before him. The announcement of his mother's death roused in him far less complex and contending emotions than did the realization of his half-brother's existence.

A suggestion of a smile struggled through the thick beard.

"Don't remember me, hey? Left home when you were quite a tad."

"Oh, yes, I remember," Griffith said vaguely. "Of course . . . I . . . It's an awfully long time ago."

"Yes," said the bearded man, "awfully long time."

There was a silence.

"They telephoned me on Friday," the man continued, "they had quite a time finding me; I'd moved three times since the old address . . . she had. I came over right away."

He paused uncertainly.

"Bates," he jerked his head with a backward movement toward the desk, "says you didn't know anything about it. I wired you on Saturday and again Sunday."

"I left there early Saturday morning."

"That was it," the other said, nodding, "we didn't know. It was very sudden; double pneumonia,"

THE EDUCATION OF GRIFFITH ADAMS 129

Again there was an interval. Griffith felt his brother was eyeing him critically, making up his mind about him. His glance wandered in embarrassment over to the two women on the sofa; one had risen preparatory to taking her leave; they continued to speak to one another at the same moment, their voices mounting as they strove to drown each other's words.

"You've been away at school?" Leslie asked presently.

"Yes, . . . at college."

"Finished there?"

"Yes."

"What're you going to do now?"

Griffith was annoyed by the questions: he shrugged his shoulders.

"Any plans?"

Griffith frowned, his eyes roving uneasily about the room.

"Find a job, I guess."

He wondered if his mother was still upstairs. She could not have been buried yet. Should he ask to see her? In a swift vision he saw her dead face in the midst of her disordered hair lying motionless upon the pillow, her flat body stretched out straight beneath the carefully smoothed bed-clothes. He shuddered; no—he should not like to see her.

His speculations were presently set at rest.

"I . . . we took . . . the . . . the body was removed to the undertaker's Saturday," said his brother. "Management here urged it. I . . . I didn't know what else to do."

So much was relief.

He was conscious Leslie's eyes were still upon him, moving over his features, noting the details of his clothing. He felt self-conscious and embarrassed; he wished Leslie would go away.

"Guess you're a bit shaken up about . . . about everything," Leslie ventured. "Let's get something; brace you up; let's go to the bar."

Griffith nodded apathetically. His irritation with his new-found brother increased. He didn't feel shaken up a bit; he wasn't in the least upset. Uncertainly, he followed him out into the lobby. As he crossed it he was conscious that the young clerk at the desk studied him curiously.

In the rear of the bar-room they sat down at a round marble-topped table. Griffith ordered a high-ball; Leslie asked for a special brand of whiskey, filled his pony glass almost full and drank with obvious enjoyment.

Gradually, as they talked, Griffith's ill-temper faded but he felt tired and his head began to ache. His brother seemed kindly disposed toward him and he found his awkwardly expressed sympathy and friendliness not unacceptable. He was gratified to observe that Leslie was naturally taciturn, spoke slowly and briefly, abbreviating his sentences, eliminating pronouns. The silences between them were soothing and companionable.

They spent the rest of the day together, wandering into the café for lunch, strolling into the Park for a time, sauntering leisurely back to the hotel, establishing themselves in two comfortable straw-seated arm-chairs before one of the wide windows in the lobby where they exchanged infrequent observations. Late in the afternoon they went up to the rooms their mother had occupied.

There was something singularly pathetic about their aspect. Griffith gazed at the denuded bed upon which his mother had died and a choking sensation rose in his throat. It was a sorry thing to realize she had died in such dismal and crowded surroundings, deserted by everyone she had loved. The futility of life oppressed Griffith. He had known so little about his mother after all! The two sons whom she had brought into the world in agony and terror, stood in the darkened room, silently, side by side, gazing down upon the bare mattress. Neither knew what the real interests of her life had been, who were her friends; who among all the thousands of people who had returned her smile and looked into her living eyes, would care that she was no longer of the world.

"Don' know what we're to do with all these things," Leslie said presently. He pulled open one of the bureau drawers; it was filled to the top with a tumbled pile of ruffled, be-ribboned *lingerie*. Another disclosed a disordered assemblage of toilet bottles, paste boxes, cosmetics, rouge sticks and cold cream jars. The scent of the powder his mother used rose delicately. It struck Griffith as an unwarrantable intrusion, a sacrilege,—this spying upon their dead mother's secrets. He turned away, averting his eyes.

"Can wait till after the funeral. When Anna, my wife, died, I gave all her clothes away to a friend."

Griffith threw his brother a brief look; he had not known that Leslie had been married. In six years he had not even heard his name nor thought of him. Life was a funny proposition; kinship was funny, too!

III

It seemed quite natural a little later, that Griffith should go home with his brother. Each realized the other had come into his life as a permanent factor, and each was cheerfully willing to begin getting acquainted. It seemed sufficiently casual at the time; Leslie had said:

"Well, we'd better go home."

"I'll get my suit-case," Griffith had answered. "They must have checked it."

They crossed the street, hailed a Riverside 'bus, climbed to its swaying roof and sat down beside one another on a narrow front seat.

The elegance of the apartment house to which Leslie took him astonished Griffith. From his brother's drab appearance, his unkempt reddish-brown beard, his unpolished shoes, his trousers that bagged noticeably at the knees, the frayed edge of his collar, he had fancied he must live somewhere in rooms even less attractive than his mother's. He was impressed with the spacious marble foyer, the paneled inserts of watered green silk, the gold decorations, the heavy brass elevator cage, the uniformed attendants.

The apartment itself consisted of six rooms. It was close and musty when they entered but Leslie raised several shades and threw open the windows, letting in the ruddy oblique rays of the declining sun. The rooms were of good size but immoderately over-furnished. Half-a-dozen chairs, straight-backed and round armed, a massive sofa, covered in scarlet satin brocade crowded the front room; its space was further congested by a mechanical piano, a small cherry writing desk and a square table covered with an oriental scarf. Statues in bisque were arranged in the center of these pieces of furniture and the top of the piano was clustered with a tumbled pile of long, oblong paste-board boxes containing the music rolls. The adjoining room was similarly over-crowded and obviously little used.

Opening off a long dark hallway which ran the length of the apartment, were Leslie's bedroom, which he had shared with his wife, a servant's room, a dining-room papered in crimson and paneled oppressively in black oak, and a kitchen.

Leslie showed his brother the room intended for a servant. It was small with but one window looking out upon an air-well and contained a white iron bed, a couple of cane-seated chairs and a varnished pine dresser.

"Don't keep house now; take my meals out; a woman does the cleaning and the wash. Prefer it that way. Think you'd be comfortable?"

"Sure," Griffith said without enthusiasm, "this is fine."

He understood his brother's invitation and, for the moment, was glad to avail himself of it. He threw his suit-case on the bed, flung back its lid, and began to put some of his things away in the bureau drawers.

Leslie was puttering about in the dining-room. Griffith could hear the clink of glasses. Presently he appeared in the doorway a bottle in his hand which he held up invitingly.

"Join me?"

Griffith shook his head; he disliked the taste of whiskey. A dozen times during the day he had accompanied Leslie to the bar in the hotel and watched him fill his pony glass nearly full and slowly drain it; it did not seem to have any effect upon him.

Presently they went out to dinner, and over this meal and during the evening which followed the last barrier of reserve between them was broken down. Restraint removed, Griffith told his brother what little he knew of his mother's marriage to Santini. He was shocked by Leslie's estimate of her; it fascinated him while at the same time it offended him.

"She was a selfish woman, vain, heartless and cruel," Leslie declared.

He smiled a small wan smile at the distress and amazement in his brother's face.

"Deceived and tricked my father and broke the heart of yours."

He nodded his head slowly in confirmation of the statement's truth.

"Nothing here," he continued tapping his heart. "She lived only for admiration; died for lack of it. She sapped others' vitality to supply nourishment for her own. Her last husband was as good-for-nothing as she; he treated her as she deserved."

Griffith burst into an exclamation.

"I don't . . . I don't see how you can *say* such things!"

Leslie wagged his head up and down and shut his eyes knowingly.

"Recall one act of hers that was either generous or unselfish? Remember anything she ever did that didn't have her own pleasure in view? It was self,—self,—self with her always. No heart—no heart. . . . I was full of the devil when I was a kid; used to chase the girls, you know, like every other young fellow. She kicked me out; it made no difference to her what became of me; I was no longer of use to her; was in the way, had been ever since she re-married, and she was glad to get rid of me. I wrote her when I married. She sent me a check for twenty-five dollars! Said she hoped I would be happy!"

He paused and drained his glass.

"She treated you about the same way, . . . a little better perhaps . . . but your father was a rich man when he died. Damned easy way to get rid of you to pack you off to boarding school. She kicked me out; sent you to school! Humph! . . . Daresay she told herself that as long as she sent you some money every month, she could squander as much as she pleased in Europe. Santini, I guess, helped her get rid of it. After it had gone and he had skipped with another rich woman, she was ready enough to come home to you."

Griffith bent forward frowning.

"Gone?" he demanded. "What do you mean?"

"Well, . . . don't know, . . . she had paid nothing at the hotel for three months. She had promised to pay up on the first of July when the interest on some bonds came due, but if she had any bonds she borrowed all she could on them. The telephone operator told me she had been speculating, and gave me the name of her brokers. Haven't seen them; tried to telephone them Saturday but the office was closed for the day. . . . Found a pawn ticket in her bag."

Griffith gazed at him in amazement. He could not believe the words. It was inconceivable! That his mother could possibly have lost all her money was preposterous! What was *he* going to do! How was he going to live! He hadn't a penny!

"Why . . . there *must* be *something!*" he cried, "a few hundred dollars!"

Leslie shrugged his shoulders.

"Maybe; if there is, it's yours. Your father left her a big fortune; there should have been thousands; she probably left only a lot of debts!"

Griffith gazed at him wide-eyed.

"Debts?"

"There're generally debts when you go see the pawn-broker; indicates your tick has run out."

Griffith continued to look fixedly into his brother's face. Hardly conscious of speaking, he said in a stricken half-whisper:

"What the devil am I going to do?"

Leslie, misunderstanding him, said cheerfully:

"Mighty hard to expect a lot of money and find out it's all spent. You're right: it's tough. . . . I can get you a job, I guess, without much trouble; I guess I can get you a pretty good job with a railroad . . ."

"I wasn't thinking about that," Griffith interrupted. "I was thinking about . . . about how much I owed myself. I'm afraid I've been pretty reckless; I owe an awful lot!"

"How much?"

"Oh I don't know," Griffith answered uneasily. "Five or six hundred."

Leslie said nothing. He ordered another drink of whiskey and lit a cigarette. Griffith lapsed into silence and his own gloomy thoughts.

He was shocked by what Leslie had said about his mother. It seemed unfilial, a disloyal, cowardly thing to criticize her so harshly when she had been dead only a little more than two days. He realized he had no tender affection for her such as other boys had for their mothers; yet he had always been aware of the bond that existed between them, something that drew him to her, something that sprang now to her defence in the face of Leslie's criticism. But he could not deny the partial truth of what his brother had said. She *had* neglected him. He had passionately wanted her during those dreadful early days at the Concord Family School; he had written begging, pleading for her to come and take him away. Before his mind rose the picture of himself as he stood, tall, thin and stoop-shouldered, in Garfield's office, and heard the fussy little man complacently announce from the pages of a letter, that his mother had written to say she had decided to remain in Italy while her husband's uncle continued so dangerously ill. It had been a brutal, cruel disappointment. Griffith remembered how dazzling the sunshine had seemed through his swimming eyes as he walked back to the great, yellow dormitory building. That had been the supreme moment of his boyhood when he had needed and wanted his mother. There was no question but that she had failed him. For what? For an old Italian's money!

A year later when she came for him, he neither needed her nor wanted her.

But looking further back into the days of childhood, he remembered times when they had been wonderfully happy together. The most perfect of these, were the months immediately following Pauline's departure, when she had undertaken to dress him each morning. She had been so beautiful and had smelled so entrancingly sweet! And there were the days when they had packed their picnic lunch the night before and they had gone canoeing or sailing with Professor Castro Verbeck in the morning. He dropped his head upon his hand as the memory of the sleek dark head of the man bending over his mother's upturned face and her soft lovely throat, rushed back to him. He shook his head impatiently, brushing the unpleasant picture aside and rose abruptly to his feet. The day had brought him many varied, and conflicting emotions; his head was aching again and he was tired to the point of exhaustion.

"Let's go home; I'm all in," he said harshly.

"Alright."

His brother rose.

"Another little nip and I'll be with you."

"Doesn't so much of that stuff play the devil with you?" Griffith ventured as they stopped at the bar on their way out.

"W-e-ll, . . . suppose it does," Leslie conceded. "I'm used

to it; never take too much; I quit for a long time after I married."

Again Griffith glanced speculatively at him. His brother must have had a curiously uneventful, hapless sort of a life. While they had sat eating their dinner, Leslie had given him a brief outline of it. He had been in the railroad business ever since his stepfather had procured him a position when he left home. For seventeen years he had continued in the employ of the same road. From a clerk at nine dollars a week, he had risen to be District Passenger Agent, had been transferred to Chicago, and then recalled to New York to be the right-hand man to the General Passenger Agent. When his superior had resigned to take charge of the Passenger Department of another road, he had succeeded him.

He had smiled the small wan sardonic distortion of his bearded lips as he spoke of this.

"My chief's name was Enos Chickering; want you to meet him some time; a good friend of mine; do anything I ask him; give you a job if you want one. He's A. G. P. A. of the New York, Niagara & Western, right in line for a big job in the Federal system."

Leslie had married while he had been in Chicago. He spoke only briefly of his wife, dismissing the subject with:

"Anna was all right at first; got kind of crazy when we came to New York; wanted to raise hell all the time. I got tired; it was damned stupid . . . she died 'bout two years ago."

Only on one other occasion did he ever again refer to her. It was the dark chapter in his life.

CHAPTER II

I

THE two brothers spent the afternoon of the funeral in going over their mother's affairs. Madame Santini had simplified the task by spending practically everything she possessed. Securities in the form of bonds had been hypothecated, and the borrowed sums used in mad stock speculation. It was evident she had attempted to regain small losses by risking bigger stakes and when these had been swept away, she had tried to recoup by even more desperate gambling. All her valuable jewels had been pawned. There was nothing left of the half-million that had once been hers.

Griffith was overwhelmed. He had promised the tradesmen in St. Cloud that he would square matters with them soon after he reached home. Now he should have to write them they must wait. He would be obliged to save the money out of what he earned. Leslie had spoken of a job. He kept wondering throughout the day, how much the job would pay.

He found the courage to speak about it when they came back to the apartment in the evening. His brother was indefinite. He said he thought his old friend, Chickering, would give Griffith a job, if he asked him, but he had no idea what salary he could offer. He promised to speak to Chickering about the matter in the morning.

A little after ten o'clock the following day, when Griffith had come in from a late breakfast and was interestedly reading the theatrical advertisements on a back page of the newspaper, Leslie called him up from his office on the telephone. Chickering had said he would like to see Griffith. Leslie advised his brother to come down "right away and have a chat with him."

A strong disinclination to follow this advice immediately took possession of Griffith as he hung up the receiver. Such an interview was intensely repugnant to him but he could think of no adequate excuse by which to avoid it. He was in an angry and petulant mood, half-an-hour later, when he descended the subway steps at Ninety-Sixth Street and slapped his nickel on the glass surface of the ticket-seller's window.

II

The offices of the New York, Niagara & Western Railroad occupied a number of floors in an immense square office building on lower Broadway. Griffith passed from the street into the vaulted corridor and a sense of his own insignificance in the rush and bustle in which he was immediately engulfed, cleared his mind of the aggrieved thoughts to which he had been a prey.

The great lobby ran the length of the building. It was wide and lofty, the ceiling curved in a spacious arch, the sides paneled in glistening slabs of mottled marble, thousands of electric bulbs flooded it with light from massive and ornate electroliers. A dozen elevators sucked in and vomited forth a constant stream of men; silently and swiftly they dropped, alighting like birds at the bottom of the shafts, disgorged their human freight, gulped in a new cargo, and as swiftly and as silently vanished, disappearing into the mysterious, vast upper regions of the mammoth structure. Only the clang of their closing gates marked their flights.

Zigzagging his way between the lines of hurrying men, Griffith was caught in a small eddy and drawn into one of the elevators, and, in another minute, stepped out upon the eighteenth floor. Bare echoing corridors stretched away on either hand, flanked by doors bearing such legends as: "Paymaster," "Department of Maintenance and Ways," "Chief Engineer." He wandered uncertainly along one deserted hall-way until unexpectedly he came to a door marked: "General Passenger Department."

He knew that this was where he would find Chickering, but again he hesitated, his distaste and embarrassment rising up strong within him. He thought of facing Leslie with an invented excuse; then, with a sigh of resignation, pushed open the door and entered.

He found himself in an unusually large room where some fifty men and boys were at work at flat-topped oak desks, arranged in groups to form, with the help of letter-filing cabinets and sectional bookcases, little separate offices. There was a sustained patter of

THE EDUCATION OF GRIFFITH ADAMS

typewriters and an incessant hum of small sounds. A sleepy-looking clerk leisurely rose from his desk as Griffith leaned against the counter and came toward him. He disappeared with the visitor's card, drifting out through a little red door and presently reappeared, nodding an invitation to Griffith to come through the swing gate in the counter.

They entered first a small carpeted room in which a freckled youth sat at a typewriter rattling off a letter at furious speed. Griffith's companion knocked softly upon an opposite door, listening attentively, then opened it, and held it so, for the caller to pass in ahead of him.

III

The office beyond was a spacious room, thickly carpeted, two sides broken by excessively wide windows overlooking the lower end of the city. On the walls were racks from which maps hung like roller shades; there were also several large photographs of beautiful bits of scenery, framed in the natural bark of trees. In the center were two large pieces of furniture: a massive mahogany table, covered with a thick plate of glass, and just beyond it a magnificent polished roll-topped desk. Between the two, in a revolving armchair, sat a grey-headed man with short closely trimmed side-chops. He had a ruddy, fat, smooth face which radiated health and cleanliness. His body was round and chunky, and a roll of fat at the back of his neck bulged over his collar. The most notable feature of his face were the eyes, wet and glistening, of a bright transparent blue that reflected sharply all the lights that fell within the range of their vision. Chickering wore a flower in his buttonhole, and his hands, folded upon the clear space of the table in front of him, were exquisitely manicured, the nails brightly polished; the cuffs about his wrists were starched and immaculately white. He gave the impression of painstaking grooming.

"Sit down, Mr. Adams."

The man indicated a chair on the opposite side of the table. As Griffith obeyed, he found the courage to meet the wet, glistening eyes a moment. Chickering both repelled and attracted him.

"You're Leslie Wagstaff's brother, . . . half-brother, hey? and you're just out of college and want a job. That it?"

The voice was friendly if the eyes were coldly critical, and Griffith felt his confidence returning. He shifted into a more comfortable position.

"Well, . . . tell me something about yourself, everything you can. I have to know something about the men who work for me."

Griffith began hesitatingly, and haltingly gave the brief sum of his experiences. When he paused with "I guess that's about all," his inquisitor was far from satisfied. He commenced asking questions that seemed quite at random. He wanted to know minutely Griffith's circumstances, who were his friends, what were his interests, how he intended to live, whether he expected to continue to remain with his brother. The boy answered him as frankly and truthfully as he was able. He had nothing to fear from this man, he told himself, but at the same time he felt uneasy and vaguely puzzled.

"I'm inclined to give you a chance here, Adams," Chickering said at length. "There's an opportunity in my office for a young man who really understands the meaning of the word 'loyal.' Don't misunderstand me: I mean loyalty to *me*. I'm boss of this particular part of the Passenger Department, and you want to keep in mind you are working for *me*. I'll look after *you*. The more I can depend on your loyalty, the more I'll watch out for your interests. Get that into your head and get it there *hard*. Your brother understands what loyalty means; he's the most staunch and dependable man I know; ask him to enlighten you."

He paused, gazing at Griffith reflectively.

"You may turn out to be just the man I'm looking for; I can't tell. I shall have to watch you awhile."

He leaned across the intervening table and tapped the hard surface of the glass with a polished finger-nail.

"Young man," he said impressively, "I'll *make* you, if you can fill the bill for me. I need a young feller like you; I need a man here whom I can trust just as I trusted your brother in the old organization."

Griffith grinned nervously, moistening his lips. He did not understand what Chickering expected of him; he was ready to do anything he was told; he felt afraid of the man who bent toward him so earnestly.

Chickering reached over and pressed a button. In the interval while he waited he drew a spotless handkerchief from his pocket and gently touched either side of his nose with it, sniffing delicately. Griffith caught the odor of fine cologne.

There was a light knock at the door and a tall man with sandy, untidy hair limped into the room. One of his legs was short and he teetered from side to side as he ambled along like the walking-beam of a ferry boat. He was slightly stoop-shouldered and had the paleness of the habitual office-worker.

"Mr. Rumsey," said Chickering restoring his handkerchief to his breast pocket, arranging its protruding ends carefully, "you spoke some time ago of needing more help in your department. This young man wants to get into railroading. See what you can teach him. Put him on your pay-roll for ten dollars a week until he's worth something more to us." He smiled pleasantly at Griffith. "When do you want to start in?"

"I don't care; any time I guess," Griffith answered indifferently. He was thinking about the ten dollars a week: a paltry sum, hardly worth working for. He had spent as much for a pair of shoes; Jack Taylor had flung away twenty times the sum in a single evening! Ten dollars a week would hardly pay for his car-fare and lunches! He couldn't save anything out of that!

"Now is as good a time as any other; suppose you start right in. Mr. Rumsey is the Chief Clerk of this division of the Passenger Department; he will take you in hand."

He dismissed them both with a glance of his wet eyes.

IV

Griffith followed his halting guide out into the larger office where the hum of the typewriters sounded like the loud stridulation of crickets. As he proceeded down the room in Rumsey's wake he felt the eyes of many of the clerks upon him. He was acutely self-conscious; the palms of his hands were moist with perspiration.

Rumsey's desk was on a raised platform half-way down one side of the room. He beckoned a young boy stenographer to him as he sat down and said briefly:

"Marlin, show this young man where to hang his hat."

The boy nodded pleasantly at Griffith, and led the way to the far end of the room, opening a door into a lavatory lined on either side with lockers.

"Most of these are already taken. The ones up top are better than those near the floor because they clean up here at night with mops and suds-buckets and the water splashes through the wire grating on your clothes. You can get a key from Mr. Sparks."

Marlin's friendliness made no impression. Griffith was becoming more dispirited and irritable every minute; he felt all this was outrageously humiliating; he might endure it if he had been promised a satisfactory salary. But ten dollars a week! It was ridiculous!

"Show him how to run those files," Rumsey directed, when they had returned to the Chief Clerk's desk.

Nearby were eight letter cabinets of oak, four drawers high. Marlin took Griffith over to them and began to explain how the Chief Clerk's correspondence was kept in order. The boy's ready flow of words and glib phrases annoyed him; he understood but little of what he was told. All the time he stood listening to the chattered instructions, he felt that others in the room were taking him in, watching him, whispering about him among themselves. He was not sure whether they considered him a fool or admired him. As he glanced about, he was conscious of his "college" bearing, his well-bred, well-groomed appearance. Marlin's collar had been worn for several days, his dark blue tie was frayed, exposing the white stuffing through a tiny slit, his nails were frankly dirty. The other clerks in the room differed but slightly in their appearance. Some of them were cleaner, but they all wore ill-fitting, ready-made clothes and their necks were carefully shaved in a neat curve at the back of their heads, and without exception they wore knobby-toed buttoned shoes. Griffith smiled to think how they would have been ridiculed at St. Cloud: rubes and rough-necks!

"Number 129 is the Q. R. & H.; that's a Harriman line; that whole system runs from 121 to 135. Masters is the G. P. A., . . . General Passenger Agent; letters to him go addressed in Chick's

THE EDUCATION OF GRIFFITH ADAMS 143

name, per the writer's initials. That's the way it is. S. V. R. are Mr. Rumsey's initials; R. P. is Plummer, the lanky steno over there. The file number 129-SVR-RP gives the whole dope on the letter. Here's the reply: it starts with 'Referring to your communication, File No. 129-SVR-RP.' . . ."

Griffith's thoughts wandered with his eyes. His instructor's words were unintelligent jargon to him; he gave up trying to understand. Presently Marlin turned to him with a bright smile.

"See? You'll soon get the hang of it; ask me any time you get stuck."

He went back to his own desk, obviously relieved at having completed the task of instruction, and began a furious attack upon his typewriter. Griffith, his heart a dead weight in his breast, dully picked up the first letter and studied it. There was nothing else for him to do but attempt to follow the directions he had been given, although he had not understood one word of them.

He read the letter in his hand through mechanically, but was unable to find either the name of the man to whom it was addressed or the name of the railroad in the card file. He laid it aside and turned hopefully to the next. This was a memorandum addressed to the Superintendent of Maintenance and Ways of the New York, Niagara & Western; he could find no card for their own road in the file. The next was a letter addressed to the General Passenger Agent of the Boston & Maine. There was a real feeling of satisfaction in finding this railroad's name in the card file and also the name of the General Passenger Agent. He poked it away and turned encouraged to the next letter. But this and the succeeding five baffled him completely. He turned to ask Marlin to straighten matters out for him but the stenographer was taking Rumsey's dictation. In disgust he faced the row of filing cabinets again, determined angrily he would stick the day out, but when it was ended he would go home and tell Leslie he'd have to get him something more interesting to do, and at the same time give him at least a living salary.

At twelve o'clock, Rumsey told him he could go to lunch at the half-hour.

"Kindly make a point of being back at one-thirty promptly," he said impersonally, "it's a rule of the office; we like to have the clerks back punctually when their lunch hour is over."

Griffith shut his teeth. It was insufferable to be talked to like that by a worm like Rumsey! God! He wouldn't stand it from anyone! The idea of telling him what time he should be back! His hours were his own and he'd come and go as he damned pleased!

However indignant he felt at first, he came to the conclusion, as he sauntered up crowded Broadway after his fifteen-cent meal, that there wasn't anything else he could do just for the present. He would have to stand idle in the street to show his independence. He'd take it out on Leslie; he'd tell him just exactly what had happened! Chickering would have to give him a decent job, or he wouldn't work for him! That was all there was about it!

Sullenly he returned to his task at half-past one and recommenced his fruitless endeavors. Again and again he was obliged to appeal to Marlin, who invariably responded good-humoredly, explaining over and over the workings of the system. Griffith's continued interruptions of the stenographer's work, finally drew Rumsey's attention and presently the Chief Clerk, himself, came over to the cabinets and explained all over again how the filing system operated, confusing Griffith completely. After this, Griffith determined he would ask no further questions of anyone. They would have no one but themselves to blame if the letters were incorrectly filed. It was going to be the only day he did such beggarly work, anyhow, and it was a matter of complete indifference to him what kind of a mess he made of the job.

By four o'clock he was half way through the first basket and the new letters and carbons which had accumulated during the day made a pile nearly twice the size of the one put away. He was discouraged, exhausted and in an ugly mood by five o'clock. The cuticle about his nails was torn and in places had started to bleed from repeated contact with the sharp edges of card-board folders and letters. For the last hour he had watched the long hand of the clock above the Chief Clerk's desk jerk its lagging way minute by minute around the circle of the dial. When it finally reached the hour mark, without a good-night to anyone, he shoved the heavy drawers of the cabinet closed, hurriedly secured his hat and gloves from the locker room and left the office. He drew a long breath as he reached the hall; he would never see any of them again; he was through forever with that kind of drudgery.

V

He found his brother already at the apartment when he reached it. From the wet hairs of his ragged mustache which clung together in little moist clusters about his mouth, Griffith saw he had just been having a drink. The boy strode past him into the close, overfurnished little parlor. He flung his hat upon the scarlet sofa and dropped into one of the deep chairs by the window.

It was not many minutes before the storm which had been gathering all day broke. It carried Griffith along with it and he found satisfaction and relief in giving way. Leslie puffed placidly at his cigarette.

"I won't stand it, I tell you; if you expect me to work for that man Chickering you've got to tell him I'll have to have a better job. I didn't go to college to learn how to stick letters away in a file. What do you suppose I can do on ten dollars a week? I owe a lot of money, I've got to pay back. I can't save anything out of *ten dollars a week!*"

Leslie smoked on, silently and thoughtfully until he had finished his cigarette.

"God damn it! Did you hear what I said?" Griffith burst out. "*I won't stand for it!*"

Leslie did not answer; he picked up the evening paper.

"You don't have to."

The tone was dispassionate, almost kindly.

Griffith's hands clinched into fists, his jaw stiffened, his breast rose on a great breath, filling his lungs; he held it there while the blood pounded in his temples, his eyeballs strained. Then all at once something within him broke. He felt the snap as if it had been the actual breaking of a bone or ligament. He sank back into his chair, weakly.

All his life, over him there had been authority. At school and college there had been the regulations of the institutions, and behind them had been his mother. These had been swept away. Leslie stood in their stead; he had no authority over his younger brother; he did not presume to exercise any. That was the staggering thing which presented itself to Griffith; Leslie had no intention nor desire perhaps, to force him to take the job he had found for him. He was free to accept or reject it, as he pleased!

It took Griffith's breath away. His mind raced on to other possibilities. What else was there for him to do? Get out and earn his living? Doing what? What was there he *could* do? He thought swiftly of David and Archie, the former with his marvelous capacity for money-earning, the latter with his powerfully rich father. He had neither the one's ability nor the other's backing. He was all alone; face to face with life. He had only this half-brother, the little man with the baggy trousers, the unkempt reddish hair, and the white expressionless face.

Leslie had said. "You don't have to."

Like a blundering persistent fly returning again and again to the window-pane, buzzing, buzzing, buzzing tirelessly at its unyielding surface, Griffith's mind ceaselessly attacked the inflexible prospect which confronted him.

He went to bed early but although he was feverishly tired, he could not get to sleep. Persistent noises kept him company: the discordant jangle of two pianos, the evenly recurring guttural rasp of his brother's snore in the next room. He tossed from one side of his narrow bed to the other, his imagination at its keenest, picturing with horrid vividness all the distasteful details of the future. He was wide awake at an early hour in the morning when the grey light filtered through the drawn window-shade. He took a bath to freshen his tired body and as he was drying himself, he heard the nickle clock in Leslie's room spring its compelling alarm. He shaved carefully and was ready ten minutes before his brother. They went out together to breakfast, each buying a morning paper at the entrance of the restaurant, poring over its pages as they ate their coffee and eggs, the newspapers propped against either side of the water decanter between them. Neither referred to Griffith's outburst the previous evening nor to what he had decided to do. The younger brother was disconcerted by the other's lack of interest. It was an aggravating thought that perhaps Leslie did not care. Possibly he had been offended by his angry explosion, and considered that his well-meant services had been flung in his teeth. Griffith was conscious of alarm; Leslie was the only friend he had; it wouldn't do to have him turn against him!

Plans to ingratiate himself with his brother were rapidly forming in his mind as he walked into the Passenger Department of the New York, Niagara & Western Railroad at nine o'clock. It was a transformed Griffith who said a respectful "good-morning" to Mr. Rumsey and nodded in a friendly manner to Marlin. He attacked his pile of letters resolutely, and tried to master the confused, contradictory jumble of directions which had been heaped upon him the day before. But if he was in a more tractable state of mind, the work itself was no more easy or interesting. It was baffling, exasperating, tiring. By eleven o'clock the skin around his fingernails was torn and raw, his back across his hips ached, his feet throbbed. The rebellion of his first day came back with the same intensity. Filing letters was no work for a grown man who had been through college!. It was a girl's work; it called for no brains, no discrimination; after one got on to the system, anyone could do it.

VI

But somehow the second day was lived through, and the days which followed. At the end of a week, on Sunday, he spent most of the day in bed, resting the tired muscles of his back and legs. His resentment against the drudgery and misery of the work decreased with his lessened vitality. He had rebelled until the work began to sap his strength, unused to any concentrated effort. But when the time came that he crept wearily into the hot, crowded subway train, profoundly grateful if he found an unoccupied seat, sat with closed eyes during the whirling journey, and, when he reached his brother's apartment, flung himself, exhausted, upon the satin-covered sofa until it was time to go out with Leslie to the restaurant they frequented, to stuff themselves with slabs of red meat and enormous helpings of vegetables and salads, he ceased to care. The things that mattered were food and sleep.

In all his life he had never done any regular physical work. He had never made an effort even to take consistent daily exercise. The muscles of his body were totally unfamiliar with steady manual labor of the mildest character. The process of adjustment lasted long with him, but eventually, he came to the grateful realization that his work was not tiring him as it had done at first. He became aware of this on the notable day when he caught up with the letters waiting to be filed, and went home with the satisfied knowledge that the wire basket contained only the mail of the previous day.

VII

One evening when he had been in the employ of the railroad about a month, his brother handed him two theatre tickets a friend had given him. Leslie hated the theatre; he never went himself.

This incident roused Griffith's mind to the fact that he had made no effort to communicate with either Archie or Margaret since he had been in New York. The latter he was certain had long ago left the city to escape the summer heat; but Archie had expected to arrive in New York the first of July and to start right in equipping himself for the position his father had reserved for him. He had probably been wondering what had become of his old school and college chum.

Griffith knew that the McCleish family when they were in the city lived at the Hotel Chelsea. They owned a suite of many rooms in that old-fashioned but ultra-respectable establishment which had been their headquarters for twenty years. They actually lived there but a few weeks in the year, but when they regarded themselves "at home" it was in the Hotel Chelsea.

Griffith was delighted to hear the even, staid tones of Archie's own voice when he telephoned on the chance of finding some member of the family at the hotel. They arranged to dine together the same evening and afterwards go to the theatre for which Leslie had furnished tickets. It was a happy meeting. Griffith had been living in a sullen, heavy-hearted state for the past month. The routine of his tiresome work had wrapped itself about him like the clinging folds of a great serpent, sapping his strength, dulling his wits. The sight of Archie's Scotch face had a marvelous heartening effect. For the first time since he had come to New York he felt like laughing; he could have embraced his placid, calm, stolid chum. The other's assumed matter-of-fact air of casuality in seeing Griffith again, was delightfully characteristic and endearing. It was

THE EDUCATION OF GRIFFITH ADAMS

so like old Mac! Nothing could affect that slow, staunch, loyal nature! Holding him by either arm, gazing into his opaque, gray eyes, Griffith realized how truly he loved him; their friendship would endure all their lives; nothing could affect it!

They dined together, went to the theatre and later dropped in at a café. Archie was full of awkward sympathy over Griffith's loss of his mother. He listened attentively to his account of his brother and the position he had secured. Griffith was inclined to embellish the latter; he could not bring himself to acknowledge the smallness of his salary or the meanness of his job.

Archie was eager to tell him in turn about his own fortunes. His father had put him in as secretary to the Vice-President of the Fourth National Bank at a salary of eighteen hundred a year. Griffith's soul rose in bitter envy of such a sum, a salary computed by the year instead of by the week. He shut his teeth as he considered the rank injustice of it! Archie's father was powerful and rich; he could find a job like that for his son immediately, and yet Archie did not possess half the natural quickness and intelligence which Griffith knew he had himself.

"I suppose he's made you a director in a lot of his companies," Griffith remarked ironically.

"Four," Archie answered simply, "they're little companies, you know; small affairs he's trying to get organized and get going. I'm just a dummy; I go to the meetings to make a quorum."

Griffith was struck dumb. Archie did not see the sullen, envious look on his face; he was anxious to tell Griffith about David and Margaret.

A special office had been created for David by the faculty of St. Cloud. He had made many friends as Secretary of the Board of Regents and now he was appointed the University's special representative to solicit funds for the endowment of a much needed dormitory. He was to travel a great deal interviewing prospective donors, encourage their well-disposed intentions, discover new generous-minded millionaires. He was guaranteed his expenses and promised a two per cent. commission. One of his trips would bring him to New York; he expected to be there for a few weeks in September.

Margaret was in Newport visiting a girl friend whom she had

known in the French convent. The National Tennis Tournament was to take place there late in August; Archie supposed she would remain for that. Barondess, he understood, had become a frantic golf enthusiast; he had laid out an elaborate course about the grounds of his country estate at Lenox. The family would probably not open their town house until November although Margaret would be in and out of the city before then. Archie proposed that when David came to New York in September, he and Griffith should give both him and his sister a wonderful time: dinners and theatres and everything that might amuse them. Griffith readily agreed, but his enthusiasm was forced. He could not but wonder where the money was to come from with which he could pay his share.

VIII

It was a warm summer night and he walked all the way home alone. The stars were blurred spots of dim radiance above the city streets, paled to insignificance by the fire signs which glowed in resplendent golden tracery upon the tops and *façades* of the buildings, and by the blaze of white light that streamed from closed shop windows and the *foyers* of apartment houses. The subway rumbled beneath his feet and taxis sped past in the street honking like hoarse dogs at the crossings. People ambled past him enjoying the cool of the evening, or gazed with mild interest into the windows of the shops on upper Broadway. Girls with their "friends" strolled up and down, simpering at their whispered remarks, conscious of their newly whitened shoes and white ankles.

Griffith realized he was happy. Youth,—confident, effervescent youth,—bubbled irrepressibly in his veins. As he walked buoyantly homeward he became aware that for the past week or possibly ten days he had begun to notice things and find amusement in them. The city itself commenced to exert a strong fascination for him as he grew more familiar with it. From his boyhood days, he had been in and out of New York, spending a night, a week, and—a year ago—more than a month in it. He had come to know the city as a visitor; New York was just a place where one went. All at once unknowingly he had become a part of the city; he belonged to it and it to him. He was a New Yorker! The phrase thrilled him.

CHAPTER III

I

DURING the year which followed, Griffith's feeling toward Margaret Sothern underwent a marked development. He was able to see a great deal of her and his first infatuation gave place to an intense admiration and deep affection. When she was in the city he saw her twice and sometimes oftener during the week. A fine intimacy sprang up between them. But Griffith could not restrain the look of longing in his eyes which expressed the turmoil in his heart. He was constantly filled with a desire to pour out his love in a mad avowal. But the girl was cleverer than he suspected. His sentiments were not only plain to herself but to anyone who observed him in her company. Margaret, skilfully maneuvering, blocked his declaration whenever its utterance seemed imminent. On the way home, or in the cold reasonable light of morning, Griffith congratulated himself upon his self-restraint.

He rarely if ever thought of marriage or of anything more definite in their relationship. He did not know what he desired beyond wanting her to like him, to approve of him, to be glad of his company. It was enough that she did not send him away. He was always welcome in the handsome city home, and she would leave the group at the tea-table to saunter with him to the hall, when he went away, or come running downstairs a quarter of an hour too early for dinner, just to stand laughing and talking to him before the library fire. Often he had acute pangs of jealousy, when she seemed to favor Archie or some sleek-headed, well-groomed New Yorker. Archie was equally devoted to her. He and Griffith recognized their rivalry but never discussed it. Margaret invited Griffith to escort her to the concerts and opera; Archie accompanied her to the theatre and to the neighborhood dances. Both were sometimes invited to the Baroness' home for dinner, formal affairs to which other people were asked.

Archie's ability to entertain her in return, provide her with a taxi, bring her flowers and candy rankled bitterly in Griffith's heart, but hardest of all was the clearly apparent preference of the girl's foster parents for his friend. Barondess greatly admired Archie's father and since their first summer together, had cultivated an intimacy with him. He showed the son much the same deferential consideration which he entertained for his powerful and influential father. Yet Griffith suspected that Margaret was often kinder to himself because of his very inability to compete with Archie's wealth and parental advantages. He was alternately elated by evidences of her kindness and depressed by the suspicion that it was actuated only by pity.

Her influence was effective in keeping him free from unprofitable associations and harmful self-indulgences. He had few interests outside of herself and Archie. Evenings in which he was with neither, he spent idly in Leslie's apartment, playing the mechanical piano, attempting to read, or maintaining a desultory conversation with his brother over the top of an evening paper.

His relationship with Leslie was unique. They had not a single interest in common, yet Griffith was aware that his brother had conceived a strong affection for him. He liked Leslie well enough himself, but he often got on his nerves. He had a contempt for his baggy, ill-fitting clothes, his ragged unkempt mustache and his whiskey-smelling breath, and yet he was grateful for all "old Les'" had done for him.

In a moment of profound depression following a call at his office of a collector in whose hands some of his college bills had been placed, he had turned to his brother and asked him for the loan of the money. The next day Leslie had brought home a cheque and handed it to him without a word. Besides, Leslie never asked him to contribute to the rent of the apartment, and when they dined together he invariably paid the bill. They never discussed finances. Griffith accepted his brother's generosity much as he had accepted it from his mother. Occasionally he would borrow a dollar or two from Leslie toward the end of the week. He never kept track of these small sums, nor did it occur to him that there was anything unusual in taking them. He always referred to them as loans but there was never any talk of repayment.

A dreary, dismal sort of life, Leslie led, so his brother thought.

It was whiskey, whiskey, whiskey from early morning until the last thing before he went to bed. He ate practically nothing. Often he went silently out to dinner with Griffith and watched him eat a hearty meal, while he sat smoking one cigarette after another, slowly drinking two, three,—sometimes four ponies of his favorite liquor. A definite aroma of tobacco and alcohol pervaded him. He did not bathe with the regularity of most men; he took a bath not oftener than once a month, and the odor that enveloped him grew more noticeable as the interval lengthened. During the day at his office he helped himself continually from a bottle he kept in his lower desk drawer. At nine o'clock in the evening, sometimes at eight he went quietly to bed, taking the newspaper with him, reading half-an-hour to an hour before getting himself his final drink and extinguishing his light.

Griffith used sometimes to wonder if his brother did not read his newspapers over more than once. A printed sheet of a morning or evening daily was constantly before his eyes; he read line by line, carefully turning the big pages, doubling them neatly back upon themselves, creasing the fold, smoothing the sheet so it would not wrinkle. He spent hours over the various news items; he never failed to read the stock market reports, the death column, the weather predictions, and frequently the want ads from first to last. These were of equal interest to him as the news that was double headlined on the first page. He never referred to what he read. The daily papers provided him with his only amusement; he read their columns to occupy his mind. The routine of office work, whiskey, and newspaper reading, were the three elements which made up his existence. He never went any place; he had no friends. He was a solitary, morose, silent little man whom nobody loved and who, outside of Griffith, loved nobody.

II

In September and again at Christmas-time, David Sothern arrived in New York for a few days' visit. His coming gave occasion for some memorable dinners and theatre parties for Margaret, Griffith and Archie. They made a happy quartette. They dined invariably together, sometimes at Barondess' house, sometimes

Archie or Griffith played host. Afterwards they went to the theatre and later to supper.

Griffith enviously noted that David was outgrowing both himself and Archie. He had become a man; there was no longer any trace of the boy about him. He impressed one immediately with his force, dynamic strength, his shrewdness and determination. He had astonished everyone by his success in collecting funds for the dormitory to be built at St. Cloud. He had no intention of renewing his year's contract for he declared the work was mean and unpleasant. He gladdened their hearts by declaring he was coming straight to New York as soon as he had completed his soliciting, and intended to start in business for himself, investing his commissions in some enterprise likely to double his capital in two or three years.

The holidays were particularly enjoyable. On Christmas Day, Margaret had a tree and there was a wonderful dinner of turkey and plum-pudding, the first real Christmas dinner Griffith had ever eaten. Two of her girl friends were present, and there was dancing and general merry-making after the feast was over. Friends of the family dropped in, during the evening. Barondess opened champagne and his fat, placid wife played accompaniments to Christmas carols and college songs which they all sang together, standing close about the piano. It was long past midnight when the party broke up.

The tones of Margaret's warm, sweet voice rising high above the others, lingered with Griffith as he walked home, his presents in their tissue paper, red ribbon and seals, tucked under his arm, his head bent to a fine driving snow that had begun to fall. It seemed to him he had never loved her so much, that she had never been kinder to him.

Wrapped in his reverie he turned his brass latch-key in the door of the apartment and opened it. The parlor was a flood of bright light, the air close and strong with the smell of stale cigarette smoke and whiskey. Leslie lay on the scarlet satin sofa, his stocking feet sticking up over one arm, his head supported by the other. He had slipped down so that his chin, covered by the unkempt beard rested flat against his chest. The arm of the sofa pressed tightly against the back of his skull and forced his head forward at right angles to his body. His nose and lips were squeezed together like the distorted features of a plastic rubber face, the ends of his ragged mustache standing out straight from beneath his nose like the uneven bristles of an old brush. He wore no collar and his opened vest exposed a soiled shirt streaked with the gray smudge of ashes. He was breathing with great difficulty, gasping and puffing, one moment struggling for air, the next sucking it in with a thick strangling gurgle. Newspapers lay in confusion upon the floor, among them butts of burned cigarettes and charred matches. Almost in the centre of the confusion, a dark brown empty bottle had rolled upon its side and another, similarly depleted, stood within arm's reach of the sofa.

Griffith bent over the sleeper and tried to arouse him. Leslie only grunted and held his breath. The boy was alarmed; he caught his brother by the feet and pulled him free from his cramped position. The man's head fell back upon the sofa's seat with a thud and a terrific snort, and Griffith saw the torso expand in a great in-take of breath.

For a moment he regarded the sprawling, dishevelled creature, shocked and revolted. It had been Leslie's way of spending the holiday: reading his newspapers and slowly drinking himself into insensibility. It was unspeakably disgusting and yet Griffith's heart was stirred.

He dragged the inert figure into his brother's room and flung it on the bed. Then he stripped off the creased and baggy clothes and thrust the ugly naked body beneath the bed covers. He opened the windows as wide as they would go letting in the sharp night cold, snapped off the light and went out, shutting the door behind him.

III

When Margaret went to Augusta in January, David returned to St. Cloud, and Archie left the city to accompany his chief on a banking inspection tour of several weeks. Griffith was deserted; loneliness descended upon him.

At his office he had long since mastered the intricacies of the filing system; it took him now not more than a couple of hours to put away the letters and carbons of the previous day. He had been assigned other work but nothing that interested him. All of it was clerical: copying names, making out requisitions, arranging cards in alphabetical sequence. He hated it all and he shirked as much as he could. To get through and go home was the feeling of which he was conscious during the day; lunch was an hour off; quitting time would be in another hour-and-a-half. It was drudgery and he despised it.

Once or twice a week Enos Chickering burst open the little red door which led from his own stenographer's office to the big operating room itself, and strode down the centre aisle on his short, fat legs, his face flushed red, his wet eyes glistening. When their chief descended upon them, it was understood he was in a towering rage. Griffith soon came to suspect that Chickering enjoyed these bursts of temper. His clerks were in terror of him. When angry, there was nothing he would not or could not say; a ready flow of words came to him at such times and his snarling, violent invectives were like a torrent of blows. The clerks cowered before him, and the more they cringed the more furiously were they abused. He relished the excitement the process of getting angry gave him, he enjoyed the terror he inspired, he loved to see his victims squirm. Griffith wondered why they stood it. He told himself the moment Chickering got angry at him and attempted to call him down, he'd snap his fingers under his nose and go get his hat and coat; he'd have no opportunity to fire him. But when his hour came, he behaved in exactly the same manner as the cringing, cowardly clerks he so despised. He hated Chickering thereafter but this feeling of resentment which he nursed from day to day, did not prevent him from being elated and thrilled about a fortnight later when he met Chickering striding briskly in the hall, his white immaculate starched cuffs pulled down over his gloved hands, and the A. G. P. A. had remarked cheerily:

"Hello there, Adams; getting on all right with Mr. Rumsey?"

It was the first recognition Chickering had vouchsafed him since their initial talk. Often Griffith speculated about that interview. He wondered if Chickering talked to every clerk the same way when he took him into the Passenger Department: promising him speedy promotion, keeping his hopes alive, while he remained upon the pay-roll at ten dollars a week. Moods oppressed him: one day he was consumed by angry impatience, the next by doubt and indecision, the third by resignation and indifference. He hated his work, his associates, his employer. He told himself it was Leslie who was responsible for his plight, and blamed him accordingly. After a particularly arduous and exacting day, he would come home sullen or viciously irascible.

IV

After his two friends and Margaret had left the city his dissatisfaction with his existence and his irritability increased. When the office closed no prospect of anything pleasant awaited him. At five o'clock he shoved his work carelessly into the little drawer of his wooden table and hurried with the others to the locker room for his hat and coat. In the stone-floored corridor, echoing to many brisk footsteps, the opening and closing of doors, he followed the small army of clerks that streamed from the offices of the railroad. With the others he squeezed into the elevator when it stopped, and swiftly, noiselessly dropped in it to the ground floor. It was when he emerged into the thronged street that the sense of his loneliness most sharply overtook him. The prospect of the same uneventful evening stretched drearily before him.

Leslie always glanced at him over the top of his evening paper as he opened the door of the apartment. He never varied the form of his greeting. It was uniformly and maddeningly the same, with the same irritating inflection:

"Hello—Hello!"

Frequently, Griffith only nodded in reply. He had anticipated his brother's greeting from the moment he had left his office. He knew just the way he would look and just the way he would say it. Sometimes he wanted to fling his arms in the air and scream at him:

"Oh, for God's sake—*change it!* Say something else!"

Raging he would seek his room, shutting the door firmly behind him, and drop upon the bed, stretching his long limbs, relaxing his muscles, while he stormed in his heart against the empty wretchedness of his life.

His brother would come presently and open the door. Griffith would hear his shuffling approach before his hand rattled the knob. He would stick his frowsy head through the aperture always with the same blinking expression, and ask in the same toneless way: "How about the eats?"

Often Griffith would not dare allow himself to answer; he would force himself to get up, would wash and comb his hair and still without speaking, follow his brother out into the noisy street where children screamed and dashed from curb to curb. There were two restaurants they patronized; one was called *The Trocadero* and the other was known to them as *Spinney's*. The former had colored lights and hanging baskets of artificial ferns; through its centre ran a railing surmounted by a flower-box in which ferns appeared to thrive; there were tables on either side of this horticultural barrier with electric lights in red candle-shades casting ruddy tinted reflections on the white cloth directly beneath them. *Spinney's* was a saloon with large round walnut tables in a back-room over which coarse table linen was spread when eatables were served; there was wet sawdust on the floor and the room smelled of boiling frankfurters.

There would invariably be a discussion as to which one of these places they should go.

"How about *Spinney's* tonight? 'S Wednesday today; they'll have bean soup an' pot-roast and noodles."

No matter which Leslie advocated, Griffith felt inclined to offer opposition. If he voiced his objection, Leslie was quite ready to give way, which would anger his brother more than if he had argued about it. The dinner at either place was insipidly the same: a vegetable soup on the surface of which thin greasy globules floated, a meat stew with pale gravy, liver and bacon or tough chicken, and mealy, tasteless vegetables, limp lettuce leaves with a strong vinegary dressing, a chemically flavored ice-cream and coffee. Griffith would have preferred the clamor and the variety of a Childs' restaurant but Leslie could not get a drink there, so such places were tabooed.

After the meal there was a general wielding of toothpicks. Griffith shuddered at first, but after a while he followed the others' example. About half-past seven they would saunter home. Life,

—gay, rioting, rollicking,—buzzed around them, whirled in great eddies about their feet and swept tempestuously past. Griffith looked and longed and hungered to be part of it. He would always be in better spirits after he had eaten; he felt good-natured again, replete and satisfied; he wanted to be amused, to play, to "go some place and have some fun." But he could not interest Leslie; his brother disliked the theatre, did not care to go to any place of amusement. He only wanted to get back to his apartment where he could take off his collar, read his paper and drink whiskey. Griffith tried to save enough each week out of his ten-dollar bill to pay for a gallery seat at a show and went alone, but it was little pleasure by himself, and he could not afford such self-indulgence more than once. The other six nights in the week he would sit at home, drowsing over his paper until recovering from a final nod with an abrupt jerk, he would find himself broad awake. Then he would rouse himself with an effort, rising stiffly to his feet, stretching himself, his hands extended high above his head, fingers wide, his mouth distended in a great yawn. It would still be only quarter to nine or a few minutes after. It was ridiculous to go to bed at such an hour. Sometimes he put a roll in the mechanical piano and ran it through. He never played with his fingers any more. The Grieg and Schubert albums with Professor Horatio Guthrie's pencilled instructions in the margins lay at the bottom of his trunk tied together with grocer's string where he had put them in his freshman year at St. Cloud. He found no pleasure in books either; reading had become a task for him. He wondered a little at the change in himself; he was not the same person who had so eagerly devoured Dickens and Thackeray, Dumas and Victor Hugo during those unhappy years at Concord when their immortal stories had been his only solace.

He would think about these things as he pedalled at the piano and the jangling harmonies filled the crowded room deafeningly. The cheap music would give him no pleasure and with a sigh of weariness, he would bang down the lid of the instrument. There was nothing left but go to bed. Good God! It was always that: go to bed!—go to bed! As he undressed, tugging impatiently at his garments, he used to wonder how long he could endure it.

V

An invitation from Mr. Rumsey to come out and call upon his two daughters some evening was gladly accepted by Griffith. Six months ago he would have politely declined. He could easily guess what kind of girls the daughters of a man like Rumsey would be; he knew they would be common and hoydenish, but in his state of friendlessness, the society of anyone fresh and young appealed to him.

The following Sunday afternoon he dressed in his best clothes and walked up to a Hundred-and-Sixteenth Street to the address that Rumsey had given him. The apartment house was one of ten thousand exactly like it that shouldered one another in that district of the city. *The Myrtle* was diagonally inscribed in flowing gilt letters across the glass panel of the front door.

Griffith pressed the button above the name of "Rumsey" and pushed open the door when the catch in the lock began to click rapidly. Inside was darkness, and close air, odorous of boiling vegetables and hot grease. He felt stifled at first, and paused a moment at the bottom of the stairs gazing up through the well that rose floor by floor above him. Vaguely, uncertainly he began to mount, pausing on the landings to read the names tacked on doors or over the electric-bells. As he ascended the suffocating smell of cooking increased. Presently he found himself before a door on which appared the name he sought.

A girl opened it. Her figure was silhouetted against the light from within; he could not see her face distinctly. Beyond her upon the couch at the opposite side of the room sat another girl, with red hair, and close beside her was a youth about Griffith's age.

There was an awkward pause; everybody was embarrassed; they all stared at one another without speaking. Then the girl with the red hair rose and came forward.

"You're Mr. Adams, I'm sure." She did not smile but her voice was warm and cordial. "Father said you might be 'round. Won't you come in?" She pushed aside the other girl and held the door wider open.

"This is my sister, Clarisse, and this is Mr. Hemmingway."

Griffith shook hands politely and took off his overcoat. A wicker arm-chair was pushed out for him.

The Rumsey sisters were widely separated types. Clarisse, the elder, was rather tall and supple, pretty too, in spite of the sallow unhealthy skin which she attempted to conceal with much powdering. Her nose was broad and flat but her eyes were soft and brown. Her full lips were brilliantly red, obviously colored. She simpered a great deal, throwing languorous, flirtatious glances under lowered lids in Griffith's direction. She had a trick of smiling slowly which effectively displayed even little rows of teeth like kernels on an ear of corn. Even from where he sat he could distinguish a strong scent of musk with which evidently she had drenched herself. Her mannerisms offended Griffith; her coquettishness was crude, her artifices glaringly transparent. She wanted to flirt, but he had no desire to respond. She was several years older than her sister; Griffith judged her to be twenty-six or seven.

The other girl, whose name was Rita, was in no sense of the word pretty, yet she appeared to Griffith far the more attractive of the two. Her hair was an unrelieved brick red, her eyebrows and eyelashes a lighter shade and her face, peppered with tiny freckles, was red like a school-boy's. She had blue alert eyes and her mouth, which was large, had a ready tendency to display the same quality of even white teeth her sister possessed. Her expression was quick, responsive and engaging. It indicated a clever, shrewd mind, and besides she had charm or that elusive something that can only be described as "smartness." There was a dash about her personality, from the way she piled her red hair on the top of her head, to her slim ankle in brown silk and her foot in its bronze pump.

Hemmingway was obviously in love with Rita. He was an attractive though odd-looking youth, with a fat round face, laughing, roving eyes, and an immense mouth that stretched across his face in a great crescent moon. His hair was coal black and grew low upon his forehead; his heavy eyebrows were also black and his beard showed dark blue beneath the skin on chin and cheeks. He was extravagantly dressed, in a low-cut, fawn-colored vest, and cut-away coat. There was a noticeably large diamond solitaire in his knitted silk tie, and the tops of his shoes were of light colored cloth with fancy glass buttons.

While Griffith was repelled by his flamboyant attire, and aware of a certain commonness about him, he was soon forced to admit Hemmingway was entertaining. He had a compelling loud laugh, as infectious as it was noisy. His wit was coarse but amusing and Griffith found himself presently laughing unaffectedly at his persistent interruptions of a recital by Rita of how her dog had been lost. His remarks generally admitted a suggestive interpretation, but they seemed not to offend the Rumsey sisters. Clarisse laughed immoderately and recklessly; Rita giggled and told him to behave.

The Rumsey parlor was ridiculously small. The couch with its Turkish covering and Indian pillows occupied nearly a quarter of it. It left room for three white wicker chairs with chintz-covered cushioned seats, and a table on which stood a cheap talking machine. Photographs of actors and actresses appeared everywhere; most of them were thrust into a crack between the wall and the trim of the windows. These alternated with colored chromos of cigar-box beauties in gilded plaster frames, and enlarged photographs of scenery taken along the route of the N. Y., N. & W.'s tracks. It was gay and comfortable, in spite of its ugliness and smallness.

Mr. Rumsey was out, it appeared. He always went on Sunday afternoons to visit their Aunt Abigail, and her flock of daughters; he always took them candy. He had spoken so many times of Mr. Adams that finally his daughters had just dared him to ask him to call; they had wanted to see what he looked like. He didn't know New York very well, did he? How did he like it? Did he think he would stay? Was father awful in the office? If he wasn't nice, Mr. Adams would have to come and tell them about it at once; they'd fix him!

Griffith smiled perfunctorily; they were hopeless, impossible; he wished he had not come. Rita was the only one who interested him, and he noticed her hand was covered by Hemmingway's big one as it lay beside her, half-concealed by the fold of her dress. Her attention was all her companion's and Clarisse embarrassed him by continuing to gaze at him affectedly under half-shut lids.

Presently he rose to go, but there was a wild protest. They drowned out his excuses, crowding about him, both girls catching him by the sleeve. Rita exclaimed they had not even had tea yet and he must stay for that. Clarisse pleaded with her eyes, and Hemmingway added a good-natured invitation to "stick round awhile" and Griffith yielded. They dragged him through a couple of dark bedrooms, a tiny dining-room,—there was no hall,—out into the kitchen. Here the men sat on the wash-tubs while Rita flung things about telling her older sister what to do. Hemmingway declared he didn't want any old tea and was promised rye and ginger-ale. Both men smoked and the conversation returned to the lost dog. Clarisse extolled the animal's virtues while Rita banged the oven door, and flipped the toasting bread over with deft fingers. Hemmingway asserted there was no dog in the world like an Airedale and quite astonished Griffith by adding that his father had fifty-two perfectly bred specimens down at his "place" on Long Island. The statement implied wealth and Griffith studied him speculatively. He was clearly no college man: he spoke ungrammatically and his manners were uncouth, oftentimes inexcusable. Whatever might be his station in life, he was undeniably amusing; he had them all in uproarious laughter as they gathered about the kitchen table, drinking tea and eating the crisp, hot toast.

VI

As he walked homeward later, the dreariness of his life was borne in upon Griffith once more. It was a pity that from sheer loneliness he was driven to seek the acquaintanceship of such girls. Rita's shrewdness bordered on sharp calculation; Clarisse was just a fool. He decided he would not go to see them again; such friendships were never profitable; they did not belong to his class and nothing was to be gained by following them up. But when Rumsey asked him to come out to dinner the following Friday night he did not hesitate in accepting. It was better, he told himself in justification, than eating vegetable soup and pale beef stew, and going back to the apartment to watch Leslie read the newspaper!

As he hurried home to dress on the day of the dinner he was

ashamed of his eager anticipation. Rumsey had mentioned Hemmingway was to be present; there would be just the five of them. Griffith was certain their commonness would offend him, but he was equally sure that he would have a good time.

He could hear Clarisse's reckless scream, Rita's giggle, and Hemmingway's blatant, infectious guffaw as he paused on the landing in front of the Rumseys' door and touched the bell. They all seemed to grab at him at once when the door was opened; they pulled him in, took his hat, stripped his overcoat from him, and shook him by both hands, they *were* so glad to see him. It was spontaneous, irresistible. Griffith's heart warmed to them all, even to Clarisse, who twisted her neck like a swan and gazed soulfully at him.

He wondered afterwards what they had talked about; he could not remember a single topic. The reserve he had promised himself should be his part in their company, was swept away like a ridge of sand in the path of a rushing tide. The tiny apartment shook with noise. Hemmingway roared and shouted, while at alternate intervals one of the girls emitted a wild scream of exuberance. Griffith was carried away by their hilarity; it was a relief to throw restraint to the winds and laugh immoderately at Hemmingway's jokes.

Presently they all trooped through the two intervening bedrooms to the little dining-room, a room even smaller than the parlor. The girls, who alternately waited on the table, were obliged to squeeze themselves between the wall and Griffith's chair each time they went to the kitchen.

Mr. Rumsey presided, his lean, cadaverous face hospitably alight with a fixed smile of approval. He was evidently determined to appear amused by whatever was said or done whether understood or not. He admired his daughters; they were smart girls. Much of their idle chatter he pondered over gravely; they both reminded him of their mother, and he confided to Griffith more than once during the evening that Mrs. Rumsey had been one of the most remarkable women God ever made.

As they began to eat, the party quieted down. Throughout the meal one or the other of the girls was continually jumping up either to remove the empty plates or to attend to something on the stove. Rita was the dominant spirit. She directed her father how to carve the roast and her sister where to find things, and all the time she rattled on to Hemmingway. Griffith thought her a remarkable girl and if Hemmingway was going to marry her he was a lucky fellow. He wished he did not treat her with such a proprietary air.

Hemmingway himself continued to puzzle Griffith. His table manners were atrocious; he had a habit of opening wide his enormous mouth while it was still filled with food, displaying the great cavern inside. Griffith averted his eyes, shuddering. Once as he turned his head quickly to avoid the unpleasant sight, he caught Rita's eye. He saw she understood, but her glance betrayed nothing.

He took the opportunity, however, when Clarisse was in the kitchen and Hemmingway had gone into the parlor for his cigarettes to ask Rita about him.

"Did you ever drink Hemmingway's Halcyon Beer?" she asked, smiling significantly.

Griffith's mouth opened in a soundless exclamation, and he nodded his head slowly. He was beginning to understand.

"He's Pa Hemmingway's young hopeful. Not much education, but he's bright, . . . don't you think? . . . and lots of fun?"

She spoke as if she sought Griffith's approval. He answered her with enthusiasm. In spite of Hemmingway's crudeness, he liked him, and now that he had gathered the facts which explained him, he was ready to approve entirely. Hemmingway's Halcyon Brew was the famous domestic beer most generally imbibed in New York City. The trucks and the huge, fetlocked horses were familiar sights on the city's streets, and the name in fat gilded letters on diamond-meshed wire screens surmounted most of the saloon *façades* in Manhattan.

After the dinner was over the two couples returned to the parlor. Mr. Rumsey explained he had some freight rates to look up and limped off to his bedroom. Hemmingway and Rita occupied the couch, Clarisse and Griffith amused themselves with the talking machine. As he stood beside the older sister he was aware again of the heavy odor of musk which pervaded her. The perfume was pungent and sickeningly sweet. As she bent over the machine to lay the needle carefully upon the revolving disk, he studied her face with interest. It seemed to him a curious fact that while she was undoubtedly pretty she was not by any means as attractive as her sister whose features were all indefinite. Clarisse had pretty hair, pretty eyes and a pretty mouth; her nose was ugly and her skin bad. But these detractions would not matter, Griffith thought, if she would only act sensibly; if she behaved more like Rita. Clarisse's affectations,—her covert glances, her arch expressions, her slow-breaking smiles, the undulations of her neck and the coy positions in which she held her head,—were as crude as the powder she heaped upon her face and the overpoweringly sweet heavy perfume she used. He wished Hemmingway would not monopolize Rita; it would have been far more interesting to talk to her, than to pretend not to take notice of Clarisse's flirtatious glances.

In consequence he welcomed Hemmingway's suggestion that they should go to some music hall where they could dance. A few confused moments of struggling into coats and wraps ensued, and presently they were out on the street, waving and whistling to attract a taxi-cab's attention. It was fun scrambling into the dark interior. There was a bewildering tangle of feet and ankles and much laughing. In a few minutes the cab stopped in front of a mammoth pavilion on One-Hundred-and-Twenty-Fifth Street. Hemmingway tossed the driver a dollar bill and they trooped in.

There was a great rectangular dancing floor in the centre of the hall and rows of tables bordering it. As the party was early, one of these was secured next to the dancing floor. The girls proceeded to make themselves comfortable: they removed their wraps, rolled up their gloves into balls, folded their veils, neatly fastening the folds together with a hair-pin, and put them away in their hand-bags. From the same receptacles they produced little round mirrors and powder-pads which they rubbed unconcernedly over their faces, Clarisse patting hers briskly against her chin where there were eruptions. Their manner was completely assured.

Hemmingway suggested "wine." Clarisse clapped her hands and made a little 'O' with her red lips, but Rita shook her head. No —no, not tonight; some other time she might not object; she would not permit it tonight. Hemmingway was disgusted and brought his black brows together in a heavy frown. He turned hopefully to Griffith, begging him to split a pint with him. Griffith would have accepted, but he felt Rita had refused the wine on his account. They all agreed finally on high-balls, except Clarisse who insisted on a cocktail in spite of her sister's head-shake.

Then they got up to dance. Griffith slipped his arm about Clarisse's waist, and started off with her. He was delightfully surprised: she was an exquisite dancer. She swayed and turned and glided in perfect symmetry of motion; her long supple body clung to his; she wreathed herself about him, undulating, twisting, entwining. They were both tall and, physically, fitted one another like saucers. Griffith had never experienced such dancing; he was wrapped in an intoxicating, sensuous ecstasy. There was no exertion of any kind; they seemed to be floating, floating, floating. The sensation was deeply emotional, soul-stirring; if there was a sexual appeal, he was not aware of it; to him Clarisse was a divine dancer, marvelously lithesome, entrancingly graceful.

The dance left him with his head spinning, his pulses throbbing, and a sudden affection for the girl. As the music stopped, their eyes found one another's in a look full of mutual delight. He did not pause to consider now whether or not she was flirting with him, in the way he had thought so silly and artificial earlier in the evening. He was aware only that they had discovered one another, that they were made to dance together. Thrilled and stirred himself, he knew she was thrilled and stirred likewise. Both were conscious of a bond.

Quite naturally, as they came back to the table side by side, their hands touched, their fingers interlocking. As they sat down, drawing deep breaths, their eyes met again in a look of feeling and pleasure. Clarisse closed hers slowly, affectedly, her breast rising on a long sigh.

Griffith had the next dance with Rita. She was a good dancer, too, but considerably shorter than her sister, so that he was obliged to stoop, and occasionally their knees bumped. Again he thought her a most unusual girl, witty, clever and interesting. Hemmingway was no match for her intellectually, she would be throwing herself away in marrying him. "But I suppose she cannot resist the money!" Griffith thought, a little jealously.

He danced the rest of the evening with Clarisse. It was a wonderful experience. Both became enwrapped in a sensuous orgy of rhythm and music. They did not speak while they danced. They surrendered themselves completely to the ecstatic harmony of their gliding, oscillating bodies. As they grew tired, they became giddy, clinging to one another excitedly, their senses swimming. They swayed drunkenly in each other's arms. In the middle of one dance, Griffith suddenly felt the room whirl about him, the floor tip beneath his feet, and he would have fallen if the girl had not caught him.

Griffith's head was still reeling as he walked back to the Rumsey flat. The night was clear and cold; nobody wanted a taxi; it was only a dozen blocks; Rita preferred to walk; Clarisse was languidly complaisant. Chattering and laughing, Hemmingway and the younger sister went on ahead. Clarisse and Griffith followed silently, dreamily conscious of each other's nearness. Quite simply, when they reached the deep shadow of an election booth, encroaching half-way upon the sidewalk, they stopped, their arms went about each other and their lips met in a long clinging kiss. As he held her to him, his lips against hers, her femininity rushed over him. He was aware of the odors of her hair, the scent of the powder on her face, the strong pungent perfume of musk that enveloped her. Her supple body yielded in his arms, her hands clasped his neck. She kissed him full upon the mouth, without reserve.

Later as he walked alone in the direction of his own home, the sensation of the kiss returned to him. He straightened himself sharply, moistening his lips. Some of the carmine paste upon her mouth had been transferred to his; he could feel it there with his tongue. It reminded him of the camphor-ice his mother had rubbed upon his chapped lips as a boy.

CHAPTER IV

I

GRIFFITH was clearly aware he ought not to allow himself to become entangled with a girl like Clarisse and yet— And yet since she had melted in his arms in the shadow of the election booth, and had clung to him, loving and ardent, yielding herself to his embrace without reserve, he could not get her out of his mind. The sensation of her hot lips against his, her long supple body in his arms, her clinging, caressing fingers, haunted him. The memory of the experience came back to him overwhelmingly at intervals. He thought about it as he bent over his little desk table in the office, as he watched Leslie reading the evening paper, as he held to a strap in the crowded car in the subway, and at night when he lay in bed.

He was ashamed of the feeling she had aroused in him, yet analyzing his emotions, he was forced to admit he loved her. It was not a deep nor lasting affection he told himself. It in no wise affected his feeling for Margaret. She would always be for him, a supernatural creature, infinitely pure and good, a glorious being to worship silently, and secretly adore.

But the thought of Clarisse Rumsey pursued him. He loved her. He could not get away from that fact; and yet he was ashamed of his love. He knew it was not the girl herself, he loved; she was light-minded, shallow, affected, a simpleton. She appealed to him neither mentally nor sexually. For a long time he could not decide what it was that attracted him. He came finally to the conclusion it was her caresses he desired. He literally hungered for these. A vivid recollection of her soft, clinging lips would make him suddenly shut his eyes, his fingers twitching, his breast heaving on a quick, hissing in-take of breath. He reveled in trying to remember his sensations of that night, composing himself as he lay in bed in the dark, sending his thoughts back to the shadow of the election booth. He yearned again for the touch of her lips and fingers. His yearning became at times a paroxysm of desire.

II

A day or so after his call upon the Rumsey girls, Archie returned to the city. He telephoned Griffith at his office at once, and Griffith dined with him and his father and mother in their apartment. Later they filled a box at the theatre. Not until the play was over and the millionaire and his wife had decided to go home rather than stay for the supper Archie and Griffith urged upon them, were the boys alone. Over beer and some indigestible chafing-dish concoction, Griffith told his friend about Clarisse.

He had been planning to confide in Archie. During the evening with the Rumsey sisters, he had mentioned McCleish's name and Rita had appeared interested at once, had asked several questions about him, and made Griffith agree to bring Archie out to call some day. When he had murmured a confused good-night, still thrilling from his experience with Clarisse, she had caught him by the arm to impress her words, reminding him of his promise. Thinking about the matter later, Griffith had decided it might prove a good scheme. Rita was the kind of girl that would attract Archie. She was not the pretty type and she had brains; the four of them might have a lot of fun together.

But Archie was not enthusiastic. Griffith realized that he had expected too much of his friend's unimaginative, stolid nature. He was not interested in girls. Outside of his mother, his sisters and Margaret Sothern, woman was an unknown quantity to him. Business absorbed him. He was engrossed in the affairs of the Fourth National Bank. He knew off-hand the market prices of standard bonds.

He listened placidly to his friend's eager sketch of the congenial quartette the two sisters and themselves would make and to his forecast of the fun they might have together. He smiled good-naturedly but shook his head. He had no time to "play 'round," was far too busy. He did not think it wise to know girls like that. Rita might be all that Griffith described, but there was

THE EDUCATION OF GRIFFITH ADAMS 171

nothing profitable in such acquaintances; he would advise Griffith to let them alone.

Griffith disgustedly dropped the matter. He knew too well that Archie's obstinacy was only increased by opposition. Two days later, however, circumstances arranged the meeting in as satisfactory a way as Griffith could have desired.

He and Archie had arranged to lunch together and the latter had dropped in at his office to meet him. At the moment Griffith joined his friend in the outer barricaded waiting-room, the Rumsey girls walked in to keep a similar appointment with their father.

Griffith's heart gave a great bound as he saw Clarisse. In spite of his emotion and excitement, his first thought was: "How perfectly hopeless she is!" His next was of the fortuitous opportunity; he introduced Archie.

Clarisse came toward Griffith, fixing him with her seal's eyes, her lids and lashes slightly quivering, her mouth parted, her expression intense with repressed feeling. She laid one gloved hand lightly on the lapel of his coat, and stood so for some silent moments, still riveting him with her soulful, fixed look. Griffith swallowed in his nervous way, and fervently hoped they were not observed. He was acutely embarrassed, and shifted uneasily from one foot to the other.

"Why haven't you 'phoned?" she breathed.

He stammered something, incoherently. Over her shoulder he saw Archie's stolid face smiling down at Rita. He had intended to get away as quickly as possible, to avail himself of any excuse that occurred; but now he hesitated. A tangle of confused impulses actuated him: it would be a satisfaction to prove to old Mac he was wrong; Rita'd get in her deadly licks all right if she only had a chance; she certainly was dressed with amazing smartness; she—she looked simply great!

He met Clarisse's ardent gaze.

"Don't look at me that way," he said crossly, "you'll have everyone in the office wise, unless you're careful."

She dropped her eyes.

"You're not very kind to me," she whispered.

He tried to explain. As he spoke, the sensations in the shadow of the election booth swept over him. He thought again of holding her close to him, of feeling her clinging to him, her arms about his neck, her soft red lips against his own.

"I . . . I've been afraid to see you."

She raised her eyes to his; he felt the blood flooding his cheeks; he caught his breath. She seemed to cast a spell over him; something drew him toward her; he was impelled to take her in his arms.

"When are we going to have another dance together?" he asked. The words were spoken lightly; he was hardly conscious of them; he was thinking: "Why does she drench herself with that suffocating stuff?"

"When are you coming again to see me?"

"When do you *want* to see me?"

Neither attached any importance to the words; the interchange was only to prolong the moment.

"We had a nice time, didn't we?"

"You're a wonderful dancer."

"Oh . . . I guess anyone could dance well with you."

Griffith thought again of her soft caressing fingers, her velvety, pulsing lips. A mist came before his eyes; her figure wavered before him.

The door from the corridor opened abruptly; someone came striding in. The interruption was like a dash of cold water, bringing Griffith sharply to his senses. He cleared his throat steadying himself.

"I want to bring Archie, . . . Mr. McCleish, . . . with me the next time I come," he said. "I think you and your sister would like him. I . . . I hope you'll let me. . . ."

"Why, of course, . . . if you'll come soon."

She turned toward Archie waiting to speak; her eye caught her sister's. Rita did not stop talking but turned a little toward the other two including them with Archie in her audience.

". . . not a word of it; father says it won't come about till election anyways. Come out some evening and we'll discuss it some more. If we get tired we can listen to the Hobgoblin March."

Clarisse laughed throatily, fixing her eyes under half-lowered lids upon Griffith's friend.

"Rita!" she said reproachfully. "That's an awful record we

have for the graphophone, Mr. McCleish. It's all scratched and dented; makes the most hideous noise; if you *do* come out, make her promise she will not put it on."

Griffith wondered she could not see how transparent her affectations were: the drawled words, the drooping head, the half-closed quivering eyelids. She attempted in a ridiculous way to assume the manner of society boredom.

Rita interrupted, putting out her hand to stop the digression. "We'll try to find something to amuse you," she said pleasantly. "Now, . . . let me see, . . . Wednesday and Thursday, Clarisse and I both have engagements . . ." she paused uncertainly.

Her methods were as subtle as they were clever, Griffith thought. He caught her purpose and turned expectantly to Archie.

"Well-a,—well-a,—how about Friday?"

Griffith smiled at his confusion.

Friday was settled upon. Rita gave each of the young men a polite smile, then turned to the sleepy clerk on the other side of the counter and asked for her father. Clarisse pressed Griffith's hand softly, thrilling him, quickening his pulse. Again he felt strongly drawn to her, and held her eyes a moment with a look full of feeling and tenderness. Then Archie pulled back the heavy glass-paneled door and they passed out into the corridor.

III

On the Friday evening when he and Archie called, Clarisse gave Griffith the first evidence of the intensity of her passion. Both girls were eager to dance, and after they had sat for half-an-hour in the diminutive parlor talking generalities, Clarisse had proposed it. The experience was much the same as it had been on the previous occasion. They went to the same mammoth dance-hall and secured a table beside the smooth, polished dancing floor. Griffith's love reached its height as he stood up and held out his arms for Clarisse as the music for the first dance began. For the moment it was a blind, fierce passion. As he whirled her away, dipping, gliding, floating, he was in the grip of an emotion poignant as pain. Clarisse never again awoke in him a feeling so intense; her appeal to him began to ebb from that moment.

He was amused and delighted by Rita's easy subjugation of Archie. McCleish had not wanted to keep the engagement, had telephoned Griffith to ask him to help him get out of it. Griffith, who had been looking forward to the event, had been exasperated and angry. He had overborne Archie with a rush of violent reproaches, and his friend, surprised by the intensity of his feeling, had hastened to agree to keep the appointment.

Glancing from the dancing floor toward the spot where he and Rita sat in earnest conversation, their heads not a foot apart, Griffith knew that his placid, conservative friend was enjoying himself. Though naturally ill-at-ease and tongue-tied in the presence of women, Rita had made him forget his self-consciousness, and he was talking as unconcernedly as if alone with Griffith. Her manner toward him was far different than with Hemmingway. There was no suggestion of the coarseness that had laughed at the other's jokes. She made no effort to awaken admiration, but carefully concealed her femininity. She was brusque, matter-of-fact, straightforward and frank. He suspected her of playing up to Archie, but she did it with such perfect semblance of real interest that sometimes he wondered if he were not doing her an injustice. She and Archie danced together almost as frequently as Clarisse and himself. Griffith met him after the music for one dance was over, and pointed a finger at him laughingly. Archie was breathing rapidly, his rough Scotch face was in high color, a broad grin illuminated his staid, solemn features.

"Having a good time, Mac?" Griffith asked banteringly.

"Sure," Archie answered, his grin widening.

After the dance they went back to the Rumsey flat for something to eat. It was cold and they walked along briskly to keep warm. A delicious supper awaited them: creamed oysters on squares of toast, crackers spread with a paste of cheese, and bottled beer not too cold. They were soon in high spirits. Griffith had never seen Archie in so festive a mood. Every little while Rita would whisper in his ear and each time he would burst out laughing. Griffith had never heard him so boisterous. Frequently Rita would lay her hand upon his sleeve and check his hilarity with a "Sish—sish—sish" and a warning look toward her father's room where Rumsey lay asleep.

Griffith could not but admire her easy manipulation of his friend. Old Mac was having a delightful evening, enjoying himself thoroughly. The supper was a great success and they were sitting about the table, smoking cigarettes and interrupting one another's happy, inconsequential chatter, when Rita suddenly stood up and catching Archie by the hand pulled him to his feet beside her, asserting she had something to show him in the parlor.

When they had left the room, Griffith's and Clarisse's gaze involuntarily sought one another's. They sat returning each other's intent look for several moments without speaking. The flat which a few seconds ago had resounded with noise and laughter was now quite still. Griffith could hear the loud "tick-tock, tick-tock" of the clock in the kitchen and the small cracking of the cooling gas-oven. Clarisse gazed at him ardently, soulfully; slowly she thrust out her chin toward him the length of her lithe neck, her eyes narrowing, her breast rising on a deep breath.

She rose and came sinuously around to his side of the table, her eyes still fixed on his. Then with a supple, graceful twist of her body, she sank down upon his lap and he took her into his arms. She began passionately to kiss him, catching him by the ears, pulling his head down to hers, running her hands over his hair and neck. Rumpling his hair and thrusting her long white fingers through his black mop seemed particularly to delight her. Griffith returned her caresses with equal intensity. It was wonderful to hold her so, to fondle her and press his lips to hers as often and with as much freedom as he desired. All his life he had wanted to kiss somebody as much as he liked; he had never before had the opportunity. He revelled in the liberty she permitted.

After awhile they both became exhausted and for a long time she lay quietly in his arms. He enjoyed this almost as much as the fervent moments of passionate caressing. It was intensely companionable to have her lie so confidently and tenderly in his arms, her head nestling upon his shoulder where he could gently brush her cheek with his own. It was like a cat purring on his lap only a thousand times more pregnant of sensation. Once in Cambridge one of his rabbits had cuddled in the crook of his arm and he had not changed his position for nearly an hour.

They were in a kind of sensual dream, half dormant, half

conscious, when Rita rattled the door-knob and after an instant's pause, opened it. It was long enough for them to struggle to their feet; they were both standing when she entered. She seemed not to see their covert efforts to straighten the derangement of their clothing and smooth their hair. Griffith's blue-black mass was in fine disorder; its confusion was unmistakably tell-tale; anyone would have suspected there had been love-making. But Rita betrayed no sign.

"It's time for you to go home now," she announced. "Archie's waiting."

"Oh . . . it's Archie already, is it?"

"Well, we get along very well together," she said smiling. "I like him first-rate."

"Better than Mr. Hemmingway?" Griffith dared.

The smile left her face; her lips twisted coldly.

"Don't be foolish; Jack Hemmingway and I went to grammar school together; I've known him for years."

"Oh, . . . I was just trying to be funny," Griffith said hurriedly. "I'm awfully glad you like Mac; he's all right and you certainly know how to handle him. He needs to be brought out of his shell, to know someone like you. He's always been awfully afraid of girls, but you . . . you made him feel quite at home."

Rita made no further comment. She left the room disappearing in the direction of the parlor. From one of the intervening dark bedrooms came the even breathing of a sleeper.

Clarisse came close to Griffith, entwining her arms again about his neck, raising her lips for a long, tender, clinging kiss.

"Oh Griffith, Griffith . . . I love you so," she breathed.

"I love you, too, dearest."

He held her for several moments looking down upon her flushed upturned face. Her eyes were closed, her slightly opened mouth disclosed the even rows of her white glistening teeth, her loosened hair hung a trifle to one side. The powder was rubbed from her face, disclosing the sallowness of her skin; the strong scent of musk enveloped her; the carmine paste was wiped from her lips. In her abandonment she was appealingly pretty. The affectation was all gone now, the artifices, the covert looks, the flirtatious smiles and languorous glances. She concealed nothing, affected nothing. She loved, whole-heartedly, without reservation.

Griffith was touched. He kissed her again, gently, lovingly upon cheek and unresponsive lips, whispering tender, caressing, meaningless words in her ear. She lay limp in his arms like a wilted lily.

A few minutes later when they joined Archie and Rita in the parlor, Griffith noticed and was immensely amused by his friend's appearance. He had been somewhat concerned about the tumbled condition of his hair which he had had no opportunity to brush; Archie would be sure to observe it and draw the only possible inference. Not that he cared whether he knew of his philandering with Clarisse or not, but he thought it possible it might prejudice Archie against Rita. He was such a peculiar person, with intolerant ideas about certain matters, and an instinctive fear of women.

But Archie's own hair had been mussed! Griffith stared at him, his face breaking into an amused smile. The smoothed and patted locks screamed their evidence; the pillows on the couch had been carefully punched up and rearranged.

A fine snow was falling as they walked over to the elevated station. Griffith accompanied his friend so far because he was interested to hear what Archie had to say. It was the first experience he had ever had with a girl. His friend, however, made no comment and Griffith knew better than to betray his inquisitiveness. They strode along silently, bending their heads to shield their eyes from the flying snow. He felt sure that Archie would be obliged to say something about the evening before they reached the stairway to the Elevated. A few feet from it Griffith could restrain himself no longer.

"Did you have a good time?"
"Sure."
"What do you think of Rita?"
"Fine."

There was another silence; then Griffith ventured:
"They tell me you're some Scotch lover?"

The other did not answer. Griffith, watching him closely, could detect no change in his face; it was as if the remark had not been heard. Archie turned as he reached the steps and said in his matter-of-fact way:

"Good-night . . . see you soon."

IV

Griffith resolved his affair with Clarisse was to be short-lived. It was merely a diversion for each of them while it lasted; it was thrilling to play at being in love. It was playing with fire and he realized they both found excitement in that. No harm could come of it if they controlled themselves. The girl might be swept away completely by the tumult of her passion, but he would always be able to hold himself in check. He was ashamed of the pleasure he derived from her caresses, ashamed of the part he was playing, ashamed of the girl herself. And yet he had no thought of terminating their friendship; he was glad to be loved even by one of whom he was ashamed; he loved her for loving him. He thought about her a great deal during the day and frequently for long intervals at night. He went to see her two or three times a week; sometimes oftener.

V

One day in March after he had been in the employ of the railroad for nine months, the Assistant General Passenger Agent sent for him. Griffith's heart sank. He saw that he had grown to be like the other clerks in the department: a cowering underling living in constant terror of a glittering-eyed bully.

Chickering however had no words of censure for him. As Griffith stood before him, his heart beating, his throat dry, his hands twitching, Chickering drew his immaculate white handkerchief from his pocket, touched either nostril delicately, and then pointed to a chair on the opposite side of the wide glass-topped table in front of him.

"I'm going to take you out of Mr. Rumsey's department, Adams; I'm going to try you in Mr. Swezey's position."

Griffith swallowed in his nervous fashion. He was not sure he had understood the other correctly. Mechanically he said:

"Yes, sir."

"That's a quick step up, Adams," Chickering continued, glancing at him for the first time, fixing him sharply with his wet eyes. "I hope I'm not making a mistake."

Griffith bobbed his head, huskily repeating:

"Yes, sir."

His mind was working rapidly. Swezey was the head of the Advertising Bureau. All the literature of the entire railroad went out under his supervision. It was the most important job in the department.

"Mr. Swezey leaves on the first of April; that gives you a fortnight to learn the ropes. I am sure he will help you in every way. I intend to take over much of his work myself, and I shall expect you to carry out my ideas. Do you understand?"

Griffith nodded.

"Mr. Swezey's salary is thirty dollars a week; you will begin to receive that after the first of April and if you *earn* it, you will get more. . . . Your brother speaks well of you and I am disposed to give you a chance."

He paused, picking up an ivory letter-opener, running his thumb along its edge abstractedly. Then he swung around in his revolving chair and gazed out through the wide windows on the other side of the room, over the roofs of office buildings and spires of churches to the distant blurred outline of the Brooklyn shore.

"You are familiar with our magazine: *The Course of Empire?* It is, as you probably know, published by this department in the interests of our road; it does excellent publicity work; I hope it will soon be on a paying basis; the advertising is rapidly increasing. . . . Mr. Swezey is leaving us to become the Advertising Director of the New Metropolitan Hotel; he is already directing its advertising campaign. In the interests of *The Course of Empire*," —here Mr. Chickering turned to Griffith, winked his wet eyes and smiled,—"I have already solicited an advertisement from him. He has placed a year's contract with us for a full page advertisement at our regular rate of two hundred dollars an issue. . . . Some time ago, in the hope of increasing the advertising revenue of the magazine, our directors made it a rule that any employee of the company who brought in an advertisement for *The Course of*

Empire should receive a twenty-five per cent commission. Now I think I am entitled to that commission for this particular ad, which I personally solicited and secured, so I have drawn up a voucher here for six hundred dollars. Our auditor, Mr. Ephraim Beals, however, is a man who is scrupulously conscientious. I esteem him highly. He is a man who by his cautiousness has saved the road many thousands of dollars. Unfortunately he does not discriminate judiciously. He's inclined to be captious and bothersome and want to know the whys and wherefores of everything. Were I to draw this voucher in favor of myself and affix my own O.K. to it, he would be sure to raise objections, and . . . and make trouble. So I've drawn the voucher in *your* favor; when you receive the notification that it is ready to be paid, you will collect the amount from the Paymaster and turn it over to me." He paused. "You understand me? . . . Your brother used to be of great help to me in the Knickerbocker & Colonial; I am trying to build up like co-operation here; loyalty is the thing that counts; I hope you will help."

VI

In the course of the next fortnight, certain hitherto inexplicable things began to make themselves clear to Griffith. Leslie helped him materially in their comprehension. He came to understand that there was an inside ring among the officials of the New York, Niagara & Western Railroad who played into each other's hands. A similar ring existed among the department heads of the Knickerbocker & Colonial. Chickering when he had been G. P. A. of that railroad had been one of its originators and organizers. The object of such a ring was to further and cultivate what were known as "P. O's": perquisites of office.

It was a finely organized system of graft. Leslie told him that there was hardly a railroad in the country whose officials did not supplement their small salaries by these "perquisites of office."

"Stick close to Chickering," Leslie counselled. "Clever man; makes lots of money. He's rich now; salary's only four thousand a year; spends that a month! Owns lots of real estate. Helped me make money, too; I had quite a pile once. Did what he told me; never asked questions; kept my mouth shut. Every once an' awhile, he'd put me in way of a good thing Chick's generous all right; likes loyalty; go to hell for you if you're loyal. He cleaned up a hundred thousand in Bayshore when the cut-off went through. He and Strozinski, the Traffic Manager, and Masset, the Chief Engineer, got the directors to decide on the cut-off. Cost couple of million. They pulled down something on every contract that was let. Made nearly ten thousand myself in commissions and what they slipped me, but it went along with the rest. Anna got most of it."

He stopped abruptly, pulling at the ragged ends of his mustache. "I used to make a lot of money, once," he continued reflectively. "Chick knew how to turn the trick. When he had my job, he made twenty to twenty-five thousand a year out of it. Guess I don't much care; I let the boys make what they can; never ask for a rake-off. You stick along by Chick; he'll be a good friend to you if you do just exactly what he tells you and keep your mouth shut."

Griffith was fascinated by this railroad gossip; his interest in the affairs of the N. Y., N. & W. was immediately awakened.

As soon as it was known he was to succeed Swezey, a marked change took place in the attitude of Griffith's associates. Rumsey asked him to lunch; Sparks, the mailing clerk, offered him a cigar and cheerfully shouted "Good-morning" when he met him each day; Marlin blushingly congratulated him, and Swezey, himself, began to Christian-name him.

The retiring head of the Advertising Bureau was a young man, not over twenty-seven or eight, yet slightly bald, with thin curling hair which waved loosely about his head. He took himself with great seriousness, and was at pains to impress Griffith with his importance.

The new work was bewildering at first. Griffith tried desperately hard to understand the meaning of the things he was told, and struggled to fix his mind on Swezey's directions. With no training in concentration, he frequently found himself listening to the other's words and wondering what they meant. Swezey would see he did not understand, and become irritated. He resorted to the expedient of dictating long memorandums, in which he explained the workings of the Bureau. These Griffith was supposed to read over after Swezey's departure.

The Advertising Bureau, of which he was to become the head, consisted of five clerks: an old man named Sickles; a copy-writer, a Jew, named Rosen; two stenographers and a young woman, the only female in the entire Passenger Department, who had a foreign-sounding name which nobody ever remembered. She was referred to and addressed invariably as "Polly."

The function of the Bureau was twofold: it wrote and placed all the advertising of the New York, Niagara & Western Railroad in newspapers, magazines, street-cars, bill-boards and so forth, paying for the same in transportation over its own lines and other roads with which it was affiliated in the great Federal System,—and it issued all the advertising literature which the Road dispersed in the shape of booklets, leaflets, and circulars. The quantity of both these forms of advertising was enormous. Thousands of newspapers all over the country ran advertisements of the N. Y., N. & W. A record had to be kept of their rates, the amount of space that had been given to the railroad, and how much transportation had been already used or was still coming to them in payment of this service. In order to get around the Interstate Commerce Law which prohibits the issuance of transportation between states in payment of advertising, tickets were purchased outright and the amount refunded on application to the Chief Clerk. This had been one of the principal duties of Rumsey's department; hundreds of requests for refunds were received every month. All of these had to be carefully kept track of in the Advertising Bureau.

The most important part of Griffith's new work, however, was getting out the literature advertising the road. Not only were illustrated pamphlets extolling the advantages of travel via N. Y., N. & W. written, printed and distributed by this bureau, but also brochures, circulars and flyers, giving descriptions of excursions, train equipment, summer and tourist travel, announcements of changes in rates and train service, and the opening and development of new land sections. Orders for the paper, printing, binding and mailing of all this literature were placed by this same subdivision of the Passenger Department.

VII

Out of the confusion, Griffith could not help but notice in most of the newspaper advertising, the street car ads, the back covers of the booklets, and in the bottom space on the circulars, a constant reference to the Old Comfort Inn at Syosset Beach. Pictures of the great, rambling structure appeared in all this literature, spread-eagling along a crescent of sandy shore, the waves breaking neatly in a series of symmetrical C's before it, diminutive figures promenading along the board-walk, prancing horses drawing carriages in which parasoled ladies elegantly reclined, trolley-cars and automobiles rolling in the foreground. He commented upon it to Swezey and his new friend eyed him quizzically a moment, then confided in a lowered voice:

"You wanter get wise, Griffith son; that's the old man's hotel. I don't know how much he owns of it outright; the big guns are all in on it; Prentiss, the G. P. A., McGukin, the Passenger Traffic Manager, and Pettengill, the General Freight Agent all have an interest. I'm not sure whether the V. P.'s in with 'em or not."

"Who's the V. P.?" Griffith asked.

"The Vice-President: Roscoe Henry Grismer," Swezey continued impressively. "He's the big Mogul of this outfit; he's only been here 'bout six or eight months; came over from the Hudson & Huron. The President of the road, Caleb Trench, has been sick for a long time; he's nothing but a figure-head; Grismer's the guy; they're all leery of him.

"Now, I don't mind making you hep to a few things you really orter know," he went on, bending closer. "There's a ring of five or six of the high-ups who work hand-in-glove with one another. You want to get in with 'em if you wanter hold your job. Chickering's the ring-master; he's only a minor official but he's got the brains of the bunch; he's sharp as a whip, and he's a damned good friend. He's worked up what they call their perquisites of office until they've become damned profitable for all concerned; you'd think the directors and the stockholders would get wise to something being wrong but he's too slick for 'em. Why five years ago the N. Y., N. & W. declared a fat dividend, something like seven or eight per cent; the stock was selling 'round 168; it had never been below par in I don't know how many years; now it's down to 88 and 87. On the street they say it's been watered but that ain't the trouble. The directors are a kind of sleepy bunch, I guess; they can't tell what's the matter; they know there ain't any more profits, the road ain't earning what it did. Chick and his crowd are milking the cow instead of giving them a chance. You can just make a guess how much they pull down every year out of the Old Comfort Inn! With all the advertising they give it, they pack it to the roof every winter and it even pays 'em to run it in the summer. It's an old barn, regular fire-trap."

Not all this information came at once. It was confided to Griffith a little at a time. He proved an eager listener and Swezey relished telling him what he knew as well as what he suspected went on among the big officials of the railroad. They hadn't been able to pull the wool over *his* eyes, you bet! He had seen what was going on, all right! He had the goods on 'em! He was only in deadly fear that Griffith might repeat to Chickering what he confided in him.

"You want to keep all this under your hat, Griffith son," he would interrupt himself to say again and again. "I'm giving you the low-down on this business; if you let on to Chick I told you this . . ."

"What do you think I am!" Griffith would reply indignantly.

"Well, I'm only tellin' you. . . . Chick's always treated me pretty white and I've got a corking job out of it. I'm tellin' you this dope for your own good!"

Griffith realized the information Swezey imparted was invaluable, and he pledged himself again and again, to repeat nothing of what he was told. He was intensely gratified at the idea of knowing Chickering's secret, and became impatient to serve him, to execute his commissions. He began now to understand what both his brother and his chief had in mind when he had been taken into the employ of the railroad: he was to serve Chickering in much the same capacity as Leslie had served him in the organization of the Knickerbocker & Colonial. Griffith felt himself singularly honored; he was fired by enthusiasm to show his willingness and loyalty.

The New York, Niagara & Western Railroad was divided into several great departments; some of these were the Engineering, the Operating, the Legal, the Commissary, the Auditing, the Freight and Passenger Departments. At the head of the Passenger Department was the Passenger Traffic Manager, Mr. McGukin, who was the senior official to Mr. V. A. Prentiss, the General Passenger Agent. Under the G. P. A. came the two Assistant General Passenger Agents: Mr. Enos Chickering and Mr. Theodore Sales. Sales, Swezey told Griffith, was merely a figure-head. Once he had been of importance in the company but had been side-tracked into his present position to get him out of the way. He was allowed to regulate traffic rates, issue employee passes and one-half rate permits. He was intimate with Ephraim Beals, the Auditor.

Chickering had under his personal supervision all the vital functions of the Passenger Department. These he distributed among seven bureaus of which by far the most important was the Advertising Bureau. The heads of the other bureaus were all old men, in type similar to Rumsey and to Sparks who had a kinky white beard and was partially deaf. Some of them had been in the service of the Passenger Department of the road for twenty years. Most of them had become indifferent to the changes which took place about them. All of them were actuated by one ever present fear: the dread that they might lose their jobs. They cringed before Chickering, they lived in terror he might discharge them.

Griffith could not refrain from swaggering a little before them as he walked up and down the long, broad aisle between the rows of desks.

VIII

His elevation was a tremendous source of satisfaction to him. He revelled in the rôle of being known as "the head of the Advertising Bureau of the N. Y., N. & W." He could not forbear to mention his title and to speak of his promotion in conversation with acquaintances. He knew they were impressed; he glowed in their surprise and congratulations.

The work itself was exciting. Salesmen from paper houses came to see him, envelope manufacturers eagerly solicited his patronage, editors and advertising managers of country newspapers dropped in to shake his hand and to tell him confidentially they could increase the amount of the railroad's advertising space during the coming summer if he wanted it. He was invited out to lunch every day. These mid-day repasts were elaborate affairs, including several courses and took place at the most expensive restaurants. Boxes of cigars were left upon his desk and he was frequently invited to split a "little bottle of wine" with his host. Often he did not get back to his office until nearly three o'clock.

At first he was haunted by the fear that he would not prove equal to the requirements of his new work. At no time had he any idea of what his own clerks were doing, or what was taking place about him. During the fortnight before Swezey left he sat next to him at his desk, listened to what he said, watched what he did, and made vague, unrelated notes of what he told him to remember. The last day of the month, Griffith was in a panic. He realized he had understood practically nothing of what he had either heard or witnessed, yet the following day he would be left alone to work out his own salvation, in imminent danger of incurring Chickering's terrible wrath. Swezey promised to help him over the telephone if anything he could not understand presented itself unexpectedly.

"If you get into difficulties ask Polly, Griffith son," he advised. "Polly's a wonder; been here in this bureau before I came, . . . five or six years. She's on to all the ropes; knows everything. You ask her if you want to find out anything; there ain't anything you c'n ask her, she can't answer."

Griffith found this to be literally so. Polly ran the Advertising Bureau herself. Griffith soon discovered that she had much more to do directly with its operation than Swezey had had. All the details were at her fingers' tips and she decided many an important matter which Chickering himself would not have known how to settle.

She was a pretty, round-armed young girl of twenty-five or six, fair skinned and smooth cheeked, with fine-spun yellow hair which she wore in twisted braids at the back of her head. Her eyes which she had a trick of keeping lowered, were dull and a deep blue; her eyebrows matched her hair and a fine yellow down covered her cheeks, her upper lip and chin. Her expression was always serious, preoccupied; in speech she indulged only in what pertained strictly to business. In an office full of men her manner was defensive. She went about her own affairs, quietly and impersonally, asking no favors, permitting no liberties, never gossiping or joking with her associates, attending only to the work of the Advertising Bureau. She wore immaculate white starched shirt-waists with high collars over which the smooth flesh of her round throat formed a slight double chin when she bent her head. Black alpaca cuff protectors clung to her wrists and forearms by elastics, and an apron of the same material was always tied about her trim waist. She gave the impression of excessive neatness and prim efficiency. Griffith soon came to regard her as his guardian angel. She was the font of all wisdom, an encyclopedia of information, a dynamo of energy, a whirlwind of executive ability, a nerveless, emotionless, tireless human machine. She never spoke unnecessarily, the expression on her face never changed, and she seldom raised her dull blue eyes unless she was addressed or needed to ask a question. Whatever information was wanted, no matter of what nature or how old, she had it ready on the tip of her tongue. She knew everything that had ever happened since the organization of the Advertising Bureau, when she had become a part of it as a stenographer. She had been retained by Chickering when the other girls had been dismissed because she was indispensable on account of the knowledge she had acquired. She was indifferent to Swezey's going as to Griffith's coming.

Griffith soon found he was merely the nominal head of the Advertising Bureau; Polly was its real director. She managed everything and everybody. She dictated nine-tenths of the letters that went out and suggested to him how to answer the remainder. Frequently when a caller was sitting beside him at his desk urging a proposition upon him, and Griffith, won by the other's eloquence, was about to accept, Polly would unobtrusively interrupt, and under cover of some correspondence she would pretend to show him, would warn and direct him. At the bottom of the letter he would see her pencilled note:

"He's asking far too much; 55 cts. per M. is all we ever pay for baronial envelopes."

"Ask for super stock; he's talking about machine finished."

"His newspaper's black-listed. Mr. C. won't do business with him."

"Tell him you'll think it over."

"Tell him you'll write him."

"Better consult Mr. C. first."

Griffith did not dare do otherwise than follow these directions blindly. Sometimes it irritated him not to be able to use his own judgment, particularly when he was won by his caller's personality and felt he wanted to oblige him. But back of Polly was the wrath of the podgy little man with the side-chops and the glistening wet eyes. He discovered her to be invariably in the right and soon came to feel warmly grateful to her for the numerous occasions when she saved him from a blunder, or pulled him out of a mess.

IX

Chickering left him to himself for nearly three weeks. Griffith studiously avoided him. Matters on which his chief's advice or decision was needed he referred to him in the form of memorandums which came back blue-pencilled "Yes" or "No" with the initials, which had grown so significant to him, "E. C."

One day toward the end of the month, the buzzer above his desk vibrated with a brisk peremptory whirr. It shocked him as if the electric current had leaped to his own body. He had to nerve himself to answer it.

The Assistant General Passenger Agent wore an amused smile as he entered his office.

"Well, how do you like your new job?"

Griffith, who had feared criticism, drew a quick breath; he could not find his voice for a moment.

"You seem to be catching on first-rate," Chickering continued. "I met your brother the other day and he told me you were behaving yourself and seemed to show the right spirit; I told him you hadn't been bothering me very much."

Griffith caught the flash of the wet eyes opposite him and smiled nervously. Chickering's praise made him more uncomfortable than his censure would have done.

They discussed several matters which Griffith had raised in his memorandums. As soon as they began to talk business, he felt more at his ease. Chickering was in his most genial mood.

"In regard to all paper orders in future, Adams," he said, "you will be so good as to place these with Blashfield and Pope. I have had a talk with Mr. Pope and I am sure we can do better by giving all our paper orders to one concern. It is more expeditious and more profitable. I have told them we would make an arrangement for a year. Mr. Blinkerhoff is their manager. You will consult him in future; tell him what we want and he will send the stock over to the *Enterprise Press* which from now on will do *all* our printing. They, as you know, print our magazine, *The Course of Empire*. I think it is much wiser to consolidate our paper buying with one firm and our printing with another. We shall be able to hold one particular concern responsible for each. It is ridiculous to shop around as we have done in the past. Also, as regards our engraving, the *Enterprise Press* has an excellent Art Department; in future they will attend to all our drawings and lettering and designing our covers, and they will engrave the cuts and plates in their own engraving plant. Mr. Atterbury is the man in charge of this work; get acquainted with him and co-operate with him in every way you can. He will know better than we will what kind of paper is needed for our booklets and circulars. In future, therefore, when a job for advertising literature comes along, see him at once in regard to it, find out what kind of paper he recommends, size, weight, color and amount, and then make out your order on Blashfield and Pope and send it along to them. Understand me: I have the highest confidence in Mr. Atterbury. I want you to do exactly as he says; don't trouble me with his suggestions; take 'em just as he gives 'em to you and put the paper order through in the regular way."

"Very well, sir," Griffith said, making a mental note of the names he heard for the first time.

"Good. . . . There is one thing more," Chickering was tapping the table approvingly with two extended fingers, "you are getting, . . . let me see, . . . thirty dollars a week. I shall expect a lot of hard work from you, . . . overtime and . . . er . . . the sacrifice of your own plans to attend to matters that may not wait; you will find the requirements of your new position increasingly exacting. It has always been one of my hobbies that a laborer is worthy of his hire and that the hire should be worthy of the laborer. I want you to feel satisfied with your work and your remuneration. Precedent makes it impossible for me to increase your salary; the clerk in charge of the Advertising Bureau in this department has always been on the payroll for thirty dollars a week, and a request for an increase would meet with serious objection, would create a prejudice against you. It has occurred to me that inasmuch as the road will make a considerable saving in our expenditures for paper by concentrating the orders with one concern in the way I have suggested, that perhaps another way could be found to reimburse you. I spoke to Mr. Pope about the matter and he saw the point at once. At his own suggestion he has offered to mail you a check to your home for fifty dollars on the first day of every month. I took the liberty of accepting for you. . . . I do not wish to excite jealousy among those who have been in my department for a long time nor to bring down upon my head a rush of requests for increases in salary, so I trust you will keep this matter *strictly* to yourself; you must confide in no one."

He paused, adjusting his immaculate starched cuffs about his wrists, pulling them down below his coat sleeves with delicate little jerks of thumb and fore-finger.

"And we will dispense with the 'thanks'; you serve *me* and I'll serve you," he added.

Griffith murmured some confused words; he was embarrassed and overwhelmed with a sense of gratitude. He wanted Chickering to know how deeply he was affected. He would have liked to take his hand and wring it, telling him he was ready to do whatever he asked him, no matter how arduous or unpleasant. God! a man who was as white as that, he was ready to go through hell to serve! A great affection for his chief filled his heart as he went back to his desk. How was it he had ever hated and been afraid of him?

CHAPTER V

I

DURING the days which followed, while spring crept upon the city unawares and all the little budding leaves suddenly spread a green mist among the trees, Griffith was in high feather. It was a great satisfaction to him to realize he was earning more money than Archie. He could not refrain from telling his friend about his raise and the important position to which he had been promoted. He expatiated on what a "prince" Chickering was.

He bought some new clothes and gave a dinner party at a down-town Italian restaurant to which he invited Clarisse, Rita and Archie. They had a gay time and all became a little hilarious from the effect of the hot spicy food and the claret. It was the first warm night of spring and after they had drunk little glasses of perfumed *liqueur* and Clarisse had daringly attempted to puff on a cigarette, they sauntered out into the street with the half-formed intention of going to some place where they could dance. But the presence of two hansom cabs at the curb altered their plan; a drive through Central Park would be delightful; laughing excitedly they climbed in.

In the seclusion of the cab, Clarisse and Griffith kissed each other rapturously. Their lips continued to find one another's until they became exhausted from their caresses. Afterwards the girl was content to lie quietly in the circle of his arm, her head upon his breast. The heavy scent of musk pervaded the cab, and Griffith could feel the carmine lip-red she used upon his own mouth. He lay back luxuriously content, resting his head upon the hard upholstery of the seat.

"When are we going to get married, Griffith?" the girl whispered.
"Pretty soon," he murmured.
"How soon?" she persisted.
"Soon as I can manage it."

"Do you love me?" she demanded pressing her head against him.

He bent down to kiss her tumbled hair.

"You know I do."

"Do you love me with all your heart?"

"Sure I do."

"Oh Griffith, I *worship you;* I adore you! My dearest, my darling boy! I think I would die if anything took you from me! . . . Griffith, do you hear me? I think I should *die!* I want you to love me like I love you; if you don't I'll kill you; sometimes I think you don't care at all! Last week I only saw you once; you didn't even 'phone! Sweetheart, you *do* love me, don't you? Oh . . . oh . . . *I love you so!* I don't know what I should do if you didn't care. I just can't wait till we are married. When do you think it will be? How soon? Next month?" She pulled herself away, twisting in the seat until she half-faced him. "Griffith," she demanded, "let's get married right away?"

For the first moment he was aware of her words. He looked at her alarmed.

"Oh God, I couldn't do that!"

"Why not?"

"Well, . . . because I *couldn't.*"

"But why *not?* Father says you're getting as much as he is down at the office. *We* have enough."

"I . . . I don't want to get married right away."

He tugged impatiently at his arm about her.

"I want to smoke."

There was an interval during which neither spoke; Griffith did not look at her; he occupied himself with his cigarettes and matches.

"Griffith . . . do you love me?" The words were slow and impassioned.

"Why o' course."

"Do you want me. . . . Aren't we going to get married?"

"Sure."

She reached for his free hand and took it softly between her palms.

"You mean that, Griffith?" she asked tenderly.

"Yes . . . I guess so."
"*Guess so!*"
"Well, I mean . . . yes."

She said nothing, but continued to look at him while he puffed at his cigarette and flicked the ashes from his knees. The cab rolled along the hard macadamized road-bed under the budding branches of the trees; the air was warm, delicately tinted with faint odors of new life. Streaming rays from the head-lights of motor cars swept around curves and flashed past. The horse's hoofs maintained an even hollow cadence, the vehicle teetering behind him. Griffith was acutely uncomfortable, content to look anywhere except at the girl beside him. Presently she put both her arms about his neck and sank down upon him, pressing her lips to his. When she drew away, she said slowly:

"That's a promise, remember. You're mine. I couldn't go on living if I thought you and I weren't going to get married. I'm going to tell Rita and father we're engaged."

II

A day or so afterwards the full significance of the entanglement in which he had involved himself dawned upon Griffith. It perplexed and annoyed him. He could not see how it had come about. The idea of marrying Clarisse had never entered his head. She was an affected, shallow, empty-headed creature. He told himself he would not want to marry her if she were the only woman in the world; she was less than nothing to him. He had enjoyed the caresses, but assumed they had been given in the same spirit in which they had been accepted. She showed what a fool she was by taking it all seriously. How in God's name had he allowed himself to be inveigled into promising to marry her! He tried to remember how the subject had come up. He was certain he had never mentioned marriage to her. How had it all happened? How had she got him to make such a damned fool promise?

Never once did he consider keeping it. He felt under no obligation to do so. Youth and freedom were the most precious things in his life and the idea of relinquishing these for a foolish, simpering creature like Clarisse Rumsey who had lost entirely whatever appeal she had once had for him, was too preposterous ever to occur to him. He foresaw there would be a row. He would have to tell her some day, but he hoped she would get over her foolish idea. She had once thought herself in love with Hemmingway, and she had got over that; perhaps she would get over this. At any rate, he decided for the time being to temporize; he would show her there was "nothing doing"; she would have to be brought to the realization he did not care, and the thing would die naturally.

III

Margaret Sothern's clear, cultivated voice over the telephone was for him like the ringing note of an anchored bell to a ship lost in a fog. The sound thrilled him, brought home to him how dear and sweet and altogether lovely she was. When had she returned? Had she had a good time? When could he come to see her? He was all impatience to be with her again.

As he hung up the receiver, he thought of Clarisse. He frowned, setting his teeth. Good God! what an ass he had been to get himself mixed up with a girl like that! It had not been right to Margaret. What would she think of him if she knew he had been flirting with a creature like Clarisse Rumsey, with her rank perfumes, her lip-red and her common ways, her sickening artifices?

There was some comfort in the thought that Archie had behaved no better than himself. He had been just as "rotten." He did not talk about it, but Griffith knew he had been carrying on with Rita in the same way he had with her sister. He had seen them lunching together in a restaurant down near Archie's office. Neither had spoken about it afterwards. It amused Griffith to think old Mac supposed he was "putting something over on him." He decided to say nothing about it. Some day he'd spring the subject on him and then he'd see what the canny old Scotchman would have to say!

As far as his own relationship with Clarisse was concerned he determined to bring it to an immediate termination. He would not care how big a rumpus she raised. She could yell and cry and call him what she liked; he had had enough, and she might as well understand it right away as later. He was *through*—that was all there was about it, he was *through*. He asked Polly at the office to tell any woman who called him up that he was out, and he gave similar instructions to the colored boy who operated the switch-board at the apartment house. The sooner she realized he was done with her, the better.

Meeting Margaret again affected him as her voice had done, only a thousand times more poignantly. She was like a clear cold rush of pure air into a hot, stale atmosphere. He drank in the sight of her face as he might have inhaled the fresh air. Never had she seemed so sweet and lovely. As he held the slim white fingers of both her hands in his, there swept over him the sudden feeling, as if for the first time, that nothing mattered in the world, so far as he was concerned, except this one gracious girl. She was the embodiment of all that was admirable and beautiful; she had more intelligence than anyone he knew; she was perfect, charming, unaffected, simple and devoted.

"It's nice to have you care so much," she said, touched by the emotion he made no attempt to hide. "I'm glad you missed me."

"Oh Margaret, . . . I . . ." He stopped, confused, struggling for words.

"It was lovely down there," she went on without waiting for him. "Augusta's a fascinating old place; the people are the kindest and the simplest . . . ! Father went perfectly wild over the golf course; it's right in the trees. I met some old friends and we became ever so fond of the army people at the Arsenal . . ."

"Margaret, . . . I . . ."

She held up her hand.

"Let's go upstairs to the library. Father's expecting some men in to talk business. I hear they've given you a splendid raise at the office and you have a fine position now! You never wrote me a word! I want to hear all about it."

She led the way up the sharply curving broad stairway to the library.

Many months had elapsed since Griffith had been alone with her. The last time he had spent the evening in one of the great leather chairs before the library fire had been in the early part of December. They had been full of David's approaching visit for the holidays then, and had talked of what they would do when he came. It seemed a long time ago.

As they settled themselves, the girl asked eager questions about his new work. Since he had been put in charge of the Advertising Bureau he had often thought how much he would enjoy telling her about it. He hoped she would be impressed. Now the moment had come, there was no satisfaction in it. He felt that she would not understand his relationship to Chickering, and he dared not take her into his confidence. He had enlarged with delight to Archie upon the importance of his new position but he could give Margaret only a bare outline of it. He was uncomfortable and unhappy. Thoughts of Clarisse came troublesomely to him. He dismissed them impatiently, and tried to listen to Margaret's account of her Augusta visit, but it was difficult to follow her. He kept thinking:

"How wonderful she is! What a wonderful girl!"

She seemed more beautiful to him than he had ever seen her. As she spoke she gazed into the fire, her head a trifle bent, the finger-tips of her hand resting lightly against her cheek. The firelight transfigured her face; shadows crossed it delicately, caressingly; the warm radiance lit her soft brown hair turning it to a burnished ruddy glory.

As he looked at her he thought how unworthy he was; remorse suddenly overtook him; his love rose strong in his heart, tumultuous, compelling. He wanted to pour out to her a complete confession, to implore her forgiveness, cleanse his heart and mind. The words struggled to his lips but he dared not say them. Instead, the long delayed explosion of his love burst from him. He fell to his knees, blurting it all out, clinging desperately to her hand, while he uttered broken phrases, repeating them helplessly over and over.

It was out before he realized it! The avowal, he had so often rehearsed, the words he knew she had again and again evaded or forestalled, were said at last. It was irrevocably done now. Fear of what might follow overwhelmed him. She might turn against him! She might tell him she would never see him again! No . . . no, Margaret listen! Margaret, . . . wait until he finished! Hear him out! . . . Great God! This was not the way he had so often imagined he would confess his love!

There was a silence while he struggled to control himself. After a few minutes he had himself in hand, but he was afraid to look at her. He could only quail at the thought of what must be passing in her mind. He sank upon the floor, his hands covering his face. Presently he began to speak again.

"You've known I cared. I've loved you from the very first day I met you. I knew I loved you then and I've gone on loving you ever since. I thought I'd never tell you; I thought I'd just go on loving you for the rest of my life, but tonight, . . . I don't know how it happened, . . . it was out of my mouth before I realized what I was saying . . ."

He paused a moment, searching for words.

"I know you don't care for me that way. I've told myself that a thousand times, but I can't stop hoping. Hope keeps on coming back and back and back. . . . I'd work hard, Margaret; I'd . . . I'd do anything you'd tell me if . . . if there was a chance. I wouldn't mind how hard it was; there's nothing I wouldn't do for you. It's almost three years since I met you and I've been loving you every minute of all that time. I'll love you for the rest of my life, Margaret, . . . and . . . and that ought to count something with you."

He felt her fingers gently on his hair. Instantly a mad hope rose within him, but she held up her hand.

"No, Griffith," she said. There was a look of pity in her eyes. She shook her head slowly, smiling kindly. "I'm fond of you; you *know* that. I'm sorry it means so much to you. I've known you cared, of course; you don't dissemble your feelings. I'm afraid others have noticed it, too, and I have felt sorry for you, and . . . and sometimes a little embarrassed on my own account. But I have always thought it was very fine of you not to speak of it. It showed me you understood and were ready to save me . . ."

"Oh, Margaret. . . . I'm such an utter fool!"

"Well, . . . you mustn't take it so," she continued, smiling gently. "I want you to be sensible, Griffith. You are hardly more than a boy, although you're twenty-four; you still think as a boy and you act as a boy. That is one of the reasons I'm so fond of you. I love you first because you are one of David's closest friends, . . . and second because you seem so hapless and helpless. I cannot feel anything but sorry for you. My heart went out to you the day your classmates marched up for their diplomas and you were not with them; I felt dreadfully sorry for you again when you were left alone in the world. I have wanted to make up to you as far as I could for these and other things, and so I have continued to ask you to come here, although I saw you cared too much. I thought perhaps you might consider my friendship some kind of compensation. I hoped all along you would understand, and often I have said to mother I was sure you *did* understand."

"But Margaret, Margaret, you know I understood all right. I never said a word to you, did I? I was certain in my heart you didn't care . . . but I couldn't help hoping. I don't know what possessed me tonight. Can't it be as if I hadn't said it?"

She shook her head.

"Those things are never unsaid, Griffith. If you really love me the way you say, is it right for me to let you go on coming to see me? . . . Griffith, my heart aches for you; you're so impulsive, so reckless, so untrained! It's hard to think of terminating our friendship."

"Ah . . . Margaret . . ."

"Well, if I thought I meant to you as much as you think I do, there would be only one course open to me. I . . . I cannot believe this is such a mad passion with you as you think." She held up her hand, silencing his protest. "If you wish to continue a friend of mine, you must not attempt to convince me that your love is undying. I should have to stop seeing you and I should miss your companionship. . . . I have sometimes thought I had a good influence over you. I have always encouraged your confidences. I've flattered myself by hoping that when you turn out to be the big man, and made the big success I believe is your future, I'll have the satisfaction of thinking I had something to do with it. Perhaps that is one of the reasons why I am so sincerely fond of you. It will never be the way you want, but I shall always love you as if you were a younger brother."

"I thought it would come to that," Griffith sniffed. "I knew you'd offer to be a sister to me."

Margaret's smile disappeared.

"You are . . . you are . . . *impossible* sometimes, Griffith," she said with feeling. "That is not the part of you I love; that is the selfish, egotistical, hateful you no one could ever like."

Again he burst into self-reproaches, earnestly repentant. He realized he was acting in a ridiculous way, insincere and absurdly dramatic. Why hadn't he had the sense to hold his tongue? In his mind there rose a vision of Archie, the essence of dignity and straightforwardness, asking Margaret to be his wife. He could offer position, power, security and wealth. He was a bridegroom among thousands, a "catch," a man any woman would be proud to marry.

"It isn't fair. . . . it isn't *right*," he exclaimed, passionately, "for him to have everything!"

The girl turned toward him inquiringly, interested.

"Whom do you mean? Who has everything?"

"Oh I know . . . I know," Griffith continued recklessly. "It's Archie, all right, . . . I know how it's been; it's always been Archie!"

"I don't understand . . ."

"Ah, . . . yes you do. You've always preferred him to me. . . . Why shouldn't you?"

"*Griffith!*" The girl gave a helpless laugh. "You . . . you . . . I don't know what to say to you! Archie McCleish? Why, its *ridiculous*. Even if I loved you deeply and truly, the way you wish, I should be afraid to trust myself to you! You don't know how to treat a woman. At the very moment when she is inclined to like you, you offend her in some way by some stupid thing you say! I love Archie McCleish; of course I love him. He's David's friend and he's mine. He's loyal and true; he's honest, chivalrous and considerate. I have every reason to be fond of him. I have no dearer friend in the world. But there is only one man whom I love with all my heart, and that is my brother, David. He has always been first with me; there is no man living that approaches him. It is impossible for me to conceive of caring for anyone as much as I do for my brother."

Griffith looked at her, amazed and abashed. Margaret, always so airy and gentle and kind, was transformed. She sat bolt upright in her chair, her slim white hands shut into fists, her breast rising, her eyes alight.

He was touched by the strong feeling she betrayed. Stirred and impressed, a tightening sensation in his throat, he rose to his feet and stood before the fire, his forearm along the edge of the mantel, his forehead resting against it, looking down into the red embers over which still wavered a little torch of flame.

He said to himself this was the end of his dreaming. There was small comfort in knowing she did not care for Archie. She had shown she would never learn to love himself. That was the unpalatable fact. What had all his constancy mattered? She gave him no credit, she was indifferent to his faithfulness, his devotion. Bitterness entered his soul. What was there left for him? What incentive remained? He thought of Leslie with his pale, expressionless face, his ragged mustache, his baggy trousers. That was what he was coming to! That kind of bloodless death in life! His work had no hold upon him. There was no honest endeavor in it. And Clarisse? He shuddered. The thought of going back to her clinging embraces and lingering kisses was revolting, disgusting. A groan of misery escaped him.

"Oh . . . oh . . . oh . . . oh!"

The girl rose and stood beside him, her arm across his bowed shoulders.

"Ah Griffith, you mustn't be so foolish!" she exclaimed. "It hurts me to see others suffer because of anything I've done; it makes me dreadfully unhappy. Griffith, . . . if you love me, don't distress me this way. I would . . . I would love you if I could, dear. I really love you as if you were my own brother and I am wretched at the thought I have made you unhappy. Don't . . . don't punish me for what I cannot help. We will try to go on being friends, . . . dear, warm, devoted friends, all the closer and dearer because we understand one another now."

"Oh Margaret . . . Margaret."

"And we'll keep on going to the opera and the concerts just as we've always done. . . . But Griffith, we must make a bargain: there must be no more of this kind of talk. I will let you come to see me just the same as always, if you will not exhibit your feelings before other people or mention them to me again. And you must try to think differently of me. Dear boy, there isn't the slightest chance in the world of my learning to love you. I would have come to care for you a long, long time ago if there had been. Can't you understand? I know you *too well.* The man I shall love must be a mystery to me. I know you, . . . your heart and mind as well as I know . . . well, I cannot think of anyone I know so well. And I love you for what I see in you, but it can never be a feeling such as you desire. Put that possibility out of your hopes. It can never, never be, dear. I should really like to love you that way, if I could, you are such a blundering boy!"

IV

A certain resignation came to Griffith after this talk with Margaret. He was glad she knew his secret,—and she had said many wonderful things to him. He liked to think about them, and repeat them to himself. She cared for him,—if not in the way he wanted, yet in a fashion which was somehow dearer and sweeter. She had told him she loved him,—and there were so few who did. He cherished the thought of her words, smiling happily to himself. He determined he would never speak to her again about his own feelings nor betray them. She knew, now; there was a certain satisfaction and comfort in that.

If he considered few people cared about him, he came rapidly to the conclusion that Clarisse Rumsey was one who cared exceedingly. He was irritated and disgusted. His interest in her had been as completely extinguished as a candle-flame is snuffed. Before his confession to Margaret he had decided he was through with her; after it, he neither wanted to see her nor to think of her again. She was obnoxious to him; thoughts of her sickened him.

But Clarisse was not a creature to be shaken off lightly. Under her seemingly shallow nature, there was passion like white heat. She had a tenacity of purpose not to be thwarted merely by an open display of indifference. She paid no attention to Polly's toneless statements that Mr. Adams was out, to the negro attendant's similar assertions when she telephoned to the apartment house, nor to Griffith's failure to answer her letters, in which she used the most loving endearments,—weird, passionate, hyphenated adjectives,—referring to him as her "husband-to-be" and signing herself "the girl who will soon be your loving wife." Her writing was almost undecipherable in its affected angularity, her spelling was ludicrously inaccurate, and her tinted notepaper reeked of her favorite scent. Griffith handled her letters gingerly, read them with distaste, and impatiently destroyed them.

At a loss to know how to extricate himself from his predicament, he consulted Leslie. It was a relief to unburden to someone, to anathematize himself and Clarisse in the terms which had been seething in his mind for days. His brother suggested the one way of escape which was perfectly obvious.

"Has she got anything on you?" he demanded.

"No, I tell you. She got that promise out of me somehow or other."

"In writing?"

"No."

"And you haven't done anything to her?"

"God—no!"

"Well . . . tell her to go to the devil."

Such advice was easy enough to give, Griffith thought resentfully. He had known as much himself before he had spoken to Leslie. *Of course,* he could tell her to go to the devil, but the damnable part of the affair was she would not go! He refused to answer the telephone or her letters, but the calls continued to come and the letters to arrive.

One day Mr. Rumsey stopped at his desk in the office, and said:

"Ring up Clarisse some time to-day, will you, Adams? She's got something important, she says, she wants to tell you."

Griffith nodded and thanked him, but felt the color rising in his face.

A few days later a small square envelope arrived in a shaded feminine handwriting he did not recognize. It was a letter from Rita.

"Dear Griffith:

"I cannot understand how you can treat anyone as cruelly as you are treating my sister. You are humiliating us all. If you did not mean what you said when you asked her to marry you, come and see her and in an honest way tell her so. If you *did* mean it, why are you making her so wretched and unhappy?

"Sincerely,

"Rita."

Griffith gritted his teeth. He felt he was in a miserable position. He could not see himself telling Clarisse to her face that he was done with her. Why in the name of God, didn't she understand that he didn't want to see her any more!

Indecision delayed action for another day or so. Then one morning Rumsey handed him a letter addressed in Clarisse's angular hand.

"Better read it, Adams," he said in an embarrassed voice, as he limped away.

It was an involved, tearful passionate appeal for him to come and see her. She understood at last, she wrote, that he wanted to be free and she was willing to break the engagement if only he would come and see her once more: the *last time*. She would expect him Saturday night. Would he tell her father whether he would come or not?

As long as Griffith did not have to act definitely, he was content to let matters drift. But he knew he could not ignore this appeal or bring himself to say to Mr. Rumsey:

"I can't come Saturday night. Please tell Clarisse."

Resignedly, wearily, he wrote a brief note to her and asked Polly to give it to Mr. Rumsey.

V

Saturday night was rainy. In long, slanting, parallel lines, the water poured down, steadily monotonous. Griffith peered through the front window of his brother's apartment, his hands cupped on either side of his face so that he could see into the darkness, and cursed the weather, himself and the girl who took him out in such a storm. A few minutes later, with rubbers, umbrella and an overcoat buttoned up around his neck, he ploughed through the downpour, angrily assuring himself that he would stay as short a time as possible and tell her firmly and definitely that he was *done*. He rejoiced he was in such an ugly, irritable temper; he did not care how brutal he was nor how soon he got the business over.

Clarisse herself opened the door. The room was in half-light; shaded candles burned here and there in little sconces on the wall.

He could not see her face at first. She was dressed in something loose and lacy; there was a ribbon in her hair which hung low upon her neck, covering the tips of her ears. At once he was assailed by the overpowering perfume she affected.

Their meeting was constrained, embarrassing. She helped him off with his wet things. He was conscious of the touch of her fingers upon his shoulders and sleeves.

"I'll take these out to the kitchen," she said and disappeared. When she had left the room, he began to feel nervous. He wished he had stuck to his determination and not come; it was going to be exceedingly difficult to tell her that it was all over. He knew instinctively that already she was at the point of tears. There was going to be a dreadful scene. Why hadn't he written her it was all off! That would have been much the better way! . . . The little flat was significantly still, suggesting there was no one in it besides himself and Clarisse.

When she returned, she closed the door slowly and gently behind her, and stood before it, her hand upon the knob, gazing at him with one of her long, ardent, affected looks. Griffith turned away, all his distaste rising up strong within him. He foresaw the poses, the tears, the accusations and supplications, the passionately phrased entreaties.

She came close beside him, but he kept his head resolutely turned from her. She whispered his name, her voice trembling. Still he would not look at her.

"Can't we get through this without hysterics?" he said irritably.

He felt one of her hands softly steal about his neck; the other touched his shoulder.

"Griffith!"

"Oh God, . . . Clarisse! What's the use?"

He drew back from her embrace, catching her by the wrists, meeting her eyes for the first time. There was something startling, tragic in them.

"Griffith! Don't you love me any more?"

There was a silence. He could not bring himself to answer her; he stared at her, frowning heavily.

"What have I done that's turned you against me? We were so happy, going places and dancing together. I never loved anyone in my life like I love you, Griffith. What's turned you against me?"

"Nothing."

"Oh, Griffith, don't tell me that! You don't know how a girl like me can love. I tell you, Griffith, I can't *live* without you."

"For heaven's sake, don't begin to cry."

"I'm trying not to. But I've been doing nothing else these past few weeks. . . . You *said* you loved me!"

She waited hoping he would affirm it.

"Griffith! Didn't you tell me you loved me?"

He nodded, reluctantly.

"Oh you did . . . you *did!*" she exclaimed exultingly. "You told me you loved me . . . and you were so *good* to me! You used to love me so nice. What's turned you against me?"

He moved uneasily, swallowing nervously.

"There's nothing doing, Clarisse."

Transfixed she looked at him.

"*Griffith!*"

"I'm . . . I'm through."

A slight convulsion passed over her. She half shrunk, half cringed, her hands raised supplicatingly toward him, sucking in her breath with a low, quick strangling noise. The silent seconds succeeded one another. Griffith stood tense, his eyes averted. Clarisse swayed toward him, her whole body quivering.

"You can't mean it, Griffith. . . . You're not going to give me up!"

Suddenly her passion was let loose.

"*I won't let you go!*" Her voice rose high, strident, almost to a scream. She flung herself against him, her arms about his neck, hugging him and sobbing violently, her face buried against his coat.

Griffith was deeply moved. For anyone to love him like that! For anyone to love him like that! The thought repeated itself, while his breath rose spasmodically, his heart beating. *This* was not acting! There was nothing affected about this! The girl really *loved* him! Limp and broken, she lay sobbing against him, her breast heaving, clinging desperately to him, her hands locked about his neck.

Why—why—why she really *loved* him!

He put his arms about her to support her, to comfort her. Her slim body was uncorsetted. With a rush of blind, unreasoning emotion he drew her to him, covering her hair and neck with eager, passionate kisses. Clarisse began to cry like a child. Words, tender, endearing,—vague, caressing, inarticulate sounds,—broke from her. She raised her wet mouth to his trembling lips and together, locked in each other's arms, they sank down upon the couch.

CHAPTER VI

I

An approved advertising scheme of the Passenger Department of the New York, Niagara & Western, was the distribution of beautifully framed photographs of wooded streams, bits of lovely landscapes or rugged mountain scenery, showing the character of the country through which the trains passed. These photographs varied in size; some were quite large. They were framed with wood covered with the natural bark of trees. At the bottom, a small, neat brass plate gave the title of the picture and then in small lettering beneath, the words: *Along the Line of the New York, Niagara & Western Railroad.*

It was the policy of the railroad to give these pictures away to anyone who would hang them conspicuously in office, club, school or hotel. Chickering, who O.K.'d the requests, was supposed to make sure they came from persons who would display the pictures in the manner intended, but Griffith noticed that every petition received his chief's neatly inscribed initials without question. He was not long in discovering the reason.

The orders for these photographs passed through his own hands, and all were given to a concern on Bleecker Street, the McIntyre, Smith Photographic Company. Bills for these pictures were received weekly and were never under four figures. McIntyre, a slim, blond young man, frequently came to confer with Chickering, and Griffith soon suspected who was Smith.

It occurred to Griffith that these pictures would be considered welcome acquisitions in the various club-houses of his college fraternity. He thought about it for a few days and then found courage to speak to Chickering.

"That's a good idea, Adams. The pictures couldn't serve the purpose of the road better. How many club-houses has your fraternity?"

"Fifty-nine."

"Good. And how many pictures did you propose to send each one?"

"One or two."

"Oh, that won't do! Send 'em four apiece. D.H. the freight. I'm sure they'll appreciate them. Write McIntyre a letter and tell him to watch out for the order and see that only the best pictures go out. Make your own selection."

Griffith was delighted, but he wondered a little, some days later, when the bill was sent him to be vouchered. His suggestion had cost the railroad nearly five thousand dollars! The item of crating the pictures alone amounted to over eight hundred.

The free distribution of photographs was but a small part of the process by which the officials of the railroad fattened their pockets. It was not long before he knew that the *Enterprise Press* was owned and operated by Chickering and his superiors. All the printing for the railroad, even the tickets, was done by it and he could only vaguely imagine the profits of the *Press*. Bills against the railroad amounting to twenty and thirty thousand dollars frequently came to him for vouchers. The company's magazine, *The Course of Empire*, alone cost hundreds of thousands of dollars annually. The advertisements did not cover one-fifth of its contents. A hundred thousand copies were practically given away each month. The bills for its manufacture did not pass through Griffith's hands; they went direct to Chickering who O.K'd them and passed them on to Prentiss, who affixed his signature and forwarded them to McGukin who did likewise. Then they went to the Auditor who paid them.

II

About the time Griffith made these discoveries, he began selling transportation on his own account to his fellow clerks at half-rates. This transportation was not wanted by the clerks themselves, who could always obtain employees' passes, but by friends of theirs and friends of their friends. Owing to the Interstate Commerce Law, Griffith could not issue transportation outside the State, but as the summer advanced, there was an increasing call for what could be used within the boundaries of New York, as certain mountain resorts and lakes where big summer hotels were situated could be reached via the N. Y., N. & W.

He manipulated his office records so as to take care of this transportation which he issued in the form of mileage books, charging them to the account of a fictitious country newspaper. Each mileage book was for a thousand miles and sold regularly at twenty-five dollars; he received twelve dollars and a half for every one he passed out.

Rumsey had suggested the idea to him. Swezey, it appeared, had accommodated his fellow clerks in this manner, and Swezey's predecessor also had done so. It was the recognized prerogative of the head of the Advertising Bureau.

Griffith soon came to learn that each one of his associates had his own special method of self-remuneration. Rumsey derived a considerable revenue in granting rebates on excess baggage to travelling salesmen, for which he received credit slips for merchandise. Rita and Clarisse obtained all their shoes, embroideries and stationery in this way. Snedeker, the head of the Land Bureau, worked in with certain real estate interests. Sparks, the mailing clerk, appropriated ten to fifteen dollars' worth of stamps each week. Chickering was pulling down thousands a year out of his job. Griffith did not see why he should not start his own perquisites of office.

Little by little he was drawn into the practise. The money was always welcome and as one instance after another worked successfully whatever apprehension he at first entertained disappeared, and he began to sell mileage books in a much larger and more open way. In July he totalled up the amount of his sales during that month, which he kept in a little vest pocket book, and was gratified to note that he had made over four hundred dollars.

He spent the money as rapidly as it came in. It brought him a great deal of pleasure and he considered himself unusually happy. David had come to New York, having completed his year's contract with the Trustees of St. Cloud. He was now on the lookout for an opening for himself and his small capital, and was living with Archie at the Hotel Chelsea, while the rest of the McCleish family was away. Margaret and her foster parents had gone to

Lake Geneva in Wisconsin and the Barondess home was shuttered and empty for the summer.

Archie had been promoted. The Johns-Mandrake Company, a large concern engaged in the manufacture of steel car-springs and iron shoe-brakes, had recently been re-organized. Archibald McCleish as Chairman of the new Board of Directors, had made his own son, Secretary of the company at a salary of six thousand a year.

But Griffith saw too little of his two friends for his own pleasure. David was eager to be in business; he was meeting men constantly, investigating propositions, seeking advice from those whom he considered able to give it. He was tirelessly active, intensely energetic. Archie was engrossed in his new work, but he began also to go out more, socially. Since his elevation to the secretaryship, his father's wealthy friends had commenced to take him up and he dined out a great deal, was invited for short cruises up the Hudson or down the Sound on beautifully appointed yachts, and was welcomed at week-end parties on sumptuous country estates. He was elected to one of the "millionaire" clubs.

III

One morning Archie telephoned Griffith, asking him to lunch. Griffith suspected there was something unusual upon his friend's mind: his voice sounded unnaturally crisp.

"This isn't any of my business, Griffith," he said in his stolid, heavy tones as he leaned across the luncheon table after they had given their respective orders to the waiter. "I thought I ought to say something, however, about the way you are acting!"

Griffith looked up at him sharply. The thought of the transportation he was selling immediately suggested itself.

"What do you mean?" he demanded.

Archie cleared his throat.

"I was thinking . . . it seemed to me . . ." He hesitated.

"Oh, fire away!" Griffith exclaimed, impatiently.

"Well, I was just . . . just wondering what you intend to do about that girl, Clarisse."

Griffith's immediate sensation was relief. To hide his feelings,

THE EDUCATION OF GRIFFITH ADAMS 211

he maintained a steady concentrated gaze upon his friend's face. It was Archie who began to blush, the color flooding his cheeks and temples.

"It's your own business of course," he continued, hurriedly, as Griffith made no comment. "A man's relation to a woman is his own affair; I don't believe it's anyone else's business; you know how I feel about that. I'm not curious or trying to interfere. You know what you are doing, and it is nobody's concern but yours. I . . . I just felt I ought to tell you that I think you're making a big mistake to marry her."

"Who said I was going to marry her?"

"Well, Rita said so the other day, . . . said it right before her father. They both seemed to think it was a settled thing."

Griffith did not answer.

"Now, let me talk to you a minute," Archie said. "I want to say a few things to you and I don't want you to get mad. Promise you will hear me out and won't be angry?"

Griffith nodded.

"You're in love with her, I know. I'm not saying anything against her, but . . but do you think she is suited to you? Do you think she's just the right kind of a woman to marry? Will she make you a good wife? Are you satisfied that you care for her so much that you can put up with her . . . with her . . . her sister and father? Look here, Griffith, . . . think this thing over a little while before you decide to go on with it. You'll be sorry some day, old man; she . . . she really isn't in your class, you know?"

"I have no intention of marrying Clarisse Rumsey or any girl," Griffith said, smiling at his friend's embarrassment.

Archie at once looked relieved, but there was still a puzzled expression upon his face.

"I don't understand . . . exactly," he said slowly.

"Neither do I."

"What do you mean?"

Griffith shrugged his shoulders.

"I'm sure I don't know where she got the idea; I never asked her."

"But Rita said you were going to be married right away. She

didn't say when, but I got the impression that it was to be soon. I couldn't believe it, Griffith; you'd never said a word to me, and I couldn't see how you could want to marry a girl like that, for the life of me! . . . Where did the family get the idea?"

"I don't know; Clarisse began talking marriage one day; she kind of expected it some way."

"Did you promise her you would marry her?"

"No."

"You never wrote her letters or committed yourself in any way? She couldn't produce any evidence? You don't want to get involved in any breach-of-promise suit, you know. Those girls are just the kind who bring 'em. You can always shut 'em up with cash. I'd stand right by you, Griffith, if you got into any kind of a mess like that. . . ."

Griffith glanced at him, his eyes full of understanding and affection.

"You always did, Mac."

"Whew!" Archie exclaimed in a relieved voice, "I'm glad you're not thinking of marrying her. Gosh! that would be something fierce!"

IV

There the discussion rested, as far as Archie's interest in the matter was concerned, but Griffith began to wonder to himself just where he was drifting and what was going to happen.

He saw Clarisse regularly now, two and often three times a week. There were no more recriminations on her part, no further talk of marriage. They idled about the city together in the evening. On Sundays they went to Coney Island or to Far Rockaway. There was no questioning the fervent, violent, insatiable love the girl bore him. She presented a pathetic figure. Her passion rode her without mercy. Sometimes she cried for long intervals merely because her love hurt her so. She hung upon Griffith's words and was as susceptible to his moods as a feather to a breeze. Often she gazed at him, her lips trembling, her eyebrows twitching from the excess of her sensitiveness. Few of her old affectations remained. She betrayed her emotions with utter abandon, exhibiting them proudly, without reserve.

Griffith always responded to an exhibition of her passion, for he was moved by the evidence of her love. He loved her for loving him, but he could not care for the girl herself. She wearied and repelled him. He was embarrassed in her company when he thought people were looking at them, and she bored him with her vapid remarks. He asked her not to use the perfume he disliked, and she willingly complied. He alternated between disgust with her and submission to the paroxysms of her mad infatuation. Days and weeks of the summer slipped by and there was no more talk of marriage. Griffith was content to let matters rest, and Clarisse having once nearly driven her lover from her, was seemingly willing to leave the topic alone. It was pleasant just to let things drift along.

Archie, however, had awakened Griffith to a situation which he knew he must face inevitably. He was sure that Clarisse, backed by her sister and her father, expected him to marry her, and this he was equally certain he would not agree to do. There remained only one way of escape, and that was to leave the city. The prospect was almost equally distasteful, as he felt he was getting on exceptionally well with Chickering, and saw visions ahead of money and preferment.

V

Therefore when his chief proposed he should go to Buffalo to execute an important commission for him he welcomed the change. Chickering invited him to lunch at the Transportation Club. A peculiar situation had arisen, the confused details of which Griffith only vaguely understood. The N. Y., N. & W. intended to move the site of their station in Buffalo. The Chief Engineer was to bring the matter up at the next meeting of the Board of Directors. He and Pettengill, McGukin and Prentiss had all agreed to the plan and options on the real estate in Buffalo where the new station was to be built had been secured secretly and were in the hands of these four officials. The scheme was to force the State to condemn the property and then sell it to the railroad at the fancy figures at which it would be condemned. The names of the road's own officials of course would not appear. Through dummies they would make use of their options, take title to the property and await condemnation proceedings.

Chickering had not been let in on the plan and he showed Griffith plainly he was disgruntled but he was not to be altogether out-tricked. He had learned of a street car franchise in Buffalo, which had for years been offered for sale. Its single track lay within a block of the proposed new site of the N. Y., N. & W. station. During the day a horse-driven dilapidated street car moved from one end of its two miles of track to the other. Chickering planned to secure an option on this franchise, which would be worth many thousands of dollars as soon as the news of the proposed station came out. He wanted Griffith to go to Buffalo, report to the attorney there who had been conducting the negotiations up to that point, meet the directors of the one-track horse-car line, hand over a five thousand cash deposit, get the franchise papers and return to New York as quickly as possible. The meeting of the Directors of the N. Y., N. & W. was imminent. It was to take place on the first of September; it was now the twenty-second of August. Griffith had a day over a week in which to carry out Chickering's commission.

He was full of enthusiasm at the trust reposed in him and elated over the importance of his mission. If the deal went through successfully, Griffith was to have his share of the spoils. That was understood. It was a wonderful opportunity, and the boy was filled with a fine affection and admiration for his chief.

It was exciting to go home in the middle of the day, pack his suit-case, telephone Leslie at his office that he was off for Buffalo, and send similar word to Archie and David. He wrote Clarisse a hasty note telling her he was not sure when he would be back, but that he would write her from Buffalo. He wanted to think things over in regard to her; he would have to decide on some course of action while he was away.

At five o'clock he met Chickering at the Grand Central Station. His chief handed him his railroad and Pullman tickets and a long sealed envelope which Griffith knew contained the money. Heartily they shook hands at the gate.

"Good luck, my boy; wire me if you get in trouble and I'll call you up at the Statler Hotel by telephone."

"All right, sir, . . . I'll do my best."

VI

He felt he had every reason to deserve his chief's approval in the way he had represented him, when eight days later he gazed from the hotel window down into crowded Swan Street, the franchise papers secure in his inside pocket.

It had required tact and patience to bring the deal to a successful conclusion for one of the directors of the horse-car line had been taken ill suddenly, another had gone to Rochester for a visit, and a third was on jury duty. A meeting of the necessary quorum of the little Board had been difficult to arrange. It was essential the option was secured before the first of the month in advance of the news of the N. Y., N. & W.'s plans. On the very last day of the month the meeting took place, the necessary signatures were obtained, the money handed over and the option secured.

With the object of his visit satisfactorily accomplished, Griffith resolutely forced himself, on the last night of his stay in Buffalo, to consider what he was going to do in regard to Clarisse. The time had come when the thing had to be settled one way or another. He was afraid of the intensity of her passion for him. He thought her quite capable of shooting him. On the other hand if it were not for the influence of Rita and her father, he felt confident he could persuade Clarisse to let things go on as they were, indefinitely. But even such an arrangement was not what he wanted. Archie had said that cash would generally take care of such girls,—keep them quiet. Undoubtedly he would receive a fair sized check from Chickering as a reward for putting through the horse-car deal so successfully; he could use this money to satisfy Clarisse and her claims. The more he thought of the plan the more its feasibility appealed to him. Rita was studying to go on the stage; she was taking dramatic instruction and having her voice cultivated. Of course Clarisse was not nearly as clever as her sister, and there was little chance of her being a success in that direction, but she might be flattered and encouraged, made to believe she could do something, if Griffith put up the money. He was confident he could persuade her to attempt it.

VII

His train reached the city early in the morning, but he decided to wait until he crossed the ferry before breakfasting, and then eat leisurely and elegantly at the Waldorf. It was after he had established himself at a table in the men's café and given a carefully thought-out order to the waiter, that he spread out his morning paper with a comfortable sigh of enjoyment, and learned that Archibald Walter McCleish, the great railroad king, had gained control of the Federal System of Railroads. His ownership had been announced by Adolph Barondess at the meeting of the Board of Directors of the New York, Niagara & Western Railroad, one of the principal properties of the Federal System, which had been held in New York the previous day. The President of the road, Caleb Trench, long incapacitated through ill health, had suddenly died and an unexpected fight had been precipitated over his successor. Roscoe Henry Grismer, the former Vice-President, had been finally selected. The purchase of the Federal system of railroads, comprising some fifteen thousand miles of track, by McCleish and his powerful ring of capitalists had been confirmed later by Mr. McCleish himself in an interview.

The item of news most surprising to Griffith was the elevation of Theodore Sales, Assistant General Passenger Agent, of the same rank as Chickering, over his head and the heads of Prentiss and McGukin, to be Vice-President in Charge of Accounts. Sales had been the joke of the Passenger Department. He had neither influence nor power, had been side-tracked years before, and endowed with insignificant authority. Griffith had encountered him once or twice in the halls of the building: a little man with a narrow, pinched forehead, a prominent humped nose like a bent knuckle and sharp animal eyes squinting through thick lenses. Chickering despised him and made fun of him to his clerks.

Griffith foresaw he would be intensely annoyed by Sales' elevation. He smiled at the prospect of hot, bitterly waged battles. He had grown sufficiently familiar with the wire-pulling and the warring cliques among the officials of the road to watch and enjoy the struggles among them, the machinations and duplicity, the secret truces and alliances. There was certain to be a determined and bitter fight with Sales.

Chickering was out when Griffith walked into the Passenger Department. He did not come in until late in the afternoon. Griffith immediately reported to him, gave him an account of his trip, his difficulties in securing a quorum of the directors of the horse-car line, his delivery of the money and his receipt of the option which he handed over to his chief. Chickering listened with indifference, nodding inattentively. He accepted the papers, glanced at them cursorily, and pigeonholed them in his desk. Griffith was disappointed. He had hoped for a friendly smile, a word of approval, as commendation of service well performed. He saw that his chief's one concern at the moment was the promotion of Sales; it was troubling more than he had imagined.

VIII

Leslie's awkward show of pleasure in his return touched Griffith. His brother consented after some urging to forego the *Trocadero Café* and *Spinney's* for that particular evening and dine at some brilliant and gay restaurant on Broadway. Griffith even succeeded in persuading him to go to the theatre, but there he sat in bored endurance, going out between the acts and during the progress of the show to fortify himself in his usual way. He showed, only too clearly, his eagerness to get back to his unread newspapers, his cigarettes and the comfort of his oppressive apartment.

When they arrived home Griffith found three telephone messages from Clarisse, the last requesting him to ring her up when he came in no matter how late it might be. Griffith decided she could wait until the morning, and in the morning he thought she could just as well wait until later in the day, in spite of the fact that her father limped over to his desk and said awkwardly:

"Clarisse was awfully glad to hear you were at home. She wants to see you; . . . little under the weather while you were away; . . . better 'phone."

Instead, Griffith telephoned Archie and David and persuaded

them to lunch with him. It struck him as curious that the fathers of both his chums,—Barondess was like a father to David,—should now be the men for whom, indirectly, he worked. Their acquaintance and friendship might be exceedingly profitable to him. Theodore Sales had been jumped to the Vice-Presidency; it was conceivable that he, too, might be advanced to a position of real importance! The knowledge of his friendly relations with both Barondess and the great McCleish might further his interests with Chickering. It was something to have the ear of such men, the *entrée* to their homes!

David was full of enthusiasm over a trade paper in which he had invested his money, and to which he had decided to devote all his personal energy. It was published in the interests of masons and carpenters and was named *The Master Builders*. It had a circulation of five or six thousand. David believed it had a big future and declared he was going to work day and night toward its success.

Archie had been up to Newport for the Tennis Tournament and had seen Margaret. She was to be back in New York in a few days, and had said she was eagerly looking forward to being with the three of them again, as they had been during the last Christmas holidays.

David wanted Griffith to come and live with him. The Hotel Chelsea was much too expensive for him, and he had found a boarding house where the two of them could have a large basement room, once a family dining-room, with a private bath, for twenty dollars a week. The food was excellent and the location ideal. The prospect appealed strongly to Griffith. He had grown to dislike cordially the close stuffy rooms of his brother's apartment and the daily annoyance of determining where they should dine. Leslie had got on his nerves more and more of late. With David there would be someone of his own age with whom to go to the theatre, someone with opinions, someone with whom he could talk. The colorlessness of Leslie's life was a weight upon Griffith's heart and mind, but he knew that his brother would be keenly disappointed at his leaving him. Whatever youth and brightness entered Leslie's bleak existence, Griffith brought to it. But he could not be expected to keep up the arrangement *forever*, he thought, resentfully. He would have to tell Leslie some time soon that he was uncomfortable living as they did. He would prepare his mind for the break and in a month or so let him know he was going to live with David.

IX

He was deciding these things in his mind as he returned to his office. When he reached his desk there was a Manila paper envelope upon the blue blotter in the centre of it, the kind used for office memorandums. He tore off a strip along one edge and shook out the contents. It read:

Mr. G. Adams:
Kindly report to my office at your earliest convenience.
Theodore Sales.

Griffith stared, convinced it was a mistake. He turned to Polly, holding out the slip to her.

"That can't be for me." He felt puzzled and annoyed.

"Yes, I think it is," she answered in her matter-of-fact way. "Douglas, the red-headed boy from Mr. Sales' office brought it; he asked when you would be back."

Griffith's mouth twitched nervously. What could Sales want of him? He had never so much as spoken to him while he was A. G. P. A.; now that he had become Vice-President, he had suddenly sent for him! Apprehensive, vaguely uncomfortable, he thrust the order into his pocket and walked out into the hallway.

The office of Theodore Sales was across the corridor from the big operating room under Chickering's direction. It was a small room, long and narrow, with one large window at the further end. A glass partition divided it into an outer and an inner office. In the first of these Douglas, the stenographer, rattled at a typewriter under a powerful electric light.

Sales swung round in his swivel arm-chair as Griffith, obeying his summons, opened the door leading to the inner office.

"Oh . . . ah! You're Adams, huh? Sit down there, Adams; I want to have a talk with you."

Griffith instinctively disliked the man with his pinched forehead, his thin bent nose and squinting eyes. Through thick lenses he peered about him as if trying to distinguish things through a dense fog.

Sales began amiably with a number of questions. His manner was chatty and leisurely. He wanted to know how long Griffith had been with the road, how he liked it, what his duties were under Mr. Chickering, and what salary he received.

His very friendliness put Griffith upon his guard; he suspected Sales intended to try to "pump" him. He confined his answers to as few words as possible, and watched him narrowly.

"I understand you're personally acquainted with Mr. Archibald McCleish and one of our Directors, Mr. Adolph Barondess?" Sales asked presently.

"Yes, sir."

It flashed to Griffith his friendship with these powerful men would really count with a man like Sales.

"You went to college with Mr. McCleish's son and the adopted son of Mr. Barondess?"

"Yes, sir."

"You are lucky to have two such influential friends upon the Board of Directors," Sales continued, smiling. "It isn't every young man who is so fortunate. Both these gentlemen have spoken to me about you. They asked me if I knew you; I was sorry to tell them I did not."

Griffith's face glowed; he made a happy sound with his lips as he grinned broadly.

"I presume you have seen the announcements in the newspapers concerning the changes which have occurred here?"

"Oh yes, sir."

"Well, you know I'm one of the Vice-Presidents of this road now. . . . Mr. Grismer and I are very warm friends. We hope to inaugurate some changes here that will make this railroad one of the best paying in the United States."

He tilted back in his seat, pursing his lips, resting his finger-tips together, his elbows supported by the chair arms.

"I'd like you to help us, Adams. There is no reason why you should not rise very high indeed in this concern with the backing of the Chairman of the Board, one of the directors, and the Vice-President, . . . hey?"

Griffith drew his breath in sharply, smiling delightfully.

"Well . . . I'd . . . like to, of course," he said, with an excited laugh.

"That's fine!" Sales exclaimed enthusiastically. "I believe you will. You're all right. You'll be a big man here!"

He paused a moment teetering back and forth in his chair.

"Well . . . now . . . I'd like to ask you a few questions." He spoke slowly, choosing his words, gazing up at the white ceiling. "Whatever you answer will be strictly confidential, . . . just between ourselves."

The smile that had been upon Griffith's face a moment before slowly faded; with a sinking heart he foresaw what impended.

"You've been with the Passenger Department here, you say, about a year and a half, and six months ago you were put in charge of the Advertising Bureau. Have you ever seen anything since you've been in charge that has impressed you as peculiar?"

Griffith gazed fixedly at his interrogator, swallowing nervously, his mouth set. He saw the choice he would have to make.

"I'll be frank with you, Adams," Sales continued deliberately. "Mr. Grismer and I have but one aim: we want this railroad to make money. It has *got* to be made to pay . . . and pay well! The stockholders are entitled to their just dividends. I've been with this company twelve years and the road showed increasing profits until about five years ago. I saw what was going on; I knew that this great property was being deliberately robbed. The Auditor has called my attention to many curious vouchers. I have suspected a great deal, but I could do nothing. Now things are different. I am determined to clean out this set of grafters. *Every one of them has got to go.*"

He waited a moment to let his words have their full effect.

"Now Adams, you see what I am getting at. I have enough proof already to go to the Directors, but these men have their own friends on the Board. I want to show them up, and I need all the facts I can obtain. I want you to tell me what *you* know. You needn't be afraid. I'll protect you thoroughly. Understand?"

"Yes, sir."

"Well, . . . what about this magazine, *The Course of Empire*, which is supposed to further the interests of the road? The Auditor tells me a voucher came through to him some time ago for ninety thousand dollars! Do you know anything about that?"

"No, sir. I don't handle the magazine vouchers."

"Don't you think some other concern than the *Enterprise Press* could print the magazine at a cheaper price?"

"I don't know."

"What about the advertising of this Old Comfort Inn at Syosset Beach?"

"I don't know."

"Did it never occur to you as odd that this hotel should receive so much space in our own advertising?"

"I . . . it didn't occur to me, sir."

"Come, Adams, I'm giving you a chance, . . . a *big* chance. Here's your opportunity to be honest, to throw your lot in with honest men. You have a powerful backing. If you will tell the truth nothing can possibly happen to you. Tell me what you know. I don't ask you to prove anything. Just tell me what you've *heard* or even what you *suspect*. I *know* you can furnish us with some valuable information, if you're willing. Now tell me, what does the manager of the Old Comfort Inn pay for all this free advertising? Does he ever give *you* anything?"

"No, sir."

"How about the higher-ups?"

"I . . . I don't know."

Sales leaned back in his chair, his narrow forehead puckered in a frown.

"Why can't you tell the truth, my boy?"

Griffith distrusted the man opposite him; there was something crafty about him. Chickering had befriended him; Leslie was his brother. To tell what he knew to this catechising official would be base treachery.

"There'll be no blame attached to you if you have personally profited by some of the deals your superiors have engineered. You won't lose by telling me what you know. . . . Come, my boy," Sales leaned toward him confidentially, "speak up, . . . tell me, . . . you know what's been going on."

Griffith was dumb. An instinctive fear of the man sealed his lips. There was no incentive to confide in him.

"Now, I'll give you one more opportunity, Adams," Sales continued. "Let me repeat once more that I'll take care of you and you won't suffer because of anything you tell me. Remember too that Mr. McCleish and Mr. Barondess will welcome any recommendation I might send them regarding your promotion."

Again Sales paused to mark the effect of the words.

"A few months ago, . . . since *you* were put in charge of the Advertising Bureau, . . . vouchers began to come through from your department in payment of paper purchased from a concern, Blashfield & Pope. I have one here," Sales indicated it upon his desk, "for seven thousand dollars, . . . another for nine thousand. Do you know any reason why this railroad should give all its paper orders to one firm? Until you were put in charge of the Advertising Bureau, we used to give our orders to several concerns. A relative of my wife's is a salesman in the Gould, Hunt Company. He used to receive some very good orders for paper from your predecessor, Mr. Swezey. Shortly after you took charge of the Bureau, you told the clerk at the desk you would see no more salesmen from paper houses. Why was that? Why did you give all our orders to Blashfield & Pope?"

"Because I was told to," Griffith answered sullenly.

"By whom?"

"By Mr. Chickering."

"And you personally did not profit by the arrangement?"

For the fraction of a second, Griffith hesitated, striving to control the trembling of his lips.

"No, sir."

Sales gave an exasperated sigh.

"What do you want to lie for, Adams? Why don't you come out with the truth?"

"I'm . . . I *am* telling the truth."

"No you're *not!*" the other snapped. He began to talk rapidly. "You're lying. It is as plain you're lying as if it were written all over your face. You know perfectly well that all the paper orders from this railroad were given to Blashfield & Pope for a monetary consideration, and all the printing orders went to the

Enterprise Press for the same reason. These changes were made *after* you were put in charge of the Advertising Bureau. You *must* know why this was done. You—know—you—got—something —out—of—it—yourself!"

Had Griffith been approached by someone of different calibre to Sales he would have willingly told what he knew. One touch of genuine sympathy or friendliness would have brought out the whole story. The man before him filled him with fear and mistrust; he disliked him; he did not know what he ought to do; he thought of Leslie and Chickering. He had a vision of the pale expressionless face of his brother, and the wet, glistening eyes of his chief. He remembered what both had said to him.

"Well, are you going to tell me?"

The boy shook his head.

"I'll make you suffer for this, my son," the other said angrily.

Griffith stared vacantly at the floor. His throat was dry; he pinched his lips together to keep them from trembling.

"You won't speak?"

Griffith did not answer.

"Very well then. . . . How about this transportation you've been selling?"

The man thrust his head out toward him, his eyes narrowed to slits behind the thick glasses, his words coming slowly and malignantly between his teeth.

Griffith quailed as if he had been struck.

His inquisitor leaned nearer, speaking deliberately, watching him intently.

"Mr. Adolph Barondess was sitting in the smoking-car of one of our trains the other day and he heard a travelling salesman boasting to a friend how he bought his thousand mile books for twelve dollars and fifty cents, . . . *half the regular rate*, . . . and how he got them from a clerk in the Passenger Department of this road named Adams!"

Sales paused. Griffith did not move. The awfulness of what was closing in upon him paralyzed his thoughts. He sat staring at the green carpet on the floor.

"Mr. Barondess and Mr. McCleish both came and asked me if I knew you. They seemed to think it was impossible for the boy who had been a college chum of their sons to be guilty of such dishonesty. It has been explained to them what thievery exists in this organization and they are ready to believe you have been a victim of the system. They are looking for the proofs of the graft I have assured them is here. Mr. Barondess instructed me to dismiss you immediately, but I told him that I was sure you were not responsible and that when the facts were laid before you, you would co-operate with me in furnishing proofs we need."

The eager words Sales spoke reached Griffith's brain as if addressed to someone else.

"Does Chickering know you've been selling transportation?"

Griffith dully shook his head.

"Then this sale of mileage books was merely a side graft of your own?"

The boy nodded.

Sales sank back in his chair and studied him silently, squinting his eyes through his thick lenses. Griffith's mind had ceased to operate; he was conscious of no sensation beyond one of mental distress. He remained gazing at the green carpet, waiting for the end of the inquisition.

"Well," Sales finally exclaimed impatiently, "aren't you going to talk *now*?"

For an instant Griffith met the thin slits of eyes. He was like a dog that is being flogged and does not understand the reason. What did Sales want? What did he expect him to do?

The man leaned toward him again, a hand upon each knee, bringing his face close to Griffith's.

"What have you got to say?"

It was a physical impossibility at the moment for the boy to have uttered a word. He shook his head, meaning to imply that he could not speak.

Sales brought his fist down with a bang upon his desk.

"You damned stubborn whelp!" he screamed. "I've had enough of you!"

"Douglas!" he called. The red-headed stenographer opened the door in the dividing glass partition, note-book in hand.

"Memorandum to Mr. Chickering," Sales began to dictate. "It has been brought to my attention that a clerk in your department,

Griffith Adams, has been apprehended in the sale of the company's transportation for his own profit. As he has made a full confession to me personally, I have taken upon myself to dismiss him at once. He leaves the company's employ today."

Griffith listened, the significance of Sales' words at last reaching his consciousness. He stood up, his hands twitching, his arms jerking, his mouth open, struggling to find his voice. When it came it was with a rush, the sounds almost inarticulate, harsh and broken.

"I'll talk . . . I'll talk . . . I'll say anything you want me to! Oh God, what do you want me to say? . . . I'll tell you everything, . . . I'll tell you the whole damned business! Just wait a moment, can't you! Just wait a *second!*"

The confession came disjointedly, in random, unrelated sentences, the stenographer racing to set down his words. Griffith sat on the edge of a chair, his fingers thrust into his mop of hair, his head bent, his elbows resting on his knees. Mechanically, he told what he knew and the gossip he had heard. He made no effort to choose his words; his language was frequently twisted, his utterances meaningless. Sales caught him up constantly, cautioning him to speak more slowly, directing him to repeat his last words.

"How's that, Adams? Say that again."

". . . McIntyre, Smith is the name. They're over there on Bleecker Street. I've been told Mr. Chickering bought a camera some years ago; McIntyre was a clerk under him. He sent him out over the road to take pictures of scenery. When McIntyre came back he bought the prints from him for advertising purposes and charged them to the road. Then he set McIntyre up in business. Smith is himself: the silent partner of the company. They commenced to make enlargements of the photographs and framed 'em up handsomely in bark. Bills for these pictures amount to several thousand dollars, . . . I don't know, . . . remember one for five thousand."

The recital went on and on. Griffith's mouth became dry; his lips and tongue made small crackling noises as he continued to articulate; his head throbbed violently. Sales prodded him with questions. It was a relentless examination. Griffith concealed nothing; he told all he knew, even the account of his recent trip to Buffalo.

X

It was dark when Sales let him go. The lights had been switched on some time during the late afternoon; he did not recall when it had been. Mechanically he went back to his desk. The great room of the Passenger Department was empty except for a single stenographer at the further end who sat clicking at his machine. Griffith found an envelope on his blotter addressed to him in Clarisse's hand. He put it into his inside coat pocket without reading it. He was conscious only of the terrific pain in his head. In a daze he made his way to the locker room for his hat and gloves, and a few minutes later boarded a subway train and was whirled uptown.

His brother greeted him with his unfailing:

"Hello—hello!" adding the unusual variation: "you're late tonight!"

Griffith could not think. He refused to allow himself to dwell on what had already happened or on what was going to happen. He was weary unto death. He shut his mind against the crowding thoughts that were ready to burst upon his exhausted brain.

Leslie was particularly irritating. Griffith could hardly endure his brother's infrequent comments as they sat opposite one another at a round table in *Spinney's* beer-smelling back room. Bluntly he told him he was going to leave him on the first of the month; he was going to live with David. He was angered by Leslie's silent acceptance of the announcement. They finished their meal without addressing one another again and walked back to the apartment. Griffith began to undress at once. He was exhausted, his head ached fiercely, and he was anxious to get to sleep, away from the ever-pressing thoughts ready to spring upon him. Just before he turned out the light, his brother came to his door and stared in at him a moment.

"Don't like it here, . . . hey?"

"No."

"We could move; any place you say."

Griffith threw back his aching head impatiently.

"David wants me to live with him."

Leslie was silent. Then:

"Perhaps he'd like to come live here with you?"

"No . . . I guess not."

"Won't cost him anything," Leslie persisted.

"No . . . I guess not."

Griffith turned out the light and dropped upon the bed, pulling the covers over him, burying his head in the pillow.

XI

He had just sunk off into oblivion when Leslie shook him by the shoulder.

Griffith started up in quick terror, gazing at his brother wildly, the electric light flooding the room.

"There're two girls here who want to see you," Leslie said. "It's that Rumsey girl, I think, and her sister."

Griffith groaned and dropped back upon his pillow.

"Oh . . . tell 'em I'm sick, Les' . . . I can't see *anyone*. Tell 'em I'm sick."

The light went out; the door closed. Presently Griffith was asleep again.

CHAPTER VII

I

THE first sensation of the morning was a feeling of overwhelming calamity. With the abrupt realization of its nature, Griffith caught his breath, his heart contracting. It was like a blow between the eyes. Now the thoughts rushed pell-mell upon him, a cataract of speculations, surging, bewildering, absorbing. What was going to happen now? What was going to happen now? What was going to happen now? The unanswerable question recurred incessantly. He was like a frail chip on the breast of a great rushing torrent, hurrying on to some destiny, terrible and unknown.

At a few minutes after nine, he walked into the Passenger Department. At once he began eyeing his fellow clerks, watching for significant looks from them, studying their behavior, dreading the detection of any unusual sign. The routine of the office proceeded unruffled. There was no indication that anything had gone amiss. He did not see Chickering. The day dragged itself out. He idled at his desk, drawing pictures, designing the floor plans of houses. He welcomed every interruption, grateful for the diversion.

Rumsey came over to him during the afternoon.

"When can we have a talk together, Adams?" he asked. "I've got something I want to . . . discuss with you."

"Oh any time will do," Griffith answered indifferently.

"Well—a, . . . could you come out to the house to-night?"

At once Griffith raised objections. He knew well enough what Clarisse's father wanted to talk about. In his present state of mind he was perfectly willing to discuss it with him or his daughter, but there were other matters troubling him a great deal more than Clarisse and her problem.

"I've got an engagement to-night," he said.

"How about tomorrow?"

"Can't come tomorrow either; got a date with my brother."

"How's Friday?"

"Friday's all right."

Rumsey hesitated.

"The girl seems kind of anxious to see you, Adams," he said bending closer. The quality of his voice had changed; his words had the tone of entreaty. "She feels pretty badly that you haven't been to see her since you got back . . . . Why don't you go out and have a talk with her?"

"I know . . . I know," Griffith said. He felt sorry for Rumsey; he sensed the man's humiliation.

"I've been terribly busy, Mr. Rumsey," he said. "I'll telephone her to-night sure."

"Thanks." Relieved, smiling gratefully, Rumsey limped back to his desk.

At a few minutes before five o'clock, the stenographer from Sales' office appeared. Griffith experienced a quick spasm; the boy was like a red flag of danger. He jerked his head in the direction of Sales' room, and without speaking turned upon his heel and went out. Griffith slowly rose and weakly followed.

As he entered, Sales peered at him, squinting first at his face, then at his feet, and again at his face, as if he had not seen him before.

"I want you to sign this, Adams," he said. He held out several typewritten sheets. "I don't expect you to substantiate every statement you made yesterday. I have just added a few lines here at the end which ought to cover everything. See here, . . ." he offered Griffith the last page. On it was typed:

"The foregoing is the truth to the best of my knowledge and belief."

"Want to read it over?" he asked.

"No, . . . I guess not."

"Sign your name underneath that," he directed.

Griffith obeyed, but he hardly knew his own signature.

"Now there's a few additional questions I'd like to ask you," Sales continued blotting Griffith's name. "The remittance you received from Blashfield & Pope on the first of every month came to you in what form?"

"A check."

"Made out 'to bearer'?"

"No, sir, . . . it was made out to me personally."

"Hu-hum. And the money you took to Buffalo was in the form of greenbacks?"

"Yes, sir, . . . fifty one hundred dollar bills."

Sales poked about among the litter on his desk and extracted from a folder a blue sheet of paper.

"You told me that when you first came here you were asked to turn over to someone a six hundred commission for an advertisement of the New Metropolitan Hotel which was to run one year in *The Course of Empire*. The voucher for this commission was made out to you and when you collected the money you gave it to Mr. Chickering. Is that correct?"

"Yes, sir."

"Is this the voucher you cashed?"

Griffith accepted the blue sheet Sales offered him, glanced at it and handed it back.

"Yes, sir."

"Very well . . . . that is all."

Again Griffith endured a wretched evening of doubt and uncertainty. He had intended to call up Clarisse as he had promised, but his heart failed him. There would be tears and reproaches; he knew all the things she would say and how his explanations would be doubted. Leslie left him to himself, for which he was grateful, but he was denied the oblivion of the sleep he had known the night before. He lay awake for many hours, twisting first on one side, then upon the other, now lying upon his back, his hands locked beneath his head, resigning himself to the tumult of his racing thoughts.

The morning's mail brought him a letter from Margaret. She was returning the end of the week and would save Friday night for him. She had had a dull summer and was looking eagerly forward to being home again. She hoped David and Archie and he could all come to supper on Sunday.

For the first time in his life, the prospect of seeing her again brought Griffith no particular pleasure. She was merely an added complication when everything was becoming bewilderingly confused.

Friday night he had promised to Rumsey; he would have to break that engagement. He resolved to confide in Margaret, make her a complete confession. He hoped she would tell him he had done the right thing. He was beginning to hunger for someone who believed in him.

The day stretched drearily before him. The morning lingered minute by minute; the afternoon slowly wore itself out. He began to feel the effect of the strain. His nerves were on edge; noises startled him, and things appeared distorted. The calm over the office seemed ominous. All his senses were keyed taut in anticipation of the thunder-clap that would break it. The clerks pattered about their work, going to and fro, answering the telephone bells, dictating their letters, attending to their duties. He wondered what they would do when the crash came, how they would be affected. He foresaw their consternation and alarm, their frightened clamor, their timid and excited conferences. He could fancy their uneasy whisperings and interchange of anxious gossip, each striving to control the surging fear in his heart about his job.

Occasionally Chickering's buzzer sounded in different parts of the room. Each time, Griffith's heart gave a quick plunge and with a racing pulse he watched the summoned clerk answer the call. He knew his own time might come at any moment. He kept his eyes upon the little red door until the clerk reappeared, closely studying his face as he walked back to his desk.

Another night brought him neither rest nor sleep.

II

A little after ten o'clock the following morning Chickering's buzzer sounded above his head. For an instant every muscle in his body sprang taut; he sat rigid in his chair, the action of his heart suspended, his eyeballs straining. With the cessation of the whirring summons, his body collapsed, a fine tremor affecting his knees, his mouth twitching. He got to his feet by pushing himself up with his hands. Uncertainly he walked the intervening distance between his desk and the little red door. He was obliged to exert himself to open it. The stenographer, bending over his machine as he cleaned the type with a bone-handled tooth-brush, paid no attention to him. With a long breath he tried to steady himself before he knocked on the inner door. Then he raised his hand and brought his knuckles feebly against its polished surface. One swift glance at Chickering's face and he realized that his chief knew. No word was spoken. Griffith stood a few feet from the table which separated them, his head bent, his eyes closed, his hands clenched, struggling against the sudden quivers that twitched his body. He had dreaded this moment, but he had not foreseen its real anguish. Chickering, he had imagined, would be the one confounded,—not himself. For the first time he realized his treachery. Confronted by the man who had trusted him and whom he had betrayed, he could only sink his head in miserable abasement.

Chickering continued to look at him. No violent denunciation nor bitter reproach could have been as stinging as that silent scrutiny. Griffith felt the wet glistening eyes upon him, moving slowly over his body, disposing of its members one by one in wordless contempt; it was like being flayed alive. The inspection was unsparing, inexorable, deliberate. Minutes followed one another and still the malignant eyes were fastened upon him. Griffith shifted from one foot to the other; the sweat began to form upon his forehead and in the palms of his hands. The silence continued, the interval lengthening until it seemed another minute of it would drive Griffith to violent outburst.

When Chickering spoke, he did not raise his voice; the words came slowly, tonelessly, their very lack of objurgation betraying the passion back of them.

"Get out of this office . . . and get out of my sight."

Griffith turned, blindly groping for the handle of the door, opened it and closed it behind him. His only thought was to escape from the man's presence, to go anywhere away from the scrutiny of those terrible eyes. He went back to his desk and sat down, resting his forehead upon both hands, gazing blankly at the spotless surface of his blue blotter.

After a time he drew a long breath, straightening himself, shrugging his shoulders as though freeing them from the great load that had weighted them down. Now that the blow had fallen, he became aware of a certain calmness.

Presently Polly stood beside him holding a letter in her hand.

"What do you want me to do about this?"

He took the sheet from her mechanically and dully read it. It was a request from a newspaper proprietor with whom he had had a sharp disagreement.

As he tried to focus his mind upon the matter, it occurred to him that Chickering had dismissed him. He stared at the letter a moment, then slowly rose and without answering Polly's question, passed out of the Passenger Department and opened the door of Sales' office on the other side of the hall.

"He's not in," the red-headed stenographer announced, "he's at a conference."

Griffith hesitated and sat down in one of the vacant chairs.

"I guess I'll wait."

"I'll call you when he comes in," the boy volunteered. "He may not come back for some time."

"I guess I'll wait," Griffith repeated.

There was nothing else for him to do. He dared not go back to his own desk and risk the chance of Chickering finding him there. He folded his hands, leaned back in the chair and resigned himself to a period of waiting.

Would Sales send him back to his desk and dictate a memorandum to Chickering that he was to remain there? Would he transfer him to another department? Perhaps he would tell him to take a vacation until Chickering himself was thrown out? He had said all the grafters had to go.

III

Abruptly the door opened and Sales strode in, crossing the outer office in three rapid steps. With him was Adolph Barondess. Neither of them saw the waiting boy; they passed on to the inner sanctum, closing the door in the glass partition behind them with a smart clatter. Griffith half rose, hesitated and sat down again. He waited, listening to the murmur of voices, occasionally distinguishing the Hollander's thick, sibilant articulation.

The telephone bell rang incessantly. Once Griffith heard Sales at the telephone say distinctly:

"I made a statement to a man from the *Wall Street Journal* . . . Yes, Mr. Grismer . . . that was what it was . . . I said nothing about that . . . Mr. Barondess agrees . . ."

The moments grew. The red-headed stenographer shut the machine up in his desk and went out to lunch. Griffith listened to the whistles blowing the noon hour. The clock on the wall he noticed was ten minutes fast.

There was a movement inside; shadows appeared on the opaque glass of the partition; he heard Sales' weak laugh. Then the door opened and the two men stood in the doorway, their hats upon their heads, their light overcoats on their arms.

They were talking as they passed into the outer office, but at sight of Griffith they both stood still, speech arrested.

Griffith rose; there was a moment's silence.

"Well, sir?"

"Mr. Chickering doesn't want me in his office; he told me to get out . . ." he paused glancing from face to face, . . . "I did not know what to do; I thought I'd see you."

Sales did not reply. He remained squinting at Griffith, his narrow forehead creased in a crooked frown.

"Vell . . . vy don't you take hiss advize,"—it was Barondess who spoke. "Ve don't vant any t'ieves round here!" His voice rose angrily.

Griffith gazed at him, wide-eyed.

"Mr. Sales," he began haltingly, "Mr. Sales said he would . . ." He stopped, confused, overwhelmed.

"What did Mr. Sales say he would do?" Barondess' companion repeated with ominous urbanity.

"You said you would look out for me," Griffith replied, meeting the squinting eyes, his spirit rising. "You said you'd take care of me, . . . give me a promotion."

Barondess laughed.

"Promotion? That iss good! Promote a t'ief!" Suddenly his manner changed. He stepped toward Griffith in anger and shook his finger in his face.

"Young man . . . vhere you belong iss in a prisson! A boy dot vould take money dot don't belong to him! Prisson iss vhere you should go! Thank God ve don't prosecute you. It iss such men ass you dot make criminals. If I had my vay you should go to prisson."

Griffith drew back before the infuriated little man whose wrath was fanned by his own words. He turned appealingly toward Sales. Sales must interfere; he would explain what service Griffith had performed; he would vindicate him. But the man he expected to champion him, averted his eyes and stepped back toward the door leading into the hall, opening it for Barondess to pass out ahead of him.

"But, Mr. Sales?" Griffith said, starting forward to detain him, "you said . . . you'd . . . you'd . . . What shall I do?"

The man studied him a moment through his thick lenses.

"I don't know," he said coldly. "We don't want you here. We only employ men who are honest."

He followed Barondess out into the hall and the heavy door swung after him in a series of lessening flights, kissing itself shut with a crisp sound of finality.

Griffith dropped back in his chair. A sudden weariness possessed him. It was a relief to know that as far as he was concerned the battle in the company was over; it involved him no longer. The sooner he got out of the building the better. He stopped at his desk and left a note for Polly, who had gone to lunch, to send him his pay envelope if it came through the next day.

He met Rumsey in the lavatory where he went to get his hat.

"Well, I'm canned," he announced.

Rumsey started, his eyes staring, his jaw fallen.

"What for?"

Griffith was about to put him off with any excuse which would serve, when he remembered it was Rumsey who had first suggested to him the sale of the company's transportation.

"Caught me selling mileage books," he said listlessly. "Result of *your* advice!"

Rumsey frowned, his face full of concern.

"Say," he said troubledly, "that's hard luck. My God, I'm sorry. I'm . . . I'm *terribly* sorry, Adams!"

Griffith did not want Rumsey's sympathy. He reached for his hat in the locker and turned toward the door. It had closed behind him, when Rumsey came limping hurriedly after him.

"See you tonight, Adams?" he called.

"Guess not; I'm all in," Griffith answered, without looking round. "I'm going home."

He passed out into the hall and descended to the street below in the crowded elevator.

"It's the last time I'll do this," he thought.

IV

There could be no more cheerless atmosphere for him on that warm afternoon than his brother's over-furnished apartment, so he crossed Broadway and went down a bustling side street to a restaurant where he and Archie often ate luncheon together. But Archie was not there. Griffith had some tasteless thing to eat, and wandered out into the bright street again. Mechanically he turned his steps toward the Johns-Mandrake Company.

He was obliged to wait until Archie came in from his lunch. He saw him crossing the street in his English walking suit, edged neatly with silk braid, which fitted his square stocky figure faultlessly, the tapering tails flapping behind him as he marched firmly along. Nothing about him suggested the college boy any longer; he was the embodiment of business responsibility, reliability and integrity, with his conservative derby hat, his tan gloves and straight silver-headed cane. Griffith knew he had been to some directors' meeting; he always wore his cutaway on such occasions.

"Hello Griffith . . . come on back to the office."

There was nothing unusual in Archie's manner or greeting, and yet in Griffith's sensitive state of mind it seemed to him that his friend had never seemed so casual, so indifferent. He followed him between the rows of dark mahogany desks and shining brass railings to the spacious office of the Secretary.

He had never been in Archie's office before; he was astonished at its luxury. The walls were paneled in mahogany, the floor thickly carpeted, two or three large leather chairs were arranged invitingly about the great flat desk in the centre of the room; an oblong green electric lamp with dull brass fittings threw a flood of light upon the surface of the desk but left the face of the worker in shadow. In the further corner of the room was the Secretary's private stenographer, tapping briskly at her machine under a similar electric radiance.

Archie stripped off his gloves, tucked them into the brim of his derby hat, hung it on a small mahogany hat-rack, and leaned his cane in the corner. Then he pointed to one of the leather chairs and sat down himself, hunching his own chair a little nearer to the desk.

"They fired me over there," Griffith announced.

Archie elevated his eyebrows.

"Is that so?" he exclaimed.

Griffith went on and told the story, his voice trembling a little when he came to the part that Sales had played. The recital brought back his outraged sense of fairness and he swore impetuously. Archie raised his hand warningly, murmuring a cautious: "Sh . . . sh . . . sh . . . sh," jerking his head in the direction of the stenographer. Griffith, abruptly silenced, nodded and sank back into the depths of his leather chair, disconcerted by the interruption. He sensed a lack of sympathy in Archie. There was a barrier between them. Suddenly he felt immeasurably removed from him; he saw in a flash their new relationship:—he, the jobless, inconsequential, moneyless acquaintance whom Archie would always befriend for the sake of their school and college days together; Archie, the secretary of a big corporation, powerful, wealthy, rising rapidly to fame and a great future. The quick vision hurt; he sat frowning, dumb, swept away for the moment by its contemplation. It would never be the same again; he could no longer regard Archie as his closest friend. It was unbelievable,—this tearing away of one of the great props of his life; it was shaking the very foundations of his existence.

Griffith turned to look at him, searching for signs in his face that might betray the change in him. The boy he had known and loved so fiercely was gone; a man with an inscrutable eye and a certain heaviness about the lower part of his jaw and chin had taken his place. Archie was drumming with his short thick fingers on the table; his forehead was heavily puckered, his eyes troubled.

"That was a pretty serious thing you did over there, Griffith," he said slowly. "I could hardly believe it when my father told me about it . . . How did you ever come to do it?"

"Do what?"

It wasn't possible, Griffith thought, that Archie, himself, would criticize him for selling the mileage books!

"Why . . ah . . . the matter of some tickets you sold. Dad told me they found out you'd been selling transportation and making no account of it . . . ."

Griffith stared at him. New adjustments, new points-of-view were rapidly presenting themselves.

"That's the fact, Mac," he admitted, "but you want to remember the whole bunch of them were grafting: the Traffic Manager, the General Passenger Agent, and all their assistants. Chickering was making thousands of dollars out of it. They were all doing it; even the mailing clerk was taking the stamps. I considered it was my right; a perquisite that went with the job I had. My predecessor did it and the one before him."

"Well that may be so, but for *you* it was downright *stealing!*" Archie spoke heatedly. Griffith gazed at him, more and more amazed at his attitude. They had roomed together for years at college, they had "swiped" chickens and cases of beer together, plundered candy stores, and gone up to their examinations with cribs in their pockets. Archie had not considered those things so reprehensible! They had thought alike regarding them. It was impossible to believe that now Archie really criticized him, and considered what he had done from the same angle as Barondess and his father!

"But Archie, old man, . . . I don't think you understand. Of course what I did was 'stealing' if you want to call it that. I tell you again that everyone else about me was 'stealing' too, and I give you my word that it never occurred to me that I was doing anything really wrong. I mean wrong from your standpoint and mine. I still don't think I have done anything of which I ought to be ashamed before you and David. Selling mileage books is no different in principle from lots of the things you and I have done together. You remember the time we swiped the college insignia out of the Philosophy building, and the time we stole all Mrs. Flannigan's ice-cream, and the photographs of the Anna Held girls out of the photographer's window down in the town, and little Johnny Sweet's bicycle?"

"Those were college pranks, Griffith. Don't talk nonsense! Swiping barber poles isn't stealing. You have robbed a great corporation of hundreds of dollars and it is a state's prison offence!"

"All right . . . all right!" Griffith exclaimed impatiently. "I'm not saying it isn't. We'll admit that; I took money that didn't belong to me and from your father's point of view and Baroness' and Sales' and most people's in general that's stealing and I'm a thief. I don't think I am. I don't think I have done the least thing wrong. And knowing me as well as you do, you ought to agree with me. I resent your condemning me when you are the same person I saw three years ago cribbing your way through that military exam., turning the pages of the manual with your feet, the book hidden under the chair of the man in front of you! That is *stealing* just the same as selling railroad transportation. You thought it was damned cute the way you got through without being caught. If you had, you would probably have been expelled from St. Cloud, and your proud father, who judges me so harshly now, would have had a terrible shock! Where do you get off, Mac? Everyone at college cheated more or less; they do in most colleges. We—you and I—saw the other students cribbing their way through their exams and we followed their example and thought nothing of it. I found everyone in the N. Y., N. & W., grafting on the road and making fat pickings and I saw no reason why I shouldn't do the same. I ran the risk and I got caught and I'm fired. That may or may not be sufficient punishment. That is not the point. What makes me sore is *your setting yourself up to judge and criticize me!*"

"You and I have different ideas about honesty," Archie said slowly. "You are trying to justify stealing by the impulsive actions of boys in college. According to you, a thief who comes along and picks your pocket shouldn't be sent to prison because students sometimes take things which do not belong to them . . ."

"Not at all!" Griffith said, rising in exasperation. "That's just like you, Mac! I'm not justifying stealing. I'm saying that *you* who countenanced what I did at college have no right to switch your point of view. You approved of me then and abetted me; now you presume to censure me."

"Griffith, don't tangle yourself up with words. You have robbed a big corporation. You have appropriated the dividends which should belong to the stockholders, the penny-savers, who have invested their money in good faith. You ask me to consider that that is not wrong! It is just the same as if you had taken money out of the till. Would you expect me to believe you were right in doing that? It is plain theft. It is impossible that you are sincere in supposing I could view the matter in any other way."

Griffith stood looking down at him, and realized the immeasurably separated points-of-view from which they argued. He knew the hopelessness of trying to convince him. Archie never admitted he was wrong. At that moment Griffith knew it was the end of their friendship, and the pity of it filled his heart. His affection for the friend of school and college had influenced him in almost everything he had thought and done during the past ten years. Now the relationship was being ruthlessly broken; it was going crashing to pieces, shattered into many fragments like a vase toppled to the floor. He gazed at him, heavily frowning, overcome by the realization, slowly shaking his head in sadness.

Archie did not understand.

"Your sense of honesty has become perverted, Griffith," he said crisply. "You need a moral doctor, someone to put a little sense of what is mine-and-thine into your head. When you have had time to think this thing over, I believe you will see the absurdity of your argument."

"Perhaps," said Griffith dully; his heart was heavy. "I'll take your advice, Mac; I'll think it over . . . Good-bye, old boy. Maybe we can get together on this thing some day. I'll try to see your point-of-view; I wish you would try to see mine . . ."

Archie shook his head firmly. He had risen and taken Griffith's proffered hand.

"All right, Mac, I understand. I'm not trying to convince you *now;* I'm only expressing the hope that some day you'll look at the matter as I do. Good-bye."

He gripped the other's hand, looked into his dull gray eyes a moment, then picked up his hat and passed out of the paneled mahogany room, out of the noisy office between the shining brass railings, and out into the bright street.

V

He walked up Nassau Street and was at the Bridge before he knew it. One thought occupied him: What would David say? Would he agree with Archie? Or would he consider him, as Griffith did at the moment, a censorious moral prig? He felt he must know at once. David should decide between them.

He found him in a back office at the top of a tall building on William Street. An air of brisk activity pervaded the three rooms in which *The Master Builders* was born each month. The doors between these rooms were open and there was a constant passing to and fro through them and frequent interchanges of loud shouts and answers. Paper in all forms and shapes pervaded the place: there were scraps upon the floor, files of newspapers dangling in racks, galley sheets and soiled proofs on hooks, bundles of magazines tied with fibrous ropes, and stacks of Manila wrappers for mailing. The air reeked with the thick, sweet smell of paste; with it was mingled the odor of ink and cheap cigars.

David sat in his shirt-sleeves at a dilapidated desk in the farthest office, the size of a hall bedroom. A green celluloid shade protected his eyes from the light of the one tall window, and a half-burnt cigar rolled about between his teeth at one side of his mouth. A thick blue pencil over his ear was thrust beneath the stiff wire holding the shade about his head. He was working at furious speed, snipping rapidly with long shears, trimming printed matter from strips of galleys and pasting it down in a rough magazine dummy of stiff paper.

"Sit down, old boy," he said cordially to Griffith. "I'll be through here in about ten minutes. We go to press at three, and they're waiting for their make-up. It's my own first number and you bet it is going to be a Jim-dandy!"

Griffith pushed a pile of trade journals from a chair onto the floor and sat down. David snipped, fitted and pasted, pounding the strips of galley proof fast to the pages of the dummy with resounding bangs of his open palm. Men and boys came to him asking directions or bawled their questions from the adjacent room. The telephone bell rang incessantly.

"Johnson on the 'phone, Mr. Sothern."

Each time he was interrupted, David disengaged his fingers from the handle of the scissors with an oath, and picked up the receiver. A rapid fire of instructions would follow, and the receiver be slammed back upon its hook. Griffith could see his old friend loved it all. The whirr and turmoil, the clamor of demands, were incense to him, the smell of battle in his nostrils.

Presently with a final whack, he pounded the last bit of galley into place, flipped the sixteen pages of rough dummy open in a last cursory examination, shoved it into a large envelope, licked the flap, and scrawled the printer's name on the outside.

When it was gone, he sat back a moment in his tilting chair, and ran his hand over his eyes and forehead under the green shade, as if he wiped away the tension of his concentrated thoughts.

"Well . . . that's the last of November," he said smiling broadly at Griffith. "I tell you what, boy, it's going to wake up the manufacturers and trade unions. I'm going to make *The Master Builders* a *power*. You wait and see!"

He considered the matter a moment further, then dismissed it and brought his beetling brows to bear on Griffith.

"What's on *your* mind?"

Griffith told his whole story as best he could. He began with the day of his mother's death when Leslie had offered him a home and promised to find him a job, and ended with his recent interview with Archie. The recital was difficult, for David was continually interrupted, and while Griffith saw he was intensely interested he saw too that he was conscious of the passing time.

"I can't see why you feel so sore with Mac," David said when he finished with an eager appeal for his sympathy. "Mac is the son of a big financier; money and corporations are the gods they worship; the safeguarding of capital is to them the greatest function of man. If you offend capital, you commit the worst possible offence. It is bred in their bones to look at things that way. Mac doesn't feel any differently toward you. He's defending his gods, that is all. He's your friend just the same as ever."

"Oh no, he isn't!" Griffith exclaimed bitterly. "He thinks I'm a common thief!"

"Oh nonsense! You've got to take your medicine, Grif, old

man. You've got caught with the goods and been shown up. The great Archibald McCleish has done the same thing as you have, but he's gotten away with it. He's honored and respected and he ought to be. Make allowances for human nature, Griffith. Nobody cares how much you swipe from the railroad as long as you aren't found out. It was that way at St. Cloud: when 'Striker' Lewis got caught cribbing, he was expelled, and we all held up our hands and said: 'My—my!' His sin was that he got caught. We went on cribbing just the same. When you are gambling on the chance that you won't get found out, and somebody comes along and shows you up, you have to expect to lose, and lose all along the line. You may not be put in prison but you suffer in public opinion. Success is what is respected in this country. Nobody cares *how* you succeed as long as you do; if you fail, your friends are only too eager to say: 'I told you so' . . . Now you've failed. Take your medicine; shut your mouth and don't go trying to justify yourself in people's minds. Begin over again . . . *My* opinion of you is that you are just a plain damned fool. The mistake you made was in selling mileage books without telling your chief. He is a practiced hand at grafting. He knows his business and would have seen immediately the risk you ran of getting caught, and would never have allowed you to take such crazy chances. You double-crossed him and now you've got to pay the piper. But don't yowl about it. Snap your jaws together and begin all over. If you're successful the next time, the world will be only too anxious to forget how you failed at first, and,—my last tip—stick to one course; don't try to run with the hare and hounds both."

VI

Griffith walked all the way to his brother's apartment—a long distance—and it was late in the afternoon when he reached home. He was disappointed in David. He had hoped to be justified, to have been able to go to Archie and say: "David agrees with *me;* you have no right to criticize me; I have done nothing you can consider dishonest." He saw too, that he had suffered in David's estimation. That lean, lantern-jawed, big-boned friend believed his cynical theory. He had begun to regard Griffith with increasing respect, as his opportunities grew for becoming a successful railroad man, and he took advantage of them. Having failed, having been apprehended for selling the company's transportation to make a few miserable dollars,—and having been "fired" like an office-boy for rifling the till, Griffith had lost David's good opinion. His manner betrayed the fact by presuming to lecture him. A few days ago he had urged Griffith to leave his brother and come to live with himself. He had made no reference to the plan during the recent talk!

Griffith's legs and back were aching and his feet were sore when he pushed open the heavy, grilled glass door of the apartment house. The foyer with its marble and panels of green watered silk, its oriental rugs and florid brass elevator cage which he had at first thought so impressive and beautiful struck him now as being inexpressibly ugly and tawdry. The mauve-uniformed negro boy who sat at the telephone board handed him a letter with a special delivery stamp upon it as he was about to enter the elevator. A feeling of abject despondency swept over him as he took it and looked at the handwriting.

VII

He did not open it until he had let himself into the apartment and had sunk utterly fatigued, into one of the heavily upholstered scarlet satin arm-chairs by the window.

It was from Margaret.

"Dear Griffith:
"You must know how hard it is for me to write you this letter. I am obeying my father unreasoningly and unquestioningly. He tells me you have done something which has angered him; something unworthy. I cannot believe this last. Whatever the circumstances may be, I know there are extenuating ones. My faith in you is not less than it has always been. I am sure you had good reasons for whatever you have done. My father—to whom you know I owe everything—does not wish me to see you again. There is no alternative for me but to obey him. I shall live in the hope that some day he may withdraw his objections or that you will vindicate yourself. Be assured of my continued faith in you and my affec-

tion. Some time this matter will be adjusted and we shall be friends again. I am heartsick at having to write you now when perhaps you need my sympathy and interest more than at any other time. Whatever befalls you, be assured of my unaltered affection and best wishes.
"Ever your friend,
"Margaret Sothern."

Griffith lay back wearily, his head resting upon the satin upholstery, his eyes closed, the letter dropping from his hand upon the floor. He had been subconsciously expecting the disruption of his relationship with Margaret all through the nervous strain of the preceding days of terrible uncertainty. He had instinctively known that Barondess would take every means in his power to punish and hurt him. It was like Margaret to declare her faith in him, but he doubted her sincerity. If Archie censured him, if he had suffered in David's estimation, and Barondess considered him a common thief, these opinions must have their weight with her. How could she believe in him despite such condemnation? She would not add her disapproval to theirs, that was all.

VIII

He was dozing from utter weariness and mental exhaustion, when Leslie's key clicked against the metal of the lock on the other side of the door as he poked about, striving to insert it in the small crooked opening. A moment later the door was pushed open and his brother came into the room.

Griffith saw at once that he had been drinking heavily. His expressionless face was grey-white and he moved with calculating deliberation. He stopped when he saw the boy in the chair by the window, then slowly advanced to the middle of the room, teetering upon his feet. He regarded Griffith a moment before he spoke.

"You said something 'bout going to live with your friend and leaving here on the first of the month . . . Don't think you'd better wait till then. You can go right away; . . . to-night . . . now. Send for your things tomorrow . . . *You're no kin of mine to betray a friend!"*

Griffith did not move; he stared fixedly at his brother, the blood surging to his face. It was a superbly timed moment, he thought in wild bitterness, for Leslie to throw him out. He struggled out of the deep chair and rose to his aching feet.

He strode past the swaying figure without speaking and went down the narrow dark hall to his little room, reaching for his suitcase under the bed. He threw back its lid and began flinging some things into it. His breath quivered, dry sobs rose in his throat. Once or twice he stopped, fiercely struggling to control himself. If he could only get out of the house before he broke down!

He was unconscious of what he did. Anything that came to hand found its way into the suit-case. Presently he was jamming down its lid, trying to force it closed, throwing his weight upon it, cursing between shut teeth. He took down his overcoat from the closet and then paused awkwardly, realizing he had left his hat in the front room. It meant he would be obliged to face his brother again. He wanted to storm out of the apartment and bang the door after him. He straightened himself, grabbed the handle of the suit-case, and stepped out into the hall.

Leslie sat in the chair he had occupied, a newspaper in his hand, his whiskey on the window-sill. Griffith's hat and gloves lay on the floor beside him. For an instant the two brothers were close to one another, Leslie's hand within an inch or so of Griffith's head as he stooped to the floor. Neither spoke; the newspaper crackled a little; the next sound was the violent concussion of the apartment's door.

IX

Griffith savagely pressed his thumb against the electric button for the elevator and held it there. He felt that his control was slipping from him and unless he gained the street within a few seconds, he must give way to his anguish. He heard the elevator boy hurriedly calling up to him through the shaft.

"Yes, sir; yes, sir, . . . I'm comin'."

Then he was in the elevator itself, sliding down past floor after floor, and then the car ceased dropping, and the gate rolled back with a shrieking clang. There was the street outside, and the autumn twilight, his goal and refuge. The brilliantly lit foyer with its gold and rugs and green silk panels, seemed immeasurably long, the time to cross it interminable. His hand was outstretched to grasp the handle of the heavy door when unexpectedly a black figure intervened.

"Griffith . . . Griffith! Just a minute! I *must* speak to you!"

He drew back, gazing at the interloper resentfully and in alarm; it was Clarisse. He swept her face, he looked into her eyes, he saw something there that caught at his soul.

"Oh my God!" he burst out.

She was talking rapidly, a supplicating, feverish, wild tone in her voice.

". . . father said you weren't coming out to-night and he said you didn't seem yourself and you had lost your position with the company and he felt he was all to blame and when I said I just had to come and see you, he said I could. . . ."

"You know I'm fired down there?" the boy asked.

"Yes, he told me. He said it was his fault."

"Did he tell you what for?"

"Yes, something about tickets you'd sold. . . ."

"Do you think any the less of me?"

"Griffith! . . . Why should I?"

"And you still love me?"

"Oh Griffith . . . you *know* it!"

Swiftly he took her in his arms and gripped her to him, hurting her with the violence of his embrace.

"Well, I love you, my girl," he said sobbing passionately, "better than any other God damned person in the world!"

End of Book II

SALT

"Ye are the salt of the earth: but if the salt have lost his savour, wherewith shall it be salted?" Matthew v: 13.

BOOK III

SALT

OR

THE EDUCATION OF GRIFFITH ADAMS

BOOK III

CHAPTER I

I

Just a week later Clarisse and Griffith were married. On the day when all his world rose up in denunciation and cast him forth, he had turned hungrily to the one person who had no thought of blame for him in her heart, who loved him blindly, unreasonably and with complete unselfishness. Affected, insipid and mentally shallow, Clarisse had yet the capacity for great love. He was jobless, friendless, penniless, an outcast from his world, shunned and disgraced, but she wanted him as he was, and several times during the few days which intervened before they were married, Griffith wondered if his misfortunes had not intensified her passion. He seemed now to belong to her alone.

It did not occur to either of them that he should go elsewhere than to her home after Leslie had turned him out. In his desolation, her tenderness and softly whispered endearments opened wide the floodgates of his heart. Alternately pleading his case and bitterly inveighing against those who censured him, he had poured out his misery to her unchecked.

Clarisse's father proved another sympathetic listener. He felt himself entirely responsible for Griffith's dismissal. Adams had lost his job! He had been fired! And just because he had taken his, Rumsey's, advice. It seemed a terrible thing to the old man. He accompanied Griffith's broken, impassioned recital with sorrowful shakes of his head and "tut-tutting" noises with his tongue.

Rita alone had been noncommittal. She had obtained a position in a one act vaudeville sketch which had been in rehearsal for about ten days and was to go on the Orpheum circuit almost immediately. It opened in Chicago, the first of the week. As she would no longer be at home, Rumsey proposed that Clarisse and Griffith when they were married should take the room in the tiny flat which the two girls occupied together. There was no reason why they should move to quarters of their own. Griffith would soon get something to do and their joint incomes would make them all more comfortable than before. They could even have "someone" in the kitchen.

Rita was only mildly acquiescent in these plans. Her enthusiasm for her sister's marriage to Griffith had apparently ebbed. She had changed in many ways during the past year. Her theatrical training had made her undeniably dainty and *chic* in appearance. Her brick-red hair she arranged in a particularly striking manner: it was swept severely off one temple and wound in a series of hard rolls and snug twists at the back of her head. Her hats were of dashing lines and her clothes smartly tailored. Her whole "get-up" was spruce and of studied simplicity. She had always puzzled Griffith, and was more of an enigma to him now than ever. He shared to an extent the awe with which her sister and father regarded her. He sensed her cleverness, and was afraid of her shrewdness.

Yet Rita advanced no definite objections to the marriage. Griffith suspected that his changed expectations readily accounted for the difference in her attitude. He could see that she had hoped for a more satisfactory match for Clarisse. Hemmingway had returned from a trip to St. Louis where he had been studying the breweries, and now resumed his attentions to Rita with renewed zest.

Clarisse confided to Griffith that Rita had suggested Hemmingway might be lured back to his first love, and that he offered a much more brilliant match than Griffith. Clarisse had angrily repudiated the idea, and Rita had shrugged her shoulders.

Despite her calculating ideas in regard to her sister, Rita seemed to have relinquished all thoughts of a rich marriage of her own. She treated Hemmingway with cold indifference. Once she had devoted herself to skilful maneuvering to inveigle him into an offer of marriage; now when he eagerly urged it, she scorned him. She was bent upon making a success of her stage career. She was away from home most of the day and night, studying elocution, singing and dramatic action during the time she could spare from rehearsals.

The wedding took place the day before Rita left for Chicago. It was a simple affair. In the morning Griffith and Clarisse went downtown and obtained their license and at five o'clock in the afternoon, after Rumsey had come home from the office,—he had asked to get off at four o'clock,—the young assistant clergyman from the neighboring Presbyterian Church came in and quietly married them. Besides the immediate family, only Rumsey's sister and her five children were present. Griffith had thought of inviting David, but he knew his friend would come only from a sense of obligation.

Rumsey's sister,—Aunt Abigail, her nieces called her,—was plainly distressed at the casualness of the whole affair. She was fat with enormous hips and, in retreat, suggested nothing so much as a ferry-boat with ponderous side wheels, laboriously propelled. Her five daughters, the oldest of whom was fifteen, and the youngest seven, were merely decreasingly diminutive editions of herself, and watched their mother's face with rigid intentness for indications of her approval or disapproval. Aunt Abigail had arrived in a stiff black silk and certain articles of her daughters' apparel were obviously new. The marriage of her niece—the first wedding in the family—she had anticipated would be an occasion. There had been a general expenditure for gloves, shoes, collars and ribbons; she and her brood had come prepared for festivities. She plainly sniffed at the tea and cake which was served in the little dining-room after the ceremony.

But to Griffith it was sufficient. He was happy in spite of Aunt Abigail's exaggerated politeness, and the graduated row of staring little girls who reminded him of the toy wherein are found smaller and smaller varieties of eggs. His old friends were gone; they had raised shocked and scandalized hands, and had banished him. He determined to accept the verdict. If his friends had repudiated him, he would repudiate them,—not without misgivings, sadness and frequent regrets,—but he no longer wished to be one of them. Among the Rumseys, he was welcome. Even Rita, in her smart black-and-white checked suit in which she was to travel to Chicago early the next day, put her hands on either side of his face and kissed him. He was of their family now, and he was content.

An inventory of his cash, revealed something over a hundred and fifty dollars. He had spent a little for a new hat, gloves and shoes, but with the remainder he determined to take Clarisse down to Long Beach for a few days. After the departure of Aunt Abigail and her family, each one of whom Griffith found he was expected to kiss for the third time, the bride and groom packed their suit-cases, said good-bye to Rita and her father and caught the elevated train for the Pennsylvania station. They decided to have dinner at their hotel, as Long Beach is less than an hour's run from the city. It was exciting and delightful, Griffith thought, starting off with his wife in this companionable fashion. Clarisse looked particularly pretty in a soft, woolly, blue tailor-made suit and a dark blue velvet hat with a turned-up brim and a curling feather. A new feeling of affection for her came to Griffith as he sat beside her in the train. She had stirred him with many kinds of emotion, but it was borne in upon him she was his *wife*. She belonged to him now, just as a few days ago she had felt he belonged to her. The sense of the relationship, his ownership, thrilled him.

There had been nothing concrete in the idea of marriage before. It always had seemed to him merely a tie which hampered a man's movements, doubled his expenses, and greatly increased his responsibilities. It had never entered his mind he received anything in return. There was something exhilarating in the thought of possessing a wife. It gave him a feeling of importance. He thought:

"Gee! It's kind of fun to be married. . . . Won't David and Mac be surprised when they hear about it. . . . She's a trusting little creature to go off with me this way."

His chivalry was awakened. He discovered there was pleasure in catering to her and in looking out for what made her comfortable. He remembered experiencing similar sensations when he had fed his rabbits as a little boy. They had eagerly eaten the lettuce leaves from his hand and it had delighted him. Now he liked to watch Clarisse drink the coffee and nibble the toast he ordered for her. It was pleasant to see her enjoy the comforts he provided. She purred like a kitten to his petting and his care.

The close companionship was wonderfully surprising too. It was luxuriously delightful to sleep with her until late in the morning, to breakfast together in bed, tub and dress leisurely and then saunter out on the Boardwalk or lie in the sand, watching the waves and the bathers until ready for a late luncheon.

She still made banal comments, affected a lisp, arched her neck and sometimes pouted, looking with soulful eyes reproachfully at him. But these things somehow did not irritate him as they had once. They all registered; but her excessive affection made up for these shortcomings. He revelled in her tender demonstrations. It was amazing that any human being could love him with such unquestionable sincerity and ardor. Ever since he was a little boy, he had hungered for affection and now it did not seem he could get enough of it.

During these first days of their honeymoon, he conceived for her the nickname of " 'Rissie."

II

While he was at Long Beach, he had written a brief note to David telling him of his marriage, and when they returned to the city on Wednesday, they found a silver and cut-glass water jug with a note from him wishing them luck. There was a sweet letter, too, from Margaret, some roses, and a crate, full of excelsior, containing a dozen china plates. A long pasteboard box from Tiffany's disclosed a tall sterling silver vase, three feet high, to which a card was attached by a tiny bow of red ribbon. On it was written: "Best wishes for your wedded happiness from your friend Archibald McCleish, Jr."

Griffith understood perfectly what different motives had prompted these gifts. Clarisse wrote letters of thanks immediately on her scented note-paper. They took Archie's vase back to Tiffany's and exchanged it for seventy-five dollars' worth of plated knives, forks, different sized spoons, cellarettes, carvers, and a soup tureen with a tiny cow as a handle to the cover.

There were other wedding gifts. Rumsey gave Clarisse credit slips on a linen house and on an importer of European laces, supplementing these with a twenty-dollar bill. Rita treated her sister to *lingerie*. Marlin, the young stenographer, sent a silver pie knife, and there arrived from Aunt Abigail a wooden plaque, tinted green, supported by a brass chain, on which was inscribed in illuminated and ornate lettering:

"Pretty good world with its dark and its light,
Pretty good world with its wrong and its right,
Sing it that way and you'll find it all right,—
Pretty good world, good people!"

Best of all was a cheque for two hundred and fifty dollars from Clarisse's maternal grandfather, who ten years before had put what profits he had made in groceries into the automobile business and was now a rich citizen of Detroit, where he lived with a married daughter. The Rumseys always spoke of Grandfather Ambrose with extravagant affection.

"He's such a dear old man," Clarisse said, joyfully, fluttering the cheque through the air. "You can always count on his doing something handsome. Mother was his favorite child; I was named after her."

It represented a bank account, if they decided to start one, but it was more amusing to lie abed in the mornings, and plan how they should spend it.

"We ought to have this room done over anyhow, Griffith," Clarisse said, gazing at the spotted, discolored ceiling. "The landlord won't do a *thing* and I'm tired of staring up at those swimming fishes. The wall-paper is awful. . . . And then I could get some furs this winter! Oh Griffith! I've never *had* any furs!"

"Don't you think we ought to save some of it, 'Rissie?"

"Oh . . . I suppose so. But we *must* have this room done over . . . and I simply have *got* to have a new hair-brush!"

"Well, I guess those things won't break us," Griffith laughed. "We can blow ourselves to that extent!"

Presently he said:

"'I've got to be hustling about to find a job pretty soon."

He was thinking about his father-in-law, who had departed for the office over two hours ago. Usually Rita or Clarisse, clad in a somewhat soiled wrapper, her hair dangling about her shoulders, and held back from the face by a single hair-pin, had risen when their father did and, while he dressed, had made his coffee and toast and set them out on a corner of the dining-room table. Now he ate his breakfast at a restaurant. Clarisse had slept soundly through her father's breakfast-time the first morning after they had come home, and since had made no effort to get up. Griffith wondered a little but said nothing. After the honeymoon was over, they would all settle down to a routine. He must soon start out to find a job, and then he would breakfast along with his father-in-law, and leave the house at the same time. Clarisse could manage their simple breakfasts and when his salary justified it they could get a maid. For the present he was living in an idle dream, happily content to let the days drift along heedlessly. He was languid, tired, indifferent, dulled to any energy, voluptuously listless.

He and Clarisse did not rise till eleven o'clock and it was afternoon before they were fully dressed. They would go to a neighboring "Tea Shop" for breakfast and luncheon combined, and often loiter over their food until after three o'clock. Sometimes they wandered into a "movie" or if it was warm, they would climb to a top of a bus and ride down Fifth Avenue. But there was always the necessity of getting back in time to cook dinner for Rumsey, when he came home from the office.

"It's *such* a bother!" Clarisse complained. "Rita always managed, and she knew just what to do. I haven't ordered yet and there isn't *one single thing* in the house! . . . Do you suppose we could afford a *table d'hote* again? It saves all the fuss of dishwashing! Oh *let's* Griffith!"

Frequently they did. Rumsey pursed his lips and uncomplainingly went along. He was kind-hearted and not exacting. After all, it was their honeymoon and they were entitled to as much enjoyment as they could get out of it. Time enough to worry about the future.

III

Griffith decided to wait until the first of October before beginning to look for a job. He had not the slightest idea where one might be obtained, but Rumsey offered to give him letters to some of the firms he had favored in the matter of the rebatement of charges on excess baggage of their travelling salesmen. Long before the first of the month, Griffith became uncomfortably aware that the two hundred and fifty dollar wedding gift from Grandfather Ambrose was almost half gone and there was nothing to show for it. He was at a loss to account for so much of it. They had gone to the theatre once or twice, he had bought a couple of shirts and a dozen collars, and Clarisse had acquired her long coveted hair-brush, but that was all. The rest had been dissipated in dinners and late breakfasts, in tips, stamps and carfare. Clarisse considered it her privilege to appropriate any loose change she might find on the bureau or lying about, and he had seen many a dollar bill he had broken for a ten-cent purchase disappear in this fashion. But a hundred and twenty dollars!

On a raw, windy fall day, armed with three letters from his father-in-law, he started out in quest of a job. As he went downtown alone on the elevated, staring into the thousands of windows that flashed past, he felt as if he was emerging from the dank humidity of a heated greenhouse into the chill penetrating air of a bleak winter's day.

Here was the fever of the streets again: the clamor and hurry, the very smell of them! Once more he was engulfed in the rushing tide; once more he was a part of it; everything spun round him: the confusion and the noise, the confusion and the noise, the confusion and the noise! He felt that for many days his senses had been befogged by thick mist. He shook his head impatiently as if freeing himself from it.

"There's nothing here. We're full up. I don't know of a concern in our line that's doing any business these days; we're all laying 'em off!"

"Had any experience with laces? No? Well . . . er . . . we haven't any vacancies just now. It is a dull season."

"Sorry. Can't do anything for you. We've got a hundred applicants waiting."

Griffith stood at the edge of the sidewalk, blinking in the pale sunshine, the wind whipping his light overcoat about his legs. There had been nothing equivocal about the answers he had received from the men to whom his father-in-law had sent him. What to do now?

It was lunch time and he found himself near the restaurant where he had so often eaten with Archie. He turned away and sought another; he did not want to run the risk of meeting his old friend. He ate in a saloon and decided to look up Swezey at the New Metropolitan Hotel.

Swezey had heard he had left the railroad and was full of the curiosity of an old employee about the office where he had once worked. He asked innumerable questions and quite forgot the object of Griffith's visit.

Tired and disheartened Griffith went home about four o'clock to Clarisse who flung her arms about him and strained him to her, covering his face and head with her quick, burning kisses, quite consoling and comforting him by her fervent and tender affection.

The following day he went downtown again and presented two other letters from his father-in-law, but he met with no better success. He called on Mr. Pope of Blashfield & Pope but found him politely discouraging. At one o'clock he telephoned Clarisse and half-an-hour later, in a wild, hilarious mood, she met him at the foot of the "L" stairs at Forty-Second Street and they went to a matinée together. Griffith was made a little uncomfortable by her silliness; he felt she was attracting attention.

The week passed. Rumsey had exhausted his knowledge of business houses to which he could give his son-in-law letters. The old man began to worry; when he came home at night he was full of anxious queries. Jobs were scarce. When a man had one it was a wise thing to hold on to it. He had been repeatedly tempted, he told Griffith again and again during these days, to quit the N. Y., N. & W. and take another job where he could make more money. He had always refused and had stuck to the old company. He knew plenty of clever men,—cleverer than he!—making such changes, who had lost their new positions almost at once and had been out of work for a year or more! His faithfulness would be rewarded some day. If Chickering was ever promoted, they'd make *him* A. G. P. A.

Griffith listened attentively and smiled inwardly. He liked his father-in-law; Rumsey was always good-natured and kind-hearted; he was never in the way at home! But even Griffith knew someone other than the limping Chief Clerk would be made A. G. P. A. in such a contingency.

He was nettled enough over his own problem. His father-in-law's solicitousness annoyed him. It might be difficult for *Rumsey* to get a job if he ever lost the one he had! But he, Griffith, was only twenty-six and had been four years at college. He felt confident of his ability to do many a high-salaried clerk's work better than it was now being performed. It was humiliating for a man of his training and brains to go about begging for work.

Invariably he was asked what experience he had had, or what were his qualifications. The question vexed him. People ought to know a college man's fitness. One did not have to have special training to hold down a desk job! Thousands of clerks in New York were running big departments who had never had more than a High School education and who knew nothing about the amenities of social intercourse. Griffith was ready and willing to work hard; he asked only the opportunity to show what he could do. He was no "gilded youth" who was afraid to roll up his shirt sleeves and "pitch in," nor had he any bad habits that could militate against him. It was inexplicable and baffling, this persistent refusal to give him a chance.

He caught his father-in-law studying the "want ads" in the newspaper one Sunday morning and the discovery exasperated him. He vented his anger and humiliation in a tirade to Clarisse. His wife began to weep, and Griffith, moodily staring at her, thought what a brainless, silly, soulless creature she was. He put on his cap and overcoat and took a long walk alone through Central Park. When he came home late in the afternoon, Clarisse wept some more, and hugged him, twisting her arm about his neck, kissing him with tearful clinging kisses, stroking his hair and cuddling in his arms. They were unusually happy going to bed, later. A mild frolic ended in a mad chase through the little flat. They began throwing water at each other and Griffith squirted a siphon bottle through the keyhole of a door, drenching her beribboned night-gown. Their shrieks of laughter brought protesting thumps, upon the intervening wall, from the next apartment.

IV

But Griffith came down to studying the "want ads" in the newspapers himself before the end of the next week, and in three or four days, he mustered up courage to answer some of them. Salesmen—salesmen—salesmen! "An attractive proposition for any bright young man not afraid to work! An easy fifty dollars a week for the right party!" Hopefully, Griffith would apply. Usually he found a score of down-at-the-heel, dark pocket-eyed men ahead of him. He would turn away sick at heart. He could not bring himself to take his place in their motley group.

Tin-ware, safety-razors, oil-lamps, grass-mowers, flower seeds, vermin exterminators, varnishes, portable houses, accident insurance, window cleansers, cement, poultry, surgical instruments, cigarettes, canned fruits, fire extinguishers, books,—poetry, home medical libraries, dictionaries and standard sets,—furnaces, candy, photographs, vacuum cleaners, rubber heels, chewing gum, soap, tires, patent medicines, fountain pens, watches and—pianos!

Pianos! There was an idea in that! He could play the piano! He knew something about music!

His mind sped back over the years to Professor Horatio Guthrie and his scrawled instructions to *Count* between the staves of the music. Well, one thing he had learned might be turned to use now in his effort to earn a living.

The next day he applied at the music department of John Wanamaker's store. The fat, jolly manager was inclined to give him a trial. Had he any references? Griffith thought of Archie and dismissed it. He knew too well how Archie would weigh the matter: could he conscientiously state that Griffith Adams was honest and reliable?

Griffith suggested David and his father-in-law.

A day or so later he was notified to report the following Monday morning; he would receive ten dollars a week and a ten per cent. commission on whatever orders he secured.

On the appointed day he arrived at the store punctually at eight o'clock. A package of cards was handed him. On each appeared the name and address of a person who had made inquiries about pianos at one time or another. The cards were soiled and obviously had been a good deal handled. All the addresses were in Newark. Griffith gazed at them rather blankly.

"Aren't there any people right here in New York City I could go to see?"

The manager smiled.

"Our city territory is the best we have, young man. The salesmen who have that divided among them have been with us a number of years."

"But I thought my ability to play the piano and demonstrate its tone would be a great help to me?"

"Well, you can't carry a piano along, can you? Invite the people you see to come here to the store and you can give them a recital. We'd *all* like to hear you play."

V

Griffith arrived in Newark a little after ten o'clock. Doggedly he inquired his way about the strange city. A long street-car ride to the first address resulted in the information that the "parties" who had resided there had moved away. Tracing the second to another quarter of the city, he found a yellow placard nailed to the porch railing on which appeared in large type the word *Diphtheria* with a notice of quarantine by the Board of Health. The third address took him to a Chinese laundry, and the fourth to a brick-faced house with pea-green shutters where a pleasant-faced woman who opened the door told him that Mrs. Gillespie had not lived there for ten years. Still he persisted. A maid informed him that no one was at home; children playing in the front yard cheerfully stated that "papa was dead"; a Scandinavian servant failed to understand his English. Late in the afternoon he finally succeeded in locating one woman for whom he inquired, only to be told she had purchased a Ford instead of a piano. He gratefully discovered then it was twenty minutes to five and wearily he turned his steps toward the dusty and crowded station and waited for the next train back to New York.

He did not go out of the house next day, persuading himself he had caught a cold. The day following was drizzling rain and Clarisse had little difficulty in inducing him to stay at home. On the third morning he made a neat package of the bundle of cards and mailed them to Wanamaker's. Swallowing his pride he went to see David.

VI

He could find no fault with his friend's cordiality. It disarmed him completely. David was full of interested questions: What did he mean by sneaking off that way and getting hitched up without letting anyone know? How did he find married life? Was it all it was cracked up to be? When could he come out and make the Missus' acquaintance? How was he getting along anyway?

Griffith thawed under his friendliness. He told him as much about Clarisse as he thought would interest him, but did not urge him to come and see them. David would look askance at his wife, he knew, and he had grown to feel sorry for Clarisse as well as sensitive about her. She was all right when you got to know her; her heart was as big as "all out-doors"; people would always misjudge her and there was no need of parading her up and down for their criticisms. They did not mention Archie but Griffith remarked on Margaret's letter, her roses, and her wedding gift, while David nodded his head, frowning a bit, and said: "That's good."

Presently Griffith spoke about a job. At once the other was all alert interest, one eyebrow elevated, the other depressed, in the way characteristic of him since their early school days together.

"You want a job, hey? Well, now let's see. What do you know? What would you *like* to do?"

Griffith described some of his efforts to land a position. David nodded, accompanying his recital with an encouraging murmur.

When he had finished, David offered no comment. He thought hard a moment, his eyes roving restlessly under his contracted brows.

"Well now, . . . what you want is something that will give you enough to live on. I suppose twenty a week is as little as you can accept, although with your father-in-law contributing, you might get along on fifteen if the opportunity justified it. . . . You've had no business training except what you picked up while you were with the railroad. Of course none of us ever learned anything in college. . . . Well, I suppose you wouldn't like trying to get a job on the elevated or subway? It pays better than anything I know of, for unskilled labor."

"You mean as a conductor?" Griffith asked in a level voice.

"Yes, . . . a guard."

"I might try," he said slowly.

"There isn't a thing I could give you here," the other said thoughtfully. "We pay the folders and addressers only six dollars a week, the girl who runs the mimeograph gets eight and the mailing clerk gets twelve; the cashier gets eighteen but you don't know anything about books!"

He paused scowling, biting his under lip. Then he threw up his hand and brought it down, smartly upon his knee, leaning toward Griffith eagerly.

"Say, would you mind soliciting subscriptions for me? You can make real money at that if you'll work at it awhile." He began to speak rapidly. "Our subscription price is two dollars. We've got to get the carpenters and masons on our books. Look here: we give this art portfolio of reproductions of the world's masterpieces in painting, this book of Home Medicine, this brass-edged four-foot rule, and this neat little pocket memorandum book, all with *one* subscription to *The Master Builders*. I'll pay you a dollar commission for every subscription you get. All you've got to do is to look up the carpenters and masons in the telephone directory and go call on 'em. Walk straight up to 'em and tell 'em who you are . . ."

David talked on, fired with his own enthusiasm.

"You ought to get from five to ten subscriptions a day. That will average you thirty-five to forty dollars a week!"

Griffith slipped samples of the premiums in his pockets, tucked two copies of *The Master Builders* under his arm, equipped himself with a pencil and receipt book, made a list of carpenters and masons, and started out.

He soon became aware that the men he sought were not at their shops but out on building jobs. He followed them to where they were at work. As he began speaking to a white-overalled bricklayer with a young friendly face, the foreman interrupted him and ordered him off the premises. He had the same experience elsewhere. At one large brick building where there were a number of men at work, he waited until the whistles blew the noon hour, but they all crowded into a neighboring saloon where a free lunch was served and stayed there until one o'clock. Completely discouraged he went back to David's office. Being a guard on the subway was better than that kind of work.

He was surprised and relieved when David accepted back the premiums and receipt book good-naturedly.

"I thought after you went out of here I had put something pretty stiff up to you. You haven't the temperament to make a man give up two dollars he doesn't want to part with. I'll keep my ears open, Griffith; I'll try to get something for you."

THE EDUCATION OF GRIFFITH ADAMS 265

VII

And David kept his word.

The following afternoon Clarisse was ironing a silk shirt-waist on the kitchen table, and Griffith was cleaning the drip-pan which slid underneath the gas burners of the stove, when a boy arrived with a note.

"Dear Grif: Trumbull & Priestman, 156 Fifth Ave.,—large mail-order book concern—are pushing a big proposition. See young Bert Trumbull at once. I think he can use you. Luck!
"D. W. S."

At a quarter to five the same afternoon Griffith walked into the noisy outer office of Trumbull & Priestman. Five minutes later a brisk, clear-eyed, sharp-featured young man came out, shook him by the hand, and asked him to come back with him to his office.

The air hummed with the buzz of typewriters; row after row of tables, piled high with stacks of mailing matter, flanked on either side by nimble-fingered girls, filled the long room from one end to the other. There was little ventilation. A fine dust choked the atmosphere, and there prevailed the unpleasant smell of many warm bodies in a close room.

Trumbull and Priestman were selling by mail a *Compendium of the World's History*, a twenty-five volume work compiled from the writings of noted historians. They were circularizing on an enormous scale, advertising the fact that the price of the books would advance on a certain date. Their present predicament was that they had run short of names. Someone with discrimination was wanted to read the directories of the principal cities in the United States, check off the persons who appeared responsible, and who might be interested in a great educational set of books. The telephone directories were not sufficiently comprehensive; a thorough canvass of the large towns was wanted. Did Griffith understand? Was he acquainted with other cities besides New York? Did he know the residential districts? He was familiar with Boston and Chicago, and had spent a few weeks in San Francisco and Los Angeles? Well, that was fortunate. They would pay twenty dollars a week. When could he start in?

CHAPTER II

I

GRIFFITH went to work the following morning for Trumbull & Priestman. An ink-stained, rickety table was cleared for him in a corner of the office of one of the "ad" writers and a boy brought him a pile of city directories. Bert Trumbull explained precisely how to discriminate in the long columns of names and Griffith settled down happily to his tedious job. It was deadly uninteresting work; he was obliged continually to bring his wandering thoughts back to the finely printed page; sometimes the type ran together in a gray blur; sometimes a wave of drowsiness passed over him; but he kept at it. It was a job, and it gave him an amazing feeling of satisfaction to be a wage-earner again. When he went out to lunch he felt he was once more back in the ranks; he was earning a salary again. He went home to Clarisse that night with a light heart.

II

A few days later Rumsey brought the news of Chickering's resignation from the N. Y., N. & W. He had not been at the office for over a month and all important matters had been referred to Sales. It was rumored that Chickering had gone to Europe.

Griffith's father-in-law was permitted to enjoy the dream of his own promotion to the post of A. G. P. A. for a brief three days, when the catastrophe which was to wreck his life fell with the directness and the blinding suddenness of a bolt of lightning. He found upon his desk one morning, a brief typewritten notification:

"Your services as an employee of this company are no longer required. The termination of your employment will take effect on the last day of November.

(Signed) "Theodore Sales."

THE EDUCATION OF GRIFFITH ADAMS

Every clerk and stenographer in the Passenger Department received a similar notice. Griffith was particularly sorry to hear that even Polly was dismissed. All were given less than a month's time to make what arrangements they could for themselves.

Rumsey's bewilderment and distress were pathetic. He would not accept the fact; it was inconceivable that they would turn him off in such a casual way. On the day he received the notice of his discharge, he came home an hour earlier than usual, bursting to impart his news, to amaze his daughter and his son-in-law with the unbelievable calamity that had befallen him, impatient to hear their exclamations of incredulity and indignation. When Griffith reached the flat at nearly six o'clock, he found Rumsey pacing the floor, his arms waving, his thin hair in disorder, while his daughter, sitting in a corner, her head buried in her hands, was convulsed with tears. His father-in-law swung around toward him, placed both hands upon his shoulders and, slowly wagging his head up and down, announced impressively:

"The corporation to which I have given twenty years' devoted service, my boy, . . . has *fired* me!"

The story poured forth in a passionate stream, accompanied by excited and vehement gestures. Constantly he turned to Griffith and Clarisse for confirmation of his statements. Habitually mild, unexacting and good-natured, he was transformed into a being who raved and railed.

Some curious chemical change began to take place in his brain from that day. The old man did not go to bed during the night. Griffith, rousing from sleep, disturbed by the noise of his movements, saw a thin streak of light beneath his door. There was a perceptible change in his face in the morning. The skin above his sandy beard was ghastly, blue shadows rimming his eyes. Griffith never heard him again express resentment. He grew moody and silent, brooding over the injustice he felt had been done him.

As the time drew nearer when he no longer would be Chief Clerk, a look of dismay came into his face. The fear of being unemployed began to take acute possession of him. To be dependent, to be beholden to someone else for his lodging, his clothes and his food! That dreadful terror had pursued him ever since he could remember, and now it threatened to become a reality. The wheel of fortune had swung around and the revolution that had carried Griffith into a job, had thrown Rumsey out. In less than a month their positions were reversed. As Rumsey had blamed himself for Griffith's dismissal, so the boy felt responsible to a certain extent for the old man's discharge. He had told Sales all about the graft prevailing in the Department and though he had not mentioned the Chief Clerk he had said that petty thievery existed everywhere, that even the mailing clerk appropriated stamps. The innocent had suffered with the others. Rumsey had had his own methods of peculation, it was true, and may have deserved his fate, but there were Marlin, and the other stenographers, and —above all—there was Polly!

Griffith spoke to Bert Trumbull about Polly. There was always room for able, intelligent girls in the mail-order business; they were cheaper than men. He succeeded in awakening that shrewd young man's interest, and Griffith was told to write her to come and see him. Her answer was a relief. She had had no difficulty in securing another position where—she knew he would be glad to know,—she received half again as much salary. She appreciated the kindness which had prompted him to write her and begged to remain, etc.

But nobody wanted Rumsey. He had not been in the employ of the N. Y., N. & W. for so long without making a great many friendly acquaintances. On the first day of unemployment, the old man got up as usual, ate his breakfast in his silent and melancholy manner, and left the flat at his ordinary time. When Griffith arrived home in the evening one glance at his face told the unsuccessful history of his day: a weary, fruitless passing from office to office, endless waiting on hard benches, the renewal of old acquaintanceships, the same story and the same plea repeated over and over, the same rebuffs, the same discouragement.

It was so day after day. The experiences of his futile pursuit did not vary, the baffled expression on his face became more set. After five in the late winter afternoons he would come limping up the stairs and, with hardly more than a nod to his daughter, would sink into a wicker chair by the window. Rocking slowly back and forth, his hands idle in his lap, their palms up, he waited until he was disturbed. He always greeted Griffith when he came in. They said little to one another but they were conscious of a bond of sympathy. Both knew what it meant to be out of a job.

III

One evening when Christmas was everywhere in the air and the first snow of the year was falling, Griffith came home to find his father-in-law sitting in his customary rocker with his overcoat still on, a forlorn and pitiable figure, huddled forward, his head drooping, his hands lying listlessly on his knees, his sparse hair sticking out over the collar of his coat. Griffith helped him off with the garment and went to find Clarisse. He heard her crying in her room. When he opened the door she was prone across the bed but she struggled instantly to her feet and threw herself into his arms.

It was the first hard pinch of poverty. There was no money to buy gifts! There was not enough even for the necessities. She wanted to "do lots of things" for Christmas, and there wasn't a penny she could spend! The laundry boy had been rude and she was tired of everlastingly buying kidneys and sausage! If father didn't get something to do, she couldn't stand it!

Griffith tried to console her. He went into the kitchen to help get the dinner. Confusion spread itself everywhere about the room. The unwashed breakfast things lay in a tumbled pile in the dish pan, while the sink was full of greasy pans and sooty pots from the previous day's cooking. The top of the kitchen table was covered by a conglomerate collection of odds and ends of food, and kitchen utensils, beside some yellow soap, Clarisse's comb and a pair of her high shoes half finished in the process of polishing. On one partly cleared corner, a half empty glass of jam, some cracker crumbs and a cup containing a few tea leaves showed where she had lunched. The floor was littered with orange peels, a piece of grocer's cord, several balls of paper and a long line of white blots where milk had spilled and been allowed to dry. Under the sink, its lid only partly covering its overflowing contents, stood the unemptied garbage bucket. On a chair seat, lay three parcels still wrapped in paper and tied around their middles with two or three turns of string indicating that at least the materials for the dinner were in the house.

At sight of the disorderly room, Clarisse burst out crying again and sank her head against her husband's arm. Griffith gazed about hopelessly. The kitchen was generally topsy-turvy but he had never seen it in such confounding confusion. A feeling of weariness and despair seized him. Was this what marriage meant? Was he in for this sort of thing all his life? Had he been trapped? He knew that criticism would merely bring a flood of tears, and would accomplish nothing. They were in trouble enough without his wife lying down on her job! In quick irritation he turned to her.

"Good God, Clarisse! I can't understand how you can be so slovenly! Your father's in there waiting for his dinner and you haven't got a *thing* started!"

The girl slid to her knees beside him, sobbing bitterly.

"I knew you'd be cross," she wailed. "I don't know how to do things. Rita *always* managed!"

"Well, Rita isn't here now, and you must *learn* to manage! We've all got to pull together and you must do your share."

"Couldn't we . . . couldn't we go out and get something to eat?" the girl said, catching her breath between sobs.

"No, we can't," Griffith replied emphatically. "That costs money and we haven't got it!"

"Oh . . . oh . . . oh," she moaned, "you're so *mean* to me!"

Her husband swore. He looked down at her savagely, and considered the idea of leaving her in the midst of the disordered kitchen and taking her father out to the corner saloon, where some sort of a hot dinner was served in the back room.

"I should like to ask what the deuce you've been doing all day?" he demanded.

She bowed her head upon her clasped hands, struggling to find her voice. A ridiculous figure she seemed, kneeling there in the doorway of the untidy room.

"I . . . I meant to start things about four o'clock but I fell asleep. . . ." Her words ended in a wail.

Griffith made an exasperated noise with his lips.

"My God, 'Rissie; . . . don't yell that way! Take a brace. There's no good crying like that. It doesn't get anything cooked!"

His wife rose to her feet shakily and blew her nose.

"I can't get along on so little money," she said, her breast still heaving. "I used to have twenty-five dollars to spend each week and what was over was my own. Now I have to get along on less than ten and feed three people. It can't be done, Griffith; at any rate *I* can't do it."

"We've been over all this before. There's forty dollars' rent due on January first; I've got to put that aside. You must do the best you can on the rest until your father is working again. I don't know what *else* to do! If we run in debt, we can't help it. . . . Come on, now, . . . what have you got for dinner? Kidneys? That will take too long; save 'em for tomorrow. I've got half-a-dollar and I'll go get some chops. Clear up your sink and shove some of this mess off the table. Let's get things started. If the dairy's open I'll try to get half-a-pint of cream on tick; make us some coffee, good and strong. Is there anything else you need?"

IV

Many similar scenes took place between Griffith and his wife during these and following days. By the first of the month, a little sheaf of unpaid bills had accumulated in his inside coat pocket. Rumsey's gloomy, despondent figure was depressing, a constant reminder of their problem. It was inevitable that Clarisse and Griffith should quarrel; they got on each other's nerves and formed the habit of cherishing resentment. The time came when the stoop-shouldered, halting old man was obliged to ask his son-in-law for "a little change," and, a little later, when Griffith was obliged to refuse his request because he did not have it.

Clarisse made an effort to be systematic. If dinner was sometimes half-an-hour or an hour late, there was at least a dinner under way when the men arrived home. But often the beds were still unmade and rarely Griffith found the bath-room in order. Lines of brown sediment along the sides of the tub marked the height of various soapy baths, and nests of dust and dirt collected in the cracks and corners. Water-bugs thrived everywhere. Over the vent in the kitchen sink there was invariably a little collection of refuse,—seeds, wet crusts, tea leaves, burnt matches, ends of string, kernels of stewed corn and chips of egg-shells. Griffith protested; Clarisse met his objections with the indifferent assertion she could not bear to touch the mess.

"It's too *ikky*, Griffith. That's one of the things I can't bring myself to do. You have to scoop it up with your fingers and I just simply can't do it."

Clarisse was an excellent cook when she put her mind to it,

but she could not remember to do things when they ought to be done. She forgot continually. She forgot to send the wash; she forgot to order sugar; she forgot to get more coffee; she forgot to put the garbage on the dumbwaiter when the janitor sent up for it; she forgot the time; she forgot all about the beds; she forgot to put the potatoes on to boil so they would be ready in time for dinner; she forgot about dinner.

Griffith rebelled at first; it disgusted and angered him. He would not have minded for himself so much, but to see Clarisse's father hungrily waiting an hour for his dinner or drinking his coffee black because there was no condensed cream, or to hear him asking for something on which to wipe his hands because there were no towels, made him ugly with resentment. He consoled himself with the thought that a smash must come sooner or later. There was no incentive to buck against his wife's slipshod methods. Things could not go on much longer as they were.

The weeks dragged on. Early in February both butchers in the neighborhood indicated by their curt manner that it would be better for Clarisse either to pay her account or transfer her patronage. Griffith was obliged to take half the month's rent he had saved, to satisfy one claim and obtain the meat needed for dinner. He had long ago given up eating anything substantial for lunch. He contented himself usually with a piece of pie and a glass of milk, but he needed meat at the end of the day; his body craved it.

V

One morning he sat on the side of his bed, dully considering a small hole in the sole of one of his shoes. It was freezing cold. His head was aching and he felt sluggish and wretched. Clarisse had gotten up in the night and closed the window. The air in the room was foul. Outside the noise of shovels scraping briskly against stone sidewalks announced there had been a heavy fall of snow.

Clarisse still lay in bed, eyeing her husband meditatively. Griffith knew she wanted him to speak to her, but he did not feel inclined to say anything pleasant. He drew on his worn shoe and stooped over to lace it.

"Griffith!" his wife said sharply.

Owing to his constrained position he could do no more than answer her with a grunt.

"Griffith," she repeated, "I think I'm caught!"

He straightened up and looked at her. They gazed at one another silently, Clarisse compressing her lips, Griffith frowning. Then the woman passed her hand over her forehead, and sighed heavily.

"I'm in for it all right. . . . I'm a week over time and I'm sick this morning. Yesterday I thought maybe it was so, but I hated to speak about it. . . . My God, . . . isn't it *fierce!*"

Griffith continued to stare at her. He was marvelling a little at the mystery of life. Her condition would be an additional complication; it meant doctor, hospital, nurse and medicines! He had only a vague idea just what the coming of a baby entailed, but he realized a great calamity had befallen them. How in the world were they ever going to manage now! It was a great misfortune! Poor 'Rissie!

What did people do? What did they do? What did they do? He kept asking himself the question the rest of the day. There *must* be *some* way out. It was terrible to be crushed out of life this way. One trouble after another was being piled upon him! It could not be borne!

At school when he had been hounded and hectored beyond all endurance, he had won his deliverance by turning and biting his persecutors. He felt much the same way now; he was desperate.

He went home at night, anxious to hear how the day had gone. Clarisse was miserably despondent. She hated the prospect of the long nine months of incapacity, the ordeal which awaited her at their end, and the exacting care and burden that a child required afterwards. She had felt wretchedly all day.

They discussed an abortion. It meant a doctor's fee and perhaps an operation,—neither knew exactly what,—but anything was better than the prospect of a child. Old Doctor Harris, who lived in the neighborhood, had been the Rumseys' physician for years. Clarisse decided to consult him in the morning.

Griffith's father-in-law listened to their discussion without comment. He had grown more silent and gloomy of late, and for long hours would sit, hunched forward in the wicker rocker, saying no word, showing no interest, staring moodily at the floor, his hands lying inert on his knees, the palms up. His daughter and her husband came to act and speak before him as if he were not present. Griffith knew he was borrowing little sums here and there among his friends to keep himself going. All his vitality seemed gone. He was simply an old, broken man who daily grew more convinced that his usefulness was over, that his existence was a burden, his thoughts and advice of no consequence.

Griffith and Clarisse realized afterwards that they had ignored him at dinner, and during the evening as they talked over the important issue they faced. Griffith had said:

"It will cost an awful lot of money . . . and I don't see where it's going to come from. We simply *can't* have a baby now!"

And Clarisse had wailed:

"I *won't* go through with it! It's another mouth to feed and clothe and . . . and . . . I haven't the strength."

In the morning Rumsey was gone.

Griffith went to his door to tell him they would be obliged to breakfast together at some restaurant, as Clarisse was too sick to lift her head from the pillow. When the old man did not answer his knock a sudden feeling of terror seized him. He flung the door open and found the room deserted. A pencilled note on the torn fly-leaf of a book was propped up against a collar-box on the bureau.

"My dear daughter and my dear Griffith: I am going to try my fortunes elsewhere. Iglehart promised me the other day a loan on my insurance policy. I shall avail myself of this for awhile until I get a position. Do not worry about me. I will write you within a few days. Maybe I will go to Detroit where I feel sure your grandfather will find something for me to do. He would be very proud of a great-grandchild. Love to you both. If I get settled I will remit occasionally. Good-bye and God bless you.

"Father."

A feeling of having been treacherously deserted came to Griffith as he read the note. He had been fooled, forsaken. He and his sick wife had been abandoned. He must face the situation now *alone!*

Clarisse's cheerful acceptance of the news, however, was disconcerting.

"Don't worry about father, Griffith; he'll be all right. If he goes to Detroit, Grandfather Ambrose will get him something to do. I wonder we didn't think about his insurance before. It would have saved us all this trouble. We could have raised a couple of thousand dollars on it! Just *think* of it!"

"How much is it?"

"Oh I don't know; five thousand, I guess. He's carried it since he was married and ten years ago he took out some more. . . . Shut that window, Griffith, . . . the smoke from that chimney blows right in!"

"Do you want me to make you some coffee?"

"Oh *no,* thanks. Just let me alone!"

"Shall I call up Doctor Harris?"

"No, I'll see him this afternoon at his office."

As he stooped over to kiss her good-bye, she said:

"If I can get rid of this . . . this trouble, we might have some fun again, Griffith, now that father is gone. Perhaps we could manage now."

"Sure, 'Rissie, . . . you tell Doc Harris to fix you up."

"Oh leave it to me. He's *got* to! . . . I wonder we never thought about that life insurance!"

"Well, I'm glad we didn't. Your father's earned all the money he's paid out in premiums. It's all *his* anyway."

"He might send us a hundred or so . . . yet!"

But Griffith hoped he would not. Several times during the day he was conscious of a lightening of his load. He was amazed to realize how much his father-in-law's jobless existence had preyed upon him. A great weight had fallen from his shoulders.

He found Clarisse in bed, when he got home, despondent and miserable, her pillow wet with angry and hopeless tears, her eyes swollen, her head aching violently. Griffith tried to comfort her, but she would not be consoled.

Doctor Harris had given her a regular lecture, scolded her as if she had been a little girl! He had crossly refused to aid her in the way she suggested. He had given her some medicine to take in the morning to help her nausea and told her a number of things she must do. She had come home furious, and having heard that a hot mustard foot-bath was efficacious in bringing about the results she desired, she had defiantly fixed one and had scalded one of her feet badly. She raged at her helplessness and vented on Griffith all her tumultuous, rebellious emotions.

He was surprised at her heat.

"Good Lord, 'Rissie!" he exclaimed. "It's hell, I know, but what can we do about it!"

"Do! Do! Nine months of wretchedness! I won't go through with it! I won't *have* it!"

Her anger changed suddenly to passionate grief.

"You don't love me like you used to, Griffith! You'd stand by me if you did! You wouldn't let me be so miserable!"

She was more tractable in this mood.

"I'll ask around, 'Rissie. I'll ask some of the boys down at the office if they know a good doctor. Perhaps Bert Trumbull can help me; he's a wise one."

Presently he discovered she had had nothing to eat all day. There was no food in the house; the kitchen was in confusion and smelled of the unemptied garbage pail.

He insisted on her getting up and going out with him for dinner. He went down to the drug store on the corner and bought some headache pills, which he persuaded her to take. Presently she felt better and an hour later in the cheap restaurant to which they went, after she had taken her thick oniony soup and was picking at her chicken, she declared she felt actually happy.

Both of them were carried back to the idle, care-free days of their honeymoon. As they talked, the prospect of a child did not seem so terrible; it was a great nuisance of course and must be avoided if possible. But Griffith, pondering the matter, said to Clarisse:

"Did you ever stop to think, 'Rissie, that all the people in the world came that way? Gosh, think of all the women who've been mothers!"

"Well I know one woman who's not going to be one," she commented firmly; "not on your life!"

They strolled back to *The Myrtle* about nine o'clock. At his suggestion they tackled the disorder in the kitchen together, and by eleven o'clock, had the row of five rooms comparatively clean and tidy. The little suite belonged entirely to them now, and it was a satisfaction to feel that it was all their own domain.

VI

An evening or so later old Doctor Harris unexpectedly dropped in on them. He had a heavy, curling, gray beard that lay on his prominent chest like a thick, dry sponge. He was bald except for two clusters of tight, gray curls about his ears. He was stout and his cheeks were firm and fat, and curved out over his beard like the halves of a shiny apple. Gold-rimmed spectacles straddled his large nose and he wore a long frock-coat and a white vest that was a little soiled around the openings of the pockets. He had brought both Clarisse and Rita into the world.

He talked for an hour, and what he said he emphasized with small slaps of his finger-tips on the palm of his hand. When he left, Clarisse was crying, but Griffith was thinking hard. After awhile he went over and sat down on the couch beside her, putting his arm about her.

"Are you sure you wouldn't like to have a baby, 'Rissie? I kind of think you'd be crazy about it after it came. They're fun when they grow up."

"Oh no . . . no . . . no," she moaned. "I—don't—want—any baby."

"Well there's a lot in what Doc Harris says . . ."

"He's an old fogey!"

"Nonsense, 'Rissie! He's a man with a lot of common sense; and he's mighty fond of you!"

"It's just one of his hobbies. I do all the suffering! It's all very well for him to say we ought to have a child; he sends his bill in just the same! I don't see how we can afford it; we're terribly in debt now . . ."

"It isn't going to cost so much! He says he'll only charge twenty-five dollars and he knows of a hospital where they'll take good care of you for ten or fifteen dollars a week!"

"A baby costs an awful lot after it's born," Clarisse persisted.

"Twenty dollars will buy all the clothes it can wear in a year . . . and it doesn't cost anything to feed. Doc Harris said . . ."

Clarisse refused to be convinced. She shook her head and cried into her handkerchief.

"Well what *else* are you going to do?" Griffith exclaimed, impatiently. "It will cost more to have an operation. Besides, it's damned dangerous, and it's malpractice, and against the law!"

"Oh . . . oh!" sobbed Clarisse. "I wish Rita was here."

VII

The next week Griffith determined to move into smaller quarters. His wife drearily agreed. She was hounded by the tradespeople whenever she went out and dared not answer the door-bell. She could no longer order by telephone, and was too miserable to walk as far as One-Hundred-and-Twenty-Fifth Street where purchases could be made for cash. The rent of the five-room apartment was twice what Griffith felt they ought to pay. There was no chance of their catching up as long as they remained where they were.

The following Sunday, he made a list of what might prove to be possible quarters for them from the "Apartments-to-Let" column in the morning paper. He spent the day, wandering from one section of the city to another, interviewing janitors, climbing long flights of stairs, examining endless suites of deserted rooms, each more dismal than the last. But late in the afternoon, weary and footsore, he found a new apartment house on St. Nicholas Avenue, which seemed to offer just what they required. It was a large concrete building composed of two, three, four and five-room suites. A two-room apartment with bath and kitchenette could be rented for twenty dollars a month. The kitchenette was no more than a closet at one side of the dining-room. Two wide folding doors disclosed a gas stove, a miniature porcelain sink, a tiny ice box, a cupboard of little drawers, a series of shelves and rows of shiny brass hooks. A round pendant electrolier of art glass indicated where the dining table was to stand within arm's reach of the kitchenette. In the other room, by opening a closet door a wire frame work and springs of a bed slid from concealment. When the bed was pulled down, a four-foot aisle on its three sides was all the space that remained. The bath-room, which was tucked out of sight behind the kitchenette, was the smallest Griffith had ever seen. He decided he could sit in the tub by drawing his knees well up under his chin.

But to him it represented a home where the problem of living could be whittled down to its finest point. There was no place for dirt to gather in that mass of steel and concrete. The halls suggested tunnels, burrowing their way into the solid grey block, the doors were of metal painted to resemble wood, the electric bulbs were protected by frosted glass. A three-inch stream of water could have been turned down any of the passages without damage.

VIII

Griffith realized from the outset that he would be obliged to borrow in order to move. He knew he would have no difficulty in obtaining the money from Archie. Utterly repellent as the idea was to him in the beginning, it persisted in recurring, until finally he found himself entertaining it seriously. He would have preferred to go to David but David had not the funds, and he even considered Leslie, but he felt he had accepted his brother's generosity in the past with too little appreciation. Archie would gladly lend it. He would not admit himself ever to have been in the wrong, but he knew he had seriously offended Griffith. A loan would help square matters between them. It was humiliating to ask for it, but Griffith no longer cared what Archie thought.

Yet when his old friend came forward from behind the huge mahogany desk of the Secretary of the Johns-Mandrake Company and gripped his hand and caught him by the forearm, the affection Griffith had borne him for so many years flamed up. Mac was a good fellow all right; they had been through a lot together; they shared some wonderful memories.

Griffith hurriedly explained the reason for his visit. He wanted Archie to know at once it was necessity, not friendliness that had brought him to his office. He remembered that the man before him had disapproved of Clarisse, had urged him not to marry her, had offered to provide money to buy off her claims if she had any. Recalling his wife's miserable figure stretched out under the tumbled bed covers, her face white and drawn, half hidden by thick masses of disordered hair, it struck him as excessively cruel that this rich, powerful, robust young magnate should have used his influence to oppose whatever hopes she might have cherished. Poor little 'Rissie, who had never harmed anyone! He was glad he had curbed his impulse to respond to the warmth of Archie's greeting.

"Why . . . *certainly*, Grif!" Archie said, interrupting his recital. He pulled out a drawer and flipped open his cheque book. "Don't mention it. I'm delighted to accommodate you. How much do you want? Five, six, . . . seven hundred?"

"Three hundred will be all I need. I'll repay you just as soon as I'm able, . . . and I want to add six per cent. as long as I keep the money."

"Tush! Don't be foolish!"

"Thank you very much."

"Oh, nonsense . . . I'm really glad you're getting on all right . . . Clarisse well?"

"Pretty well, thank you. I'm really greatly obliged to you for the loan."

"Please, Grif, . . . don't mention it. If you need any more just let me know."

"You're very kind, Mac."

There was a silence. Griffith tried to think of something to say which would prolong the conversation, but what occurred to him seemed forced. He stood up awkwardly; Archie rose too and they shook hands.

"Well, good-bye, Mac; I'm ever so much obliged to you."

Archie did not answer immediately, and Griffith noticed there was something he was trying to say.

"I suppose you've heard from David about . . . about Margaret and me."

Archie's face flushed; he was uncomfortably embarrassed. Griffith's expression changed into a broad smile as he caught the other's meaning. He tried to make his pleasure appear genuine; he wrung Archie's hand forcibly.

"Well . . . that's fine work, Mac. Gee . . . that's fine work! My heartiest congratulations! I always knew you two were made for one another. I'm *awfully* glad. When . . . when is the happy event?"

"In June."

"So soon? Well, that's certainly great. You and David will be regular brothers-in-law! Gee! I'm glad!"

But the smile dropped from his lips and there was black death in his heart, as he walked out between the shining brass railings of the outer office into John Street.

Archie and Margaret! Archie and Margaret! All the old

jealousy came flooding back. Oh, where was the justice in life that gave Archie McCleish everything and himself nothing! It was not right. Wealth and power and success and now the loveliest girl in the world! Yachts and motor cars and luxury and comfort, a country estate, a luxurious town-house! Everything for which his own heart craved! *Why* should it be so?

Margaret Sothern was to be Margaret McCleish! The pang of that! God, it wasn't *fair!*

Her husband-to-be, her brother, her adopted parents, she, herself,—they all knew he loved her. Perhaps they wondered why he had married, but they knew his heart was hers—and always would be. They talked about him among themselves. What did they say? What did Margaret say? He swore fiercely as his thoughts raced.

Oh, to go away for many years and come back a multi-millionaire, far richer than any of them, with Clarisse a cultivated woman who had travelled extensively, who knew European society intimately and could stare at them coldly! Damn them! He could see Archie and David and Margaret together sadly shaking their heads and one of them saying:

"Poor Griffith! What a mess he made of his life! He'll **never rise** above that unfortunate marriage."

Damn them! He'd show them!

CHAPTER III

I

THE move to the Selwyn Court Apartments was accomplished with surprising ease. Some of the furniture was sold to a second-hand dealer, some—together with a few battered old trunks filled to their lids—was sent to Aunt Abigail's attic.

Spring was everywhere. The sun shone without interruption, the trees were bright with their clean foliage, the grass took on a more brilliant green, the birds warbled and shrilly piped, the tulips in the window boxes of the hotels and the formal beds of the parks bloomed in violent colors. Clarisse, experimenting with the compact little gas stove, hummed happily to herself, and Griffith, lolling by the open window in the one wicker arm-chair they had permitted themselves, was aware of a peace and contentment he had not believed possible.

But his tranquillity and ease of mind were of that hour only. Clarisse's morning misery did not abate. She could not raise her head from the pillow when she woke or do more than murmur feebly a few words to Griffith's solicitous inquiries. Frequently he found her still in bed when he came home in the evening. Newspapers and underwear were strewn over the floors and chairs; his dinner was cooking in a rocking saucepan on the gas-stove, a napkin spread on the little round table and adorned with a three-sided square of a knife, fork and spoon, indicated where he was to eat it; the air was heavy with the odor of bedding and hot steam. Clarisse did not want any dinner. No, she wouldn't take even a bite; she didn't care for a *thing*. She had managed to make herself a cup of tea about four o'clock and had persuaded the elevator boy to get her a quarter of a pint of cream and a bag of chocolates. Griffith would find his own dinner right there. There were some Saratoga chips and some cottage cheese in the ice-box. Did he like cottage cheese? It looked kind of good in the delicatessen shop. She had saved him a little cream for his coffee and his frankfurters ought to be ready in a minute or so.

She just wanted to be let alone; she had had a perfectly *terrible* day; a man never knew what a woman suffered.

Griffith did not complain; he felt intensely sorry for her. She had neither religion nor philosophy to sustain her; she was motherless, and 'singularly destitute of friends. She felt her physician and her husband had failed her, and contemplated with terror the ordeal of agony which awaited her. He was powerless to aid her, clumsy and helpless. Again and again he tried to reach her tormented spirit with a sympathetic word. She had become in some way remote, mysterious. He went about the two rooms, picking up her clothes, gathering the newspapers, straightening the disarray upon her bureau. He ate his dinner, washed and put away the dishes. At nine o'clock he would sit down beside the bed with the evening paper and read whatever interesting items he could find, holding the sheet to catch the light from the electrolier in the next room.

Sometimes he was able to coax her to go out with him, and they would walk over to Broadway to grope their way to vacant seats in the darkened interior of a "movie" theatre. But Clarisse usually demurred at the trouble of dressing. Her corsets had begun to hurt her and it was too hot to cover up their absence with the only coat she had, which was heavy.

Once a week, sometimes oftener, Doctor Harris came to see her, bringing with him a fine smell of carbolic acid. He scolded her for not taking more exercise and patted her hands affectionately, as he listened to her complaints. Later he put her on a strict diet and frightened her into sticking to it.

II

One Monday morning early in June, a touch of extreme heat gave ominous promise of a hot summer. Griffith had slipped out of his coat and hung it on the chair-back, when Bert Trumbull leaned over his shoulder as he checked his way down the Joneses of Cincinnati, and asked him to come into his office. Uneasily, Griffith obeyed; such an invitation usually was the preamble to dismissal or promotion.

"We're going to shut down on the History, Adams," he said soberly. "We decided at a meeting last Friday it wasn't worth plugging any more. I guess people aren't interested in history. Summer is almost upon us and I've been instructed to shorten sail all along the line. The girls all go this week . . . I wish I had some work I could keep you to do . . . there isn't a thing."

"Yes, sir," Griffith said, mechanically.

"Let's see, . . . you've been with us . . . how long?"

"I came the middle of November."

"That's . . ." Trumbull paused counting on his finger-tips. "That's seven and a half months. Suppose we give you an extra week's salary on Saturday." He looked up inquiringly.

"You mean you won't need me after this week?"

"Well . . . I'm afraid not!"

Griffith shut his jaws tight and tried not to alter his expression. He had a swift vision of Newark's dirty streets.

He nodded without speaking and made his way back to his ink-stained, rickety table. He opened the bulky volume in front of him and gazed unseeing at the gray columns of fine type. He was out of a job again! He would have to start over! Clarisse would be sick all summer!

The glass door of the office was jerked open and Bert Trumbull's face reappeared.

"Adams!" He beckoned with a quick backward motion of his head and retraced his steps.

"You got a wife, haven't you?" he demanded when Griffith again stood beside his desk.

"Any kids?"

"In November," Griffith answered laconically.

"Humph!"

Trumbull swung around in his chair, looked out of the distant window and swung back.

"You'd like a job, hey?"

"Yes . . . I . . . I'd like a job."

"Particular?"

"I don't understand."

"Are you particular what you do?"

"No; I'll tackle anything."

"Can you take dictation? Shorthand?"

"No . . . I'm sorry . . ."

"Can you run a typewriter?"

"I used to fool with one at college. I'm pretty rotten at it."

"Well, could you write down fast in long-hand what a slow old man said, and then copy it on a machine and make up what you'd left out?"

"I guess so; I could try."

"Can you play pinocle?"

Griffith's brows contracted; he was puzzled.

"A little . . . I *used* to play it."

"Cribbage?"

"Yes."

"You like games? Checkers and backgammon and chess?"

"I don't know chess."

"You could learn it, hey?"

"I could try."

"Do you think you could read the newspaper out loud to an old man?"

Griffith smiled.

"I daresay I could do *that.*"

Bert Trumbull paused and revolved again in his chair.

"I think you might do," he said meditatively. "I tell you, Adams: Did you ever hear of Ira Quay? Ira Winterbottom Quay? He's my great-uncle, about eighty years old. He was very prominent here in the city thirty years ago, made his pile in the wool business and he's got so much money he doesn't know what to do with it. He's a curious old duffer but personally I like him first-rate. He has two daughters who will get all his cash when he dies, but he won't let 'em come near him. He's no fool, Uncle Quay isn't. He doesn't say much, because he thinks an old man is a general nuisance, but he's as sharp as a steel trap. Nothing gets by him. He don't like women; won't have one 'round him. He lives in a roomy old house on Madison Avenue, and keeps four servants: chauffeur, butler, cook, valet, . . . all men. He had a secretary but he got mixed up with a woman, . . . it was in the papers, . . . and the old man fired him. I had a telephone message from him a week ago; he wanted to find out if I knew anyone who could fill the place. I couldn't think of anyone then, but it has just occurred to me that you might like to take a chance at it. He pays well: twenty-five dollars a week. What he really wants is someone to talk to; there's no work to be done.

He dictates about two letters a day. He'll ask you to read the 'Sun' to him in the morning and the 'Post' at night; he likes pinocle, cribbage and checkers; nearly every day he takes a trip to his bank or to the business of which his son-in-law, W. A. D. Trowbridge, is now president. He'll expect you to go along with him and help him in and out of his limousine. There's nothing to the work; the hours are long, that's the only trouble. He'll want you to stay in the evenings and play cribbage with him until he goes to bed; he always turns in 'round nine o'clock. He has to have you all day Sunday, too; he hates Sunday and tries hard to keep himself amused. He'll give you a day off once a week, however . . . I think you'd like Uncle Quay. Want to go talk to him?"

"Sure," Griffith assented, a little dazed and uncertain.

"You can go up and see him now, this afternoon. There's no sense in your reading any more directories. I'll telephone and see if he's home and tell him you're coming."

Ten minutes later Griffith was walking in the direction of Quay's home. He hardly knew whether or not he liked the prospect of the position Trumbull described, but anything was preferable to going home and having to tell Clarisse he had lost his job. There would be five dollars more a week, twenty a month! They could save that; he'd send it to Archie; they could be out of debt in a year!

III

Ira Winterbottom Quay lived in a dignified brownstone house near Fortieth Street on Madison Avenue. It was one of those old-fashioned residences in that neighborhood which had definitely declined to surrender to the encroaching advance of the tall steel structures which year by year threatened to displace them. Trade like an on-coming rushing tide, beat around their feet, persistently undermining their outer bulwarks. It roared upon their backs from Fifth Avenue, it boiled mad and seething along Forty-Second Street, it foamed up, booming and thundering from below. Office and doctor's buildings, antique furniture shops, interior decorators' establishments, auction galleries, hotels, picture dealers, and the first venturesome interloper of that enterprise which eventually would complete their rout, the *modiste,*—hemmed them about on every side. There were some six blocks of these old dwellings. Every few months a defection occurred in their ranks, their number grew less and less, but the remainder stood like a squad of veterans, battered and dusty, but still vigorously defiant.

There was a high iron fence with gilded spikes about the areaway in front of Mr. Quay's residence. In its center ten square feet of dusty grass, close-clipped, advertised the care which was expended upon it. Stone steps rose precipitately to the shiny-black mahogany door which sat back in a shallow marble recess at the top of the flight. Grill work of wrought iron protected the long glass panels in the door which were covered on the inside with dark gathers of crimson silk. The brass of the knocker and doorbell shone brightly. The stone flagging underfoot teetered beneath Griffith's weight.

A solemn-faced butler with a blank, impassive expression opened the door. He showed Griffith into the darkened parlor where he had time to get only a fleeting impression of bulky furniture in Holland linen, great pictures protected by white mosquito netting, and heavy hangings sheathed in long brown cotton bags, before the man returned to say that Mr. Quay would see Mr. Adams in his library.

Ira Quay was a little man, almost weazened. He was startlingly emaciated and his face was the color of spotless ivory. There was a slight indication of eyebrows but the rest of his hair had disappeared. His skin was stretched tight across the bridge of his thin nose, his cheek-bones and forehead, and shone when he moved his little round head like the polished sides of a billiard ball. His neck suggested the throat of a picked fowl and his hairless eyelids which were darkly discolored, opened and shut like a parrot's. His lips were thin and yellow but there was no sign of puckering about them, and his eyes were as black and as bright as two jet beads. His hands were long and bony, the knuckles greatly enlarged, the finger-nails tarnished. He wore a purple dressing-gown of heavy brocade, a starched linen collar with small wings, a flat, white "made" ascot tie, and a felt skull cap that resembled a fez.

At the end of an hour Griffith took the long slim claw in his own healthy brown hand, wished Mr. Quay good afternoon, and walked out of the solemn old house, convinced he was to become the secretary of one of the shrewdest and strangest old men he had ever known.

IV

"Part of his brain knows that the rest of his faculties are impaired," he said to Clarisse, chatting with her comfortably as she struggled over the broiling of a steak in the gas oven. "He knows he isn't as keen as he was once but the part of his mind which understands that, is as sharp as ever. He wants to guard himself against slips. He believes all old people should be killed,— put out of the way. He says they have no economic value and are generally terrible bores. He pays salaries and wages to the people who live with him, for putting up with his idiosyncrasies, and he feels, when he is alone in his house, he can be as cranky and opinionated as he pleases. When they can stand him no longer, they can leave. He's lived in that house all by himself for forty years. He allows his two married daughters to come to see him only when he invites them, and then he always gives them the finest kind of things to eat and drink, so that they will be sure at least of a good dinner in return for the trouble of coming."

"I don't like that about your being down there until nine o'clock at night," Clarisse complained, sprinkling salt liberally from a canister upon the sputtering steak.

"Well, it's only five nights a week at worst, and he says that often some other old man comes in to see him, or he has a dinner party and then I can go home early."

"Does he expect you to eat with the servants?"

"Of course not. He says he wants me to lunch generally with himself, or if he's engaged, to go to a restaurant; I'm to eat my dinner out as well. At the end of each week I hand him an expense account."

"I could come downtown sometimes and have dinner with you, couldn't I?" his wife asked.

"Certainly. It's only a temporary job, 'Rissie; it will do till I get something better."

V

If he had dreamed the new position was to be a sinecure he was soon disillusioned. Ira Quay was both critical and exacting. He treated Griffith usually with the courtesy of an equal, but there were times when he spoke to him as to a servant. He was neither genial nor interesting. He was what he feared himself to be: a testy, tiresome old man. Occasional flashes showed what he had been thirty years before: an intense, purposeful, grimly determined personality, ready to make any sacrifice to gain his ultimate ends. Griffith liked him best when they played parchesi or rum or cribbage together. He was roused at such times to a spirit of competitive endeavor, particularly if an advantage over him had been gained in the game.

Frequently in the evenings, and sometimes during the day, while he was being read to, he would quietly drop off to sleep. Griffith would look up from the newspaper to observe the pallid round head fallen back against the high upholstered back of his deep-seated chair, his mouth slightly open, the thin lips stretched tight across his false teeth, his discolored lids, dark blue like a parrot's, closed over his beady eyes. He might remain so for an hour or longer. No one dared to wake him. Griffith would wait idly, reading the balance of the paper, trying to interest himself in some handy book or magazine. This drowsiness often overcame Quay half-an-hour before the time for Griffith's departure, and he was obliged to wait patiently until his aged employer woke up, and sent for his valet to take him upstairs to bed. The moment of awakening struck Griffith always as grotesquely comical. The dark lids fluttered over the unseeing eyes, there was a quick intake of breath, a sudden jerk of the shrivelled body, the mouth suddenly widened displaying the false teeth. Then with almost a convulsion the old man awoke, swiftly adjusting his displaced molars with a simultaneous motion of jaw and hand.

VI

Margaret and Archie were married on the eighteenth of June. It was an important social event. At the time the engagement had been announced, Margaret's photograph had appeared in the newspapers and society magazines. It was a particularly charming picture of her, Griffith thought, with a collar of rich fur meeting her hair,—a soft oval frame for her lovely face. Everywhere she was referred to as the *fiancée* of Archibald McCleish, Jr., son of the railroad magnate, who was himself already a significant figure in the financial and social worlds.

Both of them wrote asking Griffith and Clarisse to the wedding. There was to be a church ceremony at St. Bartholomew's and afterwards an elaborate reception at the Barondess home. Griffith was touched by their notes; the written words rang true and he felt there was genuine affection for him in both hearts. Archie said: "I won't feel I'm properly married unless you're there to see me through."

He considered going to the reception, as well as to the church, till Clarisse expressed an eager desire to accompany him. Clarisse's figure had already begun to change but Griffith had bought her a coffee-colored wrap for which she had begged, and it was pretty enough, she declared, to wear to any function no matter how "swell." She could get a new hat cheap at that time of the year and she'd just *love* to go! He could have brought himself to the point of enduring the reception alone, but not in company with his wife. He knew she would simper when she met Margaret, and look reproachfully at Archie as she held out her hand stiffly to him, asking him dramatically why he had not been to see them. She would gaze about the assemblage under affectedly lowered lids, step mincingly from room to room, pick with elaborate daintiness at whatever refreshments were served, assuming a languid, bored expression hopelessly transparent. He could not permit her to make herself ridiculous before his old friends. His face flushed and his spirit rose indignantly, as he imagined the discussion about her afterwards. It would not be fair to allow her to court sneers and disparagement. 'Rissie'd learn some day. She'd come back after a few years spent abroad, and he and she would entertain Mr. and Mrs. Archibald McCleish, invite them to dinner and show them that Mr. and Mrs. Griffith Adams knew what was what as well as they.

He decided to forego the reception, but take Clarisse to the church.

Far from obtaining good seats as they had hoped, they were

fortunate in being able to find any at all, for Griffith was fifteen minutes late in meeting Clarisse, as his aged employer had had a brief nodding spell after luncheon.

A strange young man in a perfect-fitting frock coat, with pearl gray gloves upon his hands, and a tiny bouquet of lilies-of-the valley in his lapel, came toward them and hurried them into one of the back pews. Griffith gazed into his face, his heart contracting. He was one of Archie's ushers, presumably a close friend, yet Griffith did not know him. He had read the list of names in the paper and recognized only one; that was Crittenden whom he had not seen since his first years at St. Cloud. Young Horace Mandrake was another; the rest were De Peysters and Van Rensselaers,. youths with names indicating only too clearly, Griffith thought bitterly, the class of Archie's new intimates. Of course the "best man" was to be the bride's brother. Griffith could imagine how uncomfortable David must be in his new tailored clothes, and how unhappy and nervous generally.

The organ was humming softly, a fine blending of small noises filled the church. The air was heavy with the fragrance of lilies.

"I'm going to be sick, Griffith," Clarisse whispered. "Why can't they open some windows? That perfume is making me dizzy."

Expectancy pervaded the gathering, the bobbing flowered hats of the women suggesting a florist's shop. Presently there was a diversion. Griffith, looking toward the centre aisle, saw Mrs. Baroness in a stiff grey silk, advancing self-consciously upon the arm of a stout gentleman toward the reserved pew at the front of the church. Immediately behind came Archibald Walter McCleish, tall and dignified, his forearm crooked about the white-gloved hand of Archie's mother, his two daughters each accompanied by her husband following dutifully, stepping primly, their eyes downcast. A hush, a tense moment of suspense ensued when everyone suspected a delay, then suddenly the organ boomed out the first impressive chords of the wedding march.

Griffith stood up with the others. Craning his neck and raising himself on his toes, he could see two white faces at the far end of the church by the chancel rail. Archie and David; there they were! And it was he who should be standing there by Archie's side, he who had always been Archie's chum; everyone knew they had been inseparable from boyhood.

He turned, holding his breath. The bridal procession had begun its slow progress down the aisle. He saw Crittenden, now with a small mustache, and the memory of the day he had come down to their freshman boarding-house looking for Archie came back sharply. Deliberately the ushers advanced, pausing at each step; one, two,—there were six of them, dandified, gray-gloved, elegantly groomed. Here were the bridesmaids. There was a perceptible murmur of admiration among the women, a general quick in-take of breath. The bridesmaids' gowns were of pale, pink tulle over apricot taffeta, the hats, basket-shaped, a mass of baby roses and pink ribbon that hung in long streamers to their knees. Then came Barondess and the bride.

Griffith could not see her face; the white veil hid it, and her head was bent; she leaned upon her father's arm as if grateful for the support. Far behind her stretched her white satin train dragging heavily upon the carpet of the aisle.

Griffith could neither see nor hear distinctly what followed. He was able to distinguish the priest's voice rising and falling grandiloquently, and above the soft purring of the organ, he recognized the faint whine of violins.

Clarisse clutched his arm.

"I'm going to be sick, Griffith. Take me out . . . quick!"

He looked at her skeptically, but there was no mistaking the deathly pallor of her face. Swiftly he reached for his hat beneath the seat.

"Will you excuse me please," he said to the couple occupying the end seats in the pew. The woman glanced curiously at Clarisse; the man stepped out into the aisle to allow them a freer avenue. As they left the church, the congregation with much rustling and commotion got down upon its knees.

VII

The marriage of Archie and Margaret was a hard experience for Griffith. The smouldering embers of regret and longing leaped up again in flame. The old rebellion returned, sharper, more poignant than ever. During the months when necessity had driven him, when the needs of Clarisse and her father, the exigency of securing immediate employment, had occupied all his thoughts, there had been no time to think of other things. But now,—for all his smug self-righteousness and stupid obstinacy,—Griffith realized how deeply he loved Archie,—and Margaret was as dear to him as ever. In the event which had united these two, he had had no part, no phase of their life together would he share; a door was shut between them. Clarisse was Griffith's portion! They would say among themselves that *she* had been his choice, that he had turned his back upon them, had not even come to the wedding reception though they had invited him so cordially!

Good God! If they only knew!

It was impossible to hide his depression from his wife. During the evening after the wedding she suddenly laid her head down upon the dining-room table and burst out crying. Concerned and sympathetic, Griffith came around to where she sat and put his arm about her. Her grief, he supposed, was caused by her condition, but she pushed him away angrily, and rose to her feet, tears streaming from her eyes, her lips quivering.

"I know *now*," she cried passionately. "I know *now!* You can't fool me any longer. You've *always* loved her. It's . . . it's always been her! You married me because . . . because . . ."

She choked and sank again into her chair, burying her face in her napkin, giving way utterly to her tears. From the muffling folds across her mouth, Griffith caught the words:

" . . . because she . . . because they wouldn't have anything more to do with you!"

A long, wretched wrangle followed. It was a difficult subject to argue with her, for her accusations were true. More than once he was almost driven to the point of admitting them but he caught himself in time, fearful of the infinitely more tragic scene it might precipitate. There was no end to her tears and reproaches. Determinately, wearily, he refused to reply to her. He tried not to hear her but again and again her phrases reached his consciousness with their sting. He finally sprang up, seized his straw hat, and banged the door of the apartment behind him.

He walked the streets until midnight, abandoning himself to unhappy thoughts. When he tip-toed back to their little two-room home, the lights had been snapped out and he thought Clarisse was asleep. He undressed in the dark, and when he was ready for bed, put out his hand, carefully feeling for his wife's figure in order not to disturb her. His fingers met her up-stretched arms and sobbing afresh, she drew him down to her, smothering him in her embrace, pouring out wild self-accusations, beseeching his forgiveness.

"Oh dearest . . . dearest . . . dearest," she wailed, "you're the kindest, the best husband a woman ever had!"

If doubts returned to her, she did not express them. Griffith never mentioned Archie's or Margaret's name again and spoke of David rarely.

VIII

One evening it was almost eleven before he reached home. Quay had fallen asleep after dinner and had remained so for such an interminable time that Griffith in desperation had dropped a heavy book upon the floor beside his chair. It had been efficacious, but the old man had awakened with such an amazing spring that Griffith felt certain he suspected the trick.

He found Clarisse waiting up for him, eager to discuss two things which had occurred during the day. She had received a letter from her father. He was in Detroit, and Grandfather Ambrose had obtained a position for him as time-keeper in one of the motor car factories. He received twenty-two and a half cents an hour, and worked ten hours a day. He had found a nice place to board and was comfortable, but was not especially well. The company's doctor thought he ought to go to a warmer climate. He intended to stay where he was until November, and then thought of going to Los Angeles, where he hoped to get rid of his cough.

The other unusual happening had been a call from Jack Hemmingway, who had come to find out where Rita was living. Clarisse had explained that her sister was playing a forty-week engagement on the Orpheum circuit, and that the last she had heard from her was from Spokane over six weeks before. Hemmingway declared he knew all about the theatrical engagement, and had corresponded with Rita while she was in the West. He had a more recent letter from her dated Chicago, and now he knew she was in New York. He accused Clarisse of refusing to tell him where she was living, and she had been quite unable to persuade him she was telling the truth. He had appeared excited, or as Clarisse described him, "kind of crazy." He had told her he must see Griffith right away, and not knowing what else to do, she had given him Ira Quay's address.

The following morning, while Griffith was reading the market quotations to his employer, the impassive butler brought Hemmingway's card to him. Griffith went into the library.

He had no particular liking for this acquaintance, whom he had not seen since his marriage, but he was curious to learn what he wanted of him, though not disposed to be too cordial.

"Look here, Adams," Hemmingway said brusquely after they had perfunctorily greeted one another. "I want to ask you an out and out question and I want a straight answer."

Griffith's mouth twisted dryly but he made no answer. He could see the other was agitated. Intense nervousness betrayed him; his arms, legs and head were in constant motion.

"I want to know where Rita Rumsey is?"

"My wife said *you* claimed she was here in New York," Griffith answered deliberately. "I haven't the slightest idea where she is."

Hemmingway glared at him, obviously debating whether or not to believe him; his manner was annoying.

"You have no idea where she is?" he repeated.

"I said I had not."

The other still hesitated, slowly thumping the arm of his chair with his closed fist. Suddenly he dropped his head into the palm of his hand.

"My God, Adams, . . . I love Rita Rumsey!"

Griffith's heart instantly was stirred; his sympathy aroused.

"I . . . I'm sorry," he said awkwardly.

Hemmingway looked up quickly.

"Why do you say that?" he demanded. "Why do you say you're sorry?"

The intentness of his manner was disconcerting.

"I don't know," Griffith said vaguely.

"What did you say that for?" Hemmingway persisted.

"Why, . . . I don't know," he repeated. "I suppose the way you acted made me think that . . . that . . . well, that things weren't going all right."

The other glared at him under contracted brows.

"*You* know what the trouble is all right," he said slowly. His voice rose in passion:

"By God . . ."

He did not finish. He gazed menacingly at Griffith, his fists knotted, his face working.

Griffith stood up with impatience. This kind of a scene could not go on in Quay's house.

"I must ask you, Hemmingway, to get a grip of yourself. I don't know what you're driving at; I shall be glad to help you if I can. Either be frank with me or . . . excuse me."

At that moment Griffith felt conscious of a strength and dignity that were new to him. Hemmingway, too, was aware of them.

"I'm a fool, I guess," he said, drawing a weary hand across his forehead. "I tell you I'm crazy about that girl. If I've got any chance with her, I want to know it."

Griffith sat down again and leaned toward him with encouragement.

"Come on, now, tell me what's the trouble."

"Honestly, Adams, don't you know where Rita is?"

"Honestly, I don't."

"She's been right here in New York for a whole week!"

"She has? How do you know?"

"I heard so from a theatrical agency. A friend told me he'd seen her there and I went and inquired, and they said she'd been there a week ago. Yesterday, I think I caught sight of her in a taxi on Fifth Avenue."

He paused, looking inquiringly at Griffith.

"I haven't seen her, Jack, . . . I give you my word."

"Will you find out for me?"

Griffith was puzzled.

"Why . . . how can I?"

"Ask him."

"Who? . . . For Heaven's sake, Jack, who're you talking about?"

"McCleish."

Griffith sat staring.

"Archie?" he repeated, his thoughts flying.

The other nodded.

"I thought I had a show with her," he said dropping his forehead into his hand again and smoothing back his hair as he talked. "I thought she'd stand for me and we got as far as talking plans when your friend, McCleish, comes butting in. There was nothing doing after that. She couldn't see anyone but him. Then she began talking stage and he came through with the money for her lessons in acting and singing and the rest of it. I'd've done that for her. I'd've spent two dollars to his one if she'd asked me. I ain't got what he has, but she can have every little red penny I've got . . . you bet cher . . . every little red penny. But she was stuck on him all right. You know I'm as wise as any of 'em; I've fooled 'round a bit and you can't string me along without my gettin' hep sooner or later. If she'd been after plain cash, I'd've known her game but she was stuck on him straight enough. And I thought he meant to do the square thing by her, too, until I saw his marriage in the papers . . . That's what brought her flyin' back, I'll bet a hat!"

"But . . . you mean to tell me . . ." Griffith stopped. Swift visions of understanding were breaking one upon another before his eyes.

"Didn't you know about him and Rita?"

The question staggered Griffith. He shook his head dully.

"Sure; I knew about it all the time," Hemmingway continued. "I saw I was licked and I told her I'd lie down and be good. But now McCleish goes and gets married. I don't suppose he made her any promises. I don't believe she was lookin' for 'em; it would take Christopher Columbus to put anything over on her. But you see his marrying upsets things all 'round. I suppose he's done with her . . . and I want to find out where *I* stand, whether I've got any show. I'll marry her *now*, if she'll stand for me. I just got her on the brain; she's the only thing I give a damn about . . . You might 'phone McCleish and ask him if he's heard from Rita . . ."

Griffith shook his head.

"I can't do that. McCleish and I aren't friends any more. We . . . we've had a split. I couldn't ring him up."

The other frowned, rubbing his chin reflectively.

"That's . . . too . . . bad. Couldn't you say you had a message?"

"No, it's out of the question. I couldn't do it. But Clarisse is sure to hear from Rita and if you'll leave me your address, I'll let you know the instant we find out where she's living."

Hemmingway absently thanked him.

"You'll have to excuse me for going at you so hard at first. I thought maybe all of you were sticking together to pass me up; McCleish might be running something phoney. I knew he was a close friend of yours. You brought him round to call on the girls and that was the end of me. Rita went after him as soon as she saw him."

"I had no idea you were . . . you liked Rita," Griffith ventured. "I thought it was the other way 'round, that she was crazy about *you*."

"Well perhaps that *was* the way of it at first. I guess it took somebody else poaching on my preserves to wake me up to where I stood. I was a fool all right."

He was pathetic in his distress, a ludicrous figure in his gaudy clothes, and with his uncouth manners, awkwardly acknowledging his passion.

"I'll help you in any way I can, Jack," Griffith said genuinely. "I'll let you know just as soon as I hear myself where she is located."

IX

During the rest of the day Griffith could think of nothing but Rita and Archie. He recalled the evening of his first visit with his friend to the Rumsey girls' home; he remembered how amused he had been at the rumpled state of Archie's hair. He had seen Rita lunching with him later but neither had said anything about it.

Now Archie was Margaret's husband. Rita had been away ten months. In that interval he had become engaged and the wedding ceremony had been performed. Griffith was well aware he had planned to marry Margaret in his Junior year at St. Cloud; he could not question the sincerity of Archie's affection for her. But how about Rita? And what about Clarisse? Had she any idea what her sister's relations had been with Archie? What would she say if she knew?

Griffith's disquietude on this score was immediately dispelled.

THE EDUCATION OF GRIFFITH ADAMS

He found his wife in a wild state of excitement when he got home that evening. Rita had been to see her and had spent the afternoon. They had had a wonderful time together; she had entirely explained why she had been so long in the city without coming to see her sister: there was a new show, a comic opera: *Miss Juliet of Joliet*—and she was rehearsing madly for it; she was to have the *leading rôle!* Besides she had lost Clarisse's address,—and look at all the lovely *lingerie* she had brought her! Last of all, she had been darling about the baby; had seemed quite enthusiastic over its coming and had almost reconciled Clarisse to the idea of what fate was bringing daily nearer to her.

There was no questioning Clarisse's supreme faith in Rita's wisdom, cleverness and infallibility. The younger sister had ruled her completely from childhood. Clarisse had never demurred at her decisions or thought of rebelling against her dominion.

Griffith veiled his curiosity, though full of solicitous inquiries. He began to suspect Rita's game. Of the genuineness of her feeling for Archie he had his doubts. She had perhaps convinced Hemmingway, but he believed her only passion was for her own advancement. She was calculating, shrewd, deliberately cunning. The son of Archibald McCleish had offered better material for her ends than the heir to the Hemmingway breweries. She had matched her wit against his stolid caution, and she had got what she wanted. Griffith never doubted for a moment who had agreed to finance her theatrical venture. Archie had urged him so seriously to be careful with Clarisse; he had earnestly cautioned him about evidence which could be used by such a girl in a suit for breach of promise; he had considered himself exceedingly adroit and wary! He had been caught in the very trap he had been so careful to avoid. He had not foreseen that a woman like Rita did not need evidence. The testimony of a waiter was all she required. Archibald McCleish's son was too much in the public eye to stand the publicity even of an accusation. There was no necessity to prove anything; a newspaper interview with the girl who claimed he had broken his promises to her, would spell disgrace and injure him incalculably. She had but to ask him to aid her here and help her there, buy her this, finance that, and it was easier to comply with her demands than refuse and risk the consequences. He was in her toils hopelessly for the present;

he could not brook exposure now; he was only a few weeks married! Events had played Rita's game better than she had hoped. Griffith could not refrain from smiling a little. Archie had got himself into a dreadful mess. He had considered his affair with Rita a case of inconsequential youthful philandering. Griffith knew how complacently he had assured himself that Rita was an unusual girl, she was "wise;" she knew what she was doing; they had understood one another so perfectly. But about Griffith he had been full of terrified concern, fearful lest he should involve himself unfortunately with Clarisse who, he had insisted, was just the kind of a girl to make trouble. Poor little 'Rissie, who had shown herself uncalculating, so genuinely loyal!

Griffith did not want to see Archie in any real trouble, and he would have been profoundly sorry if Margaret should be made to suffer in any way, but at the same time it gave him a certain grim pleasure to think how uncomfortable Rita was making his old friend.

He learned from Clarisse that Rita was at a hotel on Forty-Fourth Street, and the next day he telephoned the information to Jack Hemmingway.

CHAPTER IV

I

THE summer bore down upon the city with the heat of a furnace mouth. The humidity daily increased; the sun shone steadily down through a thick murky haze; the leaves hung limp and listless from the trees; on the streets and in the houses the people sweated.

Clarisse leaning upon her window-sill, gazing vacantly down from beneath the red-striped awning at the hot, dry, yellow pavements across which small distorted figures occasionally ventured, put her head down upon her crooked elbow and whimpered. It sounded like the bleating of a trapped animal.

With the passing of the period of nausea, there began the quick changes in her figure that she found was equally discomforting. She sat about the half-darkened room all day in a loose wrapper, her hair in disordered braids about her shoulders. She had begun to make some little garments for the baby, but she put these aside after she had cut them out, glad of the excuse her sticky, sweating fingers gave her to sit idly, reading the sensational fiction of a bi-monthly magazine, while the perspiration gathered on her neck and ran down in large drops between her round breasts.

Often Griffith, coming home in the evening, would find her still by the window, her head fallen against the hard ridge of the wicker chair, asleep. He came to let her remain where she was, for as the heat continued and September in hot, billowing waves closed in upon them, she found there was no comfort in lying down. She was most at ease with her cheek upon the fat cushion of her bent elbow, her arms folded beneath her head, resting on the little round dining-room table. She slept through many nights in this attitude. Griffith, prone under the single sheet that covered him, was frequently aroused from sleep by her movements.

"What is it, 'Rissie?"

"Just more soda."

"Can I do anything for you?"

"No . . . I wish you could; I can't stand this much longer." Griffith's head would drop back upon the pillow. He would blink once or twice at the grey ceiling, wondering if there was anything he had not thought of before that might ease or cheer her, and in another moment his eyelids would close and he would be asleep. Frequently he would be awakened by her tears. At such times she raged against him, against Doctor Harris, against the child. Interrupting with words and arguments grown hackneyed to both by much repetition, only drove her to stronger and more reckless language. Occasionally, she would consent to play cards with him, and two or three o'clock in the morning would sometimes find them shuffling and dealing, the early rattle of milk wagons, the deep rumble of the subway, the small noises of the city cooling under the night, reaching them through the open windows from which the curtains were carefully pinned back.

Griffith felt intensely sorry for his wife. He had no idea that she was going to suffer so much when he had joined with Doctor Harris in urging her to have a baby. It did not seem fair; it was out of all proportion to the results; no child was worth so much inconvenience and discomfort.

Clarisse fretted and fumed. She was cross and unhappy. The great heat reminded her constantly of her size and awkwardness; the quick movements of the child hurt sharply. She brooded during the day, storing up her impatient thoughts until her husband's return at night. It was fortunate that Griffith saw so little of her. He ate his meals alone, or in company of his old employer. The one day a week at home, he came actually to dread, for Clarisse complained constantly, meeting suggestion after suggestion as to how they should spend the time together with tireless objections. It was all Griffith could do to avoid a quarrel.

Her sister came to see her generally on Sunday and brought presents of fruit, flowers or *lingerie*. Griffith never encountered Rita, nor did he hear from Hemmingway.

"Ask Rita some time why she doesn't marry Hemmingway and quit the stage," he ventured one day and a fortnight later, Clarisse referring to his question, said:

"She laughed and asked me whether I thought she was crazy. She says she's got a wonderful chance in *Miss Juliet of Joliet*. The show opens in Philadelphia on the third; they've got Lester

Spooner in the cast; they'll stay a fortnight in Philadelphia and then go to Chicago for a run."

II

On a blowy November day when the last of the crisp golden-brown and yellow leaves had been whisked from their clinging perches and whirled, somersaulting, down the streets,—Griffith came home several hours earlier than usual. Ira Quay had complained of a slight chill after luncheon and a little later a headache had developed. As usual when there was anything, however slight, the matter with him he had sent for his physician. When he was ill, Mr. Quay desired only the services of his valet, at whom he swore with slow deliberation. Testily he sent Griffith home at four o'clock.

Clarisse was asleep when her husband came in. She lay upon the bed breathing heavily, her breath coming in quick gasps. Griffith stood at the bedside, hesitating to awaken her. His sympathy went out to her; it certainly was hard lines on poor old 'Rissie. It had been a dreary, terrible long pull. How much she had changed! There was little about her now that suggested the tall, slim girl who had opened the door for him the Sunday afternoon he had called on Rumsey's daughters. That seemed so long ago. He was surprised to realize it was less than two years! She had been Clarisse Rumsey then; now he thought of her only as 'Rissie. Poor 'Rissie! Her affectations had been beaten out of her; her soul had been hammered; life had laid its merciless hands upon her nature and perforce widened and deepened it. How pathetically unprepared she had been to meet the struggle!

Suddenly she opened her eyes wide, gazing at him in alarm.

"Gracious! How you frightened me, Griffith! How long have you been standing there? What time is it?"

He sat down on the bed beside her, smoothing her bare shoulder.

"How do you feel, 'Rissie?"

"Oh . . . rotten. What brings you home at this hour? You've not lost your job?"

He reassured her.

"Get up, 'Rissie. We'll go out and have a bang-up meal. It'll do you a lot of good. Or I'll tell you what: let's get something here first and go to a show. There's that stock company, on a Hundred-and-Eightieth Street; there's a good play on this week."

Indifferently she assented. But after he had helped her to her feet and she had begun to dress, her spirits rose. Griffith, shaving in the bath-room, heard her humming. Then abruptly she called him. He found her sitting on the side of the bed where she had been struggling with her stockings, one hand clutched together the gathers of a little *crêpe* wrapper, the other supported her weight as she bent forward. Her eyes were staring.

"Griffith! When did Doc say I was due?"

"The nineteenth; some time 'round there."

"Well . . . I'm in for it . . . *right now!*"

There was a moment's silence while they looked at each other.

"Go telephone him," Clarisse directed, her eyes still riveted upon his face.

Griffith turned to the instrument on the wall and as he did so his wife heavily rose to her feet. From her lips came a prolonged half-whisper, half-wail:

"Oh—my—God!"

Griffith, waiting for the negro boy downstairs to make the connection, watched her intently, a little awed, full of concern.

"You're sure you're not mistaken?" he asked.

She dismissed his question with an impatient head-shake, and stood, supporting herself upon a chair-back, surprise and fear upon her face.

"What'll we do if he isn't in?" she said tensely.

But the doctor's voice sounded to Griffith wonderfully reassuring.

"Ring me up in an hour and let me know if she has had another pain. If I don't hear from you again, I'll run out and have a look at her about eight o'clock."

Clarisse slowly paced the two small rooms, while Griffith sat and watched her, his eyes upon his time-piece. He could see that she was working herself up into an agitated state of apprehension, and seemed to be having spasms of pain every few minutes. But when he was almost sure she had been misled by some other acute ache or twinge, there was no mistaking the sudden sharp twisting of her features and the look of terror in her eyes.

He was grateful that the doctor did not ask for further evidence. At once he spoke with brisk decision: Very well,—he would telephone Miss Pebble's Sanitarium,—Griffith had better call a taxicab in the neighborhood,—he would see Clarisse at the hospital a little later.

It was a relief to have the suspense ended, to know for certainty that the supreme moment was at hand. Suppressed excitement took possession of them, and presently a general confusion prevailed. Their only suit-case was at the tailor's; the wash, an accumulation of three weeks' soiled underclothing and linen, had not come home; it would be necessary to stop at some store on the way to the hospital and buy some night-dresses; the few things Clarisse had ready for the baby must be tied into a bundle. Both were impelled with the desire to hurry; it would be terrible if anything should happen before they reached the hospital!

III

It was not until they were in the cab, spinning down Riverside Drive, that Griffith realized he had not enough money with him to pay the taxi charges in addition to purchasing the night-dresses. The few green-backs they had been able to put by were at home in the bowl of the silver-plated soup-tureen with the tiny cow on its cover. He was obliged to borrow from Miss Pebble when they arrived at the hospital.

On Doctor Harris' suggestion, some weeks before, Griffith and his wife had paid a visit to the private sanitarium he recommended and which, he assured them, was the most reasonable place of its kind in the city. Miss Pebble's hospital was located in the East Thirties and consisted of two old residences which had been connected by cutting several doorways through the intervening wall. Dingy, shabby and strongly smelling of chloroform and disinfectants, it yet looked homelike and comfortable.

In order to save expense, Clarisse was to share her room with another patient. The top floor, which was shut off from the rest of the house by a heavy, sound-proof door at the head of the stairs, was cut up into little rooms, each one of which contained two beds and was lighted and ventilated by a single skylight. At one end of the narrow hall was a nurses' lavatory, at the other a "crying room."

With difficulty Griffith helped Clarisse up the three long flights of stairs. It was cheering to hear that, for the present, she was to have no one with her. One room was unoccupied; a woman with her baby had left that morning.

Order and quiet pervaded the small hospital. The nurses, having attended to their patients, were eating their own supper. The sound of their gay talk and the clink of dishes rose faintly from the basement. Upstairs the halls were deserted; night lamps already had been lighted; the perfume of wilting flowers mingled unpleasantly with the heavy smell of anaesthetics. At the top of the last flight of stairs, the nurse who escorted them pushed open the door that shut off the upper floor of the house. At once various sounds met them: the weak puling of little babies, the moan of a sufferer and the persistent call of: "Nurse!———Nurse!" A distracted middle-aged woman in uniform was bustling to and fro. She opened one of the row of white-painted doors, and Griffith caught her admonishing voice beginning:

"Now, Mrs. Thompson . . ."

Clarisse gripped her husband's arm and stood rigid; the whites of her eyes rimmed her pupils, her mouth opened in a soundless cry.

"Right in here, Mrs. Adams," said her guide cheerily. "You'll be more comfortable as soon as you get to bed."

"I shall never . . . stand it," gasped Clarisse, her voice breaking.

"Is Doctor Harris here yet?" Griffith asked.

"Oh—oh—oh!" cried Clarisse, grinding her small white teeth together, and digging her finger-tips into the muscles of Griffith's arm. "This is *terrible!*"

"Bring your wife in here," directed the nurse.

Griffith pushed Clarisse gently into the bare little room with the two high hospital beds flanking either side.

"When did you have your last pain, dear?" the nurse asked, drawing the pins from Clarisse's hat.

"About half-an-hour ago," Griffith said, answering for her.

"So soon? Well, that's encouraging."

Both looked up at her, inquiringly, but she had her back to them, putting the hat away on the top shelf of the white-painted wardrobe. Clarisse lay back, exhausted.

Sounds from the adjoining rooms reached them: a woman was

coughing violently, and on the other side they could still hear the reproving voice of the nurse admonishing Mrs. Thompson; a hard object fell with a clatter against the intervening wall.

"It's pretty noisy here," Clarisse complained wearily.

"Is there only a wooden partition between these rooms?" demanded Griffith.

"That's all," the nurse answered placidly. Evidently she was accustomed to the complaint.

"How does a sick person ever get to sleep?" Griffith persisted, puzzled and concerned.

The nurse smiled sweetly, but she did not answer him directly Presently she said:

"Now if Mr. Adams will wait downstairs . . ."

"Oh, he can't leave me!" Clarisse exclaimed, full of alarm.

"I must get you ready, dear!" said the nurse reprovingly. "He can come up by and by."

Griffith kissed his wife and tightened his arm about her shoulders. As he went downstairs, he met the other nurses coming up from their supper.

He found a seat in the stiff little reception room and sat down to wait. Through the velour hangings he observed a nurse at a receiving desk making out bills in the light of a hanging electric. At her elbow was the telephone switchboard, which occasionally buzzed sharply. Presently he saw Miss Pebble bending over her shoulder. He expected she would come in and speak to him, reassuring him about Clarisse, but she merely glanced in through the hangings, saw him, and passed on without nod or sign of recognition.

He wondered what time it was; his watch he remembered having left on the window-sill at home. He got up to study the titles of some volumes in the shabby book-case and as he did so, Doctor Harris pushed open the front door and without looking in his direction, started upstairs with an alert step.

IV

A long time passed. Griffith's head began to ache; it occurred to him he had had nothing to eat. He was amused to discover that he had only partly shaved himself; one side of his chin was stiff with bristles. He tried to interest himself in a magazine he found in the book-case, but he was too nervous and restless. Why did not someone come and tell him about Clarisse? He felt he ought to be kept informed; he determined when he had counted a thousand to ask the nurse at the receiving desk to send word that he would like to see Doctor Harris. But before he had counted half that number the physician came running nimbly downstairs.

"Going fine, my boy; Clarisse's in fine shape; nothing could be finer. I'll be back about midnight. I guess you can go up and see her now. She's fine,—everything's fine."

Griffith looked blankly at him; he was staggered at the idea of the physician leaving Clarisse now. The doctor observed the concern in his face. He smiled, winking his eyes at him through his gold-rimmed glasses.

"Don't worry, my boy," he said, his hand on Griffith's shoulder, "I'll be back in plenty of time. Everything's going fine. You go talk to your wife and keep her mind off herself and her troubles."

He pulled back the entrance door, waved his hand toward Griffith, and trotted down the steps.

V

Griffith found Clarisse in bed, an unfamiliar drawn look across her upper lip, a haggard expression on her face. Her hair was neatly braided and her skin showed pink and soft through the cheap lace of her new embroidered night-dress. He half expected her to hold up her arms to meet his embrace as he sat down on the edge of the bed and bent toward her. But she only looked at him silently, her mouth tightly closed.

"How goes it, darling?" he whispered.

She turned her head slowly from side to side, frowning heavily, her lips white from the pressure with which she compressed them. He took one of her hands in his and began to pat it but she drew it away. Her eyes left his face and stared upward at the shaded skylight above her head. A low sucking sound came from between her clenched teeth. Griffith bent toward her, disturbed and anxious, realizing she had passed beyond the reach of any comfort he could offer.

A nurse—a younger and prettier woman than the one who had shown them upstairs—entered, a sterilizing pan and a roll of bandages in her arms. She paused an instant by the bedside. Clarisse shifted her gaze to meet the smiling eyes, but there was no answering light in her own. Griffith looked up inquiringly.

"First babies are pretty slow!" the nurse said kindly. "Doctor thinks you won't have a bad time at all." She set down the things she carried and laid a white hand on the forehead of the woman in bed.

"Chloroform before the next, Miss Pohli?"

The nurse smiled, pushing back Clarisse's hair gently.

"Perhaps."

There was something satisfying in the young woman's manner, a reassuring sense of strength about her. She had a grave, sweet face, a warm flush lay upon her cheek-bones and temples and her pale yellow hair was drawn snugly over the tops of her ears.

Suddenly Clarisse began to moan. Her hand caught Griffith's fingers, crushing them together. With a quick writhe her body twisted, a stifling cry burst through her tight shut lips.

Griffith closed his eyes, a choking sensation in his throat. It was dreadful—it was *terrible* to see her suffer that way! As the sounds of her distress increased, he looked to see if chloroform would be administered. The nurse held Clarisse's wrist firmly between her finger-tips and studied her watch, but she made no other motion.

"Oh . . . *give* it to me!" wailed Clarisse.

"My God!" Griffith exclaimed jumping to his feet. "I can't see anybody suffer that way!"

"You'd better go downstairs," the nurse whispered persuasively. "You just excite her; she doesn't carry on this way when she's alone; I'll come down in a little while and tell you how she is."

Griffith hesitated. Clarisse's body slowly heaved up, her back arching, her hands claw-shaped, digging the bed-clothes. A cry Griffith was to remember for the rest of his life, filled the room.

Miss Pebble briskly opened the door.

"You're disturbing the other patients on this floor, Mrs. Adams," she said bending over the bed. Another piercing scream rang out. Griffith clapped his hands over his ears and turned his face toward the wall.

"Take her downstairs, Miss Pohli," Miss Pebble directed authoritatively. "Put her temporarily in Number eight." She wheeled toward Griffith:

"Go down to the reception room."

Giddy and sick, he groped his way into the hall, pulled back the heavy door at the top of the stairs, and descended slowly into the quieter regions of the house. When he reached the second floor, he heard them moving Clarissa. He hurried down the rest of the way fearing he might hear her cry out again.

The ground floor of the hospital was deserted; the nurse at the receiving desk had gone and the light by which she had worked was extinguished. Griffith flung himself upon one of the hard-seated upholstered chairs in the reception room and plunged his head into his hands, thrusting his fingers into his thick hair, staring at the green arabesque of the worn carpet.

How long would it last? How long would she have to endure that agony? How long would they let her suffer?

Oh! Oh! Oh!

He sprang up and began to pace the little room, punching the palm of one hand with the fist of the other. His head was aching violently, but he was barely conscious of it in his excitement. Doctor Harris had said he would be back at midnight. *What time was it?*

He heard the faint ticking of a clock and stopped long enough to locate it; he found it in front of the telephone switch-board: half-past eleven. Half-an-hour yet! Where the devil was the doctor! They'd let her die! They'd let her die! They'd let her die! . . . God—help—her!

VI

A sleepy maid with an apron askew about her waist came stumbling through the hall to open the front door which had been locked and bolted at ten. The red apple cheeks, the spongy beard, the bald shining dome of Doctor Harris seemed to Griffith at that moment the most beautiful physiognomy in the world. With an exclamation that was almost a sob he met the physician in the hall.

"What's the trouble, boy?" the doctor demanded.

"'Rissie's having a terrible time! I ... I don't know ... They're letting her suffer up there. She's begging for chloroform and they're so damned afraid to do anything on their own initiative that they won't give it to her. They just sit 'round and grin. They're all waiting for *you!*"

"My boy ... my boy," Doctor Harris said kindly. "I guess you're as bad off as your wife. I'll run up and have a look at her and come down and tell you how she is."

He disappeared up the stairs, ascending with his usual surprising agility. In less than fifteen minutes he came running down again, but to Griffith it had seemed an hour. There was a satisfied smile upon the doctor's face.

"Nothing to worry about, my boy," he said rubbing his hands together. "Everything's going fine. She's having her pains with some regularity now. I hope to present you with a fine boy or girl about two o'clock."

"Not till *then!*"

"Come ... come, you're all upset, yourself. I want you to go out and take a walk. Go over to Third Avenue and find an all-night restaurant and get yourself a cup of coffee; fill your lungs with some fresh air and smoke a cigarette or two. ... Now you do what I tell you."

The night was cold. A vagrant wind, unwholesome and spectral at that early hour, whisked about the corners of the streets, scattering loose papers. There was a promise of rain in the air. Pedestrians hurried on their way eager to be at home; taxi-cabs bumped heavily over the uneven surface of the street; Fourth Avenue cars whirred past, sleepy passengers nodding in their brightly lighted interiors.

Griffith drank his coffee in long grateful draughts and ordered more. The restaurant was cheap and tawdry; artificial vines hung from the ceilings; a mechanical piano rattled out a tune; the bosoms of the waiters' shirts were streaked with spilled viands. In one corner of the room, a group of young men and girls were making a terrific din, the racket punctuated now and then with a shrill scream from one of the girls. Griffith thought of Clarisse and shuddered.

The coffee produced an amazing effect upon him. The creepy cold that had fastened itself upon him disappeared; his fingers ceased trembling; the pain in his head vanished. Wonderfully revivified, he hurried back to the hospital.

VII

At quarter to three, the young nurse with the pale yellow hair came running lightly downstairs, her rather serious face lighted with a bright smile.

"Congratulations, father!"

Griffith sprang to his feet.

"How is she?"

"Fine."

"Everything all right?"

"Perfect. You have a splendid nine-pound boy. He's a beauty. He's got a regular mop of the loveliest soft black hair."

"But . . . Clarisse . . . Mrs. Adams. . . . How is she?"

"Oh fine; everything's quite normal. You can see her in a few minutes."

Half-an-hour later he knelt beside a starry-eyed Clarisse he hardly knew. A gentle, contented smile was upon her lips; she seemed still to belong to another world. She was frail, weak, utterly spent, but there was a clean, spiritual look in her eyes, a beatific expression in her face, he had never seen there before. For the first time she appeared beautiful to him.

He bent over his wife's clean white hand and kissed it tenderly. The feeble pressure of her fingers on his was keenly appealing.

"Here's something you can be proud of, Mr. Adams," the nurse said coming into the room. Griffith rose. The woman held a roll of blanket in her arms; she turned back a fold of it. In the nest, like a little red puppy, Griffith beheld his son. The nurse held the child out toward him and he took the bundle in his arms. The little copper face was weazened, the eyes, nose and mouth pinched together as one might shape a piece of putty with a single pressure of five finger-tips: a curious little animal with a thick waving crown of fine-spun black hair.

"Isn't he beautiful!" the nurse exulted.

As she spoke, the baby kicked, straightening his little body vigorously. Deep down from Griffith's groin something sprang to meet that tiny heave of bone and muscle. From the depths of his soul something leaped, rising, struggling upward; a great surging, overwhelming sensation, suffocating, tremendous. He pushed the child in fear toward the nurse, tears blinding him.

VIII

The following days were intensely happy for Griffith; he was exalted by the feeling of parenthood. It was the most wonderful fact in the world that a son could be born to him and to Clarisse. It was inexplicable that he had never thought about the child before its birth; his whole consideration had been for his wife. He did not recognize any particular affection for the baby as yet; he was merely enchanted at the idea of *having* a child.

Clarisse was no less delighted with her little son. On the fourth day when he discovered for himself the trick of satisfying the craving hunger which began to manifest itself inside him regularly every two hours, she turned radiantly to Griffith, her eyes wet and shining.

"He tugs so, Griffith," she whispered fascinated. "I feel him 'way down to my toes. . . . Say, he'll be a lot of fun when he grows up; I hope he learns to love his mother like he ought. What'll we name him?"

The question was discussed at length. Griffith objected strongly to his own name. It sounded "precious" and effeminate, booky, and had been the cause for infinite regret to him at school. Clarisse's father's Christian name was Joshua, which was out of the question. They considered "David" but Griffith felt that might imply, to his old circle of friends, that he still wished to maintain relations with them. The first name of Grandfather Ambrose was John, and Clarisse begged hard for it but, Griffith thought, it was too palpable a bid for the rich old man's generosity. The boy was referred to, for the time-being, as "Jim Jeffries."

Old Ira Quay continued to be indisposed and made use of only a few hours each day of his secretary. Griffith spent all his spare time at Miss Pebble's hospital until another patient came to share Clarisse's room. Then it became impossible to remain for longer than a few minutes, for it seemed inevitable he should select the same hour to see his wife as three heavy women in black mourning veils chose to visit the room's other occupant.

As the three black figures utilized whatever space there was in the room besides the two beds, Griffith was obliged to sit in the "crying room" until the visitors departed. There were four other babies in this room besides his own. One or another of them was always bitterly complaining, but their tireless small cries did not trouble him. He was fascinated by the glorious robustness and magnificent health of his own son. The child seemed to cry much less than the other babies, but when he did, it was with an imperative lustiness that demanded immediate attention. It amused Griffith vastly. He found a keen pleasure in sitting beside his son's basket and watching him. One day he carefully undid the baby's tightly clenched fist and spread out the warm, moist hand, marvelling at the perfection of its fat knuckles and the five long firm little tendrils sticking out from it. Unexpectedly the tiny hand closed about his forefinger, gripping it forcibly, squeezing it as if it were something from which to wring the juice. It was confident, trusting, wonderfully appealing. Sensations such as Griffith had experienced on the night of his son's birth when he had felt the tiny body straighten in his arms, came rushing back.

"You little beggar," he whispered.

IX

The constant presence of the three gloomy figures in Clarisse's room made both Griffith and his wife anxious to be allowed to depart from Miss Pebble's establishment. Clarisse complained of the food, which she said reached her cold and unappetizing, and both were conscious of the expense. On the tenth day after the baby was born, Griffith found Clarisse one afternoon comfortably established in a small rocker, a pillow at her back, a blanket around her feet. She had just finished nursing and as Griffith came into the room, Miss Pohli was gathering up the baby, who had fallen asleep during the last minutes of his meal.

Clarisse answered her husband's surprised look with a radiant smile.

"Hello!" he exclaimed. "Doc said you could get up, hey? How's Jim Jeffries?"

"Oh he's the finest ever," the nurse said admiringly.

Griffith stooped over to kiss his wife. Clarisse raised her lips to his, her eyes shining happily. Suddenly she coughed, her face twitched and her head fell back upon the pillow, the eyes closing. For an instant Griffith remained transfixed.

" 'Rissie!"

He dropped upon his knees, his arms about her. Miss Pohli swiftly laid the baby on the bed and lifted the limp wrist. There was a tense, silent moment. Griffith turned from his wife's face to the nurse. He saw her eyes widen, her lips part in a quick breath; then abruptly she left the room. He struggled to his feet and bent over Clarisse, studying the calm, colorless features. He was afraid to touch her; something had gone wrong. He continued to whisper her name, striving to reach her consciousness. The woman in the other bed kept repeating:

"What is it? What happened? What is it? What happened?"

At Miss Pohli's heels came Miss Pebble. They brushed Griffith aside. Miss Pebble bent over Clarisse. She turned quickly toward him.

"Please wait outside."

He did not move. Miss Pohli laid a hand upon his arm and pushed him toward the door.

"Please—tell—me," he pleaded.

"You'll have to wait outside," Miss Pebble said decisively. "Your wife's fainted, that's all."

He knew she lied, but he allowed the nurse to push him from the room.

"Go down to the reception room," she urged, when they were out in the hall. "I'm needed here; I'll let you know as soon as I can."

Griffith paced the dingy room again, waiting—waiting—waiting. He sought refuge at the window and stared out into the street, fiercely struggling to control his nerves. Presently he saw Doctor Harris hurrying toward the hospital, the skirts of his long frock-coat clinging about his knees, his broad-brimmed hat bent against the sharp wind. Briskly he mounted the steps; the door opened; the sound of his feet upon the stairs followed immediately.

The minutes dragged on and on. The persistent questions of the woman who shared Clarisse's room, rang in his ears. What *had* happened? They had sent hurriedly for Doctor Harris and he had come at once. What was it? What had happened?

He tried desperately to reassure himself. Perhaps it was only a seizure; perhaps Miss Pebble had told the truth. Something unexpected had happened, that was all. She had got up too soon; the doctor probably had thought she was stronger than she was; it meant only a few more days in the hospital. He persuaded himself he was foolish to become so agitated and forced himself to sit down again.

He was thinking he would buy Clarisse some particularly nice-looking grape-fruit he had seen at a Fourth Avenue fruit shop, when Doctor Harris suddenly appeared between the heavy velour hangings. He beckoned with his finger.

Griffith followed him into the hall and down its length to what had been the dining-room of the old residence. Miss Pebble used it for her office. Doctor Harris shut the door after him and pointed to the chair before the desk. Griffith sat down, his eyes intent upon the doctor's face.

"It's all over, my boy," he said gently.

Griffith stiffened.

"She's gone," the physician said with finality.

"You mean 'Rissie's dead, doctor?" Griffith said evenly.

Doctor Harris inclined his head.

"It doesn't often happen: a clot gets loose in the blood; it floats along in the veins until it plugs an artery somewhere; it's called pulmonary embolism; there are no precursory symptoms; death is instantaneous; there's no way of preventing it."

Griffith said nothing. A mist gathered before his eyes; everything was dropping away from him. The doctor continued talking, but he did not follow what he said.

"She was the best, . . . the only friend I had," Griffith said when there was a pause, his lip beginning to tremble. "There's nobody left now; I guess I'm through."

"Nonsense!" The doctor's hand tightened on his shoulder. "You've got one of the finest boys I ever helped into the world. She left that for you to take care of; you've got to go on for his sake."

The recollection of the baby's firm little hand clasped tightly, confidently about his forefinger rushed back to Griffith. He laid his head quickly down upon the back of his hand on the desk's edge and began to sob violently.

End of Book III

SALT

"Ye are the salt of the earth: but if the salt have lost his savour, wherewith shall it be salted?" Matthew v: 13.

BOOK IV

SALT
OR
THE EDUCATION OF GRIFFITH ADAMS
BOOK IV.

CHAPTER I

I

AN emotional paralysis descended upon Griffith after the first moments of grief. He lived through the days that immediately followed dazed and benumbed. People treated him with singular consideration, speaking to him with lowered voices, eager to do things for him, forestalling his wishes. Telegrams, letters, flowers arrived, even strangers spoke to him in sympathy. David came, and Archie and Margaret called, and among the old and new faces appeared Leslie's.

Griffith was genuinely glad to see his half-brother again and to re-establish their friendly relationship. Leslie had not changed. He was the same insignificant figure of a man, with baggy trousers, white face and unkempt beard. In his dull, indiscriminate reading of the newspapers, paragraph by paragraph, he had come upon Clarisse's death among the death notices.

Griffith welcomed his suggestion to occupy his old room in his apartment. He slept in the little two-room suite he had shared with Clarisse for only one night, and had been saved from the thoughts and memories that might have overwhelmed him there by a dreamless sleep of complete exhaustion. In his brother's silent company he found a certain relaxation, almost comfort, for he dreaded being alone and Leslie furnished companionship marred neither by questions nor unnecessary words.

The immediate problem which confronted him was the disposition of the baby. His intense pride in his son was all the keener since he was now his alone. The child was a fine specimen of small humanity, with a fat, round torso, stocky, firm legs and a well shaped head. His little features, while still in the putty stage, were nicely moulded and his mop of blue-black hair gave him a weird expression of maturity, particularly when he opened his eyes and through tiny slits, surveyed the world from black glittering pupils. Griffith went every day to Miss Pebble's to see him and sat beside his crib talking about him to Miss Pohli who seemed to share his enthusiasm.

At first, he had been a little ashamed to show his affection for his son. He invented excuses for wishing to see the baby and to talk about him to the nurse. One day, however, Miss Pohli put the child into his arms and brought him the warmed bottle of milk; Griffith grinned foolishly as he supported the baby gingerly in a cramped position of his arm and held the bottle to his eager lips. Hungrily the few pounds of human anatomy emptied it and when the last of the nourishment had disappeared, dropped immediately off to sleep. Griffith was alone in the crying room except for the other infant occupants, who were for the moment still. Uncertainly he raised the warm moist cheek to his lips and touched it gently; the baby smelled of flannel and perspiration; there was something deliciously fragrant about him. Griffith blushed violently a moment later when one of the other nurses unexpectedly entered the room.

Rita had written from Chicago, where *Miss Juliet of Joliet* had opened with fair success, suggesting that Aunt Abigail would, she was sure, be willing to take the baby. The thought terrified Griffith, though he was obliged to admit it seemed the only logical step to take. Undoubtedly some arrangement could be made with his wife's aunt, but not without a cold shudder could he think of his little son growing up in such an environment. All day long, while he read aloud mechanically to old Quay, or listened to his crackling intonations, the idea of surrendering his son to that domineering woman's capricious dominion oppressed him.

He was in a black, despondent mood, later, as he sat down beside the basket in which the child lay asleep and bent over, studying his wrinkled features gloomily. It was then that Miss Pohli came in and suggested, with much hesitation and embarrassment, that he and the baby come to live with her family.

"I thought about it some days ago but . . . you know how you

THE EDUCATION OF GRIFFITH ADAMS 321

do about such things!" the nurse said. "It seemed so unlikely that it would come about that I didn't mention it to anyone. And then you remember I asked you what you were going to do with him? It just seemed to me I couldn't let him go away; there never was a baby like him. I suppose it was my sister getting married that put the idea into my head. We've always been crowded at home, but her going gives us an extra room, . . . and then when I talked the matter over with mother, my sister, Rosa, said she knew you and you had been very kind to her. . . ."

She paused, but Griffith looked blank.

"Rosa used to work in a railroad office; she began as a stenographer there. . . ."

His face broke into a delightful smile.

"You don't mean Polly?"

The nurse nodded, smiling in return.

"They called her that. They couldn't pronounce or remember her name, I don't know which."

Griffith could not conceal his pleasure.

"Well, . . . that's wonderful! I . . . it never would have occurred to me."

"She said you wrote her after the clerks were discharged and offered her another position; she thought it was very considerate of you."

"Why, it was nothing."

"We talked it over, and mother said that we were wasting time, unless you'd consider it. You see she didn't believe it possible you didn't have *someone* . . . some relative who was a woman who would want to take care of him."

"I haven't," Griffith said. Then he remembered Aunt Abigail and told the nurse about her.

"But I couldn't hand him over to her. She'd bring him up just as she has her five daughters: to act like her, think like her, and look like her. It wouldn't be fair to him."

Miss Pohli said nothing when he paused; they both sat staring silently at the baby.

"It's mighty kind of you to suggest it," Griffith began again awkwardly.

They both were embarrassed; the nurse rose.

"If you still think well of the plan after you've considered it for a few days you might go to see mother and talk with her about it. We live on West Ninety-second Street near Columbus Avenue," —she gave him the address. "We're Swiss, you know,—a big family. We don't put on any style; we're all packed in together in a six-room flat; there're five at home now and that's less than there's ever been."

The plan appealed strongly to Griffith; his heart was still sick over the prospect of life and the obligation of resuming relations with his fellow-beings. For the three weeks since Clarisse's death he had continued to remain at his brother's, occupying his old room, eating at *The Trocadero* and at *Spinney's* in Leslie's company on the evenings he was free, visiting Miss Pebble's for a sight of his son as often as he could manage. He shunned the little two-room suite in the Selwyn Court Apartments. Only once subsequent to the single night he had slept there, had he entered it. Then the sight of Clarisse's gay little *crêpe* wrapper where she herself had flung it across a chair as she had hurried to make ready for the hospital trip had torn at his heart. He had caught the little cheap garment up and buried his face in it. He missed her terribly; he forgot her complaints and her artificiality; he remembered her caresses, her tenderness and love. At that moment it came to him that in death he loved her better than ever he had in life.

II

The Pohlis lived in a dark apartment on the south side of the street. Columbus Avenue hummed briskly and noisily to the left a hundred yards away, and the block was bounded at its other end by the quiet stretches of Central Park.

A day or so after his talk with the nurse, Griffith went to see them. He climbed three flights of stairs through various strata of faint smells until he reached the landing where a placid-faced woman of about thirty-five or thirty-six with pale yellow hair, a white apron about her waist, stood waiting for him in an open doorway. He followed her into an unusually large room, in the centre of which, stood a great oval table littered with sewing, magazines, books and newspapers. On either side of it sat two women whose white clothing sharply reflected the gaslight above them. One of them was "Polly."

Her familiar features, the thin-spun yellow hair coiled in twisted braids at the back of her head, her dark blue eyes, the blond down on cheeks and chin, her serious expression, vividly brought back the days in the railroad office.

She was quietly cordial in her welcome and introduced her mother and sister. Mrs. Pohli was white-haired and stout, with little tufts of fine yellow hair on either side of her upper lip; her smooth cheeks drooped somewhat, making venerable dimples at the corners of her mouth. Her face was placid and gentle yet not lacking in grave dignity. Wrinkles about her eyes indicated a ready tendency to laugh. The sister who had met Griffith at the door was a younger, slighter edition of her mother.

Griffith did not remain over an hour. The three women were amused at his eagerness to come and make his home among them. The mother chuckled at his earnestness. When she laughed she shook all over, hardly making a sound but quaking like a great mound of jelly, the chair in which she sat squeaking violently.

"Vell," she said shutting her eyes and still heaving her large person expressively to indicate her amusement, "vell, you come und ve try id; maybe ve come to disagree; you may nut like id; ve are only simple, Swiss people. My daughter, Ameli, at der hospital,—she has told us aboud your little son. Your poor vife! . . . Ach! . . . Ve shall like a liddle von here, eh, Tilde? Vell, come und try id, you can go again und you dond like id!"

The older girl, Tilde, showed him the room it was proposed he was to occupy with the baby. It was at the rear of the flat next to the kitchen and had been intended originally to be used as the dining-room. The furnishings were shabby but comfortable. A large walnut bed decorated at the ends of its head and tail boards with small neatly-turned wooden urn-shaped ornaments, was pushed with its back against the folding doors to the adjoining room. In the middle of the counterpane there was a large darn, but the spread itself, the starched pillow-shams and the bed linen were spotless.

Tilde explained that the family, even when the father was alive, had taken their meals in the big living-room at the front of the flat. The last of nine children had been born when she was eighteen, and for ten years, eleven of them had lived comfortably in the six rooms. Now there were only five, and when Ameli came home from the hospital, making the family six in number, she slept with Rosa. Besides the mother and the three girls, there were two boys, Johann and Rudolf, nineteen and sixteen years old. They shared the room next to the one the baby and his father would occupy.

Griffith was deeply impressed by the strength of the ties which bound together this family group. It permeated the home which he had been invited to enter and share. He felt it almost a sacrilege to intrude, and yet, sick at heart, and worried with the problem of the baby's care, he realized that if any arrangement could possibly be made whereby he could come among them, a refuge would be found for himself and a haven for his child.

III

On the Monday after Christmas, he moved his belongings to the Pohli household. The furniture and most of Clarisse's clothes he sent to Aunt Abigail's. She offered to store the former and he knew she would make good use of the latter. It was a sad business: the folding of his dead wife's flimsy underwear,—the stockings, the stringy undervests, the ruffled petticoats, the stained and frayed corsets she had not worn for the last six months of her life,— and packing them, with her few dresses into the trays of the same trunks which they had brought with them from *The Myrtle*.

As he emptied the drawers of her bureau, suddenly in the midst of painful and comfortless reflections, he came upon a bit of brass chain. He pulled at it but it would not give. A tug brought out a piece of green board; he turned it over; it was Aunt Abigail's wedding present:

"Pretty good world with its dark and its light,
Pretty good world with its wrong and its right!"

A miserable, outrageously unfair world with only its dark and its wrong! Griffith bowed his head in sorrow upon his clasped hands.

IV

He decided to name the baby after his own father. He talked about it to Leslie and his brother's opinion of the tall sensitive shy man who had been his stepfather decided him. Griffith wondered if his strange, inarticulate parent had sometimes experienced yearnings similar to those he now felt for his own son. The pathos of his father's life struck him poignantly. He beheld him in a new light. He might not go back, with the understanding of maturity and parenthood to give him the companionship, the boyish affection the gentle-hearted man had craved, but he could honor his memory by naming his son for him: Richard Cabot Adams, Second. It would suit the baby, Griffith thought fondly, to call him "Dickey."

V

There was still much of Christmas in the air of the Pohli household when Griffith arrived to become a part of it. He found the baby already installed and his own coming warm-heartedly expected. There was a tall over-decorated tree in the spacious front room and wreaths were in the window and garlands of thick evergreen ropes were looped over the corners of the heavy gilt-framed pictures. The rooms were redolent with the spicy odor of balsam and fir. Everywhere there was a general sprinkling of tinsel, tissue paper and ribbon. The Christmas confusion penetrated even to Griffith's room, where his son's crib was decorated with chains of colored paper strung from end to end and looped in festoons over the sides.

The Pohlis made him one of them unaffectedly and without ceremony. There were several small children scampering about each day during the holidays, little sons and daughters of the Pohlis who had married, and who came to pay their respects to the old mother. Griffith was continually meeting fresh members of this amazing family: stout, kindly-faced matrons and broad-shouldered, deep-chested blond giants, accompanied by babies in arms, babies that were toddling, and babies that might no longer be considered such.

"This is my brother, Adrian," Rosa would introduce him, smiling gravely, "and this is Mrs. Adrian and here is Elizabethli and Arthur and little Tilde; and this is my sister Helen and her husband, Mr. Max Serex; these are the twins, Adrian and Max, but where is Babette? You didn't bring her? . . . Ah, what a pity and she likes the parties so much! Next time, Mr. Adams, you shall meet Babette; Babette is my favorite among all my nieces."

There was also Conrad who was twenty-eight and unmarried;—he lived over the drug-store where he was employed as chemist;—there was Paula who came in with a bride's smile, hanging on the arm of her young husband; and lastly there were the two younger boys, Johann and Rudi, who said little and impressed Griffith by the unusual respect with which they treated their elders.

On his first evening that he came to his new home after the day's work with his aged employer, he quietly let himself in with his latch-key to the back hall of the flat off which his own room directly opened. A great deal of laughter was going on in the big living-room. Griffith stood on the threshold of his room wistfully listening. He would have liked to join them if only to look on at the fun-making, but they had asked him to share their home, not to become a member of the family itself.

Dickey was asleep in his crib, fat hands tightly knotted into fists, his flushed face deep in the hot moist pillow. Griffith had removed his coat, and had one shoe unlaced when there was the sound of steps in the hall and a knock fell upon his door. Ameli stood in the hall-way.

"I didn't know you had come in; I saw the light under the door. It's time for his bottle . . . he comes in with me and Rosa at night, you know; he must have his feedings every two hours."

Griffith protested; he could do that himself. The girl laughed.

"We'll see about it; the milk's got to be warmed first; leave it to me."

"Mother was hoping you would be home early to-night," she continued, after she had placed the nipple between the baby's red gums. "We are making the New Year's punch and she wants you to help. Put on your coat and come lend us a hand."

Griffith hesitated; it was kind of them to include him but he thought he had better not join them. Ameli would not listen to him. Summarily she left him and returned within a minute with her mother. What foolishness had he been saying? He must come help them at once; yes, yes, they were *all* tired, but the work must be done, and another pair of hands was needed.

Protesting weakly, he allowed himself to be persuaded, and with one string of his unlaced shoe still dragging, he was led into the front room where the punch-making was in progress. About

THE EDUCATION OF GRIFFITH ADAMS 327

the oval table were gathered several members of the family: Rosa, Tilde, the two boys, Johann and Rudi, Conrad, and Helen and her husband. An immense china punch bowl stood in the middle of the table and on either side of it were an opened crate of oranges, another of lemons. The stamped tissue paper in which the fruit had been wrapped was scattered over table and floor. Several bursting bags of sugar lay open on the table and the party about the board were vigorously rubbing the lumps against the skin of the fruit until the sugar became thoroughly saturated with the oil in the peel, when it was tossed into the china bowl in the centre of the table.

There was a shout of welcome as Griffith appeared, and a place was made for him between the two boys. An orange and a lump of sugar were put into his hands and presently he was rubbing as energetically as his neighbors.

It was a memorable evening. After the first few minutes, he felt surprisingly at ease. The company paid him attention or ignored him as the moment required, breaking into their native language when they wished to discuss something among themselves, returning to English when the subject changed. They laughed a great deal, joking one another, explaining their jests to him at laborious length. After a while beer was brought in shiny pewter steins, foaming to the brim, and sandwiches made with great slices of onion and sausage. Griffith's weeks of loneliness and grief made the goodness and simple kindness of these people seem wonderful to him; he loved them all; he had not thought there were such gentle, unaffected, lovable folk in the world.

The punch bowl was not filled with the sugar lumps until midnight, and afterwards there was foraging in the ice-box which produced cheese, a hacked leg of lamb and a whole mince pie. Games followed the feasting. The New Year's punch was being brewed; it was festival time and a night for merry-making.

It was nearly two o'clock when Conrad stood up and announced he must get home to bed. The declaration seemed to bring the rest to their senses. Mrs. Pohli asked what time it was and, being informed, appeared horrified. She began to gather the loose tissue papers, setting things energetically to rights. Rudi and Johann indulged in a series of silent yawns and stumbled off to bed. The party unceremoniously broke up. Griffith, finding his own room, undressed and crawled into bed, his heart filled with a peace and happiness he had not known for many months.

VI

Life with this simple Swiss family that took him in so unaffectedly and wholeheartedly, soon settled into a groove. When Ameli returned to the hospital, Griffith begged that Dickey should not be moved out of his room at night. He assured the Pohlis he could attend to the baby's feedings himself. He purchased a wooden box with tin compartments to hold the ice and milk bottles, and a patent heater. The baby had a meal at ten or eleven, when Griffith went to bed, and sometimes did not wake again until Griffith's alarm rang at seven. The girls considered him a remarkably good baby.

Griffith got up and dressed at seven and left the house at quarter to eight. Breakfast for the Pohlis was well under way by that time. Rudi, who was a violin-maker, and Johann, who worked in an engraving plant, had already eaten their morning meal and departed. Rosa, whose office hours began at nine, set the breakfast hour for the rest of the family an hour earlier. Griffith frequently encountered Tilde in the short back hall-way, carrying the glistening copper coffee-pot, with steam streaming from its nozzle, leaving behind it a delicious aromatic fragrance, to the big living-room where the oval table was covered with a red, fringed cloth and where her sister and mother were setting out the sugar-bowl, the cream pitcher, the red, fringed napkins, and the knives, forks and spoons. More than once Tilde suggested that he join them, and Rosa and her mother supplemented her invitation with urging of their own, but Griffith dared not trust himself or them, fearing that the habit once established, they might come to regret the presence of a stranger always at their table.

But the one day a week which was his own, he unavoidably must spend with the people he had begun to love so dearly. Mrs. Pohli was particularly kind to him; there was no resisting her motherly heart. Griffith could refuse Tilde's and Rosa's invitations, but there was no withstanding the sweet old woman's imperative kindness.

"You come now."

THE EDUCATION OF GRIFFITH ADAMS

She would stand at the entrance of his room, her prominent figure filling the doorway.

"Dick-ee vants hees vater!" she would add, smiling and shaking her fat body in the way she had of expressing her amusement.

Griffith, who had begun to read again, would close his book and follow her into the big, front room and sit happily for the rest of the afternoon reading in the low S-shaped rocker by the window while Mrs. Pohli knitted thick woolen shawls, and her ball of yarn rolled farther and farther from her. Then there was no declining her invitation to have this day's dinner with the family. She did not ask, she commanded. These evenings became memorably delightful for him. They fell on Thursdays generally, for on that day Quay usually received a visit from a specialist who was supposed to delay the hardening of the human arteries, and his treatment lasted several hours. Ameli came to choose the same day of the week to be at home from the hospital, and Johann and Rudi, whatever other evenings they might elect to be away, saved that one to remain with their family. Conrad generally arrived in time to sit down with them and in the evening often Helen or Paula dropped in with their husbands. By degrees it became a weekly "holiday" for them all. Tilde made a huge chicken pot-pie for the dinner and great panful of hot biscuits and there was always a wonderful dessert.

It was inevitable that Griffith should be drawn into the family group. They all liked him and he suspected his presence enlivened them; unaffectedly and simply they "showed off" before him and amused themselves as well as him. For his own part he grew to love them individually and collectively, and the time came when the old mother took him affectionately in her fat arms and kissed him as if he were her own.

Dickey was the great fundamental bond of sympathy. His dawning individuality was watched hour by hour, and what indications, manifesting themselves, marked its progress, were hailed with delight.

"He reached for my bangle to-day when I bent over his basket with his bottle," Tilde would tell Rosa when her sister came home at night.

Rosa kneeling beside the sleeping child would gaze profoundly at the infant prodigy. It was amazing! It was incredible! Why he was not even five months old yet!

"I'm sure he knows the sound of my voice," she would say earnestly.

Rosa, perhaps more than Ameli or Tilde, was drawn to the child. The one was absorbed in her hospital duties, the other had the care of the house and the preparation of meals, but the baby seemed to have entered and filled Rosa's heart and life completely. She was content to stay beside little Dick's clothes' basket hours at a time, silently watching the child's sleeping face, and Griffith frequently found her in his room when he came home at night, sitting upon the floor, one arm across the basket's edge, her head resting against it.

CHAPTER II

I

ONE of Griffith's greatest pleasures on Thursdays, was to take the baby out in the Park in his perambulator. He would wheel it twice around the big reservoir before resting; it was the only exercise he got and he enjoyed the experience keenly. He met young mothers and nurses with their own charges, and frequently he was stopped and asked about the baby. It was unusual to see a young man pushing a baby carriage about alone. He and the perambulator told their own story.

It was during these solitary Thursday tramps along the bare, leafless pathways of the Park, pushing the baby-carriage on and on before him, that Griffith began to think about himself. It was April and there was no hint as yet of the loosening of winter's grip. Patches of discolored snow lingered here and there where the drifts had collected and tenaciously refused to melt. The road-beds were still frozen hard and the cold wind boisterously split itself upon the tree trunks and raced through their ranks unchecked.

Reviewing his life, Griffith saw that his parents had never given him the love he bore his own son. His father had been incapable of understanding a child, had been ill-at-ease in his company, had been shy of his acquaintance. His mother had loved him as a little boy, but when he had grown into an awkward, ungainly lout, she had abandoned him to boarding schools. Fervently, passionately, Griffith vowed Dickey should never see the inside of a boarding school. How infinitely better off he would be if he could grow up with the influence of such people as the Pohlis about him! Griffith had only to think of what manner of men and women the nine children had grown to be, to find confirming evidence of the wholesomeness of the system by which they had been reared.

College? St. Cloud?

He could only shake his head when he came to think of his four years at college: four, wasted, profitless years. He and his classmates had been sent out into the world supposedly educated and equipped for life. The folly of it! The utter absurdity of it! He had condemned Clarisse for being hopelessly unqualified to meet the demands life had made of her. He had been, he *was* no better off than she.

He realized he had no training of any description to aid him in a business life. He knew neither profession nor trade; even his mind had never been disciplined to think. If Quay fired him tomorrow, he would not know where to find another position, or for what work he had any fitness. He was able to read aloud to an old man and play games with him; he had learned to file letters, and to discriminate among names in directories. These things had taught him nothing, and he had neither the strength nor the temperament for manual labor. Schools had been supposed to help him earn his living, teach him the duties of citizenship, fit him for marriage and parenthood. It was the thought of his inability to properly meet the requirements of this last relationship that stuck in his throat. He was ready to grant he knew no profession, no trade, no recognized means of livelihood; he had no idea of what his obligations were to the State, he had not been able to provide properly for his wife nor furnish her with those creature comforts that are every woman's right. Was he equally unfit for parenthood? Was Dickey handicapped because he, Griffith Adams, was his father? Was the very fact of his being, an injury to the child he had come to love with such passionate devotion?

He went to old Mother Pohli with his troubling thoughts. It was one of the early, warm days of summer, a golden June day after a fortnight of rain. A parallelogram of sunlight fell upon the worn red carpet, the windows were open and every now and then the lazy noises of the street below were broken by the harsh roar of the elevated trains as they swept by on the Avenue. Mother Pohli knitted industriously in her low rocker, the white ball of yarn half-way across the room. It was Thursday and Griffith had had a wonderful morning wheeling the baby through the fresh green of the Park, deliciously fragrant of damp soil and new grass after the long period of spring rain. Now as he sat by the window where he had been reading, he closed his book and stared idly out at the façade of the houses opposite. Presently his eyes wandered to the basket in which his son lay asleep, the bottle he had just emptied to its last drop lying on the flat little pillow beside his soft mop of blue-black curls.

Without premeditation he began to speak about the matter of which his thoughts were filled. The old woman listened to him, placidly, occasionally pursing her lips and nodding her white crowned head as she agreed.

"I'm not getting anywhere," he finished at length. "I've got no real work; if my employer should die, I wouldn't know what to do; I'd have to go about asking for a job again. I can't go on like that all my life. I don't want to be rich; I just want to be unhampered by lack of money; I want to be free to give my time to the boy here; he's the only thing I care about now; I want to save him from the blunders I made."

"Vell, dat ist right;" the old woman said thoughtfully. Presently she began again; Griffith's problem fired a train of reminiscence. "My husband vas a violin-maker in Zurich," she said. "Ve come here ven Tilde vas a leetle girl. He say to me: 'Ve vill put der money into teaching our sons and daughters how to make deir livings; ve vill not save id; ve vill spend id on dem un ven ve er old, dey vill maybe take care of us.' Adrian vas a vise und a goot man; ve haf taught der schildren each his work. All haf gone to der schools here; dey ist good schools, und der schildren haf studied in der pooks. Adrian make dem vork hard; he say to dem all you vill learn in der pooks, you vill learn ven you er young. Dey go to der public school; dey all vork and study hard except poor Conrad. His vater ist angry mit him und make him go in der army und dree year Conrad ist a soldier. Den he come home und Adrian pay his vay in der school und now he ist a chemist und he makes twenty dollars a month more den hiss vater ever. Tilde, she vas for dree year mit a dressmaker und now she makes all der clothes here. Maybe she vill marry aber now I dond tink so. Adrian, meine oldest son, is a goot carpenter. He vas a 'prentice four year und now he makes much money; he has a goot vife und goot schildren. Helen vas a baker; she makes der kuchen und mehlspeise; she ist married now aber maybe her husband dies, . . . he ist not vell, . . . she has no fear; she alvays vill haf a goot job vaiting for her. Rosa vent to der school vhere dey teach her to be der stenograph, und Paula ist ine putzhändlerin, . . . vas ist das? . . . She makes der hats for her vomen. Und Ameli is a nurse, und Johann vorks in der engraving schop, und leetle Rudi makes der violins like his vater. Dey all haf deir vork und all meine töchter know how to cook und to sew und to sveep und take care of der house und everything. Der job for der voman is to make goot vives und goot mutters und I teach dem dot aber if dey dond marry den dey vork und dond ask der broders und sisters to help dem. Der job for der boys ist to vork hard und deir vater make dem learn how. If der boys ist goot boys und dey make der money, den der goot vomen vant to marry dem."

The old mother nodded her head sagely. She followed her own thoughts for some moments and then noticing that Griffith had said nothing looked up to observe him with his head in his hands, his fingers thrust through his thick hair.

"Vell, vat ist?" she demanded.

"Oh . . . it's just what I say," he replied drawing a deep sigh and sitting back in his chair. "I never was taught a profession or a trade; I spent four years at college getting culture and instead of getting it, I lost what little I had. It seems to me, Mother Pohli, there's no education like the education of a good home; it beats all the learning you ever get in the schools; I never had it as a boy, but I have learned a lot since I have been here. People talk about unhappy childhood and imagine poverty means unhappiness; I don't know how it is in Switzerland but in this country, nine-tenths of the big men who have made their way into history started as poor boys. Look at Lincoln and Grant and Benjamin Franklin; and the men who are alive to-day: like Rockefeller and Carnegie and Edison!"

"Vell, it ist der same vay dere; it ist so everyvhere."

"I went to college," Griffith continued with rising feeling, "supposedly to learn something but instead of being fitted for a career, prepared to meet the exactions and demands of later years and taught a means of livelihood, I lost whatever qualities I had and acquired only what served to unfit me when the test came. I'm just one of hundreds of thousands who are being hindered and handicapped instead of helped by our stupid system of education. I'm a rotten failure."

Griffith dropped his head in his hands again. The old woman nodded sympathetically.

"Ach, my poy, it ist nod too lade; you talk foolish! Vat you mean by saying you haf failed? You er young; der ist many men who haf made der stard ven dey vas old und veak. You er *young!* Meine Conrad vas tventy-six year old ven he make der stard, und now he ist a goot man und makes goot vages. Be brave; des ist leetle Dick. You can be vot you like by der dime he comes to know you. Go vhere you like, do vat you please; leave der child mit us; ve vill take goot care of him; make vat you vant of yourself; study vat you like; you haf fifty year before you er a old man."

Fifty years!

Griffith looked up and met the Swiss woman's wise old eyes.

In thirty years he could live his life all over again! In ten he could re-live the hardest part of it, the part that had told! In three or four he could learn a profession.

Mother Pohli's last words to him that afternoon before Tilde came in from her shopping trip, stayed with him for many days.

"Pig tings grow from leetle vons; maybe you tink about id avile und den you make der stard, und den you vork hard, und den . . . Ach Gott! . . . id ist done! Vile you live you dond shtop still; you alvays make der change: a goot change oder a bad change; alvays you go on oder you go back. Now you haf to make der stard, von leetle ting; der next vill come soon; von und von you make vat you vill be."

II

A day or two later, as Griffith was reading aloud to old Quay from the morning paper, his eye fell on a large display of type in the corner of the page he was about to turn. It was an advertisement of a book of knowledge: a thousand pages containing a million facts "every well educated man should know." It was headed in heavy black letters: "An average College Education costs $4076."

The statement fascinated him. His own college education had cost considerably more than that: money that had been thrown away.

Old Quay interrupted his musings with a sharp question. What was he looking at? Griffith explained and was surprised to find the old man interested.

"Takes college men five years to get the nonsense they've picked up knocked out of their heads. They don't know the meaning of the word 'work.' There are few young men now-a-days who worked as hard as I did."

"How did you make your start, Mr. Quay?" Griffith dared to ask.

The old man blinked his parrot-lidded eyes and focused his small jet-black pupils at his secretary.

"Opportunity, Mr. Adams," he answered dryly. "I saw the chance when it came, and could put my hands on the money when it was needed."

"And . . . and how were you educated? How were you trained so that you could recognize the opportunity when it arrived?"

There was a pause. Quay slowly moistened his thin lips, shut and opened his beady eyes several times.

"I worked in a bank in this city for twelve years; I began when I was thirteen years old. My father was the cashier and then he was made president. When I was twenty-five, we had a quarrel and I went to the war and nearly died in Andersonville Prison. When I got home my father was dead; he left me a few thousand. There was a woolen mill in Providence which was going to close down because the banks couldn't float any additional loans: war times; there wasn't any money to be had. They came to me and asked me to help. I was just recovering from a long period of sickness. The proposition seemed right; I drove a sharp bargain with them; in six months I owned the business."

"Did you know anything about . . . about wool?"

The old man shook his round yellow head.

"No . . . but I knew money and I was able to recognize a profitable investment. The mill had a good business; it was sure to show profits; it needed a little money to bring it to life. Conditions everywhere were chaotic; the war was just over; the country was getting adjusted. I believed in the future of the wool business provided we had a high enough tariff. I financed a United States Senator's campaign and the protective tariff was assured me. In the next ten years I bought six other mills. In '79, I started up a mill in Brooklyn. Four years later the city condemned the property in order to erect the Brooklyn Bridge. I made money out of the sale and in '93 when the wool interests combined and formed our present business, I was the largest and strongest wool manufacturer in the country . . . Sixty years of work, young man, and it has been all that has saved me from the mad-house. Try work when trouble comes, Mr. Adams; it is an infallible cure."

Quay stopped speaking and stared for some minutes in front of him. Then the discolored lids closed over the bright little eyes, his lips compressed themselves in a sharp line like a crooked crack in a billiard ball. Griffith, watching him, wondered what memories had risen in his mind, bringing back their hurt, opening old wounds.

"How would you start in, sir, if you were going to do it all over again?" he asked.

The eyes opened and there shot from them one of the old man's quick beady glances.

"You don't like your present work, is that it?" he asked.

"No, sir; but it's not getting me anywhere. I want work that will teach me to do something better. I want to progress, . . . get on."

Quay hunched his frail shoulders. There was a brief silence and then unexpectedly the old man barked at him:

"Do you want to learn the wool business?"

"Why . . . why I guess so," Griffith began vaguely; then with more positive assurance he added: "Yes, sir."

"You'd have to begin at the very bottom," Quay warned him.

"I'd expect to."

"You wouldn't earn enough money the first year to buy a patch for the seat of your pants."

Griffith clicked his teeth together. Swiftly he made up his mind. Wool or cotton, books or briefs, pills or figures, it made no difference what he did; he grasped the fact that the chance of a vocation was offered him.

"I'll tackle anything," he said earnestly, "that will teach me something. I don't want any money to be taught."

The hairless lids closed and opened again.

"I'll send you to Trowbridge tomorrow. He'll give you a chance if you really want it."

"But . . . but I don't want to quit you, Mr. Quay, . . . not as suddenly as that. You've been very kind to me."

The shrivelled frail figure croaked. The sound was like the cluck of a hen.

"My old secretary wants to come back. I'm used to his ways and he to mine."

III

Griffith had met the President of the Woolen Company before. Trowbridge sometimes gave him a brief nod when he appeared in his employer's wake. The interview the following day in which his future was settled did not last ten minutes. At the end of that time, Trowbridge placed his finger on a push button and when a brisk young man appeared in response, said casually but concisely:

"Write Cravath at Dover that Mr. Griffith Adams will report there . . . on Monday?" He paused an instant on the interrogation, glancing at Griffith. "Ask him to make arrangements to take him in hand as soon as he arrives," he continued, at Griffith's confirmatory nod, "and get him established; find him a place to board and start him in as usual. I'll write about the matter myself in a day or so. Make a note to remind me."

"It will require two years," he said to Griffith when the clerk withdrew, "to familiarize yourself with the process of wool manufacture. Until you can tell the differences between serges, worsteds, cassimeres, tibets, venetians, broadcloths, kersies and flannels, and know just why and how they are different, you can be of no use to us. Mr. Cravath will put you through the mill and you will work there like an ordinary employee; he'll start you in the sorting room. From there you will follow the processes by which woolens are made, . . . the weaving, finishing, perching and so on, . . . until you come to where the goods are designed. When you have learned how to design goods yourself, we'll give you a chance out here on the floor for awhile to show you how to sell goods and then perhaps you will try designing your own fabrics. That is the process by which we train our men; we send 'em to school; you're worthless to us until you've learned the manufacturing end and until then you will receive only apprentice wages: six dollars and sixty cents a week. Do you think you can live on that?"

"Yes, sir."

Griffith did not hesitate. The Pohlis would take care of Dickey until he could repay them; he himself would manage somehow.

"Very well, then, I'll write Cravath about you and ask him to let me know from time to time how you are getting on."

CHAPTER III

I

Dover, New Hampshire, a quaint little town of white clapboarded houses standing flush with uneven brick pavements, lies peacefully under thick foliage of elm and locust trees which closely line the streets and meet overhead. It is old-fashioned, prim and sedate, a little rambling, a little dreamy, tranquil and Arcadian.

It seemed to Griffith it had been predestined he should come to Dover. He felt that his place in the little home of old Mrs. Carmichael on Silver Street, had long awaited him, that his seat at the table of little O'Rourke, the chief engineer, and his red-faced buxom wife had been ready for him months before.

He arrived on Monday with a letter from Trowbridge to Cravath, the Superintendent, and by Wednesday it was as if he had been in Dover too long to remember just when he came. Mrs. Carmichael had a back room she would let for two dollars a week; O'Rourke thought the "Missus" could board him for four. Without preliminaries, without ceremony or delay, his education,—his vocational instruction, began.

He rose every morning at five as a mile walk lay between him and Mrs. O'Rourke's overloaded breakfast table. The chief engineer lived in one of the Company's houses, which stood across the road from the mammoth, many-windowed mill, a little, gray-painted, two-story house with a peak roof like a score of others similar to it that lay scattered about the rambling mill.

Work began at half-past six; there was an hour at noon and the whistle blew again at six in the evening. It was a long day and in the beginning it seemed unendurably tedious. During the first fortnight Griffith questioned his strength and his determination to go through with it. The time came when he whipped his flagging courage by resolving daily he would remain just another twenty-four hours; each day of grinding fatigue represented a milestone to be passed.

He was put to work in the sorting-room. Here the wool in great cumbersome bags of burlap was received and here the fleeces were separated into different qualities. All day long he had to stand in front of the sorting board, pulling the fleeces to pieces, throwing the good wool,—the second, third, fourth and fifth grades and the skirtings, the half and the quarter clips,—into bins, arranged in a semi-circle about him. Two or three minutes were all he was supposed to allow to each fleece and his hands must fly, and his eye not wander, to dispose of it within that time. Thurston, the old foreman, was patient and encouraging. He had seen other young men come up from New York to learn of wool, and perhaps Griffith impressed him by his earnestness. It was exhausting work and he knew it. Towards the middle of the day, as the summer advanced, the temperature in the low room steadily rose. The air was full of fine floating hair and dust and the choking smell of unwashed fleeces, redolent of animals and the sheep-pen. Once a week a few bags of "pulled" wool made their way into the sorting-room to be handled, and then the stench was so great, one must breathe only through the mouth. As the long afternoons wore on, and his feet ached and throbbed, and the muscles in his back and the space between his shoulder blades seemed on fire, Griffith used to smile at the recollection of his rebellion over the fatigue he fancied he had endured before the filing cabinets in the railroad's office.

He was astonished, however, at the rapidity with which he grew accustomed to the work. He ate enormously of Mrs. O'Rourke's abundant meals; he slept profoundly nine hours each night in the springless, slatted wooden bed in Mrs. Carmichael's back spare bedroom. He rose refreshed and full of energy.

In the mornings the sun was always throwing the outline of his window casement in a bright triangle upon the wall beside his bed when his alarm clock awoke him, the birds were twittering cheerily and busily in the narrow rose-beds of the tiny garden, an early-hour haze hung softly, almost caressingly, over the white houses and the motionless foliage of the thickly-leafed trees; here and there wreaths of white smoke floated in trailing scarfs from square brick-capped chimney tops. The mile walk before breakfast was exhilarating; the air was fragrant of wet grass and early morning smells; as he strode along the foot-path that followed the road to the mill, he filled his lungs exultingly to their capacity and expelled the air in great bursts.

All day long the clack of the looms and the carding machines, the plunge of the water over the dam, the throb of the engines, the roar of the great mill above and about him, beat upon his ears. As he became accustomed to the terrific racket, he grew to enjoy it, and to like the fine tremor of things beneath his hand. At the end of a month when he found that without effort he was keeping pace with the other wool-sorters, it sometimes seemed to him he had never known any other existence.

At the beginning of his sixth week, Cravath sent him word to report to the foreman of the scouring-room, and Griffith was put to work mixing alkali soap and cleansing acids, and to dumping bins of sorted wool into great boiling vats, sending it down the chute into whirling scouring machines.

The weeks slipped by almost unnoticed. At the end of another month he passed on to the picking-room where the blending was done, thence to the carding-room where great sliding machines with a clang, clap and slither, slipped to and fro and carded out the wool into thick hairy ropes. October found him among the looms, where he had to pay one of the weavers for his instruction, to reimburse him for his own loss of time. The work absorbed him; it was fascinating to see the thick matted fleeces slowly taking shape and finally being woven into the soft flocculent fabrics. Winter was upon him before he was aware that the leaves were gone.

Weekly he received letters from the Pohlis; Rosa wrote long typewritten chronicles of Dickey's days, Ameli dashed him hurried postals, sometimes Mother Pohli achieved a curiously worded, strangely spelled epistle. He lived for these, revelling in the news of his son. Dickey crowed and gurgled all the time he was awake; he slept sixteen hours out of the twenty-four; he could raise himself to a sitting posture now; he had a tooth, a little glistening pearly chip in his red gums. In November there had arrived three small snapshots, to Griffith the most precious pictures in the world. They had been taken on the baby's first birthday and showed him manfully clinging to an iron railing in the Park, and there was another of him in Rosa's lap, holding out a bit of cracker to a venturesome squirrel. Something reached out from the little photographs and caught at his heart. His love for the boy was a frenzy, absorbing, consummate, exquisite; it possessed him mind and body. The long hours in the mill, the aching muscles, the tired feet, the long tramp to and from his work, the separation from the child itself, the loneliness and home-sickness were all for his son. There was a fine satisfaction in the sacrifices he was called upon to make.

Winter swept down on Dover with all the rigor of New England snow and cold. The morning came when he found a thin coating of ice over the water in the pitcher in his room, and the day arrived when there was no way of getting back from the mill because of the drifts and he spent the night on the couch in O'Rourke's parlor, a rug from the floor supplementing the blankets the fat, good-natured wife of the engineer was able to spare him. This was the hardest time of his exile; six months were behind him; another year and a half stretched drearily before.

II

Griffith had little opportunity to read the papers; he rarely saw them and it was only on Sunday that he ever glanced at one. Mrs. Carmichael took a Portsmouth daily and occasionally a bulky Boston Sunday paper found its way into the house. It was not strange therefore that he did not hear anything of the double tragedy which came so near to him until it was several days old, and then it seemed too utterly awful, too unreal and impossible, for him to believe. At first he was more violently shocked than even he had been when Clarisse smiling happily up into his face had suddenly ceased to live. Then it had been only his own loss, the loss of her intimate companionship and warm love, that had mattered.

But this——! He wanted to rush into the street and tell those he met, all his fellow towns-people, he had known them both,—that both were friends of his—yes, yes, intimate, dear friends,—*both* of them! Excitedly he bore the newspaper to little Mrs. Carmichael and struggling to control his agitation informed her of the fact.

He was amazed she was not impressed; her "Tut-t-t-t . . . shure 'tis a dreadful matter-r!" and her mournful expression and sorry headshake seemed to him to scream to heaven with their pitiful inadequacy.

He turned from her in despair. He felt he must do something about the matter at once; he must hurry; there must be no delay. Only he, Griffith Adams, knew the motive that had prompted the murderer. The papers said that there had been an altercation and the clerks in the outer office had heard high words and then suddenly two quick shots, one upon another, and after an interval, a third which had sealed the slayer's lips as firmly as his victim's. No one knew why they had quarrelled; the police admitted they could find no motive for the crime and the secret of the two dead men would never be learned. But Griffith knew; he could explain the provocation behind the shot that had laid low his friend.

He felt he *must* tell someone in authority what he knew, that it was his duty, and with trembling fingers he struggled into his great coat and was floundering through the snow-drifts on his way to send a telegram to the Chief of Police, when the folly and absurdity of the act flashed across his mind. He stood still, the snow crowding his heavy coat up around his body as he stopped in the knee-deep drifts, and stared about him. What consequence was it to the police or to the public to know the reason that had actuated the murderer's hand? Who would be the happier or be better satisfied by knowing the sordid cause? His information would furnish sensational material for the newspapers and nothing else!

Into these reflections came the thought of another who like himself—wherever she might be—must hear the news and accept the grim facts alone, for solitary anguish. He wondered about Rita; he had not heard from her in nearly a year. Was she still playing in *Miss Juliet of Joliet,* and was it her fate to assume her motley, rouge her cheeks, sing and simper through her lines and songs as usual on the very night when the evening papers were screaming the murder and suicide of the man whose quarrel had been provoked by her? Mad, infatuated Jack Hemmingway, tortured by doubts and the torment of love, had not been able to see that it was her ambition which would not yield to his persuasion. It was not her preference for his rival. Rejected, spurned, he had turned in fury upon the man he believed had won her favor and had determined, with his own death, the other should share his fate.

And Archie? Prudent, discreet, cautious Archie had paid dearly for his lapse from rectitude. Abhorrent as the realization of the emotion was to Griffith, as uncharitable and unworthy as it appeared, he could not but be aware, together with his shock and sorrow, of a certain faint, almost an inappreciable feeling of satisfaction. He refused to allow himself to entertain the thought or his mind to consider the fact, but yet he was conscious it persisted. There had been something always so righteous about Archie, not smugness exactly but a vein of self-sufficiency that had always vaguely irritated. He had paid the gravest price for his transgression, and Griffith would have given generously of himself, his blood and body, to have been able to restore him again to the world of living men, but there was gratification in the words he caught himself excitedly whispering:

"God! He *got* it! He *got* it, all right!"

Again and again during the night or as he bent over mending the broken warp of a loom, the frightfulness of the tragedy rushed over him. He saw the dim luxuriousness of Archie's office, the rich mahogany and leather, the green light and the dull brass fixture; he saw Archie's set, calm face, the steady opaque gray eye, the cool stolid expression, the firm lip and the look of dogged obstinacy he knew so well; and across the polished surface of the table, the congested features of poor, exasperated Jack Hemmingway. No one had heard the violent accusations, the mad demands, the insane threats. The sound of the angry voice had passed beyond the glass-panelled partitions, but Archie's cold, passionless, phlegmatic answers reached only the ears for which they were intended. Griffith knew so well how he had considered Hemmingway's accusations impertinent, his catechizing effrontery. His calmness, his unruffled dignity and imperturbable self-possession had been just the things that had roused the other's inflamed wits to madness. The weapon had flashed in his hand, a choking oath from his lips, and the crashing detonation of the two shots had filled the whole office; once more the report shook the glass panelling, and then there had been silence, profound, unbroken, deathly, while the white-faced clerks, some crouching behind desks, some half-risen from their chairs, had stared at one another wide-eyed, waiting for another sound to break the tense stillness.

They had found Archie sitting in his desk-chair, his hands lying slack, half-open upon the shining desk-top, his head a little to one side, a sad smile upon his firm, tight-pressed lips. Hemmingway was on the floor flat against the partition, the revolver still in his hand, an arm across his face.

And Margaret? How had they told her? How had she received it? Had David been beside her at the time? Had it been his lot to tell her? His imagination gave him no rest. He saw her with the black *crêpe* shrouding face and figure; he saw the black-edged handkerchief pressed again and again to her brimming eyes; he saw the darkened carriage, Barondess beside her,—David leaning forward holding her limp hand. He saw her in the arms of her tall, stalwart father-in-law, his tragic face bent close to the burnished glory of her dark hair, his tearless eyes shut in agony of grief. He saw her staring with vacant eyes as she moved listlessly about her empty home. He knew the desolation in her heart and the bleak loneliness that wrapped her.

He wrote her as best he could. There was little he could say; the words as he had penned them seemed so pitifully, so preposterously inadequate. How write of his sorrow and his horror or express his extravagant sympathy! His heart cried out to her but he could only inscribe conventional phrases. He had a letter from David presently, pathetically eloquent of his own distress in its crude wording.

Things were in pretty bad shape, he wrote. Margaret was ill; she was under the care of physician and nurses; as soon as she could be moved Archie's father and mother were going to take her with them to Europe; she had stood it all bravely and had tried hard not to break down, but the strain had been too great and now they were closely watching her heart; for awhile they had been afraid she might go into brain fever but that danger had passed. He hoped Griffith would understand why he hadn't written before; there had been a lot to attend to;—and he hadn't felt able to manage a letter.

Some weeks later Griffith heard from Margaret herself. The letter had been written on board the steamer and was postmarked *London*. It began:

"My dear, dear Griffith:
"I have been thinking of you very often these past few days and blaming myself that in my own loss and grief, I have not remembered yours. I was too sick to appreciate your letter when it came but the other day among the things I brought along on the steamer, I found it and it suddenly occurred to me how much he was to you and how unselfishly you loved him. It came to me, too, that I had no idea of what your own bereavement must have been for you so short a time ago. Such sorrow is not understood short of the terrible experience itself. Now you and I know, and the knowledge must bind us all the closer to one another.

He loved you, Griffith, more than you realized; among all his men friends you came first; not even David was so deep in his affections. I know how sincerely you returned it; perhaps I know this better than even he did. He was not exacting in his relationships; he was too generous, too big-hearted . . . . ."

The rest of the letter was devoted to a passionately-worded tribute to the man whose wife she had been. It was incoherent in spots and its sentences frequently unrelated. The thought that had actuated her to write it was forgotten; at times it was evident she was not conscious to whom she wrote; she poured out her grief in an extravagant eulogy. She made no mention of her probable return nor gave any address.

III

The winter in Dover shut down determinedly; storm after storm piled foot on foot of snow in the streets; the cold was intense.

Griffith struggled to and from the mill, plunging through the drifts, catching a ride now and then on an early milk sleigh, or spending the night on the sofa in the O'Rourke's little parlor. The mill pounded and roared, the looms clacked and clashed, the spinning mules slammed and banged; a fine vibration shook the rambling structure constantly.

He thought of his mother, of his wife, and of his friend,—and, with passionate love, of his son.

CHAPTER IV

I

ONCE every two or three weeks, Griffith received a letter from Leslie. These were dictated epistles, typewritten at the office, and invariably contained the information that the weather was hot, cold, pleasant or disagreeable in the city, that Leslie, himself, was "pretty good," that things were as usual, and concluded with the hope that Griffith would soon be back. Enclosed was usually a five-dollar bill. Griffith kept the notes until he had twenty of them and then returned them asking his brother to credit the amount to what he owed him. Leslie did not send the bills back as he feared, but thereafter when his communications contained money, the letter was affixed to a ten-dollar note.

Griffith had come to love his brother with real affection, and it was therefore with a sense of one calamity being heaped upon another, that he received a letter from a physician the following July informing him that his brother had had a paralytic stroke and hoped that Griffith might run down to see him, if that could be conveniently managed.

There was no difficulty in obtaining permission for a week's absence from the mill. Griffith found Leslie in a private sanitarium on Manhattan Avenue, in a little white-walled room, propped up in a semi-reclining attitude with many pillows. He was sadly changed; his shrunken body was more shrunken, his pale emaciated face more wasted and haggard. All his right side was paralyzed; he talked with the greatest difficulty and was just able to masticate his food. He presented a pitiable sight with his distorted features, his ragged, unkempt beard, his rumpled pajamas open at the throat disclosing his corked neck like the strings of a harp, his twisted mouth and drooping eyelid, his frowsy head that looked so small among the pillows! On the chair beside his bed was the crumpled newspaper and a tumbler with a swallow of whiskey at its bottom.

" 'Bout finish . . ." Leslie whispered. "Just one . . . two little things want y't'do f'me."

None of these had been of any consequence, it seemed to Griffith. Certain shares and stocks were to be sold; a bank-book had to be balanced; a few documents and papers locked up in his safety-deposit box; his attorney consulted. The apartment was given up and the furniture, including the red satin parlor set, was sent to an auctioneer to be sold. Leslie offered to keep the place in case Griffith should care to establish himself there with his son when he returned from Dover and get a nurse-maid in to take care of the baby.

"Won't cost you anything," he urged.

Griffith could not find it in his heart to explain that through the toiling lonely months of his exile in Dover, it was the prospect of coming back to the genial, affectionate Pohlis that spurred him on and encouraged him when his purpose flagged.

He spent all the few days of his visit with Leslie at the hospital, reading the newspaper to him and trying to put hope into his heart that he would be about again before long. But Leslie was resigned to his fate. He had no complaints to make. He hoped only that he would not live too long; it was so difficult to manage his paper with one hand that he grew too tired to read, and the doctor only allowed him twelve ounces of whiskey a day.

Griffith parted from him with sad misgivings. He never saw him again. Two months after he returned to Dover he had a letter from the attorney, informing him of his brother's death. Leslie's dead wife's sister and her husband had taken charge of his interment and had laid claim to the estate, which amounted to several thousand dollars, on the strength of a will dated eight years before in which Leslie had bequeathed all that he owned to his wife who was then living. Another will, of later date, had now been brought to the attorney's attention by Mr. Wagstaff's stenographer in whose keeping it had been placed. By its terms Griffith was named sole legatee. Unfortunately Mr. Wagstaff had neglected to sign it but there was every likelihood that in court the document, to the validity of which and its purpose the young woman who had taken the dictation from Mr. Wagstaff's own lips, was ready to swear, would have consideration. It was the lawyer's opinion that if the matter was brought to court, the other parties could be persuaded to settle on some equitable basis and in this adjustment as in other legal affairs, the attorney would be very pleased to represent him.

Griffith did not take long to decide his course of action; the dispute over the money seemed sordid. His title to whatever Leslie had left on the strength of an unsigned paper struck him as hardly justified. He did not question his brother's purpose but if through an oversight his inheritance was invalidated, then the result of his brother's negligence ought to stand. More than all, he was actuated by a lack of desire to possess the money. He did not need it; it was not of his earning; it would hamper his purpose. Once accepted, it would influence him, cloud his vision, weaken his determination. Had the legacy been his beyond a doubt, if it had come to him without dispute, he would have accepted it even though he did so with misgivings; but he would not fight for it.

II

His deliverance from exile in Dover came sooner than he expected. He was put in the designing office when he returned to the mill, and here was shown how to write the formulas by which the patterns are woven, to lay out drafts for blankets, and to work up designs after the suggestion of the "styler" from the New York office. It was more interesting work than any to which he had as yet applied himself, and he was soon absorbed in planning, and having woven on the small looms in the designer's office his own special combinations of the colored yarns.

The styler came up from New York for a fortnight's stay in October. John Osborne was not many years older than Griffith, but he was a man of experience, and had a family of three children, of whom he loved to talk. Perhaps it was this which resulted in mutual confidences, perhaps it was some of the samples of cloth that had been woven after Griffith's ideas, and which pleased the man's fancy. Whatever it was, Griffith made a new friend in John Osborne, and a month after the latter's return to New York, Griffith had word direct from Trowbridge, informing him that there was now a vacancy "on the floor," and requesting him to report for duty on the first of December, when his salary of a thousand dollars a year would commence.

Yet, when the moment came, it was hard to part with Mrs. Carmichael, and fat buxom Mrs. O'Rourke, from Cravath, and Thurston and O'Rourke, himself, and from some of the men in the mill whom he had come to know, and warmly like, after the intimate companionship of a year and a half. It would have been pleasant, Griffith thought, as he sat in the dusty train, and saw the prim white houses and the tree-lined streets begin slowly to slip past him, as the train gathered headway,—to have made Dover his home, to have raised Dickey in this quiet New England town, and to have worked all the rest of his life in the mill beside the simple-hearted, kindly people he had learned to respect and like. Mrs. O'Rourke kissed him when he said good-bye, and Mrs. Carmichael placed in his hand a little scalloped silver medal of the Blessed Virgin, as he stood for the last time on the rickety stoop before her little home, that had been his so long.

"Kape it f'r the choild, Misther Adams, and let him wear it, sorr. 'Twill be like a cha'rm to him, and kape the ould b'y away! Father Fitzpatrick blessed it for me h'mself when he was here awhile back!"

"I'll bring him to see you, some time!" Griffith said, touched. He and his son had not so many friends that even this humble one could be lightly spared.

III

To surprise him, Tilde and Dickey met him at the Grand Central Station. Half-way down the concrete platform Griffith, struggling to retain his suit-case under an onslaught of red-caps, recognized his son,—the dark mop, the sturdy square little figure, and the red-gaitered legs. Tilde was sure that the child knew his father, too, but Griffith could not admit it. He was willing to surrender his luggage at last to one of the persistent porters, in order to take his son into his arms. He would have liked to have crushed the child in the violence of his embrace.

There was a big family dinner in the Pohli household that night, to celebrate his homecoming, and before it was over he kissed in turn each one of the women about the oval table, and there was great merriment when he came to Rosa and Ameli.

IV

He had not seen David during his brief visit to New York in July. His old friend seldom wrote letters, and it was only at long intervals that Griffith heard from him. He had been greatly surprised to discover, when he went to call upon him, that the offices of *The Master Builders* were occupied by a tailoring establishment, and to learn that that periodical was now a part of the United States Trade Journal Corporation, which occupied an immense building of its own, somewhere in the West Forties. Upon inquiry at its imposing headquarters, he was informed that Mr. Sothern, its General Manager, was in England. Since Archie's death he had not heard of, or from Margaret. But a few weeks before he left Dover, he had a few lines from David, once more in America, demanding to know what had become of him, and when he expected to return to New York. The day following his arrival, Griffith went to see him.

Awed a trifle by the size of the building, the enormity of the whole establishment, the brisk efficiency of elevator boys and office boys, Griffith had no time for any misgivings. He was instantly admitted, and David's cordiality, and his delight in the meeting, were too spontaneous to doubt. David wrung his hands, and clapped him upon the back, and was eager to hear all his news, to hear of everything that interested or concerned him.

"It's been close to two years, Griffith old boy, since we've seen one another! By George, you've changed, I'd hardly know you! You've got bigger, somehow, and more serious; you've changed a lot. You've grown handsome, do you know that? Margaret will be overjoyed to see you. You must come out to dinner tonight. She's been back about a month, she doesn't find much pleasure in life, Grif. But she was asking me about you yesterday, urging me to find out from your office when you'd return to New York . . . Why can't you come out and have dinner with us tonight? I came back before she did, and got things in order as well as I could! I had to get the house ready for her; it's been closed since she went away . . . There were lots of things we had to get into shape, but now it's pretty well settled, and she's very brave, and she's decided to make her home here, and . . . you know, . . . start over. But she's got nothing to interest her, I think that's more the trouble than anything else. Old Barondess' death on top of poor Archie's . . ."

"Barondess?" Griffith cried sharply.

"Why . . . yes. Both Barondess and his wife! Didn't you hear that?"

"Good God, . . . *no!*"

Griffith sucked in his breath sharply.

David nodded.

"They were on the *Titanic;* Margaret waited over in London to meet me. She would have been aboard herself if I hadn't been delayed here."

Griffith closed his eyes.

"I didn't know . . . I hadn't heard . . ." he said, shocked and in deep sympathy.

"Well . . . she hasn't anything to keep her mind busy. She took up singing again when she was in Paris, and she may do something with her voice now. You'll cheer her up a lot if you'll go and talk music to her, and take her to the opera, and to concerts. She goes alone most of the time. I can't tell one tune from another!" David confessed, with his old smile. "The other night I annoyed her by doing some figuring on the back of a program, while some woman was singing! . . . She'll be terribly pleased to know you're back again, and to stay. I'll be through here at about five-thirty, and we'll run out in the car."

Griffith shook his head.

"I can't tonight, David, thanks just the same. I've got an engagement with one of the girls at home, . . . the Swiss family I live with; she wants to go see her married sister tonight, . . . it's one of the kids' birthday, . . . and I promised to take her. But I could come tomorrow."

"All right, I'll tell Margaret." David looked pleased, and Griffith felt strongly the return of his old affection for him. They presently lunched together, and to Griffith the relationship between them had not seemed so evenly balanced since the early days at St. Cloud. He had not David's income, of course. But David had no black-haired son. And Archie—once so far ahead of them both—

They talked of Archie, while the orchestra played, and the waiters noiselessly came and went. An hour later, Griffith walked into the clear winter sunlight with a new-born content, even a faint stirring of complacence and self-respect in his heart.

V

On the following evening he was obliged to telephone and postpone his dinner engagement. It was his second day at his new work, and John Osborne, who was now in charge of the clerks on the floor, wanted Griffith to dine with him. The invitation was too important, and too graciously extended, Griffith felt, to be declined. The atmosphere of the great woolen company's offices delighted him, and he liked his fellow-clerks, who took him in without reserve, and made him one of themselves.

On the third night after their luncheon together, he and David went to dine with Margaret.

She was much changed. Griffith had expected that, but he had not foreseen in just what way she would be different. He remembered her as a girl, a pretty, sweet, light-hearted girl. The Margaret he met tonight was a woman, still sweet and kindly, but with the merriment and cheerfulness gone. Not that she was sad or mournful. She impressed him rather with her calmness and dignity. The lines of her figure were rounder and more generous, her face fuller, she was riper, and far more lovely. He caught his breath as she stood a moment in the wide doorway of the room in which he and David, with their backs to the fire, were waiting for her to come downstairs. It was an exquisitely beautiful woman who advanced toward him, her round arm extended, a sweet welcoming smile upon her lips, her soft gray draperies trailing behind her. A beautiful woman, but she was not the same person who had lightly touched his hair, and urged him to forget his passion, a few years ago.

"Well . . . *Griffith!*"

She was charmingly cordial. His affection warmed to her, his staunch, devoted friend!—Dear Margaret!

There was, however, no longer the boy-and-girl relationship between them. He and David were men now, and she was a woman. A sadness came over Griffith as he sat listening to her. Here she was, Mrs. Archibald McCleish, in her richly furnished brownstone house, a lovely woman, exquisitely gowned, about her the elegant appointments of her home, the polished dull woods, the soft-toned tapestries and Persian rugs. The servants, from the obsequious butler at the door, to the maid who came to throw another log on the fire, from the French cook to the liveried chauffeur, all strove to make the life of their mistress as frictionless, as happy and contented, as possible. And here was her brother, the manager of a great corporation, his alert mind forever turning over schemes, juggling figures, weighing and rejecting propositions, whose limousine and chauffeur waited hourly his wish, the call to whirl him to one appointment fast-following another, to whirl him home to dinner, and whirl him downtown again to a directors' meeting. And here he was himself, a father and a widower, with so many illusions vanished, so much young faith dissipated! Youth had forsaken them all. The ardent impulsiveness, the self-assurance, the trusting confidence of early years, were gone; the golden season had passed them by; springtime was over.

And yet Griffith experienced a sense of security as he watched Margaret's face, animated and alight now, as she spoke of her meeting with David in London. He had no apprehensions for the future; the illusions and the dreams might have vanished, but his vision was clear. He had himself in hand, he was prepared to meet whatever he confronted, he was master of himself.

The butler approached, and deferentially announced dinner. The three linked arms and walked between the heavy tapestry curtains into the brilliant dining-room beyond. The fine linen cloth sparkled with polished glass and bright silver, there were flowers on the table, and flowers glowed everywhere in the room.

Formally the meal proceeded, the butler whisking off the silver lids of dishes, and proffering the appetizingly arranged viands. A rare Madeira in thimble glasses appeared with the broiled fish, an amber-toned Burgundy in frail rainbow-tinted glasses was served with the spitted fowl. It was all harmonious, gratifying, exquisite, and Margaret, sitting between the two men was a vision of beauty: her lovely soft throat delicately bordered by the silver-gray lace, her rare smile flashing over her small white teeth, her blue eyes alight with warmth and interest, her fair skin framed by the warm tints of her hair.

It was widely different from the noisy group about the oval table at home, with Tilde piling the soiled plates upon one another as soon as they had been emptied, Mother Pohli wiping a spot from the front of her prominent bust, Rudi loudly laughing. . . .

After dinner David left them, and Margaret and Griffith spent the evening alone. She sang for him, and he was astonished at the new, rich, resonant quality of her voice. She had studied the part of Sieglinde, and knew it thoroughly. They discussed the possibility of an operatic debut; Griffith was enthusiastic, Margaret rather preferring the thought of concert work.

"You'd make a sensation, Margaret. You have every qualification; the public would go mad about you. Oh my dear, dear girl! It would be an astonishing thing . . . it would be wonderful . . . to see you at Carnegie! I can just picture you in that golden bath of light, with all the little musicians perched about you, bending over their racks, and the crowded house eagerly waiting to applaud!"

Her eyes reflected his enthusiasm. Transfixed by the picture, she watched his face, her own alight and smiling. Then she drew her breath sharply, her eyelids fluttering.

"My dear Griffith, you almost make it seem worth while!"

She left the piano bench, and crossed to the fire, where she stood gazing down at the languid, waving little flames that embraced a half-burned log.

Presently they began to talk of Archie, and of the other sorrows that had changed Margaret's life. The world had gasped for many months over the great sea-tragedy that had snatched Baronedss and his wife from the world of the living, but it seemed a fresh and living thing tonight, when Margaret spoke of it.

"Of course it wasn't like . . . the other, like Archie's . . . going," she said, tears in her eyes. "But . . . coming so soon after it, it seemed to make the whole world a black place of cruelty and suffering and loss, to me. They weren't really my parents, Griffith, and in many ways we weren't alike. But they were always so kind to me, . . . they were ties, you know. And now, now there's only you and David . . . who seem to . . . to belong to me. You two are the only ones to whom I can really speak . . . of Archie, and the old days."

It was a sad, an affecting talk, to them both. They sat side by side before the languishing fire, in the deep armchairs, and found certain comfort in it. The tears occasionally flowed from the woman's eyes; she checked them with a small, damp handkerchief.

VI

"There is one thing that has haunted me for this whole year, day and night," she said uncertainly, "and there is just one person in the world who can . . . who might . . . throw light upon the matter, Griffith, and satisfy my doubts . . . and my . . . my fears. That person is you."

He looked up, troubled and concerned.

"You knew . . . the other, I know; Archie mentioned him to me once. I cannot remember what he said about him, but I know that he spoke of him as . . . as your wife's friend." She began to speak rapidly. "Griffith, what was it they quarreled about? What was it they discussed? Oh, Archie could be cold and unreasonable . . . he could be maddeningly provoking, . . . I know that. But there was a grievance; the man had been wronged, or fancied he had been! What was it? There was something Archie kept from me? I have tortured myself with thinking about it, I've waited and waited . . . one can't write of a thing like this! I've said to myself that you would help me, that we'd puzzle it out together! . . . What was it, Griffith? What had he done?"

Griffith was looking steadily into the fire. No flicker of a muscle betrayed him, as she finished speaking. He had long ago decided upon his course, when this moment should come. It was Archie's secret, and Hemmingway's. He could not betray the dead. It would do Margaret no good to learn the truth. Archie was dead, his honor, in his wife's eyes, lay in the hands of his friend. Griffith thought of Archie's loyal championship of himself in boarding-school days, his devotion thereafter. How safe a secret of his own would have been in Archie's hands! He shook his head, and gravely met her anxious eyes.

"No, there was nothing, Margaret . . . nothing that I know about. We weren't as close to each other . . . the last year, you know. I've . . . I've wondered myself, very often."

Margaret drew her breath in again quickly.

"But you *knew* . . . the . . . the man . . ." she said after awhile, her voice trembling.

"Yes, I knew him," he admitted. "He was once in love with Clarisse, and she with him, but that was no affair of Mac's. He was excitable and vehement . . ."

"There . . . there was some talk . . ." Margaret began, hesitated and stopped. She chose her words painfully, crushing down her emotion. "I heard," she continued presently, "it came from his people, I believe, . . . some paper hinted, . . . that it was a woman they quarreled about . . . a girl . . ."

Griffith met her eye unflinchingly.

"Oh *no*, Margaret!" His voice was steady, the inflection he threw into his words sincere. "Archie was as straight as a string! There was nothing like that. Hemmingway perhaps wanted to borrow money, or was going into some deal with him, or he wanted to break a contract. It was something like that . . . nothing else."

The dark head dropped forward into a fine white hand. She looked up presently, and sighed.

"Well," she said slowly, "I hope it was so. Archie loved me, I am sure of that. He was wonderfully considerate of me, was devotion itself. But it might not be so hard if it had come in some other way . . . an accident, or a sudden illness. Somehow I think I shouldn't have minded it so much if it had been so, but . . . but to have him brutally shot, in his own chair, , . . with no effort . . ."

She began to sob brokenly.

VII

An hour later, when Griffith stood holding her hand a moment, as he said good-night, she was her composed self again.

"I've never seen your son," she said. "Won't you bring him and let him spend a morning with me, so that we may get acquainted?" She shook her head, smiling gently at him. "You . . . a father, Griffith! . . . I can't accept it! It seems so strange that it is you, of all of us, who has a child. Is he like you, or like his mother?"

"He's like my father, I think."

"Oh, I know he's wonderful!"

"Well, he's companionable, and *fairly* intelligent," Griffith admitted proudly.

"I want to see him! When can you bring him; tomorrow? Saturday? Sunday? Or shall I send Felice and Stuart for him? The car's a closed one; let me have him tomorrow? Do you think he'd come? I'll call for him myself if I may have him!"

Her eagerness was touching. Griffith could not have refused her, even if he had had a reason for so doing.

"You . . . you haven't an idea, Griffith, how you've cheered me! My dear, you've really put the heart back into me with your encouragement, your good advice . . . and the prospect of your son's affection, which I promise you I shall win!"

"You've always had his father's."

A warm color flushed her cheek.

"Griffith, you're a goose! But I'll be after your gosling at ten tomorrow, and I promise to have him home again for his lunch and nap at twelve!"

VIII

The Pohlis moved for the summer down on the ocean shore, into a storm-beaten cottage that stood with a swarm of others like it on ranks of short, round piles a hundred yards or so from the pounding breakers. The waves, flattening themselves on the hard sand, slid, thin and foaming, across more than a third of that hundred yards toward the dry, clean, unpainted steps leading from the wide, railed porch, to the hummocky sand. A colony of these battered cottages huddled together on a strip of beach, several miles long, and half a mile wide, and separated from the mainland by spreading marshes. Through these wound a deep channel, and down it several times a day came the sturdy little gasolene launch that was the only means of communication with the village, a mile or so inland. Forty or fifty persons could be carried by the launch, and from the Long Island village, the city was only a fifty-minute train trip. Nearly every family had its commuter.

Wreck Leads was impossible for habitation in the winter, but in summer some two hundred families thronged the strip of sand, and held clamorous possession of the white beach from June to September.

The Pohlis' bungalow boasted but five rooms, and three of these it was necessary to use for sleeping purposes. The remaining two were devoted to eating and cooking, and the wide porch supplied a comfortable and intimate place to congregate and lounge. There were grass rugs and sagging wicker chairs here, and the family spent the day in this spot, when its members were not down on the white glistening beach, dancing and shouting among the great rolling combers.

It was a roisterous, familiar, tomboy sort of life, but even the Pohlis declared that they had never had so much unalloyed fun. They all breakfasted at six in the morning, sometimes with the soft fog pressing thick about them, sometimes with sparkling sunlight flooding the restless, tossing floor of the ocean, and the bleached, parched sand.

Rudi, Johann, Rosa and Griffith departed together for the city when the launch left the rickety dock at a quarter to seven. Dickey in Tilde's arms would wave an energetic farewell, as they trooped off across the sands.

There was some quality that was regal about the child. Under the stimulus of the ocean winds and the salt air he throve marvellously. All day he pattered back and forth barefooted on the sand, pail and shovel busy, digging, crawling, burrowing, retreating with shouted glee from an unexpected wave that swept up about his ankles, wetting his diminutive overalls. The bloom of his skin turned a warm, dark russet brown, a triangle of deep tan lay on his chest where his shirt was left open at his throat, and the ends of his short sleeves marked a sharp line between the milk-whiteness of his body and the tawny hue of his arms. Beneath the hair that tumbled about his neck was a strip of white skin, and his lids, when closed, were like silver leaves across his eyes. Griffith's heart would suddenly contract as he watched him. Had he been puny and homely, his father told himself he would have loved his son equally as well. But this magnificent and brawny child in his faded overalls, his scant shirt blowing free about arms and chest, his small feet planted so firmly on the hard, wet sand, as he manfully strode about his forts and tunnels, his thick dark hair waving carelessly about his head, seemed to him the most beautiful scrap of humanity that had ever been born.

IX

It was pleasant, travelling to and from the city with Rosa. Rudi and Johann left them in the train, and went off to the smoking-car. Griffith preferred to remain with the girl. There was not the slightest trace of anything sentimental in their relationship. Rosa was an unaffected, straightforward, simple-hearted girl, who was frankly his friend, his closest perhaps, at this stage of his life. Griffith thought her amazingly clear-sighted and clever. Rosa was sensible, there was no nonsense about her. What she said was sound and discriminating, she was wise and—and sensible.

Her passion for Dickey was undiminished, and the two never grew tired of discussing him, his clothes, his meals, his punishments, his budding personality. Day by day they rode together in the train, meeting under the clock in the Long Island waiting-room a few minutes before train-time, threading their way through coach after coach in the long train until they found an empty seat. Griffith came to tell the girl unreservedly of his own life, his schools and college, his marriage and his wife. She commented, sympathized, agreed. Dick must be saved from that kind of upbringing, there should be no boarding-schools in his life, and if he went to college he should at least learn a profession.

"What we learn from books," Rosa reflected one day, looking out of the car window at the flying country, "doesn't help us so much as we are taught to believe. Our mothers and fathers, who have lived fine, self-sacrificing lives, cry out for education, the thing they missed themselves, in work. Education! Their sons and their daughters must be taught Latin and chemistry and history, the things they have hungered to know. They lose sight of the fact that they themselves have had the only education that really counts. Book learning is an excellent thing, I wish I had more myself. But it is not, by any means, so important as learning of life itself. Life is not pleasant; there is far more sorrow in the world than happiness, and happiness only comes in one way, and that is in service. My mother is the happiest woman I know. She has toiled for sixty years, for others, and while she has had sorrow, she hasn't found her contentment in the study of books."

"I don't decry the education of books either," Griffith said,

"I criticize the environment where education is disseminated. Boarding schools are an abomination. They are unnatural institutions. They propose to take the place of the father and mother at a time when a boy needs more careful supervision than at any other time in his life. They are nests of cruelty and iniquity. Nothing can justify an institution where a boy of twelve years is flung into a cell and kept in solitary confinement for three days and nights, nor one where a boy can be subjected to such cruelty as I knew from my fellows at Concord. I have talked to other men about their experiences at boarding school. There *are* exceptional schools, I daresay, but the evidence is overwhelmingly against them."

"Parents send their children from home at the very time when they begin to appreciate what a home is," Rosa contributed. "How can the children make homes if they don't know what good homes are like?"

"Exactly." Griffith spoke eagerly. "But if boarding schools are bad, colleges are far worse. I do not quarrel with the immorality that exists at college,—though Heaven knows it's bad enough,— nor have I anything to say about the kind of book learning that is taught there. I leave it to the educators to decide whether Latin should or should not be inculcated into the undergraduate mind. I attack the mental attitude, the code and the point-of-view of the students themselves in our great state colleges and big universities of the West with which I am familiar. In nearly all these institutions, cheating in recitation and in examination prevails. The adoption of the honor system such as exists at Princeton and Williams, was put up to the student body at St. Cloud when I was a sophomore. It was defeated three to one. Fifty-five per cent. of the undergraduates were women; think how many 'co-eds' must have voted against the measure to defeat it! The fraternities foster this loose sense of honor. The club men went up in a body and cast their votes against the proposition. It should be the fraternities, in whose ranks are supposed to be the best bred men in college, that stand for the sacredness of the given word, for honesty and integrity. Yet I was urged and persuaded by the fraternity I joined to break my pledged word to another club; I was told such pledges were constantly broken, and I found it to be the fact. One freshman I knew, who had promised to join another society, was deliberately gotten drunk and when he didn't know what he was doing, was initiated into a fraternity."

"But what did he do when he was sober again and found out what had been done to him?" Rosa asked.

"Nothing. What could he do? It was too late then. . . . Last year at Cornell, the fraternities made a solemn agreement among themselves that freshmen should not be 'rushed' until they became second year men. They pledged their words not to cultivate any freshman's society nor entertain in any way. The agreement did not hold good six months. The fraternity men could not keep their words."

"But why do parents send their sons to institutions where promises are so lightly made and lightly broken? What is the use of all the early teaching?"

Griffith shrugged his shoulders.

"It comes closely home to me," he said sadly. "I was taught to lie at boarding school and to regard my pledged word as valueless at college. Cheating was practised by everyone I respected and petty thieving was considered an amusing escapade. When it came to accepting a bribe after I graduated, and taking what did not belong to me, it never occurred to me that these were reprehensible things to do. Our universities are making thousands of such loose-principled men year after year and turning them out all over the country."

"Then what is the sense of ever sending a boy to college?" Rosa demanded.

"There isn't any, unless he goes where such conditions do not prevail and where he learns something definite like engineering or electricity or law,—something by which he can earn his living after he graduates. I look back in deepest sorrow and regret at my undergraduate career. I was urged to vice and robbed of my natural instincts for what was decent. I knew nothing of life when I finished my four-years' course but my head was full of false ideas and false standards. I had to unlearn what I'd been taught and through hard experience find out for myself the real values and truths of life."

"I hope you'll never send Dickey to college."

"I can't keep him from it, if he wants to go," Griffith answered. "He'll have to want very badly to go, however; he'll have to work to get there; and he'll go with his eyes open. I'd prefer to have him learn a trade like your brothers. They've learned of life along with their jobs."

"I think I agree with you," Rosa said meditatively. "I've worked for eight years in business offices. It's been a wonderful education for me,—the best, I think, a woman can have."

"But haven't you found it drudgery, Rosa?"

"Oh, no! I'm always interested in my work. It's much better than sitting at home waiting for something to happen, as most girls do."

"Waiting to be asked to marry?"

"Yes. But I shall never marry."

"How foolish, Rosa! Of course you'll marry!"

She did not answer, and presently began to speak of Dick again.

X

On Saturday afternoons and Sundays the Pohlis spent all their time on the beach. These were glorious hours for Griffith. He hurried into his bathing suit as soon as he got home on Saturday, and tumbled and splashed in the water with Rudi, Johann and the girls. He coaxed Dickey into venturing in his arms out into deep water, where the bubbling wave-rips swirled white and foaming about his waist. The child's confidence in him was enchanting, and when with his brown little arms clasped tight about his father's neck, he clung frantically to him, as the rushing surf swept down upon them, and cried a supplicating and excited "Dad—Dad—Dad! . . . Oh, Dad!" Griffith strained the small figure to him in passionate embrace.

Later, they sprawled on the dry sand, and drowsed, heads pillowed on bent elbows, the hot flagellating sun beating down upon their prostrate bodies. Dickey, under a weighted umbrella, and stretched upon a fringed shawl, took his midday nap, a little flounced pillow beneath his head. Frequently they had their supper down by the waves, a clambake, with piping hot corn roasted in the ashes, broiled chops, apples and potatoes, and even fish, rolled in cheese-cloth and steamed, served with a marvellous sauce of Tilde's concoction.

The strip of shore below the cottages was lined with these evening fires, and there mingled in the air a not unpleasant blending of the music of phonographs, guitars, and harmonized singing, subdued by the pound and rush of the surf. On calm nights the moon shed a white glory over the beach, and blazed across the surface of the water an iridescent path of silver. Far out, dots of light like brief rows of pinholes, marked a steamer ploughing its way up the coast. In August phosphorus appeared in the water, and the breaking waves were alight with a ghostly emerald shimmer. Rosa and Griffith, who loved the water best, often slipped again into their damp bathing-suits, and hand in hand raced down the flat hard shelf of sand, leaped across the shallow tide, plunged through the luminous, churning surf, and with backs turned, hurled themselves into the descending combers, that burst with lustrous splendor into a thousand flashing jewels.

XI

In September Griffith received his first promotion. He was assigned a small mill in Providence, for which he was to become the "styler" and selling agent. He had worked hard since he came to New York, and his devotion and enthusiasm had not escaped the attention of those above him.

He spent a month at the Providence mill, and during that time he had the good fortune to see a good deal of Margaret. She had come to Newport to visit her friend of convent school-days, and he was invited down for the week-ends. He had never met Mary Schiller before, although he had seen her at Margaret's wedding, and had heard her so often mentioned and quoted that she was far from being a new acquaintance. She was the same age as Margaret, enormously wealthy, and went in heavily for society. Her home was one of the granite palaces that form Millionaires Row, and during the season she and her mother entertained elaborately.

The visits to Newport were delightful, though Griffith was uncomfortable at first with so much grandeur about him. He had explained before his arrival that he had brought no evening clothes from New York with him, but Margaret had urged him to come nevertheless. He decided that he would make no useless apologies.

He was not in "society"; he had no place among these wealthy men and women. He determined to appear simply what he was, a salesman in the wool business.

Mary Schiller was devoted to Margaret, and she eagerly watched for opportunities to give her friend such pleasures as could reach Margaret's still empty heart and life. During Griffith's visits she contrived to leave them as much as possible to themselves. It proved to be the most enjoyable entertainment she could have provided for either. They were not interested in the polo, or the golf tournament that was in progress. They liked best to wander out through the garden, and across the lawn,— strewn in spite of the gardeners' efforts with the crumpled red and yellow leaves that floated from the surrounding trees.

They talked often of Archie, his loyalty and steadfastness, his generosity and thoughtfulness, reminding one another of this and that that he had said and done. Gradually they came to talk more of little Dick. Margaret had taken the boy to her heart from the moment she had first seen him. Nothing since her husband's death had brought the interest back into her life, as had this small person, Griffith's baby son.

Before the Pohlis had moved down to Wreck Leads, she had come almost every morning, in the open car, for Dickey, and had taken him for long drives with her. She would buy him expensive toys and clothing, little sweaters, Chinese wrappers, gloves, elaborately embroidered rompers, and hem-stitched night-gowns and handkerchiefs. She lavished gifts upon him until Griffith begged her to stop. He had been glad when Dick went off to Wreck Leads, but even there Margaret's affection pursued him, and once a week, sometimes oftener, packages had arrived, containing toys or presents of some sort. Griffith gave these to other children on the beach; Dickey had too much as it was. But he took some kodak pictures of the baby, bending over, in his water-soaked overalls, vigorously spading his sand ramparts, and sent prints to "Aunt Margaret." Margaret wrote that she had cried over the pictures, and begged for the films, so that she might have enlargements made.

Now she wanted to hear about him, and how he had spent his days, and whether or not he remembered her, or ever spoke of her.

"Ah, the darling! The dear . . . ! He's all I care for now,

Griffith; my heart's wrapped 'round him. . . . I couldn't love a child of my own more. He's like my own!"

The last Sunday spent at Newport was the most perfect of Griffith's visits. There were no other guests, and he and Margaret took a long motor drive as far as Falmouth, where they had lunch in a quaint white farm-house, the last of whose summer boarders had departed. The autumn glory was fading, but there was still a prodigal blending of yellows, reds and browns among the trees. The air was soft and hazy, the ocean a Prussian blue, with white sails scattered over it like fallen petals. Margaret was unusually gay and light-hearted, and at a spot above the cliffs the motor car had waited while they climbed down to a rim of white beach, laughing like children, as they slipped and scrambled over the rocks in an effort to reach a wave-encircled boulder without mishap.

CHAPTER V

I

BUT there was a sense of relief when he got back to the Pohlis. The flat smelled of boiling onions, and the small kitchen was filled with drying clothes, for outside it was raining. Johann was in the bath-room, shaving, and Ameli, who was doing private nursing now, was ironing one of her stiff piqué uniforms in his own room; Tilde, in the midst of making dresses for Rosa and her sister, was busily buzzing the sewing machine in the front parlor, and Dick was charging about from room to room on an improvised hobby-horse, shouting a jargon of inarticulate commands.

There were no servants, no beautiful brocades, no vistas of great rooms, no stately carved oak furniture, antiques, nor works of art here. It was just a busy happy family who dropped their tasks, and gathered round him to laugh over his return, to kiss his cheek and wring his hand, while the smallest member desperately hugged his knee until he was gathered into his father's arms.

II

Griffith was permitted just one week's enjoyment of being home again among these people who were now to him like his own, when the sun was wiped from his sky.

He had left the office a little earlier than usual, one afternoon, and had walked over to meet Rosa and ride home with her on the elevated. They arrived at the house in high spirits, and reached the top landing laughing and breathless.

Tilde opened the door for them. Griffith knew that something was wrong the instant he saw her face.

"What is it?" he demanded.

"It's Dick," she said slowly. "He not well. I think . . ."

His heart froze.

". . . I thought it best to send for the doctor."

The child lay on the bed, with wide starry eyes, his cheeks aflame, his lips bright red.

Griffith sat down beside him; Rosa sank on her knees. He touched the forehead and cheek gently as he bent over him, pushing the mop of hair out of the baby's eyes. The skin was hot, like the surface of thin iron in the sun.

Mother Pohli sat in a rocker at the other side of the bed. At once Griffith's eyes sought hers; she did not answer his mute question directly.

"Der docktor vill come soon, den ve will see!"

Half an hour later the grave-faced physician was taking temperature and pulse. Anxiously they watched his face, and presently he met their gaze, but there was only uncertainty in his eyes.

"Well . . . we'll see. It's not going to be one of those indefinite ailments. He's got a hundred and four now. . . . I think we can say in the morning. I'll be in early."

An endless night of wakefulness and fear ensued. Ameli, who had come off a case only two days before, assumed charge of the sick-room. Dick moaned and whimpered, and strung unintelligible phrases together, tossing from side to side. Toward three o'clock he dozed off. Griffith lay flat on his back in one of the boy's beds, in the next room, staring wide-eyed into the darkness above him.

"I think the doctor will be able to diagnose the sickness this morning," Ameli said significantly, over an early breakfast in the gas-lighted kitchen.

"I'll wait. . . . I've got to know," Griffith said hoarsely. An hour or two later the physician confirmed Ameli's prediction.

Scarlet fever! The terrible word paled all their faces. But the doctor was reassuring.

"You've got an excellent nurse right here in the house, and we know what we have to fight. That's the main thing. I'll have to quarantine you, I'm afraid."

They looked at one another blankly.

"You mean . . . ?"

"You'll all have either to stay here altogether, or move away at once. Some of you go to business? So? . . . Well, you can find other quarters?"

"But, doctor," Griffith burst out, "it can't be! There are four in this family who go to work in different places!"

The physician frowned.

"We can send the child to North Brothers' Island, or perhaps they'll accept the case in the contagious ward of the Willard Parker; I'll telephone right away, and find out. We can get an ambulance immediately . . ."

"Good God! . . . Isn't there some other way, doctor?"

The physician shook his head.

"I'm afraid not," he said. "Unless you have some friends who could take him into their home, and who don't have to go out!"

There was silence among them. Griffith shut his eyes fiercely. He couldn't let Dickey be taken away from them! He couldn't turn all the Pohlis out of their house! . . . Someone?

There was Margaret! She was home again, she had returned from Newport only two days before. She was alone, with her servants, in the big house! Dared he ask her? Would she consent? He did not wait to consider long. Blindly he went to the telephone.

There was no questioning the sincerity in her voice.

Why, Griffith, of course! The limousine would be there in twenty minutes. Stuart had just come from the garage for his orders. She would go with him . . . or would it be better for her to stay at the house and get the room ready? Then Griffith could bring Dick. There was plenty of room for Ameli; of course, she must come. Dickey must be wrapped warmly for his drive, and in half-an-hour he would be tucked safely into bed in Aunt Margaret's house. She would not think of allowing an ambulance to be sent for; the car would be fumigated afterwards. But they must guard against his catching cold. Had they a good physician? And Griffith must not worry, lots of children had it. And he needn't explain, and he needn't thank her . . . there was nothing to thank her for!

Intense confusion prevailed. And yet Ameli's bag was packed, and the baby's few necessities tied up separately, and Griffith overcoated and hatted, impatiently waited beside the bed to gather the little trussed bundle in his arms, long before the twenty minutes Margaret had mentioned were over, and the bell sounded from below announcing that the car had arrived.

In spite of the excitement of the moment, and the haste that actuated them, Griffith turned affectionately at the last moment toward Rosa and her mother, as they stood beside one another in the doorway, and smiled a wordless good-bye. He felt the love that flowed from their hearts as Mother Pohli with compressed lips waved a good-bye, and Rosa, tears upon her cheeks, whispered, "God bless you."

III

Ah, he had friends, at last! They stood around him now, eager, loving, anxious to help. As the motor sped along the smooth pavement, and he and Ameli sat side by side in the car, the silent staring child pinned snugly in double blankets in his arms, there rose before him a memory of the moment when all his world had risen against him, and drove him forth, an outcast! Was he the same person? Was he still Griffith Adams?

IV

Margaret herself opened the door.

There was nothing said. He heard her catch her breath as she caught sight of the child's face, then she turned and hurried upstairs, beckoning them to follow.

In half-an-hour the quiet room had been metamorphosed. The hangings were gone, the heavy velours and the fine lace undercurtains; the pictures had been taken down, the unholstered furniture removed. Nothing remained except the great mahogany bed, a couch, a table, and three or four straight-backed chairs. The room had been gutted of luxuries.

In this denuded chamber, suddenly equipped for the grim battle, little Dick Adams fought for his life during the next three weeks, and Ameli and Margaret and the doctor fought with him. Griffith was not permitted to see the boy closer than through the crack of the door which Ameli held ajar for him, and these glimpses lasted but a few minutes. All day long the black terror that lurked in the shades pursued him; he felt it hourly at his back, waiting the moment to suddenly spring upon him, and shatter his reason.

"Oh, God, I couldn't stand it. . . . I couldn't stand it!" he muttered through the days and nights, "I've endured enough! I don't deserve that I should lose my boy! Spare him, God! Grant me my son!"

V

He had moved out to Margaret's house, at her urgent request, and they passed the long evenings together by the fire, their words halting at the slightest suggestion of sudden haste in the feet on the floor above.

Steadily, the fever mounted, reaching its terrifying height as the afternoons lengthened. One hundred and five and two-tenths, one hundred and five and four-tenths, one hundred and five and seven-tenths,—and eight—nine-tenths. *One hundred and six!* And still there was no checking it.

"It's got to break some time!" the doctor assured them.

The child's delirium was harrowing. They could hear his treble mutter going on monotonously, endlessly.

Griffith would sit with fiercely gripped forehead, teeth clenched and eyes tight shut, until the murmuring died away. As the tense muscles relapsed, he would turn wearily to the woman beside him, to find her eyes full of affectionate sympathy.

"Oh . . . Margaret!"

"Dear . . . *dear* Griffith!"

VI

Swiftly, unexpectedly, the crisis developed. There came the dreaded hurry of feet, and the voice of Susan, the maid, at the telephone. Griffith stood in the doorway below, clinging to the heavy portière, his face buried in its folds.

"Yes . . . Doctor . . . Miss Pohli thinks you'd better come over right away . . . she didn't say, sir. . . . She just told me to telephone you to come!"

Margaret was running upstairs. Griffith stumbled to a chair, and fell upon his knees, struggling to form the words of some forgotten prayer of earliest childhood.

An hour went by. It was life or death for Dickey now. . . . And then Margaret was beside him, her arm about him, her warm breath upon his cheek.

"It's all right, Griffith dear. It was just the last spurt of the fever. It's broken now, and he's sleeping peacefully!"

VII

The days of convalescence followed. There was another nurse now to relieve Ameli, who had firmly refused help before. This was the time when the greatest care must be exercised, the temperature of the room watched, the dimness of the light filtering through the drawn curtains vigilantly maintained. The two nurses, the maids of the house, and Margaret, herself, guarded the precincts of the sick-room as if for each it held the most precious thing in life.

There came a day when Griffith was allowed to come in, and sit beside the bed, and try to return the radiant smile from the gaunt white face. But he must not touch the fragile little hand. Thereafter he was allowed to come daily, and the visits lengthened gradually to an hour. He racked his brains to find things that would amuse the boy: flash-lights, paint-boxes and a stuffed, brown furry bear. He haunted the toy stores.

But Margaret put his efforts miserably to rout. There was nothing she would not buy, reckless of cost, no trouble to which she would not put herself and her household, to provide half-an-hour's distraction for the little convalescent. One day it would be an electric railroad; the next a circus, with half-a-hundred animals, clowns and acrobats. Griffith was troubled, but he could not hurt her by denying the warm-hearted generosity, prompted by an affection comparable to his own.

VIII

When first the suspicion awoke in his mind he could not have told. From the outset he rejected it indignantly, but it persisted. Again and again he attacked himself for the absurdity of the idea; again and again it recurred. He dismissed it resolutely, and the firmness of his purpose was still hot when new evidence reawakened the disquieting speculation. He found confirmation all about him in David's brusque heartiness, in Ameli's silence, even in Dick's artless prattle.

These he might discount. But the hour arrived when there was no disregarding the blush on Margaret's cheek, and the light in Margaret's eyes. No matter how incredible it appeared, he came finally to the point when he must admit that it was so. The realization staggered him, but his heart rose to meet it tumultuously. Could it be possible? After all these years? Was the old hope and desire to be quickened and stirred again? Was the thought of Margaret as anything else than Archie's wife and widow to reassert itself?

The wonder of it filled all his days, but he could not consider it rationally. How was he different from the person who had pleaded his case five years before? What had he done to deserve her favor now? In the beginning he had suspected that it was Dick for whom she cared, and that her love for the child was so intense she might consider the father in a more intimate relationship, in order to call his son her own. But he was presently compelled to admit the real truth of the situation.

As the inexplicable fact became less strange to him a vague misgiving grew into something like alarm. The days were passing, the weeks lengthening into months. Dick, warmly bundled, had taken his first ride in the car, Ameli was talking of going home. It was this announcement that forced him definitely to face the situation. When Ameli went, he and Dick must go too. He had been looking forward impatiently to being back among his old friends in the pleasant warmth of their kindliness and simplicity. Dick had spoken of it, too. They had been away now for nearly two months, and were all anxious to be home again.

Griffith had gone two or three times each week to see the Pohlis, and had frequently had dinner with them. Of late they had been eager to know when he was to return. Tilde and Mother Pohli had gone to see Dick, and had taken him little presents, but it was not the same as having the child among them; they missed him dreadfully, and after Rosa went away——

The statement was surprising news to Griffith. He had not heard of her plans; when had she decided to go, and where? It occurred to him that he had not seen Rosa for weeks. Twice he had come to dinner and not found her; she had been obliged to go to Helen's, or she was spending the night with the Adrians. On another occasion when he had dropped in, late in the afternoon, he had been told that she had gone to bed with a headache. She had come nearly every day to ask for Dick at Margaret's house, but at such times Griffith had been at his office.

Rosa had resigned her position, it appeared; she did not like it now that a new man had been made manager, and Cousin Ferdinand had written her to come to Philadelphia, to his office, and he would pay her thirty dollars a week.

Griffith was angry that Rosa had not sent him word, or written him a note. They had been such good comrades all summer, riding to and from the city in the trains, racing into the surf, and idling on the sun-flooded beach. He could not understand how she could treat him so, and he went in an indignant mood to Ameli.

And Ameli, for the first time in her life, was short with him. She resented his tone, told him brusquely she saw no reason why Rosa should feel any obligation to consult him about her plans, and she did not like his cross-questioning, nor his attempt to take her to task for her sister's actions.

He was hurt and mystified; he felt he had in some way offended Ameli, and with his heart overrunning with gratitude toward her for her wonderful nursing of the boy, he could not understand what he had said or done to vex her. He decided to have Mother Pohli straighten the matter out for him.

IX

But he allowed his intention to grow cold. Margaret filled his thoughts. Sleeping, waking, his mind dwelt on the miracle that had befallen him. She loved him; that was the overwhelming fact, she *loved* him. The flattery of it left him breathless. She stood before him one of the beautiful women of the world, kindly, sweet, tender and loving, prodigiously rich, the sister of his closest friend, ready for the question that would make her his. Yet he hesitated.

It was too much; it was more than he wanted; it was confounding. He loved Margaret;—he *dearly* loved her. She had been first in his heart from the day he had met her. He had burned his incense to her, and given her his devotion for so many years that she had grown to be an institution in his life. He wanted her to remain as she was; he did not want her to love him. By stress and travail he was working out his own scheme of life, and his destiny lay clear-cut before him. His soul had been tortured, scarified and hammered, and strength and courage and righteousness had been born into it. And now this lovely woman,—even though she was Margaret,—threatened his new-found resoluteness, his new faith in himself, his fresh spirit and confidence with her beauty and her wealth. He feared his hard-won fortitude might break under the test.

A picture rose before him of himself as Margaret's husband: no need to go on designing fabrics, no need to work, no need to think longer of wool. There would be no call for self-abnegation. Luxury and bodily ease awaited him, a great fortune was his for the asking; motor cars, yachts, country estates, lackeys, grooms and valets, fine raiment, silver and gold,—and the lovely mistress of it all!

He saw himself luxuriously seated in the fawn-lined interior of a great motor car, riding leisurely down the Avenue, he saw himself directing the new work on the great estate at Lenox; he saw himself and Margaret being lavishly entertained. He saw Europe and the Orient,—a vista of the golden years before him, cloudless, frictionless. Margaret and himself returning from the opera, Margaret and himself looking out across the oceans, or gazing from Alpine peaks on greater heights. Margaret and himself growing peacefully and contentedly old together, while Dick—while Dick—while Dick grew up—while Dick—

That was where the vision vanished, and a heavy frown creased his forehead. His son—his Dick—the child of his heart—where did he fit into the picture?

A shudder seized him. He visualized Dick's share as vividly as he saw his own. Good God! The conventional schools and the conventional college, the conventional training! He saw the great handicap of money like a huge stone about his son's neck. He saw Dick's wishes immediately gratified, his fancies eagerly humored. He saw himself, robbed of his hard-won wisdom, his strength and courage sapped by luxury and ease, pandering to his son's laziness, improvidence, and extravagance.

And he saw Margaret, well-intentioned, generous, and loving, but undisciplined, denying her stepson nothing, enfeebling his mind and soul, with her misguided generosity. He knew Margaret's greatest weakness was her good nature, her desire to please. He had seen the improvident way in which she had lavished gifts and toys upon Dick. He had seen her hand her gold jewelled lorgnettes to the pleading child, and had seen him promptly break the delicate mechanism, by which they opened and closed. He had seen her stealthily slip a chocolate wafer into his moist little palm, right under the eye of the watchful Ameli, and he had listened to her warm golden voice singing the child to sleep when her physician had forbidden her to use her throat.

Dick was her idol, now. But Dick might not always be so bewitching. Dick might one day be a shy, unattractive, inarticulate boy, a boy who needed his father. Suppose that father were loitering abroad, that boy left in charge of someone like——

He might fling away his own life; he could not sacrifice Dick's. The nervousness that had become fear, and the fear that had become alarm, sharply became terror. He was afraid of Margaret, afraid of himself, afraid of the temptation facing him, afraid now to allow his mind to dwell an instant longer on the prospect he had permitted himself pleasantly to consider during the past weeks. His heart cried out, he longed for escape,—for *refuge!*

Refuge! Ah, that was what he desired with all his soul. Refuge for himself and his son. His thoughts swept the horizon of the people he knew,—David, Mother Pohli, Ameli, Tilde——

Swiftly, like the quick rising of a curtain, like a bandage being swept away from before his eyes, his vision cleared and he saw what a fool he had been. What a blind, blundering fool! There was only one refuge in the world for him. Burning with shame, sick with humility and mortification, he longed to throw himself at the feet of the woman whom he knew at last to be his natural mate.

Simple, gentle, unassuming Rosa! So wise, so lovely, so good. He saw her standing, serious and silent, hands locked, eyes drooped, a sad smile faintly suggested about her lips, a flush upon her warm cheek, rosy like her name, her fine-spun yellow hair framing her face, clinging close, covering her ear-tips. Ah, there was never such a woman! And she had been beside him, all through the summer, in the same house with him for two years and more, and he had been blind, and had not recognized his fate.

Rosa, of course. His heart leaped at a thousand memories of her, leaped as it had never leaped at the thought of Margaret. Rosa, who was so firm an authority with Dick; Rosa who loved all children. Rosa who could tie an apron about her trim waist and cook a dinner, or clean a room, who was healthily radiant over a picnic, who was always in ecstasies over a baby. She would be a helpmate to any man, steady, busy, proud of her husband, proud of her home. She could no more spoil a child than she could neglect him, there would be no pandering to extravagant tastes in Rosa's house. And she—she *loved* him! He understood Ameli's behavior now.

Griffith felt he could not wait to heal the hurt his slow wit had caused her, to console her troubled heart. She had deliberately avoided him, and had planned to go to Philadelphia, that she might not see or hear of his happiness. The doubt and anguish of her heart must be ended, her purpose checked. Griffith was on fire to tell her all his thoughts, to unburden himself of his yearning, to throw himself at her feet and avow his love.

But he was too late; Rosa had gone.

"On Saturday I have to go to Philadelphia," he announced as he sat at the Pohlis' cheerful dinner-table that night.

"Maybe you'll see Rosa?" Tilde ventured. Her mother frowned, but Griffith smiled.

"I am going just to see Rosa," he answered gravely. He saw the quick glance the women exchanged, but nothing more was said. But later as he bade them good-night, the old mother drew his face close to her own and kissed him.

X

He found Rosa in Cousin Ferdinand's garden. It was an overgrown tumble of wild things, surrounded by a tall iron fence, fashioned from the barrels of rifles used in the Mexican war. She sat on the low, worn seat that encircled a thick old locust tree, and leaned against the rough twisted trunk, reading aloud to a little boy of nine, who lay sprawled at her feet in the long grass. To Griffith it was like some quaint old picture, needing only the hoop-skirt and the water-fall to put it back in the early sixties. He paused outside the railing.

Quite involuntarily Rosa glanced up and saw him. She started, and closed the book with a faint clap. Griffith holding the iron bars as he looked through them, smiled, drinking in the sight of her, with a fast-beating heart.

"What is it, Griffith? Not Dick?"

His eyes shone with his love.

"No . . . no, Rosa, it's not Dick. Ameli brings him home again on Sunday!"

"Ah . . . !"

He opened the tall gate, mounted the little flight of chipped brick steps, and came forward, holding both hands toward her, his face glowing.

Swiftly the color flooded her own. Frightened and embarrassed she turned to the boy.

"Run tell your mother a friend has come, Walter. He will stay to dinner . . . won't you, Griffith?"

"If it's all right."

He could not check the happy smile he felt upon his lips. He watched the boy disappear into the house.

"Rosa!"

She did not look at him, but sat down on the bench again, and picked up her book. He dropped down beside her.

"Rosa!"

He saw the leaves of the book tremble as she turned them.

"You know why I've come?"

Her hand paused, and she bent closer over the book.

Her dearness and sweetness rushed over him in a flood. He put his fingers over hers, and the words burst from him in a tense and passionate avowal. It was turbulent, broken, vehement. There were no flowery phrases, none of the neatly-turned expressions he had planned as he had gazed from the windows of the train on his way from New York. It was the cry of his heart for her love, and herself, the cry of a soul storm-tossed and weather-beaten, longing for the safety of a harbor, a refuge from rough waves and winds, and the rocks that lay concealed, waiting to destroy.

There was no resisting the appeal. Thirty years of the hunger for human love were back of it. It was irresistibly eloquent. Rosa covered her face with her hands, and began to cry softly. Screened by the tree he slipped his arm about her, and gently drew her to him, and raised her wet face to his. Her long dark lashes fluttered an instant, and then she met his kiss with full lips, tenderly, ardently, lovingly.

And so he entered into his rightful heritage. The years of his childhood, boyhood, and early manhood lay behind him, years full of hard and fearful lessons, from which he had learned bitter truths. It had been an arduous path by which he had come, devious and difficult, but, with Rosa's love won, he believed he had his face turned squarely towards the heights, his feet securely planted on the right road.

XIII

Life never marks time. New experiences, events and circumstances, sorrows and joys, death and new life bring their lessons and their greater knowledge. These lay ahead, and the only road by which they could be reached rose precipitous and crooked as before. But the mistakes, the misjudgments and the blunders lay behind, together with what had been the hardest and the saddest part of the education of Griffith Adams.

THE END

Afterword

By Louis Auchincloss

Salt, published shortly before the end of the First World War, marks the end of the period in which naturalist fiction could still shock American readers. For more than two decades novelists such as Charles G. Norris's more famous brother Frank, Theodore Dreiser, and Upton Sinclair had been creating fiction that purported to tear aside the shimmering veil of the American Dream and reveal the sham and despair behind it. They carried on in America the crusade that Zola had started in France. But after 1918 a new age of tolerance nullified the shock effect of such writers, and *Salt*, for all its vivid characterizations and for all the tenseness of its plot, seems now simply the herald of a day whose loud voices are less noted because all voices are loud.

Salt is also a literary oddity, a determinist novel with a happy ending. Norris has to do some violent things to his plot to make his ending happy, and the husband of Kathleen (a popular and prolific sentimental novelist) triumphed at last over the brother of Frank. But until those final chapters he has a number of interesting and provocative things to say about the education of American upper-middle-class males.

The subtitle of the book, *The Education of Griffith Adams* and the birth of its hero in Cambridge, Massachusetts, suggest that some humor or irony may have been intended in relation to *The Eucation of Henry Adams*, published in the same year but already widely known in privately printed editions, but just what humor or irony is not clear. Henry Adams's thesis was that his education had been useless in the world in which he had had to live, and this is also true of Norris's hero, Griffith, but for totally different reasons. Henry's education in a world of unity was to prove irrelevant in a world of multiplicity, but Griffith's education was simply nonexistent. He cut all his courses in the University of St. Cloud.

The subtitle is further confusing in that Norris makes nothing of his hero's Boston background. Griffith's father, Richard Cabot Adams, is represented as rich and well-born, presumably a member of two famous and prolific New England families. Yet nowhere in the novel is there so much as a hint of the effect of two such powerful tribes on the boy, either morally or psychologically, and never does an uncle or aunt or a cousin on his father's side intervene to offer him the smallest help or encouragement, or even hindrance or discouragement. The factor that most determinist writers would have pounced upon as the single most decisive one in the development of such a protagonist is simply ignored. The only way to read the novel is to assume that Griffith's Adamses and Cabots are for some reason the "wrong" kind of Adamses and Cabots and push on to the author's main thesis.

Norris is intent upon creating a protagonist with a maximum surface area for the prods and pricks of his environment. Griffith's father is a cipher, a cold preoccupied scholar; his mother, a vain and fatuous creature, concerned only with her own sexual adventures. There are no siblings, except for a much older alcoholic half-brother, with the result that the boy is brought up in an atmosphere of essential lovelessness. He is sent to a ferocious military academy and then a rotten little boarding school, in neither of which does he learn anything but the technique of survival with his fists, and when he goes at last to a big midwestern university he has developed neither a moral character nor the realization that he lacks one. At St. Cloud he follows the norm of social aspiration, turning down a fraternity to which he is already committed for a more exclusive one, and being saved from an elaborate cheating scheme on his final exams only by a friendly professor who discovers his plot and prevents it. Then his mother dies, having dissipated his father's fortune, and he drops to a lowly job with a railway where he joins an office gang that is padding expense accounts and milking the company's revenues. Not only dishonest but clumsy, he is caught, tries vainly to save himself by turning in his confederates, and is fired.

Up to this point Griffith's story is not only convincing but interesting. But now the reader's credulity is stretched. Granted that he would cheat and steal and let down his associates; would he really be astonished that two of his old college friends should find his conduct reprehensible? Even his creator seems to go along with Griffith's idea that the only thing he has done wrong according to the prevailing code of American morals is to have let himself get caught. But just as the reader is beginning to speculate that Griffith is really too stupid and too unimaginative to provide a case history of any social significance, Norris produces the love affair that saves his novel.

Clarisse Rumsey is the only character who, until now, has loved Griffith. She is cheap, lazy, and pretentious; she is dull and almost illiterate; she is absurdly affected, but she has two qualities that enchain her reluctant lover: her obvious passion for him and her skill at dancing. Today, her dancing would be love-making, but before 1914 a girl who tried to be respectable would endeavor to put the latter off at least until she had hooked her man. I can think of no novel where the power of sex to overcome a man's deep distaste for, almost revulsion from, a woman's personality, is more convincingly portrayed.

Lester Adams, Griffith's half-brother, also cares for him, but in a somnolent fashion. Lester's days and nights are mired in an unchanging routine of newspapers and whiskey in which he still manages to preserve a small semblance of heart and an odd little spark of integrity. Like Griffith, he has made money with the railway gang, but unlike Griffith, he has not betrayed them. F. Scott Fitzgerald considered Lester, along with George Hurstwood and Tom Buchanan, the three best characters in contemporary American fiction.

And then, in the final chapters, the novel simply falls to pieces. Griffith must be redeemed, and all the characters in the way of his redemption must be disposed of. Poor Clarisse is carried away by a pulmonary embolism; Griffith's oldest friend is murdered; two characters even go down in the *Titanic*. Griffith goes off to educate himself by working for two years in a New England textile mill, and when he returns he has developed enough sense to choose for his second wife a sober, industrious, loving girl over a spoiled, self-indulgent heiress. The author now steps out from behind his pages to denounce as the villains of the piece the American boarding school and college. Apparently it is not the capitalist system and *laissez-faire* that are so much at fault as the inability of academia to educate the young to deal with them! But at that point one can turn back to the chapters where Griffith and Clarisse are doing a fox trot at a dance hall. That, at least, makes sense.

Textual Note

The text of *Salt, or The Education of Griffith Adams* published here is a photo-offset reprinting of the third printing (New York, E. P. Dutton and Company, 1918). No emendations have been made in the text.

Lost American Fiction Series
published titles as of April 1981
please write for current list of titles

Weeds. By Edith Summers Kelley. Afterword by Matthew J. Bruccoli.
The Professors Like Vodka. By Harold Loeb. Afterword by the author.
Dry Martini: A Gentleman Turns to Love. By John Thomas. Afterword by Morrill Cody.
The Devil's Hand. By Edith Summers Kelley. Afterword by Matthew J. Bruccoli.
Predestined. A Novel of New York Life. By Stephen French Whitman. Afterword by Alden Whitman.
The Cubical City. By Janet Flanner. Afterword by the author.
They Don't Dance Much. By James Ross. Afterword by George V. Higgins.
Yesterday's Burdens. By Robert M. Coates. Afterword by Malcolm Cowley.
Mr and Mrs Haddock Abroad. By Donald Ogden Stewart. Afterword by the author.
Flesh Is Heir. By Lincoln Kirstein. Afterword by the author.
The Wedding. By Grace Lumpkin. Afterword by Lillian Barnard Gilkes. Postscript by the author.
The Red Napoleon. By Floyd Gibbons. Afterword by John Gardner.
Single Lady. By John Monk Saunders. Afterword by Stephen Longstreet.
Queer People. By Carroll and Garrett Graham. Afterword by Budd Schulberg.
A Hasty Bunch. By Robert McAlmon. Afterword by Kay Boyle.
Susan Lenox: Her Fall and Rise. By David Graham Phillips. Afterword by Elizabeth Janeway.
Inn of That Journey. By Emerson Price. Afterword by the author.
The Landsmen. By Peter Martin. Afterword by Wallace Markfield.
Through the Wheat. By Thomas Boyd. Afterword by James Dickey.
Delilah. By Marcus Goodrich. Afterword by James A. Michener.
Fast One. By Paul Cain. Afterword by Irvin Faust.

Contending Forces. By Pauline E. Hopkins. Afterword by Gwendolyn Brooks.
Infants of the Spring. By Wallace Thurman. Afterword by John A. Williams.
The Great Big Doorstep. By E. P. O'Donnell. Afterword by Eudora Welty.
Rain on the Just. By Kathleen Morehouse. Afterword by the author.
Aleck Maury, Sportsman. By Caroline Gordon. Afterword by the author.
The Plastic Age. By Percy Marks. Afterword by R. V. Cassill.
Salt, or The Education of Griffith Adams. By Charles G. Norris. Afterword by Louis Auchincloss.